IN DAYS OF YORE—

The image of the Knight in shining armor is as much at the heart of fantasy as it is a part of a highly romanticized era of history. From the Knights of the Round Table to lone paladins bent on legendary quests to both champions and despoilers of fantastical realms, the men and women warriors to whom honor means more than life itself have won the loyalty of fantasy readers everywhere.

Now, in fourteen stories of tragedy and triumph—plus one truly memorable ballad—some of today's most talented bards bring us powerful tales of heroes faithful to their knightly vows, and others who must struggle to free themselves from seemingly overwhelming ensorcellments. So take your seat for an unforgettable fantasy tourney filled with such spellbinding combats as:

"Red Cross, White Cross"—He had sworn to fulfill a mission for his dying lord. But could he deny his own brother to complete his quest?

"Nights of the Round Table"—Though knights were a powerful force in the realm, it was easy to see who had become the real power behind the Round Table. . . .

"In a Lifetime"—He had lived beyond the scope of any mortal man's years, but now he had been drawn on a quest to reclaim a life he could no longer remember. But even if he succeeded in breaking through his spell of forgetfulness, would his victory bring him peace?"

KNIGHT FANTASTIC

KNIGHT FANTASTIC

EDITED BY

Martin H. Greenberg and John Helfers

DAW BOOKS, INC.
DONALD A. WOLLHEIM, FOUNDER
375 Hudson Street, New York, NY 10014
ELIZABETH R. WOLLHEIM
SHEILA E. GILBERT
PUBLISHERS
www.dawbooks.com

First Printing, April 2002
1 2 3 4 5 6 7 8 9

Acknowledgments

INTRODUCTION © 2002 by John Helfers.
RODERGO'S SONG © 2002 by Jane Yolen and Adam Stemple.
RED CROSS, WHITE CROSS © 2002 by Andre Norton.
SQUIRE THORIAN'S TRIAL © 2002 by Mickey Zucker Reichert.
THE CROSS OF GOD © 2002 by Brendan DuBois.
NIGHTS OF THE ROUND TABLE © 2002 by Tanya Huff.
BURIED TREASURES © 2002 by Jean Rabe.
FATHER OF SHADOW, SON OF LIGHT © 2002 by Russell Davis.
IN A LIFETIME © 2002 by Kristin Schwengel.
AND THE WIND SANG © 2002 by Bradley H. Sinor.
KILLER IN THE REIGN © 2002 by Rosemary Edghill and India Edghill.
IN DAYS OF OLD © 2002 by Esther Friesner.
KNIGHT MARE © 2002 by Josepha Sherman.
FAINT HEART, FOUL LADY © 2002 by Nina Kiriki Hoffman.
THE CAPTAIN OF THE GUARD © 2002 by Fiona Patton.
THE KNIGHT OF HYDAN ATHE © 2002 by Michelle West.

CONTENTS

INTRODUCTION

by John Helfers

OF all the concepts that have survived from the Middle Ages, few have been idealized as much as the knight. Medieval kings were often only concerned (and rightly so) with keeping and expanding their kingdoms and fending off those who would take from them. The evils they would commit to ensure their reigns would fill volumes. The Church held sway over the masses, spreading its version, depending on which group one listened to, of God's word. Wielding as much power as some sovereign nations, prelates were often involved in the political machinations and intrigues among the various European kingdoms. The nobles were busy currying favor with the monarchy or the Church to increase their land and influence and spending the money earned from the taxes paid by their serfs. Merchants then were the same as merchants now, their primary concern being selling their wares at a profit. The peasants also had one concern—survival. Between bandits, crushing taxes, starvation, disease, and being conscripted for any one of the innumerable wars that broke out between lords, daily life was oppressive enough without anything to look up to. Until the larger-than-life figure of the knight appeared.

While historians aren't exactly sure when the idea of the knight was created, the origins of a landed warrior can be seen as early as 732, when Charles Martel, leader of the Franks, destroyed a large Muslim raiding party that had sacked Bordeaux and was marching north. He requested large land grants from the Church and rewarded his followers with parcels on the condition that they fight for him on demand. And so the warrior knight was created.

During the rise of feudalism, lords were expected to fight for their king when asked. If the lord's holdings were extensive, he was also expected to provide trained fighting men as well as himself for battle. The lords swore fealty to their king, and in return, were allowed to keep their lands on the condition of service rendered to the king.

During the eleventh century, two advances in armor and weaponry helped form the basis for the knightly mounted warrior. First, the chain mail shirt, a staple of armor for the past century, was extended into a knee-length hauberk, often with leggings and mittens of mail. Second, the concept of the charge with a couched lance was developed, which led to the knights' military supremacy.

Along with the idea of this armored, mounted warrior, there arose the idea of a code of conduct that these specially-trained men-at-arms should follow. This led to the rise of chivalry in medieval Europe, which combined a fairly straightforward warrior's code with more civilian virtues such as loyalty to one's lord, personal integrity, compassion, and courtliness. Songs and poetry of the time only reinforced this notion of the chaste, virtuous, noble, generous, honorable, trustworthy, loyal knight. Indeed, writings such as the allegorical poem *Piers Plowman* supported the concept that the knight is expected to do menial work and help those who cannot manage for themselves.

By the end of the eleventh century, knighthood had become a position to aspire to, and the "dubbing" ceremony, a ritual full of pomp and circumstance, was in full force. Mass knightings were not uncommon for dozens of men who showed loyalty and courage in serving their lord. With the rise of romance in the eleventh century, aided by such epic poems as

Chanson de Roland, which tells of one knight's overwhelming, and some would say foolhardy, bravery in having the 20,000 men under his command hold off a force of 100,000 to satisfy his pride, the knight's reputation was lifted even higher.

And, in 1136 came the story that would forever immortalize the code of knights and all they stood for, Geoffrey of Monmouth's *A History of the Kings of Britain* in which he detailed and embellished the life and times of that greatest of English kings, Arthur. With the advent of the Round Table, the Quest for the Holy Grail, Excalibur, and the idea that "Arthur will rise again when his country needs him most," the social class of knight passed from necessity into legend.

Today, in this callous world of school shootings, domestic abuse, rampant drug use, and crimes against humanity in general, the ideal of the knight seems to have fallen by the wayside, abandoned as an impractical and outmoded tenet of living that would only get in the way of anyone trying to survive today. And yet there are those who still hold to a sense of purpose and strive for honor, courage, and forthrightness in their everyday lives. I'm sure if you look around, you can probably spot one near you. Someone who upholds the way of the knight as his or her way of life.

In the following fifteen tales, the epic character of the knight is revealed by some of today's top fantasy writers. From grand master Andre Norton comes the story of two brothers, each in different knightly orders, forced to make a decision that pits their honor against their pride. Fiona Patton takes a look at a knight who is torn by his duty, even as he faithfully serves his master. The lighter side of the knight is revealed in Tanya Huff's story of who really calls the shots at the Round Table. And Michelle West tells of a place where the knights are not only sworn to protect the land they come from, but do so much more.

From valorous deeds to epic quests, the knight in all his (or her) armored glory stands ready for the command to sally forth into battle. So turn the page and enter the fantastic world of the knight!

RODERGO'S SONG

by Jane Yolen and Adam Stemple

World Fantasy Award winner Jane Yolen has written well over two hundred books for children and adults, and well over one hundred short stories, most of them fantasy. She is a past president of the Science Fiction and Fantasy Writers of America as well as a twenty-five-year veteran of the Board of Directors of the Society of Children's Book Writers & Illustrators. Recent novels include *The One-Armed Queen* and *Odysseus in the Serpent Maze*. She lives with her husband in Hatfield, Massachusetts, and St. Andrews, Scotland.

Adam Stemple has been playing one kind of instrument or another since he was three. He has performed professionally since he was eighteen, steadily touring the US and Canada for a period of eight years in the 1990s. Currently, he is based out of Minneapolis, playing guitar and singing lead in two bands, Boiled in Lead, a world beat band, and The Tim Malloys, a popular Irish pub band. He has a number of children's books out, short stories and poems in several anthologies, and is the owner/producer of Fabulous Records which puts out both music and spoken arts recordings.

Rodergo's Song

Words by Jane Yolen

Music by Adam Stemple

Chorus: I - ron rose flow - er of steel

Knight of the white plume and shield. On - ly to you will I

yield. Brada - mant - - - - e.

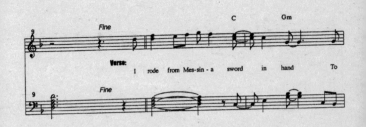

Verse:
I rode from Mes-sin-a   sword   in   hand   To

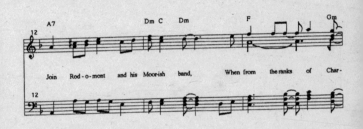

Join Rod-o-mont and his Moor-ish band,   When from the ranks of Char-

le - magne   A knight in shin - ing   ar - mor came   To

trade us blow for shatt - 'ring blow, And was the ve - ry last

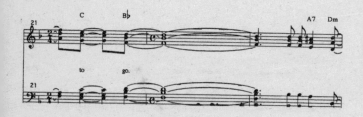

to go.

D.C. al Fine

Chorus:
Iron rose, flower of steel,
Knight of the white plume and shield
Only to you will I yield
Bradamante.

2:
"Good knight," I cried, "we brothers be,
I all for you and you for me.
For never will I hurt such a knight
Who shows such courage in a fight.
Know me then, Rodergo, raised
By a wizard in his lonely days."

Chorus

3:
"And I a Clermont," the knight replied.
"I shall be with you side by side.
Perhaps my brother is known to you,
Rinaldo his name, good man and true."
"I know him well as any other,
But did not know he had a brother."

Chorus

4:
Then taking helm from head, revealed
The lovely maiden behind the shield.
"No brother has mine, but here I stand
To take you by your Moorish hand."
And long they gazed on one another,
Closer became than sister and brother.

Iron rose, flower of steel
Knight of the white plume and shield
Only to you will I yield,
Bradamante.

RED CROSS, WHITE CROSS

Andre Norton

Andre Norton has written and collaborated on over 100 novels in her sixty years as a writer, working with such authors as Robert Bloch, Marian Zimmer Bradley, Mercedes Lackey, and Julian May. Her best-known creation is the Witch World, which has been the subject of several novels and anthologies. She has received the Nebula Grand Master Award, The Fritz Leiber Award, and the Daedalus Award, and lives in Murfreesboro, Tennessee, where she directs High Hallack Library, a facility for genre writers.

THE land was the same. Below the hill upon which Michael lay, it stretched golden to the edge of the orchard. He strove to see any evidence of neglect, but none could be sighted from his resting place. Locksley-on-the-Marsh . . . he had worked in its fields during his novitiate, had ridden forth as a squire from the cluster of buildings half-ringed by the arms of an orchard. And here he was once more, spying upon a land that now might well be a trap set to close upon such as he.

Yet he had sworn upon the cross-hilt of a broken sword— a weapon not even his own. Fortunate indeed had been the brethren who had died at Acre in all honor, defending to the last a Christian hold against the infidels in the Lord's Holy Land. Michael was too late to march in that company, even as the least of fighting men.

The scene that lay before and beneath him wavered as though wrapped in shifting mist. He was feverish—his healer's training was enough to tell him that. And the pain had been with him always since—Michael forced himself up, nursing his right wrist, its bindings now filthy, against his breast. Wrist? Naught but a crushed stub answered to that description. Right hand—sword hand—wild laughter bubbled to his parched lips, and he held it back only with an effort. A handsome jest *they* had thought the deed: no sword hand, no sword! But some men in this world wielded blade with the left hand, as well, or even both with equal ease.

How many days had passed since Sir William, Senior Knight Commander of the Convent of Locksley-on-the-Marsh, died in a rough nest of grass among the bushes? Sir William, betrayed by a mob of villeins in a stinking huddle of huts, his white robe with its blood-red cross torn from him. At least the old Templar did not die at the hands of that rabble who shouted for a fire to send to hell such a son of Satan. Those muck-crawlers had thought Michael dead from the wound he now nursed; but his commander's sword, caught up in his left hand, had driven them off. Then one of the wretches had sighted men-at-arms approaching from the castle, and the rabble had taken to their heels.

Michael had made no move against the soldiers of the castle guard, aware as he was that all hands were now raised against the Templars. Instead—he would never be sure how—he had managed to get Sir William down to the river and into the skiff he had earlier noticed there.

From the boat, the young knight could see the party from the castle heading toward the village and knew that he and his precious charge could be seen in their turn. As he paddled the unsteady craft out into the current, he murmured one of the prayers he had learned from much repetition: a plea for aid. The True God had answered, for the two men had crossed the stream without being sighted. And, once ashore, Sir William had been granted enough strength to work his way into a thick maze of brambles that grew near the water's edge.

Michael had not dared to try a fire, even when the chill from the river reached them. Fevered by the great gash on his head, Sir William rambled, repeating orders once issued in battle, fragments of the Divine Office, or mere wordless mouthings, and it was necessary at times to lay fingers across his dry lips as he raised his voice. His subordinate could offer no more ease to either of them than to apply crude bandages, torn from their shirts and wetted in the stream, first to his commander's gaping wound and then to his own wrist, lifting the latter to his teeth for knotting. Michael seriously questioned whether the older knight would ever raise himself out of this hole.

Sir William, standing tall, his hand resting on his sword hilt, the spotless white of his cloak making a frame for the great red cross . . . that was how the young man had seen his superior on the day he took his own vows. The Commander was a man of honor and a mighty fighter, yet at times—even as did the lowliest of the Brotherhood—he had tended the injured and ill, cared for the homeless and poor. To be his squire had been— Michael fought against a darkness that seemed to be rising about them both in spite of the coming dawn. Sir William, who had stood witness in his own hastily-held initiation and had thereafter been as much mentor as master . . . Sir William . . .

As if he had spoken that name aloud, the man he supported spoke, not in a mumble of half-consciousness but with the strength of the past.

"Michael?"

"Brother!"

"You must do it . . ." The voice faded.

"What must be done, sir?" Michael prompted gently when the other did not continue.

"The safekeepings—for others." Again a pause.

"At Locksley?" Michael guessed.

"Yes—widow of Lord of Lauchon—needs funds. King Philip and Hospitallers must not take—*no!*" The old knight coughed heavily with his vehemence. "You must get—to Lady Gladden—what is hers." The next silence was unbroken.

Wordless, too, Michael cradled the cooling body against his own. The Templars had served not infrequently as custodians of the funds of merchants and nobles; in London, they were wardens of even King Edward's treasures. It was greed that had brought about their destruction—not the knights' own, but the gold-lust of Philip of France, who wished all the wealth they guarded—as well as their holdings—in his own hands. Vile lies had been fostered to achieve this end, some by the very Church that had once trembled before the Infidel and clamored for aid to the Brotherhood of the Red Cross.

But persecution did not justify the dereliction of duty to God—or men. The Templars had acted as faithful stewards, and such service must continue to be rendered even were the Order to be scourged from the Earth.

Michael's heart felt numb, but his mind was clear, and so was his way. Groping in the brush, thorns tearing at his flesh, he grasped the broken sword.

"Brother," he whispered, "it shall be done." Then he swung its cruciform hilt into the air and, as the morning light blessed it with gold, added fervently, "Upon this Cross I swear it!"

That same oath had brought him here. There had been no reverent burial within the shadow of any Temple for Sir William; maimed as he was, the young Templar could only heap a mass of leaves and drag loose branches over his commander's body. Prayers—yes, that much else he could do; but he was no priest to give rest to his dead master. Surely, however, that Lord whom both served, knowing the truest treasure coffered in a faithful soul, would accept this warrior long in His service.

Now Michael himself was near the end of his task. Three days it had taken him to reach Locksley since Sir William's passing. Hunger gnawed him like a beast, its pain near as bad as that tearing ever at his ruined hand. So far he had seen no sign of life below him; the convent might well be deserted. Doubtless—he grimaced at the thought—when the soldiers had swept in to arrest the brothers, they had done some looting. The safe-room, though, was always well hidden. When he had been here with Sir William during the months of danger, he had been shown the secrets.

It was common knowledge that King Edward and those descended from the families who had given rich gifts of land to the Order in the past opposed the Church's recent command that Templar holdings be yielded up to the Knights Hospitaller. But this convent had been hardly more than a grange, and as such it would be under the care of a custodian who visited it only at intervals.

He knew he must move, and soon, or he would not be able to move at all. Noting ahead the bushes that might afford him cover, Michael started down.

No noise could be heard of cattle or horses, and no watchdog gave tongue in warning. Crouching low, the knight approached the enclosed farmstead. At last he pulled himself to his feet, aided by the gate of the wall that encircled the main buildings.

The door of the inner one facing him had been beaten in, and nothing had been done to repair it. Michael drew a deep breath and lurched forward. Did its damage betoken plundering? He could only believe that it must. But who had wrought the ruin—king's men, villagers roused by a priest, or mere outlaws emboldened by the news that the Templars were to be taken?

Staggering to the broken door, he worked his way inside. All the simple furniture of the large meeting room had been smashed into kindling, and from the fireplace rose a greasy reek where half-bare bones had been thrown—the remains of a pig's carcass.

Food—the first in three days! Michael bent to twist free a bone that still held blackened flesh and clutched it possessively. However, the need to discover what had happened in this place was a stronger hunger than an ache in the belly, and, without eating, he moved on to the other rooms.

The chamber where Sir William, nigh on a year ago, had written his reports to the Grand Master had been stripped of all furnishings save a broken chair. Beyond lay quarters for knights or visitors; the dormitory for the sergeants was on the second floor.

At the door that led to the chapel, the young man hesitated. It was closed, and no signs of assault were evident; but creeping from within came a strong and evil odor—the unmistakable stench of death.

Entering, Michael pressed his shoulder against the right wall to steady himself and so made his way into the sacred chamber that was the center of every Templar dwelling. As he reached the altar, he stopped, rooted by shock at what he saw, unable to believe that any born in Christendom had committed such foul sacrilege.

He wheeled around, unable to fight down sickness, but though he heaved, there was nothing left in his stomach to void. Sliding down the wall that had supported him, the knight lay too weak to move, closing his eyes tightly to shut out the abomination around him. Then a deeper darkness mercifully veiled it from him.

*   *   *

"May they be damned into hell for this!"

Sharp as the sword that had severed his hand, the curse cut through the inner night that had held him. Michael was forced to open his eyes. Light from a torch struck them, flaring and fading, but enough to show him two men standing close by and to glimpse others in the shadows behind.

The companion of the torchbearer drew a step closer. Fire glinted on well-kept mail, though much was hidden by an overgarment. A cloak, a cross—not white with a blood-scarlet sign, but rather black with white. Hospitaller! Come to see what the Church had declared now belonged to his Order, was he?

The Templar's lips flattened against his teeth. Let them cut him down here and now, he thought savagely; to the end he would keep the oath he had taken. And he would not die like a cringing slave. Bracing his arms to raise himself up, he struck his mangled wrist against the floor. Agony lanced through the wound, and he screamed.

In the moment it took for the fiendish torture to subside, Michael found himself fronted by the cloaked knight, who knelt swiftly beside him and steadied him with a strong arm. Then the torchbearer came forward and, in spite of pain-blurred vision, the young man had clear sight of the mail-framed face now close to his own.

"Ralf—?"

Perhaps no one heard that whisper save himself, or what he saw was but a cruel delusion born of the fever he carried. Yet new-kindled hope made him strive again for an answer:

"Ralf—brother—"

"Michael!"

The arm about the injured man tightened, holding his body more securely than before; but the wave of weakness and relief that washed over him swept his mind away into darkness once again.

"Michael—here!"

A whisper, then a tug at his hand. He was back in the great hall at Colmount, and someone was striving to draw him into the shadows near a tapestry that hung on the wall behind the high table. Ralf, of course.

"What—" he began, realizing as he spoke that a strange glamour seemed to be holding them both. Ralf looked as he had the last time they had been alone together—a boy in a rumpled smock. And he—he was in the same state.

"Be still!" commanded his brother. There was only a year between them, but Michael was the elder and did not take kindly to such orders. He had just opened his mouth to protest when he heard another voice—one he hated. Scowling, he edged still closer to the dais and the tall-backed chairs that held and hid the speakers.

"Have you thought upon Stephen's advice, my lord?"

"Yes." The single word was a grunt.

A moment of silence followed. Michael could hear his brother's quick-drawn breaths as the two rubbed shoulders in the small space.

"You would be choosing well, my lord." The first speaker's light voice carried a trace of impatience. "They would bring honor to themselves and their house, and you have another son—"

Michael wanted to spit. Oh, yes—Udo!

So he and Ralf stood and listened to the decision that would change their lives forever, removing them from the world they knew and taking from them all they had, to favor the half brother they despised.

That their father was under the will of their stepmother the boys had learned even before the marriage. With the birth of Udo, they had also become aware that the Lady Anigale wanted the heirship for her own stupid cub.

And her scheme had borne fruit true to its seeding, for

Michael and his brother were separated. Ralf had gone to the Hospitallers; he, to the Templars.

"Michael—"

Faint and from far away came that voice, but it was enough to break his dream. He returned to himself enough to sense that he lay not on stone now but on a softer surface.

"Drink!"

A rim of metal was pressed against his lips as his head and shoulders were lifted. Unwilling to open his eyes, he drank, and his mouth filled with a taste of blended herbs; then he was allowed to lie down again. The darkness was waiting, but this time he made no return to the past.

When at last he roused completely, Michael found himself staring up at a white ceiling like a cloud, cleft by the lightning of a jagged crack. This was not the chapel—it was one of the rooms of the infirmary, his torpid memory supplied that much. Two burning torches were thrust into rings on the wall. By their light, as he slowly turned his head, he was able to bring into focus the back of a man who stood by a table, counting liquid drop by drop as he held a small flask above the mouth of a larger.

As though sensing his patient's gaze, the other turned; then, with one long stride, he was beside the Templar and on his knees. Again Michael was looking up into the face of his brother.

"I am meat for the sheriff." He was able to think clearly again, and his voice was stronger. "Best let me go—"

Bound as Ralf was by the Hospitallers' rules, could he—or would he—do otherwise, or did too many years lie between them now?

"No!" The word was spoken with force. "How came you here, and—"

"—why?" Michael could readily guess that second question. "Tis simple enough. I am under oath to the Senior of this holding, which is now—" he strove to keep his voice free of passion, "—sealed by Church and King to your Order. But what brings *you* to this place? Is not Rhodes the land where the White Cross holds sway?"

"I was on caravan," began Ralf, then paused at the bewilderment on his brother's face. "Oh, yes—we are now wedded to ships, but a scouting voyage is still deemed a 'caravan.' Our vessel was dispatched out of the Middle Sea to London on matters of the Order—" Once more he fell silent.

Michael thought he had a good idea of what such "matters" might be. "You and your brethren are to survey your new properties here."

"You have the right of it," said Ralf, looking relieved at not having to speak a painful truth. "But, know this, Michael—" He leaned closer over the pallet and spoke in a near whisper.

"In the past there have indeed been times when the White Cross has differed in creed or deed from the Red. But the foul lies that have brought low the Knights of the Temple—have sent them to torture and death—those we do *not* believe. Some of your brothers have even taken refuge with us, have changed their white cloaks for black. Our Order still battles slavers; the blood of Turks—and not all who are of that cruel mind dwell in the East!—is drink for our swords. Yet we also labor to heal those struck down by either steel or plague."

"'Put not your trust in princes,' brother," Michael quoted. Then he added with a bitter smile. "Or in Church fathers; perhaps your day of doubt, too, will come.

"As to why I am here," he continued, "I gave oath to my leader, even as he died, to carry out a mission. You know that we of the Temple have had safe places wherein merchants, lords, and even kings have stored their treasures. These riches are not ours, yet much has lately been seized, and the true owners fear their wealth is gone beyond recovering."

Ralf straightened a fraction. "Men's worldly goods pass not through our hands!" he retorted hotly. "Lands we will do with as the Church decides, but we claim nothing left in trust;

we are sworn even to refuse those charges ourselves. You now seek such an object of safekeeping?"

"Aye—there is a lady very needful of what lies here. The Lady Gladden—"

Ralf stared, then drew back a little. His mouth set in an expression of truculence his brother knew of old.

"What mischief roils the kettle now?" Michael repeated the question that had been so often aimed at them by Dame Hannah, their mother's nurse, in those lost days.

Ralf ran tonguetip over his lips as though to open them for the passing of words that were hard to utter.

"Our father died six years ago."

"What of that?" Michael made answer to this news. "I have no thought of seeking out Colmount again. Udo may sit in the high seat there until his beard turns white, as far as I am concerned! Too well I know that the countess stands always behind him, quick with her suggestions—"

"Udo died of a putrid fever," Ralf cut in. "Our late lady stepmother gained nothing in the end from Colmount; she had to satisfy herself with another lord—Gladden! And *he* met with the Scots, to his swift undoing. She is now without lord or land; yet you say she has some treasure here."

Michael lay very still. His eyes met those green ones, so like his own, set in his brother's face, and saw them suddenly become hooded, withdrawn.

"I know what Sir William wished of me," he said at length into the silence, "and to that I must hold." He struggled up, Ralf doing nothing to help him, until he was sitting on the rough bed of cloaks and time-tattered blankets. "I *must* hold," he repeated, but he made the vow only to himself.

The Hospitaller rose to his feet and, once erect, gazed for a long moment down at the Templar. "A man does what his honor demands," he said formally. "Lady Anigale may be the

witch we always deemed her, but she will still have your service, it seems—"

Michael had known the blinding pain of having his hand
severed, the withering of spirit brought by the knowledge that
his life had been shattered beyond mending. Those sufferings,
however, diminished to nothing when compared with the thrust
Ralf had just delivered.

"I have heard nothing of Lady Gladden." Ralf spoke
slowly, giving each word more than its usual weight. "I have
found one set upon by outlaws, and to him I have given aid, as
my Oath demands. We await Sir Jean de Averele, the leader of
our party, who is to meet us here. I have seen no Templar, only
a wayfarer—perhaps a merchant. Who and what you are you
must decide for yourself. Understand this."

"I understand."

Ralf turned on his heel and was gone. And so their first re-
union ended.

Nothing was left to him except, as Ralf had said, honor. After
his brother had left the room, Michael crawled on hands and
knees to a table close by and used its sturdy trestles to pull himself to his feet. At least he knew this building and the exact
place of his goal.

Suppose he did bring what he had sworn to retrieve out of
its safekeeping; how could he return it to—*her?* During the
past few days, he had never thought beyond opening the cache.
He did not even know how much was to be transported. And
there was none to turn to—his younger brother's parting words
had made it plain that there was little in common between them
any longer. It was small comfort that no amount of planning
could have prepared him for the ironic twist this tale had taken.
He was now severed from everything and everyone more

surely than he had been in that hour when the rabble had held him down to maim him in body and soul.

The windowless hall beyond the door was deep in darkness. Michael judged that day had passed into night, though he could not depend upon his perceptions, being unable to reckon how long he had lain unconscious. However, the Hospitallers had not ridden out, and they might still be in the process of evaluating their new holding. Yet, as the Templar scraped his way along the wall, he heard no sound and saw no further dance of torchlight. It might be that Ralf, knowing now what had brought him to Locksley, would be waiting to use him as a guide and thereby discover the safe-room without difficulty or danger.

Rounding a corner, he came to the entrance of the chapel. Even in this place, he heard and saw nothing to suggest that others were still present under this roof, though there could be no service here. Those who had despoiled the chapel had also desecrated it, and it would have to be cleansed before the Host could once more be brought within.

But there was light—moonlight; a portion of the roof had vanished not far from the altar. Michael took step by wavering step until he caught at the massive block, then used it for support as he steered himself around to the other side.

Once more on his knees, he sought the wall behind it. The effort to arrive here had winded him, but he breathed as shallowly as possible to avoid drawing in the air about, fouled as it was by what had been nailed to the Cross: the body of Nigar, Sir William's hound. The space behind the altar was pitch-black, and Michael, shuddering, had to run his hand down the besmirched stones, counting the mortar seams between them.

Twice he made that tally; then, certain, he spread his left hand flat on the block he had selected. With all the force he could summon, he set his weight against it. Again he placed his hand, this time at another section of the same stone. Four times, all told, he repeated the action—one he had performed before under Sir William's eye.

At first Michael thought he had failed; then the blocks gave a little. With renewed hope, he put forth the last of his strength, and suddenly the whole wall grated loudly and swung forward. Stumbling to get out of the way, the young knight fell again and lay gasping.

After a moment, he rolled over awkwardly and got back to his knees, an effort that made moisture run down his face until he tasted salt on his lips. Half-crawling, he pulled himself to the doorway, then through it. Just inside he hunkered down, breathing in stale air scented with unidentifiable odors, some of which surely arose from what lay in the chamber.

And where among its contents was he to find what he sought? This ignorance seemed, somehow, the final defeat. With its realization, Michael cast himself prone on the dust-carpeted floor. Once more he murmured prayers—not the ritual entreaties of any service, but broken phrases wrung from a soul near to the mortal sin of despair.

Then came the sound of boots, and fingers of torchlight probed within the treasure place. Those who approached had the glow at their backs, so Michael could not see their faces until one swung around and reached a torch into the room.

It was Ralf—and he was not alone in wearing the cloak of a sworn knight. As he brought the light closer, Michael could see his companion. The other man was much older, and his face was graven with the same lines of authority that had seamed the countenance of Sir William. Here was surely the superior of whom Ralf had spoken.

"Be this your invader, brother?" the elder knight asked. "It would seem that he is also a master of secrets—which is a curious thing, since the mighty among our brethren of the Temple were not wont to share hidden knowledge beyond their own tight-held circle."

Michael braced himself up on the elbow of his left arm.

"I am Michael of Colmount, Knight of St. John of Jerusalem, and now prey to any enforcer of the law. Take me in to Dorchester and get the glory of it! I came here at the orders of the Senior Knight of Locksley-on-the-Marsh, but I have failed. There is no more to be said."

Sir John de Averele stood beside him now. The two men were pressed close by the number of chests and coffers crowded into the small chamber.

"Sir William de Vere—you served him?" he asked. "He is with you, here—?"

The Templar's throat was thick with grief, but he forced himself to reply.

"He is dead," he answered shortly.

"So?" the Hospitaller glanced around at all the wealth that had been concealed in this place. "Your leader being dead, you came to fill your pockets? Such tales are now told of your kind in the courts!"

This offense against his honor gave Michael a last strength to front his accuser. He threw his maimed limb over a chest beside him and pulled himself upright; then another arm—a strong one—was about him, and he was held on his feet by a body solid as the neighboring stone in its aid. Ralf!

"Sir William died, yes, pulled down by the scum of a village," the young knight answered evenly. "I gave oath to complete his mission."

He wanted so much to strike that face, framed in its shining mail-coif, with his wounded wrist, to show what it meant when all the world turned against a man—one, moreover, who had sworn to protect that same world from the ravages of evil.

Sir Jean now tried another tack. "You name yourself of the House of Colmount. Another of that House stands beside you—does he speak for you and your presence here?"

"Ralf and I be brothers indeed by birth," Michael replied

carefully, "but we have known naught of each other since we were children. What is warded here is no affair of his, nor is my purpose."

"Which is to plunder—"

"No!" the Templar's voice rose to a shout. "I take no man's goods for myself! There is a treasure here that does not belong to the Temple but was sent to this place for safekeeping. Sir William heard that the rightful owner was in great need and promised to find and deliver it to her."

The senior Hospitaller gave a strange smile. "This lady is also known to you, Sir Michael, and not happily. Oh, yes, Sir Ralf has told me a curious story, one almost too hard to believe; yet proof exists that it is true. Can you now find this so-precious thing? If you can, and it proves to be, as you say, the property of another, then it will be returned without any report to that owner."

The Templar turned his head a fraction to survey the chests, the boxes, the bags. He had no idea as to the nature of what he sought; he could only hope that the Lord in Whom he had placed his trust for so long would guide him—it might be for the last time.

He would have moved unaided in his search, but Ralf resisted his efforts to tug free and instead matched steps to his. Sir Jean, taking the torch, walked behind, keeping its gleam on the storage containers as well as he could.

Then there came an answer. The light showed it plainly: a small coffer, resting on a second, larger chest. And on the carven lid—an owl. The Owl of Colmount!

Michael did not hail his discovery by voice or touch, merely pointed. Sir Jean called, and the sergeant still at the door strode forward to take the torch, while the senior knight stretched hand to the wooden box. "We shall examine this in more suitable quarters," he announced, motioning to Ralf, Michael, and the others to follow.

The Hospitaller looked to the Templar as the group

emerged into the gloom of the chapel. "You can close what you have opened?" he asked, indicating the door.

Michael nodded. "Swing it shut again and press three times on one block down from the opening at the top, then at the left edge and the right." He watched, fearing that his instructions might not work. They did, however, and the knights proceeded without hindrance to the room that had been Sir William's chamber. No chairs had been left there by the vandals, but saddles had been brought in to serve as seats. Ralf lowered Michael onto one and stood behind him to keep him steady.

Sir Jean pried up the lid of the coffer. Then, as though the age-bitten wood had been dead ash to be swept from living embers, a glittering fire was revealed at its heart. Jewels, as Michael had expected. The older man lifted every pendant, bracelet, and hair-band, examining each in turn.

"A fortune for the lucky, yes," he commented as he worked.

But when one necklet was drawn forth, Michael blinked. The ornament was a chain of silver, hung with what seemed drops of frozen moonlight. That was a Colmount jewel only by default, thought the Templar angrily; their mother had worn it once. He remembered, and, by Ralf's sudden clutch on his arms, his brother did, as well.

"A fortune for the Lady Gladden—"

NO! Michael wanted to howl. The fingers of his left hand balled into a fist. For a long moment, he fought within a battle such as he had never faced in the field—perhaps his personal Acre. But this time there was victory.

"Sir William deemed it her right." He thought the words would choke him.

"Very well, then, it shall go to her." Sir Jean closed the coffer. Then his full attention returned to Michael.

"And what will you do, loyal Knight of St. John of Jerusalem?"

"I can die like the rest," the Templar made answer, "and I shall if any take me. They have not yet laid heretic fires here, but God alone knows what will happen." With this final defiance, Michael felt as though all the strength that had upheld him through his ordeal had seeped away. He no longer cared for his fate, except that he wished to have it done.

"Brother—" Ralf was speaking to his superior. "Others who wore the Red Cross have turned to the White."

"They were not cripples who would be pensioners." replied Sir Jean.

The maimed Templar was too worn to resent that truth. No, he would not appeal to be put into a hospital for, though his body might be tended in such a place, his mind and soul would shrivel for lack for purpose.

"Brother—" Ralf again, "—he is left-handed."

Sudden as lightning, the Hospitaller's sword appeared over Michael's shoulder. Instinctively, the Templar seized the hilt with his remaining hand. Ralf half-loosed his hold upon the blade, and it swayed for a moment, then straightened up.

Michael's head no longer drooped in defeat.

"Take me to your practice-field, if you will," he said, his voice firm, confident. "I was blooded in Spain against the Moors, and I won my cloak with the consent of the Brothers in assembly, as is the custom. I was also trained to fight two-handed, a swordsman right or left. I can be so again."

Sir Jean studied him. "I cannot speak for the Masters," he said quietly. "But ride with us, and we shall see."

Thus, as had been perhaps ordained long before by a Power beyond both, the Red became White, and heart sworn to one Cross found service beneath another which was, in truth, the same.

SQUIRE THORIAN'S TRIAL

by Mickey Zucker Reichert

Mickey Zucker Reichert is a pediatrician whose fantasy and science fiction novels include *The Beasts of Barakhai, Flightless Falcon, The Legend of Nightfall, The Unknown Soldier,* and several books and trilogies about the Renshai. Her short fiction has appeared in numerous anthologies, including *Battle Magic, Zodiac Fantastic,* and *Wizard Fantastic.* Her claims to fame: she has performed brain surgery, and her parents really are rocket scientists

A BREEZE grazed the hillside, twining through the line of six mounted knight hopefuls, chilling the sweat beaded across Squire Thorian's brow. Third in line, he scanned the crowd over Dalton's and Fenestamdt's heads, seeking his wife and infant daughter among those gathered to see which three completed their training and which three retired before their lives began. Helmet clenched between his knees, he let the wind riffle through his sandy hair, knowing it would become suffocatingly warm and dusty once he donned his headgear. The mail chafed through his padding; he had had to choose between too thin or too hot. He would pay with abraded skin, but he still believed he had made the right choice.

Thorian had known for fourteen years that he would eventually reach this point, yet it still seemed overwhelmingly sudden. Every other year, a dozen promising seven- and eight-year-old boys joined the king's staff as pages. Most made it through the first seven years, when they became squires and their duties shifted from general servitude to assisting the knights. From that time, accidents, changes of heart, or incompetence always claimed a few, leaving four to ten to compete for the knighthood.

So far, all of the hopefuls had made it through the tests of knowledge, strategy, honor, and leadership skills. Hand-to-hand combat had left them with rankings that could so swiftly change in tourney. It all came down to this last crucial event. Win, and Thorian achieved the life he had chased since childhood. Lose, and the dream collapsed. The next hour or so would determine, irrevocably, whether or not Thorian and his family had a future.

Discovering Lyntara in the stands, clutching tiny Dalia, Thorian smiled. Waves of long, brown hair cascaded to his wife's waist, her green bonnet holding the hair back and framing her face. Dalia perched on her lap, her soft round features angelic and her cheeks a brilliant pink. The bright bonnet, a twin of her mother's, brought out the emerald glow in eyes that changed with the colors around her, like his own. Gaze stopping there, he could forget why so much more than his own happiness depended on the results of this tourney. He could choose not to look, but he could not change fate. Dalia's right arm ended in a stump halfway between elbow and wrist, and her badly deformed left foot would never support her weight. These things had happened in the womb, yet they would determine the rest of her life.

A tear stung Thorian's eye, and he angrily wiped it away. His time of mourning had ended at sundown on the day of Dalia's birth. She was his daughter. He would love her forever, unconditionally, no matter what cruelties the world dared to inflict upon her. He had dedicated himself to protecting her from them, when possible, to teach her to handle them with dignity and respect, when necessary, and to never add to her burden. He held that vow as strongly as those that came with knighthood, yet he knew he might stand on the verge of failing both. Should his skills not prove good enough, should he not win a place in the top three of his class, he would not only lose the Order of the King's Knights but also the lifelong pension for family members widowed or orphaned by his death.

Sir Elander, the knight's captain, called the hopefuls to order while a page announced their arrival to the waiting audience. An enormous covered box with lavender draperies held the king and queen, the prince and two princesses, several of the higher ranking knights, and a visiting duke. Positioned just over the center of the lists, they would have the best view of the proceedings where they could judge and award points. The surrounding stands held those knights not participating in setup, rules, direction, or arbitration. Joining them were castle staff and the families of the participants. The peasants assembled haphazardly, children on the grass in front of the stands, adults on fence posts, rooftops, or perched in the branches of trees. The cynic of the hopefuls, Byrinith, had said the vastness of the crowd reflected some who came only to see if someone got killed in the tourney. Thorian suspected he might be right.

The competing squires circled the field on their horses, displaying the colors that festooned their mounts. As the winner of the hand-to-hand competitions, Dalton led the parade, clutching the flagpole. The banner fluttered and snapped behind him, exhibiting the rippling ambers of the two rearing lions, each with a forepaw firmly planted on a silver crown.

The golden fringes danced on the breeze, outlining the kingdom's rich, deep purple.

The muscles of Thorian's bay mare bunched beneath him as she executed the tight, high-stepping canter she'd been trained to since birth. She was only five. Thorian would have preferred a more experienced mount, but he accepted the lot he had fairly drawn. The knights did not have a single bad steed. He only wished he could have pulled a familiar horse, like the massive gelding he had ridden during most of his practices. He currently held the third position of six, better than he had expected yet right on the edge of resigning his commission. Any tiny detail could make the difference between the life to which he had dedicated his entire youth and something unknown and lesser.

As the horses skirted the perimeter of the jousting lists, Thorian tried to imagine his life without the knighthood. In the past, nearly all the fallen squires had joined the king's army. It made sense, yet the option did not seem open to Thorian. He could not risk leaving Lyntara widowed without the pension money his knighthood would grant her and Dalia. He would have to choose a safer profession, though it meant sacrificing a lifetime of training. An apprenticeship would require years of unpaid labor, which his family could not afford. Laborers did not command the kind of income necessary to support a disfigured daughter forever. She would not likely marry and could never earn money for herself.

Dalton completed the circuit and rode to the youngster he had chosen to become his squire should he leave the tourney victorious, as seemed likely. Already the point leader, he had demonstrated great skill at jousting in the past. Thorian studied him. He would never speak ill of anyone, but he could not control his thoughts. He did not like Dalton. Though a dedicated young knight prospect, the burly, pinch-faced man had remained aloof from most of the camaraderie, preferring to view his fellow squires as competition rather than peers. Thorian would trust Dalton with his life, but he would do anything to avoid a situation where he might have to.

Fenestamdt headed toward his squire, and Thorian scanned the area for Orthan. He found the stocky thirteen-year-old waiting for him beneath a broadly branching tree. A patch of his black hair stuck up in the front in the familiar, untamable cowlick. His broad nasal bridge made his eyes seem not to focus quite together, but his stunning ability with a bow belied the image. He had extraordinary depth perception. Appreciating the shade his squire prospect had chosen, Thorian reined toward him.

As Thorian approached, Orthan snapped to attention. He drew up to the horse and immediately started working on her: adjusting blankets and colors, polishing boots and stirrups, scraping sweat and neatening mane and tail.

"At ease, Orthan," Thorian said, wishing he could obey the command himself. "Right now, I need emotional support more than grooming."

"Yes, sir," Orthan replied. He back stepped and smiled thinly. "Right now, sir, I think you need both."

Mind spinning with thoughts, Thorian considered the words. "Do I look that bad?"

"No, sir." A flush passed across the familiar, flat-faced features. "I didn't mean that at all. You just don't have the necessary . . . um . . . perfection for this all-important tourney."

"Perfection?" Thorian repeated, then laughed. He wiped his brow with the back of one hand, using the other to steady his helmet in his lap. "I don't think we have an *entire* century to prepare."

Orthan could not even maintain his weak grin. "Sir, the way I figure things, you'll have to win two of your three matches to become a knight. Lose two and . . ." His gaze went distant.

Thorian followed his squire's regard to the speck of his own family in the stands. He sighed, then sat up straighter. "I'll just have to win two, then." It was not an impossible feat. Though average at jousting, the points he had gained in hand-to-hand would carry him reasonably well. At least, he could lose once. As things stood, Orthan knew more about the upcoming procedure than he did. "Who am I fighting?"

"It's random, sir. We won't know until just before each match." Orthan returned to his attending duties as he talked. "They wave flags. Yours is green. I'll let you know when your turns come up, sir." He glanced toward the nearby lists.

A burst of applause greeted the current competitors.

"Who's up now?"

"Dalton and Fenestamdt." Orthan ran a brush over Thorian's mount with stiff strokes. He stopped suddenly. "Here, sir. Take this."

Thorian's gaze dropped to Orthan's free hand. A wax pellet balanced on the palm. "What's that?"

"Sir, it's better if you don't ask questions."

A cheer went up from the crowd as the competitors lined up for a second pass.

Thorian took the pellet into his own hand and examined it. Pale blue light shimmered through the opaqueness of the wax.

"The king's magician gave it to me, sir," Orthan said hurriedly, without meeting Thorian's gaze. "You're supposed to keep it in your mouth. Bite down when you need it."

Thorian blinked. The description made little sense to him. "When I need it to what?"

"To win, sir."

Louder cries came from the spectators. A red flag waved in triumph. Forced to look up to see who would fight the next match, Orthan dodged Thorian's stare.

"To win?" Thorian repeated, scarcely daring to believe he had heard correctly. "You mean to . . . cheat?"

Orthan continued as if Thorian had not spoken. "It only works once, and—"

"I don't care if it works a million times." Thorian's respect for Orthan plummeted, and sorrow spiraled through him. He tried to focus on the coming battle, to abandon the fear that he might have joined himself for two years to an untrustworthy squire. "Orthan, I won't be a part of—"

Orthan did not allow him to finish. "Sir, I appreciate your sentiments, but we don't have time for arguments. Your family's future, as well as your own, rests on how you do in the coming battles."

A picture of Dalia filled Thorian's mind's eye, unbidden, accompanied by a rush of warm affection. "But I won't—"

"Please, sir. Trust me. Just put it in your mouth. You have plenty of time to make the decision about whether or not to bite." Orthan jabbed a hand toward the lists. "Right now, sir, you're being summoned." He balanced the shield against the saddle and handed over Thorian's lance.

Thorian studied his squire's lopsided face and the urgency stamped across it like a mask. The boy had never given him reason for suspicion in the past. Against his better judgment, he popped the capsule into his mouth, tonguing it against his cheek. To his surprise, it settled easily into place, without affecting his speech, breathing, or concentration. He placed his arming cap and helmet over sweat-plastered hair and took the shield and the lance in hand. Within a few strides, he had wholly forgotten about the pellet snuggled against his cheek, and his horse loped smoothly toward the sparring field.

The crowd murmured as Thorian took his place at the far end of the second lane. At the opposite side of the field, he saw a distant figure looking glorious in armor and colors, astride a well-muscled black stallion. Thorian recognized the horse before the man. *It's Listir.* Even the knight hopeful in last place would not prove an easy opponent, but Thorian appreciated that he would warm up on someone he had beaten more often than not during practices.

The eldest princess rose from her seat and tossed down a handkerchief. It fluttered in the gentle breeze, ghostlike, toward the ground. When it touched, the two knight hopefuls charged down their lists. Thorian braced his shield against his chest, fist curled as tightly as his gauntlets would allow. He aimed his lance dead center for Listir's shield, targeting the silver crown between the lions. He tensed for the coming blow, watching the bobbing tip of his opponent's lance over the low fence that separated their horses into lanes. Some of the oldest knights maintained that their trials were harder, since they had had no such security between them. Their horses occasionally slammed together or entangled, and a man unseated faced the very real risk of being trampled.

Realizing his mind had wandered, Thorian shoved his thoughts back to the pertinent a moment before the collision. The shock drove the hilt of his lance into his own chest, and he felt the crash of Listir's weapon against his shield. The sound seemed to come an instant later: the ear-splitting clang of metal meeting metal followed by thunderous applause. Thorian wobbled but managed to keep his seat. He wheeled his mount for a second pass, only to see Listir on the ground, the black nuzzling its rider.

Thorian reined his horse toward his fallen rival, dragging the helmet from his own sweat-smeared head. He drew up beside Listir just as his squire did the same. Listir sat, then stood with the boy's help. The younger squire saluted Thorian to let him know Listir was all right, and Listir waved to the victor. Polite clapping met the gesture that confirmed what the audience already knew. Thorian had won the match.

I won. Thorian tempered his joy with the realization that, from his gain had come a friend's loss. The crowd, he knew, expected some sort of happy gesture from him, so, bracing his shield and lance, he swung his helmet through the air. Another loud wave of applause passed through them.

Orthan met Thorian at the end of his lane. "Good job. One more win, and you're in." He eased the heavy gear to the ground. "And you should know, you're fighting Dalton next."

Dalton. Thorian chewed his lower lip. In spar, only Fenestamdt consistently bested the man who now stood in first place, and Thorian never had. Tourney did not seem like a likely time for an upset. The best with shield and lance, Fenestamdt might even draw ahead of Dalton, which would please Thorian. The man with the highest point total at the end of the contests became the captain of his year; and Thorian would far prefer taking his orders from friendly Fenestamdt than self-involved, humorless Dalton. *Assuming I manage to pull out those two wins.* "No problem," he said, trying to sound upbeat. "There's always a first time."

"Right," Orthan gave back, with the same strained bravery. "You should know. Dalton beat Fenestamdt."

So much for Fen making captain. "Really?" he said thoughtfully.

Byrinith rode to the list Thorian had just vacated, saluting as he passed.

"Good luck, Byr." Thorian doubted his fellow heard him. Ranked fourth, the slender pessimist would prove Thorian's greatest threat; but he bore the man no ill-will. He only wished both of them could win, though it seemed more likely one would steal the knighthood from the other. "Who's he fighting?"

Orthan glanced up, then went back to gathering Thorian's gear. "Charlemott."

Thorian nodded. *Fourth place against fifth.* "Sounds fair."

Orthan lifted his head again, this time turning his gaze directly on his superior. "Charlemott beat Dalton."

The news shocked Thorian silent.

Orthan returned to his task, while Thorian watched the match, mulling the information his squire had delivered. If Dalton had bested Fenestamdt and Charlemott beat Dalton, it changed the whole dynamics of the tourney and the knight hopefuls. He watched Byrinith's gray charger bear down on Charlemott's white. The two slammed together, lances thudding heavily against shields. Charlemott swayed dangerously but managed to stay a-horse. The two realigned. Then, each in its own lane, the steeds leaped toward one another again. In front of the royals' stand, they crashed together. As the beasts charged past, Charlemott tumbled from his seat amid a wild roar of applause and cheering. Glad for his friend, Thorian clapped one gauntleted hand against the helmet in the other. It made a muffled clunking sound.

Orthan shoved Thorian's shield toward his hand. "You're up next, sir."

Already? Though it seemed soon, Thorian realized his second battle was Dalton's third. He had come out better than the front-runner, at least when it came to drawing positions. Unable to tear his eyes from the scene, Thorian fastened his helmet methodically. "Byrinith won against Charlemott who bested Dalton."

"Yes, sir." Orthan pressed the shield more persistently against Thorian's arm, and he accepted it without a word.

Thorian also took his lance. His arm still ached from the impact against Listir's defense. His skin felt raw and stung by sweat. He doubted Orthan had taken all the upsets into account when he calculated Thorian's chances for success and wondered if that meant he would now have to win every one of his battles. *All I can do is my best.* The tip of his tongue touched the pellet still wedged in his cheek. *No.* He jerked his tongue away, wishing he had never agreed to put the thing in his mouth. As he rode into position, his gaze found his family again. Lyntara leaned forward in the stands, gaze clamped on her husband, crippled daughter clutched tightly in her arms. *I've got to win. For them.*

His mind on his family, Thorian nearly missed the signal. Dalton's sudden forward movement cued him, rather than the princess' handkerchief, which had already touched the ground. He barely grazed his mount with a heel, and she sprang forward, already a stride behind her opposite. Dalton looked like some huge, silver monster gliding toward him, single long horn outstretched, vitals shielded by the familiar colors of the kingdom. Then, abruptly, they were on top of one another. Thorian's lance arm jerked backward so hard pain howled through every muscle. The edge of his shield dug into his chin, and he felt himself thrown forcefully backward. Desperately, he scrabbled for balance. And lost. Before he even realized he had fallen, he found himself sprawled in the dirt, applause for Dalton hammering in his ears.

Orthan appeared at his side, and Thorian allowed his chosen squire to assist him. The heavy armor made rising difficult, especially in concert with the strains and bruises from this and the previous battle. Every joint of armor stabbed through his flimsy undergarments, inciting the pain of abraded, sweat-stung skin. "Are you all right, sir?"

I'm sitting on my ass in the dirt. What do you think? Trained to gentility, Thorian did not even consider speaking such sarcasm aloud. "I'm fine, Orthan. Thank you." Only then, did he assess the damage from the fall. His arms ached and his back felt sore, but nothing seemed seriously damaged. With his squire's help, he waved Dalton's victory and then limped from the field. A groom brought his horse.

Thorian watched as Charlemott faced off with Listir. Likely, Charlemott would win, which, combined with his victory against Dalton might well give him the points to pull ahead of Thorian.

As if reading the knight hopeful's mind, Orthan said softly, "You have to win the last match, sir." Thorian clamped his mouth to a line, knowing Orthan spoke the truth. He would have to face either Fenestamdt or Byrinith, and he would have to triumph. Losing to either would probably put him in second to last place. *One loss. One predictable loss, and look how far I've fallen.* He shook the thought from his mind. *Unless I win this match.* Uncertain he really wanted the answer, he asked, "Who am I up against?"

Orthan's hard swallow told him enough, and the words only confirmed it. "Fenestamdt, sir. Your opponent is Fenestamdt." His smile looked forced, stretching between the broad-set eyes. "You can do it, sir."

Thorian's nod clearly did not convince Orthan.

"Dalton beat him."

Then dropped me on my butt. "Yes."

"Have faith, sir. Charlemott bested Dalton, and they had him ranked fifth. You're third. Fenestamdt's only one ranking above you."

Thorian knew all that, and it did not soothe him. Though second going into the competition, Fenestamdt held the highest jousting record. Unexpectedly bested once, Fenestamdt would surely evoke the same fire Thorian needed now, the same desperate lust for victory.

Desperate. The word seemed apt. *I have to win. For Dalia, I have to win.* He closed his eyes, summoning all the will and power of his mind, fusing it with bodily strength and experience. Each deep breath funneled through his mouth, released in a concentrated cycle through his nose. He pinned his thoughts to the task at hand, imbuing himself with the savage, unstoppable power of an earthquake, the ruinous quickness of flame. "I'm ready," he said, only then realizing that his aches had disappeared, his helmet lay strapped on his head, lance and shield at the ready.

"Do right, sir," Orthan whispered. Though spoken earnestly, they were a far cry from his usual words of encouragement. "Do well."

Thorian never remembered seeing the handkerchief, never remembered giving the order to charge. He found himself airborne, surging toward the inevitable collision. Then, lances met shields with a crash that pounded his ears. He felt himself slipping. *NO!* He flung his weight forward, trying to merge with the power and motion of the horse. Together they thundered to the far end of the list, and together they whirled for a second pass. Together, they leaped into action, and one doubt managed to weasel through the web of power and need Thorian had constructed. *I can't take another hit like that.*

Four strides separated the combatants, then three, then two. The wax pellet seemed to burn into Thorian's cheek, calling to him in his daughter's bell-like voice but with Orthan's words. *You have to win the last match, sir.* Dalia's bright, young face, so ripe with unfulfillable promise, flooded Thorian's mind's eye. For her, he had to triumph. For her to have a future. He maneuvered the pellet between his teeth. *Guaranteed success. One time. Just one desperate time.* The world seemed to freeze in that moment. *Do right, sir.* Deeply ingrained honor would not allow Thorian's jaw to close. For a fraction of a second longer, time stood utterly still. *A victory without principle is the worst damnation.* Thorian spat the magical pellet from his mouth. Intact, it slid down his cheek, warm and wet with saliva, and fell through the neck hole of his helmet to the ground. Then, the lances and shields smashed together. Momentum flung Thorian from his horse, and wind whistled through his ears. He struck the ground, breath dashed from his lungs, helmet rolling from his head.

Orthan appeared like a wraith beside him, assisting Thorian to his feet. "Are you well, sir?"

Thorian battled for breath and finally found it. "My body's well enough, Orthan." He did not need to finish.

"Your spirit will heal." Orthan turned his charge a wan smile. "I'm proud of you, sir."

Though it came from a thirteen-year-old boy, Thorian found himself warmed by the praise.

The six knight hopefuls gathered at the edge of the lists, sans horses and helmets, beneath the watchful gaze of the captain. Sir Elander threaded through the ranks, examining them from head to toe, nodding disinterestedly as a page announced the winners of each match. The words struck Thorian especially hard. Hearing his two losses to one win pronounced in a loud monotone brought home fully the realization of what they meant: no knighthood, no prospects, no security for his daughter.

As if to add insult to injury, Sir Elander had each man describe his record for himself while he studied their faces impassively. When they finished, he nodded and mounted his horse.

"Men, you all did very well today. I'm proud."

The trite words did nothing to comfort Thorian's aching heart. His squire's tribute, from the heart, meant infinitely more. He wondered if Orthan had spoken the truth, if his spirit would ever heal.

Elander made a flourishing gesture. "I want the following knight hopefuls to step into list two: Squire Dalton . . ."

Nods swept through the ranks. No one had ever doubted

that the front-runner would become one of the chosen. ". . . Squire Charlemott . . ."

Thorian had expected Fenestamdt next and hoped his loss to Dalton had not crippled his ranking too severely. He suddenly realized he did not know whether or not the man who had held second place, the best jouster usually, had won or lost his last match. Now, it seemed clear that he must have gotten unhorsed. *At least I'm in good company.* He could not help feeling sorry for his fellow, a good man who would have made an excellent captain of his year.

Sir Elander continued, ". . . and Squire Listir."

No name could have caught Thorian more by surprise. "Listir?"

Beside Thorian, Byrinith nudged him. "He beat Fen."

"Fenestamdt?" Thorian shook his head to clear it. At any moment, he would wake up in his own bed, full of dreams of the upcoming competitions; but the world remained the same. Dalton, Charlemott, and Listir stood in the second combat lane with Sir Elander.

Elander's massive chestnut pranced a high-stepping course around all of the hopefuls. "Gentlemen, you've worked long and hard for an honor so few attain . . ."

Thorian winced, uncertain he could listen to an inspiring speech after losing so much.

". . . Anyone can learn to fight. But only a slight handful have the courage, the fortitude, and the honor to gain the Order of the King's Knights. This last test was not about combat, but principle. Not about who has the strongest arm or the finest shield, but about which men have the virtue to call themselves members of the king's elite. For integrity, once sacrificed, can never be made whole."

Integrity. Realization dawned. *The wax pellet. Everyone got one.* Suddenly, all became clear to Thorian: Orthan's giving the magic to him, the shocking upsets, the wrestling of conscience. He glanced at the ground toward the center of lane three, where he had spat out his unused pellet. A blue splotch soaked into the dirt, the same dye that surely stained the mouths of the hopefuls called forward. *No wonder Sir Elander had each of us speak.* Thorian's lips twitched into a smile of understanding as the captain of the knights rode toward them. *A moment of weakness resisted for a lifetime of happiness.*

"Sir Fenestamdt, Sir Byrinith, Sir Thorian. Welcome to the Order."

Sir Thorian. It sounded so good.

THE CROSS OF GOD

by Brendan DuBois

Brendan DuBois is the award-winning author of
short stories and novels. His short fiction has appeared in *Playboy, Ellery Queen's Mystery Magazine, Alfred Hitchcock's Mystery Magazine, Mary
Higgins Clark Mystery Magazine,* and numerous
anthologies. He has twice received the Shamus
Award from the Private Eye Writers of America,
and has been nominated three times for an Edgar
Allan Poe Award by the Mystery Writers of America. His most recent novel, *Resurrection Day,* is a
suspense thriller that looks at what might have
happened had the Cuban Missile Crisis of 1962
erupted into a nuclear war between the United
States and the Soviet Union. This book also re-
cently received the Sidewise Award for best alter-
native history novel of 1999. He lives in New
Hampshire with his wife Mona. Visit his website at
www.BrendanDuBois.com

IT was the middle of the night when the pounding on the door
awoke Frederick of Munchen, the monastery's abbot. He sat
up in his plain bed, feeling the hay mattress underneath him

rustle in the darkness, his hands clutching the coarse woolen blanket.

"Who is it?" he called out. "What is the matter?"

"Quick, Brother Frederick, please come quick," came the muffled voice. "There is a visitor here to see you."

"At this hour?" he said. "Who is it, then?"

"Your cousin, the knight Sir Godfrey!" the voice said, now recognizable as Brother Heinrich. "He's here to see you! All the way from Jerusalem!"

Jerusalem! Frederick felt a flash of excitement at hearing that holy word, almost as much excitement as at hearing his cousin had unexpectedly arrived. He got out of his bed in the darkness and put on a wool cloak over his bedclothes, then struggled for a moment, pulling on wool socks over his bare feet. He padded across the stone floor and opened the door to his cell, revealing Brother Heinrich standing outside, a lit candle stub in his dirty hand. He was one of the youngest monks in the monastery, and his skin was blotchy with boils and sores.

"Sir Godfrey, are you certain?" he asked.

Brother Heinrich nodded enthusiastically. "Yes, Brother Frederick. Quite sure. He has come to see you, all the way from Jerusalem. He said it was urgent, most urgent, that you come at once."

"Then move on, Brother Heinrich. Move on."

He followed the young monk through the stone corridor, led by the faint light of the flickering candle. There were whispers in the darkness, as other monks came out of their dormitory, to see what was happening, but he paid them no heed. Godfrey! Here to see him! All the way from Jerusalem, all the way from the Great Crusade, the Great Crusade started by Pope Urban II, to wrest control of that holiest of cities from the infidels of the East. He felt his heart surge with pride—and then asked God's forgiveness for having done so—at having his knighted cousin go on such a holy quest, and to return here—here, and not his home at Nuremberg—to visit.

Down stone steps they went, he still following the young boy ahead of him. Years . . . it had been years since he had seen Sir Godfrey. At least four, perhaps five. He had seen Godfrey just before he had ridden south, to meet up with the great columns of knights and peasants and merchants, all marching across the lands of the infidel, to meet and free Jerusalem and its Christian people. Godfrey had been on his white stallion, his face strong and eyes bright, his red hair and beard flowing, his chain mail and armor bright and shiny. He leaned down from his horse and offered his gauntleted hand to his cousin.

"Will you give me a blessing, then, Brother Frederick? The journey ahead will be a long one, and I make no secret that I fear what might be ahead."

And, his voice choked with emotion and love for his brave cousin, he had given him God's blessing. "You will journey far, but you will return, with God's love and blessing," he had said. And with a laugh and shout, his cousin rode away, wearing the white tunic and red cross that marked him as a member of the crusade, his confidence and strong bearing bringing tears to Frederick's eyes.

All those years . . . They came to the main floor of the monastery, and Frederick looked around in confusion. The entrance hall was empty. "Where is he?" he demanded of Heinrich. "Where is my cousin?"

Brother Heinrich stepped away, now looking frightened, cowering before his abbot. "Brother . . . Brother Frederick. Sir Godfrey is outside."

"Outside! At this hour, and in this cold?"

"But that's what he requested, Brother Frederick. He said he would not tread these holy stones, until you came before him, to see him and bless him."

"Open the door, then, brother. And hurry up about it!"

They walked the short distance to the oaken door that led outside, and Brother Heinrich pulled at the iron handle. The door groaned as it opened inward, and Frederick shivered and gathered his cloak tighter about him. The wind was strong tonight, coming from the haunted peaks of this part of Bavaria, and he shivered again, thinking of the monsters and spirits that lived up there in the dark hills. Some flakes of snow whirled in and he stepped out, Brother Heinrich next to him, shielding the guttering candle flame in his dirty hands.

"Godfrey!" Frederick called out to the darkness. "Sir Godfrey, are you there?"

Then Frederick stepped back in horror, as a shape stumbled out of the darkness, moving slowly toward the open door. A terrifying thought came to him, that some devilish spirit had confused young Heinrich's mind and was now going to open up the entire monastery to the devil's work. But he muttered a quick prayer and called out, "Who are you? What do you want?"

The shape revealed itself to be a man, wearing a tattered sackcloth about his thin shoulders, and some bits of chain mail, broken and rusting, and the shreds of a tunic, the red cross having been torn away. His hair and beard were long and gray, and as he came closer to the light, the dull eyes looked at Frederick and the man said in a hoarse voice, "Frederick . . . is that you . . . is that really you?"

He blinked his eyes against the sudden rush of tears. The strong and confident man who had been his cousin and the bravest knight in the land was no more. But still, his soul was there. Frederick reached out, grabbed his thin arm. "Godfrey . . . come in, please come in. You're welcome to stay—"

Godfrey shrieked and fell to his knees in the snow, and Heinrich jumped back, almost causing the candle to go dark. Frederick reached down with both hands, holding onto his cousin's shoulders. "Godfrey . . . please, what is it? What has happened?"

"I'm not worthy," he said, his voice raspy. "I'm not worthy to enter this house of God. Oh, blessed Frederick, please forgive me. For I have seen such horrors, such awful things, and I have lost my faith."

Brother Heinrich muttered something but Frederick ignored it, squeezing his cousin's shoulders even tighter. "Speak not of that, cousin. You are certainly welcome here, no matter what horrors you have seen, no matter what troubles have befallen you. Please, stand up. Please, enter my home, and the home of my brothers."

Godfrey slowly stood up, wiping at his eyes, and Frederick again said a quick prayer for this man, who had once been so strong and fearless. He leaned into him, so Brother Heinrich—who could gossip for hours in the kitchen or the laundry—would not hear what was said between them.

"Was it . . . was it the infidels?" he whispered.

"No," Godfrey whispered back. "No, it was much worse . . ."

"Worse?"

"Yes," Godfrey said. "A wizard . . . a wizard in the Holy Land, he has cursed me and my descendants . . . all of us here, Frederick, he cursed all of us here."

This time, Frederick started pulling his cousin through the doorway. "Then you will tell me all about it, and fear not, Godfrey. This wizard's reach cannot come this far and through these walls."

And Godfrey burst into tears, saying, "Oh, I pray it's so, Frederick. I pray it's so."

He brought his cousin into the kitchen and told Brother Heinrich, "Build a fire. Warm this place up. And find some food for my cousin. A sausage, some bread, and broth. He must be quite famished."

Godfrey shook his head violently. "No . . . no Frederick, I've been fasting ever since my journey home . . . no meat, no meat at all . . ."

Frederick still found it hard to believe that this gaunt and pathetic creature before him was his once strong and noble cousin, a knight in service of the local lord, whose piety and bravery was known throughout the valley. He cleared his throat. "Nonsense. You are under my care, in a house of God. You will do what I say."

The look of hope on the man's face was like that of a child, and Frederick brought him to one of the long tables, where the monks took their meals. He sat his cousin down on one of the benches and then called out to Heinrich. "Hurry, now, for my cousin is famished."

Godfrey started rubbing his hands together, and then the room lit up some as Brother Heinrich threw some branches and bits of wood on the embers. The knight turned to the fire and said, "I've not felt such warmth in months, cousin. In months. I must tell you something, something that frightens my soul, for what I saw on the crusade."

"Wait," Frederick said. "Wait until you've eaten. Then we can spend all night here, if you wish. But only after you've eaten."

Godfrey pulled his tattered clothing about him. "Very well, then. After I've eaten."

It was good to see his older cousin eat, for Frederick was concerned about what had seemingly struck his mind and his soul. But his old appetites returned and he ate well, his gaunt jaw moving back and forth. Brother Heinrich silently provided him with ale, sausage, some old black bread and broth, and Godfrey finished the broth by wiping the wooden bowl down with a final piece of bread. "This food . . . this blessed food . . ." he murmured. Brother Heinrich stood there and Frederick dismissed him with a motion of his hand. He didn't want the younger monk to hear any strange stories that his cousin might tell, stories that could cause someone so young to turn away from God.

Godfrey looked up, his eyes dark. "At the beginning we ate so well, as the noblemen we were. We ate the finest foods, drank the best wines. But the trip was harsher than anything we could have dreamed of, traveling into the land of the Turks and the infidels. Soon, our food ran out. We were forced to eat our pack animals, and sometimes, God forgive us, our best mounts."

Knowing the love that Godfrey had for horses, Frederick could only nod. His cousin went on. "We had to fight our way south, through cities such as Tarsus and Tripoli and Acre. There were times, on the long march to Jerusalem, when we were so hungry, we ate the foulest things. Offal and trash that even the worse peasant here in the valley would turn away from. Yet we went on, fighting and singing and praying, knowing our crusade to liberate Jerusalem was a holy one, blessed by the Pope and by God. *Deus lo volt.* God wills it! That was our battle cry, all those days we marched and fought."

Outside the wind hammered at the wooden shutters, and Godfrey managed a weak smile, the first smile Frederick had seen since his cousin had arrived. "But that is not the tale I must tell you, to save my immortal soul. No, Brother Frederick, you need not hear the tales of a knight, on crusade for the Lord. No, I must tell you of what happened to me, after a small battle, near the city of Jerusalem."

Despite himself, Frederick murmured, "Jerusalem. The Holy City. You did see it, then, did you?"

Godfrey nodded. "Yes, I did see it, yet I would have gladly

given away everything I owned and loved, for that not to have happened. For after I had seen that glorious city, shimmering in the distance, I and a few other knights fought a minor skirmish, with some mounted infidels. We had won the day, but in the clash, I was tossed off my mount and injured my head. When I awoke, night had fallen, and a mist had come down. I was alone and I was lost, and—I am ashamed to say—I was frightened. There were shapes out there in the mist, and strange lights, and muttered voices. I called out, in a challenge, but no one answered. I seemed to have walked for many hours, until, exhausted, I fell down near some rocks. Then, a strange light dawned. I could see a bit but not too far, into the mist. Then . . . then . . . he came to me."

Brother Frederick knew that the look on his cousin's face would haunt him the rest of his days, but he pressed on. "Who? Who came to you? The wizard?"

Godfrey nodded and pulled his pieces of clothing tighter against him, as if trying to ward off the bad memories. "Yes . . . the wizard . . . but he did not seem to be a wizard. He was just a short, squat, swarthy man, with a long beard. Dressed in dark robes. Nothing strange for such a country. But he knelt beside me and offered me a drink. A drink of the sweetest, purest water, Frederick. It flowed through me and made me feel strong, as strong as I had been before I left on the crusade. The man looked at me and asked me my name, which I told him, and he said, 'You have come a long way, brave knight.'"

"I replied that I had, in the service of God. The man shook his head and pointed to my tunic, with the red cross, and said, 'what manner of symbol is this?' At once, I knew him to be an unbeliever, but because of the water and comfort he had supplied me, I kept talking with him. I explained that the cross was the sign of the Son of God, that it represented the one true faith, and that my brothers and I were on a crusade, to free the Holy City from the infidel. Then, then . . . then he laughed at me."

"He laughed?"

Godfrey seemed angry. "Yes, he laughed. The unbeliever. He laughed. He said that the cross was nothing holy, but was a symbol of death and destruction. And I replied that no, it wasn't. That it was the cross of God, that it was here to serve His name, and to free His city."

"What then?" Frederick asked.

"The wizard . . . he said, no, it was a cross of death. He said that all we had done, in our marches across the diverse lands, in our travels to Palestine, was to spread hate and death and destruction. That this was the true meaning of our cross. To spread death, nothing else."

"And what did you say?"

"The truth," Godfrey said, anger still in his voice. "I said that the cross was for the people who had chosen the true faith, that if in our journeys to free the Holy Land, unbelievers and infidels and pagans perished, then that was the price to be paid, that God would reward our labors. I said none who believed in the true faith should fear the cross of God."

"A wise statement," Frederick said, now feeling proud that his cousin would have the courage of his beliefs, in such a dangerous land, with such an evil man before him. "And how did the wizard reply?"

Then the anger in his voice seemed to drift away, to be replaced by the tones of a scared young page. Godfrey seemed to huddle even tighter in his tattered clothes. "The wizard . . . he asked me if I was a true believer, if I believed what I had just said, if true believers should not fear the cross of God. I said, yes, that I believed that. And he asked, 'And your followers? And your descendants? And their descendants, all through the ages?' Of course, I replied. Even a thousand years from now, none should fear the cross of God. Then . . ." And Godfrey's voice lowered to a whisper. "Then . . . he said, 'Well, brave knight, let us see for ourselves.' And I said, 'What do you mean?' And he laughed, an evil sound. 'If you are so strong in your beliefs, then we shall show you, right now, what your descendants shall be like, they and their cross of God.' And he seized my hand. Oh, God, he seized my hand!"

For the last few moments, Godfrey's voice had been getting stronger and stronger, and the last sentence was almost a shout. Frederick clasped his cousin's wrist. "You are in no danger here, Godfrey. You are safe. Pray tell me what happened to you, after the wizard clasped your hand."

Godfrey stared over Frederick's shoulder, at a far point on the wall, his voice low and even. "There was a thunderclap, like a large storm had erupted. I tried to pull away but the wizard's clasp . . . it was like the strongest iron. Yet I could not see him. I could only feel his grasp, and hear his words, like he was whispering into my ear, and he said, right after the thunderclap, 'A thousand years, you said? That sounds about right. Let us travel and see what we can see.' And then, we were lifted up, Frederick, lifted up and we flew like birds. I could see the lands beneath me, the rivers, the seas. I closed my eyes and prayed to God and tried to awaken myself, as if I was having a dream, yet the wizard laughed and laughed. He said, 'Your God is not hearing you, is he? There is only you and me and our travels.' And we flew quick, like a dream, Frederick, and I don't know how he did it, but I knew that in a manner of moments, we were back in my own country."

Frederick murmured a quick, silent prayer, and said, "How did you know?"

"I don't know," he answered simply. "It felt that way. We were still in the air and I was so frightened, and the wizard whispered again, 'Now, we are in the right place. Let us be in the right time, shall we, brave knight?' And then . . . the land beneath us began to change, Frederick. Began to change. Oh, cousin, you don't think I'm mad, do you?"

The monk shook his head, patted Godfrey's hand. "No,

dear cousin. You have had an extraordinary event, meeting such an evil man. No doubt he clouded your mind through some wicked alchemy. Please, tell me more. Confess what did happen to you, and your soul will find comfort. I promise you that."

Godfrey nodded, and said, "The land . . . I saw cities and villages grow. I saw lights beneath me, and then, lights in the air. And the noise . . . a murmuring noise, like many water wheels, working as one. Like many smithies and forges, banging and grinding. And the lights . . . it was like all the cities were ablaze, yet none were being destroyed by fire. I yelled, I screamed, I howled . . . cousin, I admit it to you, that I was so frightened. I have faced death on the field many times, yet the fear I felt there . . . I was like a child, wetting himself. I tried to close my eyes, but the wizard must have worked more magic upon me, for I could not turn away. I saw everything below me, and then . . . the wizard, he said, 'Now we are at the right time. Let us see what your descendants are doing . . .' And I felt myself being brought to the ground. I was falling, faster and faster, the wind whipping against my armor and my clothes. I yelled again, but before the ground met me, I was slowed, like a feather, drifting. And then I saw the knights, marching in a column . . . yet, so strange . . . so very strange."

"How were they strange?" Frederick asked, and then turned, seeing a shadow move back there. Brother Heinrich, perhaps, listening in, but he did not want to interrupt his cousin's tale.

"They were clean-shaven, all of them, and they wore uniforms of cloth. Nothing else. Oh, there was armor of a sort, about their heads, but that was all. And any horses were being used to drag wagons. There were no mounted knights, not at all. Very few banners. No shields. No lances. And the noise! Like armorers hammering and water wheels clunking, there was so much noise. And then I saw them. There were . . . I don't know how to say this without sounding mad, cousin, but there were wagons, moving, with no horses."

There was a gasp behind Brother Frederick, and he knew without a doubt Brother Heinrich was listening in. Yet he was determined to hear this entire tale, and would deal with the young monk later. "Fret not, cousin. Obviously the wizard clouded your mind. Report everything you saw, everything, and trust me to believe what you saw. Go on. There were wagons, moving by themselves. What next?"

Godfrey nodded. "The wizard whispered, 'Can you see your crosses, can you?' And I did, Frederick. I did. On the side of each wagon was a cross, a cross of God. It was black and bordered in white, but it was a cross. There were other crosses as well, strange ones with hooks at each end. I was cheered then, at seeing the sight, and though I could not see the wizard, I knew he heard me. I said to him, 'Look. Even in the future, my countrymen march under the cross of God.' And the wizard "replied, 'So they do, so they do. Look at how they are greeted.'

Then, Frederick, we flew again, in a heartbeat, to another place, farther to the east. There were peasants there, by their farms, and they were tossing flowers at the knights as they marched. They did not speak the same language, but they recognized the cross of God, Frederick. They recognized it and kissed it on the wagons, and they presented gifts of bread and salt to the knights. And it was good. I asked the wizard, 'Who are the foes of these brave knights?' And he said in my ear, 'Unbelievers who rule this land. Who do not believe in God. Who have torn down churches and murdered priests and nuns.' Frederick, I must confess at hearing those words that I felt even more prideful at what my children's children were doing, so far into the future. They may have wagons without horses and strange clothing, but the cross . . . the cross was still there. They were still fighting God's fight against the infidels. I felt so proud and yet . . . that damnable wizard, he must have sensed my thoughts. He laughed again and said, 'You seem filled with pride at what your children of God are doing. Here, let us see further what they will do.' And I felt like . . . I felt like time had passed again, Frederick, and . . . then . . ."

Frederick got up as Godfrey composed himself, and threw a few more sticks of wood upon the fire. His hands trembled as he stirred the embers with another length of wood. He had prayed over many a troubled soul these past years, souls filled with guilt or terror or even possessed on one or two occasions, with demons that needed to be expelled, but never had he heard such a tale. And to be hearing it from his own cousin, his own brave knight!

He returned to his bench and Godfrey went on. "Then, one right after another, I saw visions. Quick visions, like tapestries being held up before me and then taken away, and then followed by another. And all of the visions had the same knights I had seen marching, and . . . and it was different. Bad things were happening, Frederick, very bad."

"Tell me," Frederick said.

Godfrey took a deep, shuddering breath. "I . . . I saw dragons in the air, dragons flying that bore the same cross. The dragons were going over cities, tall cities, and the dragons were dropping eggs . . . eggs that exploded with flame . . . I saw women and children, burned alive . . . it was horrible. The eggs were dropped everywhere across the city, even on cathedrals and what I believed was a hospital . . . and the fire spread and spread. The screaming from the men and women was quite loud. And there were smaller dragons as well, who chased after the people from the air, and dropped eggs on them, killing them and rending their bodies asunder."

"Dragons," Frederick said simply.

"Dragons," Godfrey replied. "Then, another vision. I saw a long line of men and women, digging a trench in the soft soil. It was hard work in the sun, and they labored all day, with no rest, no water. The knights kept view on them, laughing among themselves, and sometimes . . . sometimes they were breathing smoke through ivory twigs brought up to their mouths . . . I watched and I could not fathom why such a long ditch was being dug. Then . . . the knights, started shouting at the men and women. They beat them, abused them, until they were all unclothed, in the most shameful fashion, men and women, mixing together. They were forced to stand in a line, their backs to the knights, who then—Frederick, they had strange swords and lances in their hands, that could strike from a distance . . . it made the loudest noise and spat fire, and each time the swords and lances moved, the men and women . . . great wounds would rend through their flesh, striking them down, and then, I knew with even greater horror why such a ditch had been dug. It was to be these poor people's grave . . . and I looked around, searching for a priest or a nobleman or anyone to stop the slaughter. But the only ones there were the knights, the knights who were doing the killing. Some of them were even laughing. Then, one more vision . . . worse than the others . . . oh, Frederick, please . . ."

Again, Frederick reached out with a hand to grasp his cousin's thin wrist. "Is it the last vision?"

Godfrey's eyes were filling with tears. "Not . . . the very last one . . . but the worst, the very worst . . ."

"Then go ahead, and all will be forgiven, Godfrey," Frederick said. "All will be forgiven."

His cousin wiped at his eyes and coughed. "The last vision . . . it was a vision of hell, Frederick. All about was a sea of mud and in the sea of mud, were low cottages, made of timber. The wizard brought me to each of the cottages, brought me up to the doors to look inside. And inside, on beds of straw and wood, rising up to the roof, were men and boys, and in other buildings, women and girls . . . but they were like nothing I had ever seen. All had been starved in the most brutal manner . . .

Frederick, they were like skin, stretched over bones. My own poor tattered clothing was better than what those tormented souls were wearing. Then I was brought out and around this place, and I saw battlements and towers and fences, and the fences seemed to be made of some kind of silvery rope. On the other side of the place, were more dragons, land dragons that belched smoke and sparks, and each dragon was used to drag some type of wagon . . . and in each wagon were more and more people . . . there were knights there, knights with hounds leashed by their sides, who terrified the people . . . who forced them to march and then forced them to strip, just like the ones who had dug that hole in the ground . . . again, the horrible mixing of unclothed, men and women, boys and girls . . . and then they were brought inside this dungeon . . . I was outside and the wizard whispered to me, 'Watch closely, brave one. Watch closely, and see why your children's children, the ones bearing the cross, will be cursed for generations to come, for what they are about to do."

Godfrey looked about him, as another gust of wind disturbed a wooden shutter. He shuddered and said, "I saw some strange type of alchemy occur there, Frederick. Some creatures, not like man, were upon the roof of this dungeon, dropping stones inside through some opening. And from the inside of the dungeon, came a great, shuddering cry. A cry of such anguish that it tore at my soul. I could not stand it and I begged the wizard to bring me back to Jerusalem, to kill me, to strike me blind, but he would not. 'Look on, knight. Look on and see what they do, those who wear your holy cross.' So we stayed there, for a long while, as the cries and screams from inside the dungeon faded away. Then, the doors of the dungeon were opened . . . the bodies were dragged out with metal hooks . . . the old men, the women, and God, the children, Frederick, the poor, dead innocents. And they were carted away, to another place, a place of hell, Frederick. It was a larger building than the dungeon . . . there were roaring fires in there, in brick hearths . . . and the dead . . . the dead were placed into the fires and burned, after their heads had been shaved, some of their teeth pulled out . . . and the smoke rose up over everything, Frederick, over everything, and the wizard laughed once more. 'There,' he said. 'You have seen the future, of your children and your cross,' and then, in a twinkling, we were back to where we had started, outside of Jerusalem. I was on my knees, and the wizard was before me."

Godfrey looked down at the stone floor, speaking in a quiet tone. Frederick moved closer, to hear him better. "I thought of many things, cousin. I thought of my journeys, across all those lands, and the good knights we had lost, to free Jerusalem. I thought of the good men who had fallen from disease or starvation, the ones who had gone mad when the water was gone. I thought, too, if my sword was with me, to drive it through the wizard." But Godfrey raised his face and smiled. "But do you know what I thought, even then?"

"Do tell me, cousin."

Godfrey smiled, his teeth brown and yellow. "I thought, even then, that the wizard had played tricks with me, had shown me strange visions, things that did not exist, like the mirages on the hot desert floor."

Frederick nodded. "True. That is what I thought, as well, as you told the story. That through some strange powers, he placed you in a deep sleep, and caused you to dream the most fantastic dreams."

His cousin giggled, but it was the sound of a man nearing his breaking point, not that of a man amused by what he was about to say. "Yes, that's what I thought. Fantastic dreams. And when I was back there in the Holy Land, after seeing all those visions, for the briefest moment, I regained my strength. I was a brave knight again, for just a moment. I knelt on the good stony ground, the soil of the Holy Land, and I prayed to the

Lord and I looked at the wizard and cursed him. I said he was an infidel, an evil spawn of the devil, someone who had the power to cloud men's minds. I said that despite the dreams and visions he had shown me, that I was still a believer. That no visions would disturb my faith."

"The wizard," Frederick said. "What did he do in reply?"

"He laughed!" Godfrey said, his voice rising in amazement. "He bent over, grabbed at his belly, he was laughing so hard at me! The wizard said, 'Such thick-skulled knights they must breed from the barbaric land you call home, where you can't even see the truth before you.' He kept on laughing, and I raised my voice at him, telling him to be still, and he wiped tears from his eyes and said, 'Still? You demand me to be still? You are in no position to do so, knight. For you are about to travel one more time, so that you will know, in the deepest recesses of your soul, that what you've seen is true.' Then, he came before me, and struck me so fast and hard, that my eyes were darkened by the force of the blow. I felt the ground move beneath me and then . . . I was back there. . . . Oh, God, I was back there."

Godfrey clasped his trembling hands together, the fingers growing white under the pressure. "It was a different place, but the same . . . I was in a village, in a square . . . a gallows had been set up, made of the finest wood. The villagers were gathered around and there were a few of the wagons with no horses, the wagons with the crosses painted on the side. By the gallows were the same type of knights I saw before . . . and there were young maidens with them . . . maidens who were weeping, who wore God's cross about their necks. And then, I . . . I moved. I could feel the ground beneath me! I could hear the murmur of the crowd, could smell their fear, could taste smoke on my tongue. Frederick, it wasn't a vision! I was there! Alone, without the wizard! And I saw the maidens being led up to the gallows, and parchments in some foreign script were hung about their necks. Then . . . some of the knights, they placed nooses of rope about the necks of the maidens, and in a flash, it was done. They were hanged. The crowd moaned and even I said something, and that's . . . that's when they began looking at me strangely. And I knew why. I was a stranger in their midst, with even stranger clothes, and I made to move and one of the knights came to me, shouting at me. And the odd thing is, Frederick, I could understand a few of his words. Some Latin, some German. Yet even though I could not make out what he was saying, I knew he was demanding to know who I was. And what I was doing there. And why I was dressed so differently. I tried to talk back, but he talked over me, and then . . . he struck my face. The blow hurt, Frederick, not as bad as blows I have experienced before, but it hurt. And then I was upon him. We fell to the ground and I grabbed his throat and pulled at it and then . . . another blow, larger, and I was back in the Holy Land. Alone."

"The wizard?"

"Gone," Godfrey said. "The mist had risen and the land was clear, and there was no wizard. None. I stayed on the ground for a day and a night, weeping and praying, and then . . . forgive me, Frederick, for I had lost my faith, seeing those knights, bearing our cross, hanging young maidens." He reached under his cloak, pulled it aside, displaying his tattered tunic. "See? I tore off my own cross, the one that marked me as a crusader, and I deserted my fellow knights, deserted everyone, and I started walking back home. That's all, walking back home, in penance, as a sinner. It took me so many months, Frederick, walking as if I were a pilgrim, when in fact, I was nothing but a sinner. An unbelieving, despairing sinner. Heading back to my home, heading back here, to see you, to ask forgiveness."

Frederick placed his hand upon his cousin's forehead. "All is forgiven, cousin. And fear not. Your faith will return. I know it."

Godfrey shook his head wildly. "No, it will not. For I was there. I saw what our children's children will do, under the cross. I saw such evil, Frederick, that I will never regain my faith."

Frederick made his voice soothing. "Of course you will, Godfrey. For it was just another trick, like the other tricks the wizard played upon you. He made you see visions. Could he not make you smell them, taste them, feel them, as well?"

The strained smile returned to Godfrey's face. "Then how do you explain this, Frederick? How?"

His cousin reached into his clothing and pulled something out, which he placed in Frederick's hands. It was heavy, cold, and metal, and he looked down upon it. A metal cross, shaped oddly, but still . . . a cross, with bits of colored cloth at the top. Godfrey leaned forward, moved his fingers along the metal. "The knight who struck me, at that village . . . he was wearing this cross about his neck. I tore it off during our struggle, and when I awoke in the Holy Land, it was still in my grasp. Do you understand? Feel the smoothness of that metal. Is it not better than anything our metalworkers could make? Is it?"

Frederick ran his own fingers across the dark metal, marveling at its quality, but feeling a growing sense of horror and fear at what it meant. Godfrey pressed on. "I was there! I saw the future, Frederick, I saw the future and it frightens me so!"

He kept the metal cross, touched his cousin on the forehead again. "It is late. We will talk again in the morning. You will sleep in my cell tonight."

Godfrey made to speak, but Frederick hushed him. "No. We will talk later. Now, you will sleep."

Later that night, standing by an open window in the monastery, Frederick looked out at the dark valley and the bright stars overhead, shivering from the cold and the touch of madness which his cousin had placed upon him. He had listened to the tales of his cousin with an open heart, but knowing that they were just tales, like those of any other traveler who had gone afar, say to Cathay. Yet what was different about these tales was that it was his cousin—his brave, sober cousin—who had told them, and what was even more different was what Godfrey had placed in his hand. The metal cross.

He removed the cross from his clothing and felt it again in the darkness. Heavy and smooth and not of this land. No, Godfrey was right. It came from someplace else, perhaps that dark future his cousin had seen. He shivered again, sensing that he could feel the evil from that time, living in this piece of worked metal, and with disgust, he tossed it out the window, where he knew it would fall into a snow-covered ravine, to be washed away by the spring rains.

Frederick turned and touched the simple wooden cross hanging around his neck. A symbol, of course, and a holy symbol at that, but still . . . something worked by man's hands. And man's hands can be worked for good or for evil, and God's symbols could be corrupted. That much was true.

But faith? He sighed and started walking back to where his cousin, the brave knight, slept like a terrified child. Faith could not be corrupted. It could not be changed. And that was the only comfort he had in this cold darkness.

NIGHTS OF THE ROUND TABLE

by Tanya Huff

Tanya Huff lives and writes in rural Ontario with her partner, four cats, and an unintentional chihuahua. After sixteen fantasies, she wrote her first space opera, *Valor's Choice*, the sequel to which, *The Better Part of Valor*, is just out from DAW. Currently she is working on the third novel in her Keeper series, which began with *Summon The Keeper* and *The Second Summoning*. In her spare time she gardens and complains about the weather.

THEY met outside the chamber door, the old woman and the young. Camelot slept; the night so still and quiet within its walls, they might have been the only two alive.

"Are you ready?"

The girl drew in a deep breath, dark eyes wide, thin cheeks flushed. "I'm—I'm not sure."

"You've no time to be unsure," the old woman snapped. "We do what has to be done."

"What has to be done," the girl repeated, as though the words gave her courage.

Lifting her basket in one clawlike hand, the old woman

laid the other against the ironbound door. "Bring the torch," she said.

The Chamber of the Round Table danced with shadows. Thin bands of moonlight poured through the arrow slits and drew golden lines across polished wood, illuminated the rampant stag carved into a slab of oak, gilded pale blocks of stone.

As the door closed behind them and the shadows wrapped around them both like shrouds, the old woman set her basket down in the rushes, placing a fist on each bony hip. "How the blazes they expect us to clean this place in the dark, I'll never know. They got me comin' in to clean up after 'em once a week since they built this great pile of buggering rock, but does any of 'em think to leave a torch lit. No. My cat's got more brains than the whole sodding lot of 'em."

"But, Gran, it's so romantic."

Her grandmother snorted. "You'll think it's a sight less romantic if you step on one of them morning stars left lying around. Now light us up, Manda, they ain't payin' us to waste time."

Six torches lit. Seven. The light began to reflect off the pale stone walls, filling the room with a soft diffuse glow. Nine. Ten. Manda carefully extinguished her own small torch. Only one of the shadows, pooled in the depths of a massive chair, remained.

"Oh, criminy. Not again."

Manda clutched at her grandmother's homespun sleeve. "Who is it, Gran?"

"Sir Gareth, nephew to the king. Used to work in the kitchens with our Sara."

"He what?"

"Long story. You get busy turnin' them rushes now. Any big bits of stuff that ain't supposed to be there, pitch out the window. Unless it looks edible, then tuck it away for later."

"Gran!" Her cheeks were bright pink as she stared across

the room at Sir Gareth. "That's one of *the* knights. I can't be doin' cleanin' in front of a knight."

"You can do what you're told, girl, while I goes and has a word with ol' mournful Morris. Odds are good," she added, shaking her arm free of Manda's grip, "he won't even notice you. Servants is invisible to his sort."

"But you're a . . ." Her grandmother's glare wedged the final word sideways in her throat. "Won't you be invisible?" she rephrased after she stopped coughing.

"No. He knows me." Prominent gray brows drew in and, girded for battle, the old woman stomped around the table. "Well?" she demanded glaring up at the fair young man in the chair, who, even sitting, was taller than she was. "Don't you got a home to go to?"

He opened a pair of brilliant blue eyes framed by long lashes. "Is that you, Mother Orlan?"

"No, it's the sodding queen of the fairies."

"Ah, fair Tatiana, who doth tempt with silvered words and capricious beauty."

"And I hear she does windows. Spit it out; what was it this time?"

"A raspberry flan."

"Uh-huh."

"Fain, but it came to my table with a soggy center and yet the syrup did not reach the edge. Two of the berries maintained still their stems and others had been crushed beyond recognition. And the cream, well whipped as it was, was nigh to butter. I vow by my faith as a knight, I could have made it better in my sleep."

"You said that?"

He sighed an affirmative. "And my lady has banished me from her chamber."

"We've been through this." Grabbing the front of his tunic, she dragged his head around until she could capture his gaze with hers. "Don't criticize the cooking. Your missus don't like being reminded of that year you spent in the kitchens."

"Two of the berries maintained their stems." The fingers he held up wore a lacework pattern of scars. "Two."

"I heard you the first time."

"And a large fly had been cooked into the syrup."

"Protein. Some of us are thankful to get a fly or two cooked into our flans." Releasing him, Mother Orlan folded her arms and stood quietly for a moment, brow creased in thought. "All right," she said at last, "here's what you're gonna do. Since you can't keep your mouth shut, we gotta work with what we have. You're gonna go home and clank your knightly way down to the kitchen, and you're gonna make that flan the way it's supposed to be made. Then you're gonna take it to your missus and get down on your knees and feed it to her. If you're still as good as our Sara says you used to be, you'll have her eatin' out of your hand."

"But I am a knight of the Round Table," he protested weakly. "I am a protector of the realm, a slayer of evil, I defeat all those who raise their swords in opposition to Arthur, King of all Briton."

"Trust me, kid, women prefer a man who can cook."

"But you said my lady preferred I not remind her of my time in the kitchens."

"Are you arguing with me?"

"No, ma'am."

"An incredible dessert," Mother Orlan said slowly and distinctly. "Presented to her on your knees. She'll come around. If fact, if'n it's just you and the dessert, she'll come around faster, if you take my meaning."

"Just me and the . . ." His eyes widened as understanding dawned and his fair cheeks flushed. "I don't know."

"I do. Unless you'd *rather* be sittin' here in the middle of the night moanin' to me when you oughta be home in the sack with your missus."

"No. I wouldn't." The flush vanished as one gray brow rose. "No offense."

"None taken."

"Very well, then." Broad shoulders squared, Sir Gareth laid both hands against the edge of the table and, with a mighty heave, pushed back his chair. A martial light gleaming amidst the brilliant blue of his eyes, he surged to his feet. "There is no dishonor in a flaky pastry. I will do as you advise, Mother Orlan."

"Atta boy." She watched him stride manfully from the chamber and then returned to her granddaughter. "Lad's a dab hand with a pudding by all accounts."

Tossing an armload of rushes back to the floor, Manda straightened and brushed a lock of hair from her face. "Will it work? What you told him?"

"It'd work on me."

"But, Gran . . ."

"What goes on between a man and his missus is nobody's business; especially where dessert toppin's involved."

They finished the rushes in silence.

"Nice to have that done with no unpleasant surprises," Mother Orlan sighed, pulling one of the chairs out from the table and lowering herself carefully into it. "I found half a wyvern's tail in them rushes once. Them boys'll drag the darndest things back from foreign parts."

"Gran! That's the king's chair!"

The older woman made herself more comfortable. "And how do you know that? Every last one of them's the same and his bum ain't in it now."

Manda pointed with a trembling finger. "That's his name there, in gold."

"And his name makes it his, does it? Makes a fiddly bit of

polishing if you ask me. Besides, I don't expect he'd begrudge an old woman a chance to rest her weary bones." She dragged her kirtle up so that bare legs the size and coloring of dead twigs swung free. "Ah, that's better, that is. Come on, then, and I'll show you what's to be done to the table."

The Round Table had been made of a single section of an ancient and venerable oak, carved and polished. Resting on stone pillars the same pale gold as the castle, it ensured that no knight sat above any other; that all were equal in honor.

"If'n I told 'em once, I told 'em a hundred times; if'n you gotta bang on the table take your bloody gauntlets off! Sir Kay's the worst; he's got a temper on him like a weasel in a sack. Look at that gouge. Never thinks he's makin' work for others. Oh, no. And there, just look there."

Manda followed her pointing finger and blanched. "Someone's carved their initials."

"Carved something anyways." Mother Orlan squinted down at the marks. "If you can see that's initials, you're doin' better than me. Whole lot of 'em's got bloody awful penmanship." Her remaining teeth gleamed between the curves of a salacious grin. "One of 'em's got some drawin' talent, though. And an imagination about the sorts of positions a man and a woman can get themselves into."

"Gran!"

"Oh, I know it's the . . ." Both hands waved for emphasis. ". . . Round Table. You needn't look so horrified. What do you expect when you sits a bunch of men around a wooden table with blades in their hands? They're no different than your brothers. 'Ceptin' they're bigger and they clank," she added after a moment's thought.

"So what do we do?"

"We sands it out, that's what we do."

They'd nearly finished when the chamber door crashed open to show a distraught young knight standing in the doorway. Chest heaving, muddy helm tucked under one equally muddy arm, he swept a near desperate gaze around the room and cried, "Mother Orlan! Mother Orlan!"

She sighed and straightened, one hand in the small of her back. "Stop shoutin' Sir Gawain, I ain't deaf."

He raced around the table and threw himself on his knees at her feet, the force of his landing flinging up a great bow wave of rushes. "Mother Orlan, I pray you will grant me the boon of your wisdom!"

"Stay away from the seafood at an 'all you can eat' buffet."

Golden brows drew in over brilliant blue eyes. "What?"

"Oh. You wanted specific wisdom. What's wrong, kid?"

"Dost thou remember how a year hence, a huge man all of green didst interrupt our feasting? How he did challenge one among our proud company to take his noble ax and strike a blow, having first vowed that twelve months hence that knight would stand and take an equal blow in turn? And dost thou remember how I rose and asked my lord king and noble uncle that the adventure be mine, and when he did full grant me that boon I took up the ax and cut through flesh and bone, beheading the green giant?"

"Remember?" The old woman snorted. "Who do you think had to clean up the mess? Sure, he took his sodding head with him," she explained to Manda who was listening with her fist pressed hard against her mouth, "but first it rolls halfway across the floor. Oh, there's no blood, thanks very much, but we got knights and their ladies throwin' chunks left, right, and center. Had to toss out half the rushes in the bloody room." She turned her attention back to Sir Gawain. "Let me guess. Year's up?"

"The year has passed full swiftly, yes, and . . ." He glanced over at Manda and back. "Mother Orlan, we are not alone."

"Don't worry, that's my granddaughter, it's her first night. She's learnin' the ropes."

One gauntleted hand clutched at faded homespun. "But this matter is, I fear, of a delicate nature."

"Good. So's she." As Gawain tried to work his way around that, Mother Orlan sighed and prompted: "The year has passed full swiftly . . ."

His brow unfurled. ". . . and I rode out to find this Green Knight and keep my vow."

She covered her mouth, turned her head, and coughed. *"Patsy."*

"Didst thou say . . ."

"No. Go on. Get to the needing my wisdom bit, we've still got to scrape under the chairs."

"I did not come first to the castle of the Green Knight, but another. The lord of the castle and his lady bade me welcome, fed me well, and bade me rest. As night fell, the lord went out to hunt and the lady to my bedchamber came."

"Uh-oh."

"Though she was fair and didst long beg for my attention, pleading and throwing herself upon me, pulling the covers from me and laying her hands upon me . . ."

"Do yourself a favor, kid, and get to the point; armor ain't made for those kinds of memories."

Gawain shifted uncomfortably, and nodded. "For the sake of my oath of knighthood, I allowed her but one kiss and then, struck with guilt, leaped from the bed and rode back to Camelot as fast as my horse could run. On the morrow, when the lord of the castle returns, what shall I tell him?"

"You're gonna ride right back?"

"I must, for still my vow to the Green Knight binds me."

"And you don't know if you should tell this fella what's off huntin' that his missus was trying to play hide the sausage with a pretty stranger?"

"Not those words, perhaps," Gawain allowed, after a moment's consideration, "but yea."

"Give him what's his."

"But I have naught that does belong to him."

"You gotta kiss from his missus, doncha?"

"Give him the kiss?"

Mother Orlan nodded.

"But he's got this beard, and his lips are chapped, and . . ."

"Look, sweetcheeks, I ain't suggestin' you slip him the tongue, but you can't go wrong givin' a fella what's rightly his."

"Give mine host what is rightly his," he murmured, thoughtfully. "I did ask thee for thy advice."

"Yeah, you did."

"So it would fain me to listen to it."

"Yeah, it would."

He stood and, towering over her, smiled a brilliant smile. "Thank you, Mother Orlan."

"Glad to 'blige. And, Sir Gawain?"

He paused just outside the chamber and turned.

"Next time, lock your buggering door." When he waved a little sheepishly and clanked away, she turned to Manda. "What the blazes does 'fain' mean?"

"I don't know."

"I thought it might be one of them newfangled words you kids are usin'. Like gadzooks and fizig."

"No, Gran. You know, he's got an awfully pretty smile for someone missin' so many teeth."

"You'd be missin' teeth too if'n you spent your hols sittin' up on a big horse with a big stick while a nuther guy sits up on a nuther big horse with his own stick and you rides full tilt at each other until one of you gets whacked and goes ass over tip."

Manda winced. "Why do they do that?"

"For the glory, they reckon."

"Doesn't it hurt?"

"Glory usually does. Now, get your putty knife and take a looksee under them chairs."

"What am I lookin' for, Gran?" she asked, dropping to her knees.

"You'll know it when you sees it." The old woman grinned as the visible bits of her granddaughter stiffened.

"Eww. I didn't even know you could *stick* that to a chair."

"Don't touch anything with your bare hands; half of this lot are dealin' with wizards and the like."

"And the other half?"

"Are also morons."

The torches had burned down over half of their length by the time Manda stood. "'Bout time." Her grandmother took her arm and pulled her around the table. "Give us a hand getting up on a chair, I ain't as young as I used to be."

Manda dug in her heels. "If you gotta stand on a chair, Gran, this chair's closer."

Dismissing the offered chair with a disdainful snort, she dragged the girl on by. "I ain't standing on that. That's what they call Siege Perilous."

"Why?"

"I doesn't know 'bout the siege part but the perilous is plain enough if'n you ever stand on it. It's got a right dicky leg. This here's good."

"It's Sir Percival's chair."

"Just get me up on it. I ain't as tall as I used to be either, and I can't reach it from the floor."

With one hand tucked in her grandmother's armpit and the other clutching her elbow, Manda heaved. For a skinny old lady, her Gran was a lot heavier than she looked.

"What is it you need to reach, Gran?"

"That." Squinting a little, she reached back. "Pass me the can of polish."

Eyes wide, Manda did as she was told.

The cup pulled from the light had been made of plain hammered brass and had clearly seen better days. Holding it firmly in one hand, Mother Orlan rubbed it vigorously with a soft cloth.

"It's the . . ."

"Oh, aye. Comes in every week regular, just about this time. All the sodding damp round here dulls it down somethin' fierce, but it's gleamin' when I'm done with it, let me tell you."

"But I thought it gleamed because of . . ."

"Elbow grease. And a bit of polish on an old pair of knickers."

There was no denying that the cup was looking better. Manda cocked her head to one side. "I always though it'd be, I dunno, more fancy. All over jewels and stuff."

"And does our Shaun have fancy cups all over jewels and stuff?"

"Gran, our Shaun's just a carpen . . . Oh."

"Exactly; oh." Rubbing the rim against her sleeve, Mother Orlan nodded approvingly. She set the cup back where it had come from, and for a heartbeat the chamber filled with a brilliant light, brighter even than the most beautiful day of summer, and with the light came the sweet scent of roses, and the sound of pounding.

Light and scent faded. The pounding not only continued, but grew louder and picked up a metallic ring.

"Gran! What is it!"

"No need to panic, girl. Just help me down and stay away from the door."

Heart pounding, Manda did as she was told. No sooner was her grandmother standing on the rushes, than the door burst open and a knight in dark red armor charged into the room. "Is it here?" he cried, dragging his helm from his head. "The scent of roses led me here, and . . . Mother Orlan." He paused, took a deep breath, and looked around the chamber as though suddenly realizing where he was. Broad shoulders sagged, red metal plates whispering secrets against each other. "Did *you* see it, Mother Orlan?" he asked hopefully. "Or you, fair maid?"

Manda's mouth opened.

The old woman shifted slightly, her heel coming down hard on her granddaughter's instep. "Sorry, there, Sir Galahad. You was followin' the smell of the rose water I use to freshen the rushes again."

"But I was so sure this time."

"I know, kid. I know."

"But it has been prophesied that I will be the one to find the lost Grail."

"Yeah, well, if you remembered where you put these things, you wouldn't lose them." She patted him on the vambrace in a motherly sort of way. "Off you go now, kid. I got work to finish."

"But I shall never stop searching."

"No one's asking you to, kid." She pushed him toward the door. "You might want to think about oiling your culet though, or it's gonna chafe."

They stood together listening to the thumping and clanking fade as Sir Galahad made his way back down the stairs.

"Why'd you lie to him, Gran?"

"The poor kid's got enough problems, bein' chased and all but never bein' caught. He don't need to know he just missed it again."

Eyes locked on the knot she was twisting into her apron, Manda sighed. "Yeah, I guess."

"Well, *I* know."

"He called me fair lady." A soft smile curved flushed cheeks. "He's dreamy."

"Now don't you be getting mixed up with that lot, girl. Not one of them has what might be called a normal relationship with a woman. Take Sir Percival, for example." She smacked his chair. "Stumbles on this castle, spends the night, falls in love, rides off the next day, and can't ever find the sodding castle again. Swears he wasn't drinking either. Knights. If you ask me, they all wears their helmets too tight. What you wants is a nice boy who comes home nights instead of buggering off on a quest just when there's work to be done. And speaking of work to be done, check the arrow slits for pigeon bits. Merlin's bloody owl sometimes stuffs them in there. Nothing like the smell of rotting pigeon when you're trying to keep a kingdom together, that's what I always say."

"Nothing there, Gran."

"Good. Then we're done and headin' home."

The door opened again—slowly, this time—and a large fair man slouched into the room. His brilliant blue eyes were shadowed and his golden hair looked as though he'd been attempting to pull it from his head. "Oh," he said upon seeing the two women. "You're not done yet, Mother Orlan. I saw Galahad leave and . . . well, it doesn't matter. Never mind me, I just need to sit and . . ." His sigh was deep enough to cause two torches to flicker. ". . . think." Dragging his feet through the rushes, he circled the table, pulled out a chair, and collapsed into it.

"It's Sir Lancelot!"

"You've met?"

"No, Gran, it said so on his chair."

"Said King Arthur and Sir Percival on the chairs I was sittin' in; that don't make me them."

"Oh."

"But, in this case, you're right. It's Sir Lancelot." One

hand dove under the edge of her wimple for a contemplative scratch. "He's always been a bit moody."

They stared at him for a while.

"They all look kinda alike, don't they?" Manda said at last.

"'spect it's all the poundin' they take, beats 'em inta one shape. Well, wait here, I'll go talk to him."

"Let me, Gran."

"Let you what?"

"Talk to him. Give him advice."

"You wants to give advice to Sir Lancelot, a knight unequaled in worldly fame, in beauty, strength, honor, and great deeds?"

"Well, yeah."

Her grandmother shrugged. "Why not. Best you take a crack while I'm still around to fix the mess if'n you screw it up. Well, go on before he sighs again and we're all standin' in the dark."

Rearranging her features into something essentially sympathetic, Manda scuffed through the rushes to the knight's side.

They spoke too softly to be overheard, their conversation illustrated by Lancelot beating his chest and the girl shaking her head. Finally, she grabbed his fist in one small hand and laid the other over her heart. A slow smile spread over the knight's face. He nodded and hurried out of the room, rushing past the older woman as though he'd forgotten she was there.

"So?" Mother Orlan asked when the girl came back to her.

"It's so sad, Gran. But so very romantic." At her grandmother's impatient wave, she picked up her basket of cleaning supplies. "He's been in love with this girl for years, and he's pretty sure she loves him, but he's never said anything and neither has she."

"So, what did you tell him?"

Basket on her arm, Manda relit her small torch off the now sputtering room torches. "That nothing's more important than love and he should follow his heart."

Picking up her own basket, Mother Orlan followed her granddaughter out of the chamber. "Follow his heart," she snorted, glancing back at the Round Table as she closed the door. "Well, seems harmless enough."

BURIED TREASURES

by Jean Rabe

When she's not typing away at her out-of-date computer, Jean Rabe watches the goldfish swimming happily in her backyard pond, tugs fiercely on old socks with her two dogs, listens to classical music and noisy cows, and thinks up things to write about. She is the author of ten fantasy novels, including her first hardcover: *Downfall, The Dhamon Saga Volume 1,* and more than a dozen fantasy and science fiction short stories. She lives in rural Wisconsin across from a dairy farm.

A PINK ropey scar ran from just above where his left eye had been and disappeared beneath a thick, salt-and-pepper beard. The eyelid had been sewn shut, the stitches crude and uneven. There were other disfiguring marks and burns on his forehead and all along his sword arm. And on his back and chest, hidden beneath a threadbare white tabard, were dozens of welts from a harshly-wielded whip.

Despite these and other injuries, the Knight carried himself proudly, standing at military attention with his unusually short hair carefully combed, his broad shoulders squared, and his angular face a stoic mask hiding the pain he obviously felt. His stiff posture was threatened only for a moment, as the ship he rode in the belly of rose with a great swell and then abruptly settled back down.

Leaning on a spear for support, head held high, he made his way across the cabin and to a small table, slowly easing himself onto a stool that had been bolted to the floor. The lantern that hung from the ceiling directly above him highlighted the deep lines on his face and hands, revealing him to be an old man.

"Thirsty, Knight?"

"Yes," he replied, gently laying the spear on the floor, then digging into a pouch at his side, withdrawing a battered goblet and placing it on the table in front of him. He smiled slightly when his host filled it with sweet mulled cider, and he was quick to take a deep pull.

"Delicious. Thank you, Captain Rogan," the Knight said, the words hoarse, a whisper folded around the edges. When Rogan pushed a wedge of sharp cheese toward him, he quickly accepted it and added, "Thank you for your kindness and generosity."

"You are most welcome, Knight. But I am not a kind man, and I'm *generous* only because you are paying me."

"I thank you anyway."

Captain Rogan was easily half the Knight's age, a wiry man with curly black hair framing an unblemished boyish face. Flashing blue eyes took in the Knight's tired gray ones, holding them as surely as any vise and measuring the man. He found one who had been beaten to the point of death physically, but not spiritually, and one who had somehow managed to cling to a sense of duty and chivalry. Rogan took the stool opposite the Knight, eyes still locked, still measuring.

"And speaking of payment . . ." Rogan prompted. "You promised me gold."

Three bites and the cheese was gone. "Payment if you could get my cargo and me safely away, Captain."

"We are well away."

The Knight skeptically raised an eyebrow.

"Nearly an hour out and still no sign of pursuit. I've just come from the fo'castle. And my mate in the nest gave the all clear. So I tell you again, Knight, there is no sign of pursuit."

"Yet," the Knight said. He wrapped his fingers tightly around the goblet and took another swallow. "No sign of pursuit—yet."

Rogan drummed his fingers on the tabletop. "You are safe, Knight." There was more than a hint of indignation in the younger man's voice. "Aye, my ship is an old one, but she's seaworthy and fast."

"Someone may have seen me get onto your ship, Captain Rogan. And for enough coin they'd be quick to tell Philip's men—who would be just as quick after us. Still . . ." The Knight reached for another pouch, a small one, which he untied from his belt and tossed on the table. "Perhaps you are right. Perhaps I am finally safe. Here is part of your payment."

Rogan grinned widely as he stirred the pouch's contents with a finger. "You lied, Knight. You've not paid me with gold. These are diamonds."

"More than enough to buy you a small fleet of ships, Captain. And far more than enough to pay my fare to the island."

Rogan wagged his head as he stuffed the pouch of gems into a deep pocket. "Aye, Knight, well more than enough to take you wherever in this world you want to go."

"The narrow island, as I requested when I came on board. And once we reach my destination, I shall pay you more. In maps the likes of which you've never seen. Worth a fortune to a seaman."

Rogan craned his neck to glance at a large, tattered map tacked to the cabin wall. France and a watery-pale rendition of his home—England—dominated it. There were three smaller maps hanging near it, these given to him by the Knight and displaying lands and islands he'd never seen, all precisely marked with navigation routes. Rogan gestured at one of them. "Knight, what could you possibly want with that place? So far from France and England? A place unknown, it is. Perhaps not real."

The Knight didn't answer, dropping his gaze to the surface of the cider and catching a glimpse of his battered reflection. He frowned at the sight.

"And *if* it exists, there might be nothing at all there, Knight. No people." Rogan closed his eyes, leaned back and listened to the rhythmic creaking of the timbers and faintly above that the snapping of the sails. "Certainly no Frenchmen. No English. A place unknown." He heard a sailor walk across the deck above, followed by another and another. He heard the bark of his first mate, instructing someone to trim the sail. In the distance was the shrill cry of a seabird. He felt the ship turn gently, heading farther out as per his orders. "But that narrow island it is," he said finally. "For God and for these diamonds. And for the promise of these maps you claim you carry and will give me, I'll take you there." Much softer, he added. "If *there* exists."

The Knight raised his head, again meeting Rogan's vise-like gaze. "How long?"

"To get there?" Rogan squinted, studying the maps a while. "The wind is against us. And the distance is considerable. A few months, I'd wager. We'll stop somewhere for a hold full of supplies before we head out across the sea. And I'll have to come up with a tale for my men about where we're going and why—or they'll get restless. Good that they are all English and are loyal to me, and that most have a sense of adventure about them." Rogan paused. "But I'm curious, Knight. Just what is your cargo? What is it you possess that would cause you to run to an island so very, very far from home?"

The Knight merely shook his head and turned to study the maps.

"For that matter, Knight, what would cause the pope to order all the Templars hunted down and prompt King Philip to torture the lot of you?" Rogan's eyes drifted from the maps to three large satchels that rested in the corner of his stateroom. The Knight had brought them. Atop one satchel was folded a red-and-white silk flag that Rogan recognized as the Templar's battle banner.

The Knight's face took on a hardness that held a warning. "You've been paid well, Captain. That is *my Order's* treasure."

"Aye, Sir Knight. I am an opportunist, and a merchantman, and occasionally I raid an enemy ship. But I am not an outright thief. I am a God-fearing man, a Christian, so you've no worry that I'll take your . . ."

"Holy relics," the Knight finished, tipping his head back to gesture at the satchels. "I've brought onto your ship the greatest of all the Templar treasures."

Rogan's eyes gleamed, and his eyebrows rose in question.

The Knight let out a deep sigh, the sound of sand blown by a gust of hot wind. "Silver chalices from long-abandoned churches, golden crosses studded with emeralds and rubies, strings of rare black pearls, bejeweled brooches and rings once owned by a French queen. There is a singular topaz, the size of my fist. And more, much more. If you've a need, you may look at them."

Rogan shook his head. "I am a merchantman. I am a Christian," he repeated firmly. "I said I'd take no interest in your treasures. But I truly don't need to be tempted." He pointed to the Knight's tabard, eyes lingering on the eight-pointed red cross, the symbol of the Templar Knights. The stitches around one edge of it had become loose, and so it flapped down. "But I am also a curious man. All that wealth, Knight, and you wear a rag."

The Knight stiffened, the motion causing him pain and making him flinch. "I wear only the garb of my Order."

"And with silver chalices in your satchels, you drink from an old wooden one."

"The silver chalices belong to my Order. They are not for my personal use."

"And you carry an old spear for a weapon."

"Philip's men took my sword, a beautiful long blade given to me by Grand Master de Molay himself. Fortunate I was to be able to acquire a weapon at all when I fled."

"And your armor? I've never seen a Templar Knight without armor."

"They took that, too. They took everything I owned. "

"Why? Why all of it?" Despite the question, Rogan didn't give the Knight a chance to answer. "It was the treasure, wasn't it? You Templars hoarding gold, amassing a fortune to rival any king's. That's why they brought you down. You were too wealthy. They couldn't stomach someone having greater riches than themselves."

"That's not entirely the reason. We had loaned Philip money. And we knew it wouldn't be repaid. We saved his life when the mobs of Paris struck." The Knight let out a clipped laugh. "He owed us. But it was power, more than wealth, I believe, that caused our persecution. And his debt to us did nothing to soften his attitude. King Philip feared the Templars' increasing influence."

"Feared the power of a band of warrior-monks?"

"And hated the rejection. He asked, once, to join the Order."

"And the Order refused."

The Knight ran his fingers along the edge of the goblet, staring at the cider but seeing something far beyond it and the confines of Captain Rogan's cabin.

"The Poor Knights of the Temple of Solomon," Rogan

continued. "You should have stayed poor, should have stayed away from kings and governments, relegated yourselves to only protecting Christian travelers to the Holy Land. That's what you did in the beginning, didn't you? Before you gained vast holdings of land all across the face of France and the rest of Europe. Before you accumulated so much wealth during the time of the Crusades and collected more than what . . . nine thousand . . . manses and castles. You should have stayed poor. You would have stayed safe that way, wouldn't you?"

A shrug.

"So why all of it? Why were you such a threat to their authority? Were you too popular with the people? Why *exactly* did the king go after you?"

Another shrug, then a sigh. "Grand Master de Molay said Philip went to Rome and managed to convince Pope Clement that we were not defenders of God's faith, but were—in our rituals and secret meetings—working to destroy it. King Philip must have been convincing, for the Pope ordered him to arrest all of the Templar Knights in France."

"Ah, the start of Philip's holy inquisition," Rogan supplied. "On Friday the thirteenth. But the king didn't get quite all of you."

"Though he tried. We had warning and were ahead of Philip," the Knight continued. "When Philip's men arrived in force at the Templar castles, he found most of them abandoned. A week earlier our brethren had managed to get a few large wagons out of the country."

Rogan slammed his fist on the table. "Ha! And so that's why the rest of you went to Philip like sheep to the slaughter! Your surrender distracted Philip from the wagons spotted leaving the Paris Commanderie. So consumed with his Templar prisoners, he didn't pursue the wagons. Ah, but they must have been filled with things of incredible value for your fellow Knights to face torture and death."

"They were."

"Rumors are you Knights possessed religious artifacts. The Shroud of Turin."

"The Shroud is safely away, well beyond Philip's grasp."

The admonition startled Rogan. "Word is you possessed much more."

No answer.

"And these wagons? Where did they go?"

"To the port. The treasure was divided and taken out on ships."

"Explaining why your naval force in La Rochelle set sail."

The Knight gave a nod. "They sailed away with the wealth we had accumulated through the decades, all tucked safely in the holds. Holy relics Philip wanted more for their monetary value than their divine significance. But only two dozen of my brethren escaped on those ships."

"With all of the rest of you tried and found guilty by Philip and Rome."

"Guilty of sins against God," the Knight finished sadly with a shake of his head. He drained the remainder of the cider and nudged the goblet forward, silently requesting more. "I watched many of my brethren tortured by Philip's decree, and watched too many of them die."

"You nearly died as well from the looks of you," Rogan said. "I'm surprised you managed to escape from Philip's dungeon."

The Knight smiled again when Rogan poured more cider. "I am surprised, too," he admitted. "But the hand of God intervened. A devoutly Christian jailer helped me escape. And so I was able to return home, to recover these relics I'd carefully hidden and that I hadn't been able to get to the wagons before my arrest."

"And you were able to make your way to the docks before Philip and his men noticed your absence."

Another nod.

"Where, by chance, you found my ship ready to cast off."

"Yes."

"Perhaps the hand of God led you to me." Rogan again looked at the satchels. "And now you want to go to an island across the sea, an island off the coast of a land I didn't know existed. That perhaps might not exist."

"To the narrow island in the north to bury the treasure," the Knight said.

Rogan shook his head and made a tsk-tsking sound. "A shame. All that wealth to be hidden a world away like a forgotten, nameless corpse. All that wealth you accumulated in the name of God. But God doesn't need it."

"And Philip doesn't deserve it." The Knight leaned on the spear and rose from the stool. He drained the last of the cider and replaced the goblet in his pouch, then smoothed a wrinkle in his tabard. "I wish to go on deck, Captain Rogan."

Rogan stood and gestured to the door, taking one last look at the satchels before climbing the stairs behind the Knight.

Above, the wind struck them, brisk and strong and biting with the scent of salt. The Knight turned his face into it and relished the fresh air, wanting it to chase the last of the dungeon's staleness from his lungs. There were seabirds in the distance, circling something, white slashes against a dark blue late October sky. He could hear them, oh-so-faintly, and imagined that they must be causing a ruckus that would be annoying much closer. They dove and climbed, and he found himself mesmerized, roused only when he heard a shout from the crow's nest.

"Ship, Cap'n!"

Narrowing his eye to a thin slit, the Knight saw just what the birds were circling. A sail as white as the birds came into focus. The ship had been turned so the mast and sail were needle-thin, almost invisible.

"She's got speed!" the mate continued.

There were murmurs on deck—speculations that the ship was nothing, another merchantman heading out on the trade route. But as the minutes passed, and the sail grew larger, there were also speculations that it was a military vessel, that the Templar had come aboard in a hurry, fleeing King Philip's men, that the Templar had brought danger on his heels.

From over his shoulder the Knight heard the first mate, the whispers barely carrying over the shush of the waves against the hull and the flap of the sails. "Cap'n, the Templar's brought bad luck on us. That ship's on an arrow course." After several more minutes had passed. "She flies Philip's colors. We've no business stirring trouble with France."

"Tack into the wind," Captain Rogan replied. "Bring her to starboard and we'll outrun our shadow. We've a fast ship."

But it wasn't fast enough. And in less than two hours Philip's ship had closed to the point Rogan could clearly see the men on the deck. Philip's ship was larger, though the crew looked scant compared to its size, assembled in a hurry, he suspected.

"They'll ram us, Cap'n!" this from the first mate. "Give 'em the Templar and we might get out of this. Can't afford to make an enemy of the French."

Rogan defiantly shook his head. He looked to the Knight, who was standing at the rail, shoulders square and still leaning on the spear for support, eyes trained on the French ship. "They'll not ram us," Rogan said. *They'll not risk our sinking, sending the Templar's holy treasure to the bottom,* he thought. "I swear to you they'll not ram us. And I swear we'll not surrender the Knight."

The first mate cursed and relayed a string of orders to the men, one last attempt to outrun the other ship. Several minutes later, he was ordering the men to gather crossbows and swords. Indeed, it looked like the French ship wouldn't ram them. But it was turning to pull alongside, and Philip's men were readying grapples and crossbows.

"One knight ain't worth it, Cap'n!" the first mate cried, as he snapped up a crossbow and took aim. "Ain't worth us dyin' for!" Near him a man fell to a French bolt.

"Aye," Rogan admitted too softly for the first mate to hear. "The Knight's not worth dying for. But his treasure is. And it's ours if he dies defending it." He clenched his teeth as the sound of wood scraping against wood cut through the air. The thunk of the grapples digging into his ship's deck came next, the repeated "thwuck" of crossbows being fired as Philip's men began to come aboard. Rogan tugged his sword free from his belt, set his feet, and made ready.

The Frenchmen were practiced at boarding, one rank continuing to use their crossbows to help cover the men climbing across to the English ship and to keep Rogan's men from crossing onto theirs.

A half dozen of Rogan's men were dead to the quarrels before the French had secured the two ships together. Another half dozen were down to sword blows. Rogan's first mate had waded into the thick of the fight, cursing the Templar as he went, howling that the French were welcome to take the crippled old Knight.

And the Knight? Rogan caught sight of him just as a Frenchman darted in and slashed, the blade dancing off his own. The Knight was surrounded by Philip's men, who were alternately slashing at him and parrying the thrusts of his spear. Though the Templar was outnumbered, he was not outskilled. He drove the spear forward, skewering one man. At the same time, he brought his leg up and around, sending another man to the deck.

The Templar shoved the speared man forward, pitching him over the side of the ship. Without pause, he brought the spear around, swinging it to keep Philip's men at bay, using it alternately as a staff, thwacking opponents behind him with the butt of it, while jabbing at those in front. Within the span of a few heartbeats, eight men lay dead at his feet, and another three had been knocked over the side. Philip's men were beginning to give him a wider berth, one waving his hand and calling for the crossbowmen to target the Templar. They did, though each bolt miraculously missed, some striking Frenchmen, most biting into the deck.

Rogan watched all of this as he continued to struggle with two foes now. "God-touched," he breathed, as he spied the Knight slay another one and then another, bat away crossbow bolts, and send swords flying from the Frenchmen's hands. "Twice my age and twice the warrior." Rogan had downed only one man in the time the old Templar had slain a dozen.

"The Templar!" Someone from Philip's ship hollered. "Everyone at him!"

Everyone, to Rogan's eyes, appeared to be two dozen men, the rest of those on the deck of the French ship. They dropped their crossbows and began to clamber over. Rogan's sword arm worked faster, parrying one blow, then slicing in to cut through the man in front of him.

"Two down," Rogan groaned. "Too many to go." He continued to fight, three men in front of him now. He could no longer keep his eyes on the Knight, and he had only a brief moment to glance about at the rest of men to see how they were faring.

The deck was red with blood and littered with bodies, an equal number of French and English. The first mate was among Rogan's casualties, going down still cursing the Templar. Rogan shouted his own curses, all these directed at the French and meant to bolster his men's spirits.

"Surrender!" someone hollered, by the accent, one of Philip's men.

"Should we?" came an English voice behind Rogan.

Rogan shook his head, not knowing if the man saw him. The French would slaughter them if they surrendered; they would have no witnesses to their taking of the Templar's treasure. Philip would brook no wagging tongues.

"Die!" Rogan shouted to the largest of his opponents. "Die!" His blade flashed in the afternoon sun, an arc of scarlet following it. His arm throbbed from the constant swinging, and his chest ached from the exertion. The largest Frenchman indeed fell, but there were two more to take his place, and Rogan knew it would be himself who would be dying soon.

"Never should have brought you on my ship, Templar," he said, as he drove his blade down, then dropped beneath the swing of an especially-adept Frenchman. "Never should have been tempted by your treasure. Never should have . . ." His mutterings were interrupted by a cheer—his men hollering.

Rogan pushed forward, knocking one of his opponents back and buying him a moment to get his bearings. "Templar . . ."

The old Knight had a dozen dead around him, had waded over the bodies and was slaying man after man with that spear, the weapon giving him a reach that was turning the tide. The French couldn't get close enough to him—he was running them through as they darted forward. One after another. The cheering grew, and Rogan found himself whooping, too.

"You surrender!" One of Rogan's mates called to the French. "You give!"

But the French continued to fight, and the old Knight continued to drop one after the next, moving from one English sailor to the next, aiding Rogan's men and dropping their foes. Within moments he was at Rogan's side, driving the captain's opponents back, slipping in the blood and staggering with the sway of the ship, but never falling and never faltering.

"Templar," Rogan managed as he caught his breath. "My thanks."

The Knight didn't reply, he merely continued to worry at Philip's men. Rogan's sailors picked up the infectious energy and surged forward, driving the French back, the survivors scrambling onto the deck of the larger ship and working to separate the vessels.

"Let them go!" the Templar hollered, waving for the men to regroup around him.

"We can take them, Cap'n!" the bosun cried. "We can scuttle their ship."

"No more dying," the Templar said.

"But if they make it back to port," Rogan posed, "Philip will know for sure you've escaped. He'll know you've treasure for certain."

The Templar smiled.

In the days that followed three more French ships came after them, each larger than the first and each repelled when the Templar took command of Rogan's men. There were no fatalities on the English side.

"A miracle," the bosun pronounced.

"Perhaps," Rogan said. The captain banished all thoughts of taking the Templar's treasure. *The diamonds are enough,* he told himself, though he continued to eye the satchels that rested in his stateroom. *The diamonds and the promise of the maps.*

There were no more attacks when they were well out on the sea, away from any hint of land and traveling on waters Rogan was certain no Englishman had sailed. He studied the maps each day, and he headed the ship north, where the wind blew cold and sent his men deep into the folds of their coats and blankets.

The old Knight refused the comfort of additional clothing, insisting he would wear only the "garb of my Order."

And Rogan was not surprised when the Knight paid the price for his stubbornness.

"Consumption," Rogan told him one evening.

The Knight was stretched out on the floor of the captain's cabin, refusing to take Rogan's bunk—despite the Englishman making offers repeatedly.

"You've got sweating sickness, my friend." Rogan paused, touching the Knight's fiery forehead. Friend. Indeed they'd become friends in the three months since they'd sailed from the French port. They'd spent their evenings discussing religion, sometimes praying together, spent their mornings on deck—as the Knight wanted to familiarize himself with the operations of the ship.

"Sweating sickness," the Knight acknowledged. "A bad thing for an old man like myself."

"We shouldn't keep sailing north," Rogan said. "Too cold. And the cold's not good for you." *Not good for any of us,* he added to himself. He hadn't been warm for weeks.

"To the narrow island," the Knight insisted. "The one on the northern map. I paid you well enough."

"Aye," Rogan said with a nod. *Aye, you stubborn old man, I'll take you to the island.*

It was in the heart of February that they arrived, at an island no more than a mile long and half a mile across, all covered with oak trees and blanketed with snow. The Templar had managed to hang on until they neared the shore. He was on deck, still refusing to wear anything over his tabard. It wasn't that he didn't like coats, he had explained earlier to Rogan. But there were no Templar coats aboard. And he'd vowed to wear nothing that was not of his Order.

"The treasure is to be buried here," the Knight said, leaning heavily on the spear and the railing for support. He pointed to the southern end of the island. "There will do, beneath that one very large oak, I think." The Templar turned to Rogan, a restful expression on his lined face. "Will you see to it? Bury it deep, where Philip or no man can reach it. Bury it as I've instructed?"

Rogan nodded.

"And see to my burial as well? On the opposite side of the island, somewhere in that stand of trees. I would fancy that."

Another nod.

"Bury the spear with me, Captain. And the goblet."

"Aye, my friend. I'll bury your treasures."

The Knight died less than an hour later.

It was a simple ceremony, but one that had considerable work behind it. The ground was frozen, and it took days to bury the Knight deep in it, spear at his side, goblet clutched to his chest.

The English sailors waited another month offshore, subsisting on fish that were abundant in the area. Then the air started to warm, and with it the ground. They could dig much deeper now, on the southern part of the island. They buried the satchels filled with silver chalices and bejeweled brooches, golden crosses and a topaz the size of a large man's fist. They retrieved the maps the Knight had promised them, along with one strand of black pearls—wanting something of the Templar horde. They took nothing else.

Then they stocked up on fish and sailed east, certain the Templar's maps would return them to England.

"Cap'n?" It was the bosun. He edged into Rogan's cabin and found the captain studying one of the wondrous maps.

"D'ya think anyone'll ever find the Templar treasure?"

Rogan looked up, a crooked smile on his face. "Perhaps," he said. "And perhaps the Knight intends someone to. Some day. If they find the things that sparkle, they'll stop looking for the things that matter."

"All them gems," the bosun mused. "They'd matter a lot to me."

"Not the real treasure," Rogan said.

The bosun cocked his head.

"That, we buried with our friend. In an unmarked grave."

"Couldn't mark it. Didn't know his name," the bosun admitted.

"I never asked him it, and he never volunteered it," Rogan said. "All that wealth to be hidden a world away with a forgotten, nameless corpse."

"Sir?"

"Never mind." Rogan dismissed the man with a wave of his hand. When he was gone, the captain breathed deep and leaned back in his chair. "All that wealth. The Grail." One day he'd gotten a good look at the battered wooden goblet the Knight kept close to him, at the bloodstain at its bottom, realizing its significance. "The spear he wielded against the French. The spear of Longinus that pierced Christ's side. The Holy Lance." He'd gotten a good look at that old spear, too, and by the bloodstains and by the aura he felt, and by the way the Knight never let go of it, Rogan had realized just what it was. Holy relics the Templar hid in plain sight and demanded be buried with him. "Buried. With a forgotten, nameless corpse," Rogan sighed. "The real buried treasure."

*   *   *

Notes about the Templars: *Some scholars are certain the Knights Templar were the guardians of religious relics such as the Shroud of Turin, the Holy Grail, and the spear of Longinus. Too, some believe that the Templars buried their greatest treasure on Oak Island, a small island off the coast of Nova Scotia.*

*Treasure hunters continue to this day to search for it on that is-
land, which is roughly a half-mile wide by a mile long.*

*King Philip's hostility toward the Templars reached fever
pitch when he was refused admission to the Order. He mounted
false charges against the Knights, and on Friday, October 13,
1307, he directed his armies to attack the Templar headquar-
ters. Hundreds of Knights were arrested and tortured. Historians believe Philip's true target was the Templar treasure, which
had been carted away on wagons to the port of La Rochelle.
The treasure was placed aboard the Templar ships, and the
fleet disappeared.*

*Among the Templar's treasures were said to be exceptional
maps and navigational charts of the oceans.*

FATHER OF SHADOW, SON OF LIGHT

by Russell Davis

Russell Davis lives in Maine with his wife, their children, and a psychotic cat. His short fiction has appeared in numerous anthologies including *Merlin, Single White Vampire Seeks Same* and *Civil War Fantastic*. He coedited the anthology *Mardi Gras Madness* and the forthcoming DAW anthology *Apprentice Fantastic,* both with Martin Greenberg. He is currently at work on a novel, *The Crown of Sands,* and numerous other writing and editing projects.

GENERAL Seth Rellick led the vast army of the Kahm-Ridhe over a hill and reined in his mount. In the valley below, the elven city of Parthanor waited like a shimmering jewel nestled in a skindancer's navel. The forest of Riantha, which spread over the better part of the elven kingdom, was not as thick as it could have been—a fact which pleased Seth to no end. It was difficult to fight a mounted campaign among the trees. From here, Seth could see that the gates were closed and the bray of horns sounding the alarm echoed across the remaining distance. Several hours earlier, his scouts had reported that most of the citizenry had either fled or was ensconced in the fortified city.

Not that the fortifications would matter. The outcome of the battle, as far as Seth was concerned, was a foregone conclusion. The advance elements of the Kham-Ridhe, ten thousand foot soldiers and five thousand mounted cavalry, were more than adequate to the task. There were even more men, foreigners and mercenaries who had joined as the campaign wore on, waiting to come in behind his troops.

He raised his right arm, made a fist, and the six primary commanders rode forward. There was no need to discuss the plans, which had been finalized the day before. Seth waited until they were arranged in a semicircle around him and then pointed at the beautiful city below. Legend had it that the first buildings constructed in Parthanor had been created by ancient gods. "Destroy it," he said. The commanders nodded in unison and turned their horses at once, barking orders as they rode.

The gods, Seth knew, had surely forsaken the elves. Otherwise, this war would have been even more difficult. The first ranks of the army began moving down the hillside. Parthanor was fortified, but the gates wouldn't hold for long, and most of what remained of the elven army had withdrawn to the capital city of Kathas to make their final stand.

One of his personal guard, Marikus, rode forward and inclined his head. "General?" he said.

Seth sighed. "Yes?" he said. Marikus was the leader of his personal guard, but he was not one of the Kham-Ridhe. He was a foreigner, a mercenary from the free city of Accord. Upon learning the army rewarded their warriors by physical challenge, he immediately had earned his place by besting the other five bodyguards in single combat. The previous leader, whose name Seth remembered but didn't allow himself to think of, had been killed. By right of challenge, Marikus had taken his place, though Seth was still not completely comfortable with the man.

"A messenger has arrived from the main encampment.

Your wife has begun true labor, and the child will be born soon," Marikus said. "She requests that you return to the camp."

Seth felt a chill run along his spine. The thought of having a child was exhilarating and disquieting all at the same time—that it should be born as he laid waste to the second finest city in the elven kingdom seemed an omen . . . but of what? "Very well, Marikus. Send the messenger back. Have him tell her that I'm currently busy trying to overrun Parthanor, but will come or send for her as soon as I'm able." His voice was stern, though not cold, and it held the tenor of command from long practice.

"Yes, General," he said.

Seth noted a slight tone of humor in the other man's voice. "Marikus, try to get hold of yourself. I wasn't trying to be funny. Just have the messenger explain that I'm . . . oh forget it. Don't bother. The battle will be over soon enough."

Marikus nodded. "Will you be going down to the front, sir?" he asked.

The first wings of he Kham-Ridhe were in position. "Yes," Seth said. "Any moment now." On the walls, the elves could be seen running about, getting their archers into position.

"Sir?" Marikus asked. "We're not waiting for sunrise?"

"That's what they'd expect us to do," Seth said. "So, no, we're going to attack now." Though it appears, he thought, that they're trying to get ready as quickly as they can.

"I . . . I had thought everyone was just getting into position."

"They are," Seth said, his eyes taking in the scene before him.

From the trees, six horns sounded the readiness of his troops. Seth turned in his saddle, surveying the strength of the army. The foot soldiers would go in first, drawing the fire of the archers and attempting to gain a foothold on the walls. Their armor would protect them against the arrows for the most part—the elves' bows did not have a strong enough pull to pierce plate mail. They'd never encountered an organized army with the strength and resources of his people. Their armor and weapons had been forged by a veritable fleet of dwarven black-smiths, taken prisoner when the Kham-Ridhe had first begun their conquest of the continent.

After the foot soldiers took the wall, the mounted troops would sweep in behind them, going through the gate, and lead-ing the charge into the city. Seth and his personal guard would lead the charge against the gate. It was possible, he thought, that they might be able to take the gate—which looked as though it hadn't been used in quite some time, and only re-cently strengthened with logs—in a single strike.

"What is our role to be in the battle, sir?" Marikus asked.

"The gate," Seth said, donning his helm.

"The gate, sir?"

"The gate," Seth repeated. "Are you ready?"

Marikus waved a hand, and the five other men in his per-sonal guard rode forward. "Yes, sir," Marikus replied.

"Excellent," Seth said. He raised a hand high over his head. "Attack!" he yelled, spurring his horse forward.

They hit the gate and the walls with everything they had, but by the time darkness fell, the desperate citizens of Parthanor still held the city. Fear of death was a powerful in-ducement for fighting your best. Seth settled in for a more pro-tracted siege, but it mattered not, he thought as he rolled into his blankets that night for a few hours' sleep. Parthanor, like the other cities before it, would fall before the might of the Kham-Ridhe and another piece of the western mass of the continent would be his.

*   *   *

In the distance, the elven city of Parthanor burned. From his vantage point on top of a steep hill that overlooked the city, Seth could see the glow of the flames spreading into the sky, the black clouds of smoke reaching up like the fingers of the damned to join with the approaching night above. Had it been the city before this one, or the one before that, the sight would have brought him pleasure. The faint echoes in the wind that hinted at the screams of the dying would have brought a grin of victory to his lips. But now . . .

Seth crossed to the small cook fire he had made and sat down before it. The rabbit was almost done. Behind him, the six knights who made up his personal guard stood in attendant silence, waiting for his commands. Their armor, like his though less ornate, showed gold and red sand dragons on black that seemed to writhe and dance in the flickering light. His thoughts returned to the burning city again, as he turned the spitted rabbit over the flames.

Parthanor was the next to the last. The next city, Kathas, was the elven capital. There was little doubt in his mind about the outcome of that battle. There weren't enough elves left to defend it. He'd laid waste to their army, cutting it to pieces one battle at a time, though they'd made a valiant stand here. The siege had lasted for over two days. Why then, he wondered, did he feel so restless?

Using a long dagger, he pulled the rabbit out of the fire, removed it from the spit, and placed it on a tin plate. Seth contemplated the glow on the horizon and his own dissatisfied feelings while he waited for the rabbit to cool. When it was ready, he began eating. The knights behind him were silent, though he knew they were probably hungry by now.

He shrugged and, between bites, said, "Marikus."

Marikus stepped forward, his blond hair the color of blood in the firelight. "Yes, General?"

"Go down to the main camp and ask Lianre to come up and

bring the child. Get a meal for yourself. When you return with them, send the other men down to eat. You will remain on guard here." He speared another piece of rabbit, put it in his mouth.

"As you command, General." Marikus bowed again, turned, and left. His horse made almost no sound on the soft grass of the hill.

Seth finished the rabbit, and threw all the bones except a tiny rib into the fire. He hadn't seen Lianre since the birthing began several days ago, but word had been brought to him that she had fared well through the birth. And that he had a son.

He nibbled absently on the rabbit rib, using it to pick his teeth clean. A son. Lianre had given him an heir. Perhaps that was what he felt—a need to see the boy and take his measure.

Lianre was his third wife, and the only one to bear him a child. The others hadn't conceived, no matter how many times he'd slept with them. It was a damnable thing, and had shaken his confidence, at least in the private chambers of his mind. But finally there was a child.

Seth contemplated the stars again, noting that the fire glow was dimming in the distance. It was almost over. His empire, born of blood and death, the entire western half of the continent, was nearly complete. His urge to conquer it all had led him here.

And now he had a son to give it to. But would the son prove worthy?

Lianre was sitting outside her tent and nursing her son when Marikus rode up and dismounted. He bowed perfunctorily from the waist, and said, "The general has asked me to bring you and the boy to him." He paused and when she arched an eyebrow at him, added a belated, "Honored Mistress."

"I am feeding him right now," Lianre said. "I will come as

soon as he is finished." She was feeling waspish, and Marikus' half-hearted bow and his tone of feigned diffidence annoyed her. It was the tradition of the Kham-Ridhe people that men should be respectful of women in their actions and in their hearts, but many of Seth's knights were foreigners and only obeyed out of necessity. A man accused of treating a woman badly among the Kham-Ridhe risked scorn at the very least. A man found guilty of mistreating a woman risked death.

Marikus bowed again. "I will get a meal for myself and return to you then, Honored Mistress."

Well, Lianre thought, *at least he's bright enough to have picked up on my tone.* "Very well," she said. "I will be ready." She made a brief shooing gesture, and Marikus strode away, heading in the direction of the cook tent. She sighed. Marikus was an insufferable snob, and he disdained her claim of royal blood.

It was odd for Seth to be summoning her now, she realized. Under normal circumstances, he would be down in the ruined city of Parthanor, watching over the looting and making certain that none of the captives were important persons of rank who could be pressed for information or ransomed. She had last seen him when the birth had started, though she had made certain to send word that all was well and that he had a son.

She looked down at the infant suckling at her breast. The boy was special, she knew, so different from the other children she had seen. He had not cried when he was brought into this world of bright light and loud noises, had not in fact, cried once since. He just stared at her with eyes so blue they were almost black. When he wanted to nurse, his lips and arms stretched outward in a grasping motion that seemed out of place on an infant only a few days old.

But the twin-moon birthmark on his right cheek marked him as much more than just a strangely quiet infant whose awareness was a bit more acute than normal. The birthmark was a part of an old prophecy among the Kham-Ridhe—and she knew the prophecy by heart. It was said that one day a child would come, marked by the twin moons, and born under the banners of war, who would cause the Kham-Ridhe to put down their weapons and take up the cause of peace forever.

In the past few days, Lianre had thought of little else, and an odd combination of wonder and worry filled her each time she gazed upon her tiny son. What kind of a man would he grow to be? What strength must he one day be destined to possess, if he could cause the Kham-Ridhe to become peaceful? She shook her head.

The prophecy, like many of them, was regarded with a mixture of awe and fear by her people. They did not just practice war, it was a part of them, in their blood from the first days of their creation. The Elder Gods had made them that way, and though they were long since gone, the Kham-Ridhe remained.

Lianre was unsure of how Seth would take the sight of his son, destined to be a peacemaker, when the father led an army of thousands. It might well be very difficult for him to accept.

She looked down at the boy, as yet unnamed, who blinked at her sleepily, burped, and fell asleep. She smiled, pleased to have him be happy and content. On the other side of the fire, Marikus was walking toward her and she sighed again, wishing that Seth had sent someone else to escort her.

Nonetheless, it was time to go and show Seth his newborn son. Later, she supposed, there would be plenty of time to think about destiny.

Seth watched as Marikus and Lianre rode into the light from the fire. Wrapped in her arms, and secured against her chest by a clever scarf, was his son. Seth stood up and crossed the small campsite, offering his assistance to Lianre as she dismounted.

She nodded her thanks, and once her feet were on the ground, Seth bowed at the waist.

"Lianre," he said, smiling. "I'm pleased that you've come."

"I'm pleased to be here, my husband," she said. Her voice was moonlight and silk, and Seth wondered again why she hadn't pursued more than a passing interest in singing.

Marikus dismounted and tied up both his and Lianre's mounts, then dismissed the other members of the guard to their well-deserved dinner. Without comment, he posted himself on the far side of the fire, distant enough to be out of earshot.

Seth gestured at the fire. "Come and sit with me, Lianre. I want to see my son."

She nodded and he guided her to a comfortable camp chair. "Will this do?" he asked. "Are you comfortable?"

Lianre smiled. "Yes, Seth, I'm comfortable enough." She laughed. "I didn't ever imagine you fussing over me like a mother hen."

He felt himself blush, and was glad of the flickering light that hid his reaction. "I don't mean to fuss," he said. "You probably get more than enough of that from your women."

She nodded. "I did, but I sent them away after the birth."

Seth felt a moment of alarm. For a woman of her rank to be without attendants was unheard of among the Kham-Ridhe. "Why?" he said.

"For fussing over me like a piece of Andari glass art," she said. "They were driving me crazy. I told them to come back after they'd learned how to behave around a new mother." She arched an eyebrow mischievously. "They may never return," she added in an ominous voice.

Seth tried not to laugh, and failed. "It's not proper, Lianre. You know that."

"I know," she said. "I'll recall them in a couple of days. I just needed to find my balance."

He nodded. "Very well. I wouldn't presume to understand what you've been through or what you may need at this time." The urge to ask about the child swaddled at her breast was there, but he restrained himself. Tradition dictated that the woman present the child to its father, and he believed very strongly in those traditions.

"Of course," she said. "Do you want to see your son?"

As she spoke, Seth saw something—he was unsure what—pass across her face, and he felt another moment of anxiety. He nodded.

Lianre rose from the camp chair, her black hair swirling almost to her waist. Carefully, she unwrapped the child, then stepped toward him. She held the infant up in both hands, and said the ritual words. "Seth Rellick, General of the Kham-Ridhe and Knight of the First Rank, I present to you the blood of your blood—your son. From the loins of a warrior and a princess, he comes forth, awaiting your blessing and your teaching. From his mother, he shall have nourishment, love, and the comforts of home; from his father, the ways of the Kham-Ridhe, the path of the warrior, the honor of knighthood, and a name." She offered the child to him. "What do you name him, Seth Rellick?"

For the space of perhaps ten heartbeats, Seth said nothing. He stared at the little form before him, wondering if all fathers saw such perfection in their newborn children. Then the child turned its face toward him and Seth saw the intense blue eyes, and the birthmark. He wanted to cry out, to say something that would make what he saw different, but the child's gaze held him, pulled him into its depths, and offered a vision. . . .

The banners of the Kham-Ridhe flew over the elven capital of Kathas. Parts of the city still burned, but it was over—the elves were defeated and even now, the last of them were being led to the temporary prison camp. The campaign to take over this part of the continent had been successful.

On the steps of the palace, Seth stood over their King, Thalon, and spoke some silent words. Thalon responded, defiance in his every gesture. With a sweeping gesture, Seth drew his long sword and took Thalon's head. . . .

The city of Kathas had been restored. How much time had passed? In the sky above, flights of dragons, black and cruel, were sweeping down on the terrified populace. Archers fired arrow after arrow to no effect. From the south, the enemy rose up in ranks of black-skinned elves, pouring out of caves and underground warrens, to fall upon the citizens of Kathas. Elsewhere on the continent, the last flickers of civilization were being eradicated by this unstoppable force from below the soil. . . .

The vision faded, and Seth drew a shuddering breath to speak, but the child's gaze took him again. . . .

Seth was leading the Kham-Ridhe across a vast desert. Their armor and swords, the path of knighthood and war, were behind them, discarded like so much useless baggage. Before them, lay a harsh realm that could not be conquered, only endured. In time, perhaps, they would learn to thrive here. There would be no choice but to become nomads, moving as the seasons and the shifting sand winds dictated. . . .

More time passes, and Seth senses that his bones are long since dust. But the Kham-Ridhe still survive, have thrived, living in silk tents and raising horses bred to this harsh environment. Their skills as swordsmen have endured, too. Become greater, in fact, for the long years of solitary practice. And he can see them, after generations of peace, being the saviors of this world, their swords flashing in the sunlight of a hundred different kingdoms to bring smashing defeat to the black-skinned elves that in another vision conquered the world. . . .

Seth drew a long, almost painful breath. His knees felt weak. Lianre was speaking to him.

"Seth? Seth? Are you all right?" Lianre was saying, while

she held the child and tried to shake his shoulder at the same time. "Seth?"

Seth shook his head. On the other side of the fire, Marikus sensed a problem and began making his way toward them. Seth held up a hand and shook his head, and Marikus retreated to his original position.

"I'm sorry, Lianre," Seth said. "I . . . I was distracted for a moment. Where were we?"

She looked at him carefully. "You were about to name your son," she said. "Where were you just then? Your eyes were far away from here."

Seth held out his arms. "May I hold him, please?" he asked.

Lianre handed over the child, and Seth saw that the blue eyes had closed and the child was sleeping again. On his face, the tiny birthmark seemed to glow with an inner light for a moment, then faded to a mundane reddish-black.

Seth was unsure of what he'd just seen, just experienced. A vision, yes. But of what? Possible futures? The price of leading the Kham-Ridhe to victory over the elves? He shook his head and sighed, knowing that Lianre was waiting for him to complete the ritual.

The child in his arms frightened him. The prophecy the child represented frightened him. What were the Kham-Ridhe if not warriors born? How could he lay down his sword and lead them off into the desert because of a . . . a child, a story? The very idea shook him to his core. How many of his people had died as he'd led them across the western half of the Astran continent? And how could he turn his back on that conquest now?

Lianre put a hand on his shoulder. "Seth? You must name him."

"I don't know if I can, Lianre," Seth said, whispering. A horrible thought crossed his mind then, that the prophecy had no power over him or his people if the child were dead. He cradled the boy in his arms, arms strong enough to snap a man's neck or throw a spear with enough force to shatter a shield. To kill the child would be nothing, no effort at all.

"You must," Lianre was saying. "He is your son, regardless of the prophecy."

"He will destroy us all," Seth whispered. "We are the Kham-Ridhe. Without war, we will be nothing."

Lianre's eyes narrowed. "Is that how little you value your people?" she asked. "That without the task of killing others, they will blow away on the wind? Is that what you saw?"

"I saw a world I didn't recognize," Seth said. "I am a knight, Lianre. What else could I be?"

" A father," she said. "A teacher, a leader. Perhaps taking the Kham-Ridhe somewhere they've never been before."

"Or somewhere they don't belong," Seth said.

"How long have you wanted a child?" she asked. "How long have you waited for a son to follow you?"

"Many years," Seth said. "But I didn't want this."

"But it's what you have," Lianre said, "want it or not."

"I . . . I don't know what to do, Lianre." Even to himself, his voice sounded weak and unsure, and it brought a twisting feeling to his gut.

"You must do what is right," she said. "Not what you think is right, but what *is* right. The prophecy doesn't say what will happen to the Kham-Ridhe if the child never comes. Perhaps this is because without the child, there will be no Kham-Ridhe. Would you try to trick the universe?"

It was an old question, a philosophy game among his people. It was often jested that every side of a rock, once lifted, was the top side, and the universe would have its way, a force unstoppable.

"This isn't the universe," Seth said. "It's just a child, and an old prophecy. How will I tell the people? How will I explain that we've come so far only to leave the field?"

Lianre nodded. "It will be difficult. They've been following you for a long time, and following the way of war longer still. But they will do as you say, Seth. They will look at the child and see a prophecy fulfilled and the Kham-Ridhe have been following prophecies since memory began."

For a long moment, Seth said nothing, his head bowed and his eyes fixed on the infant in his arms that would change his world forever. "Very well," he said. "It seems I have little choice when faced with your determination and the visions given to me by a child without a name." He lifted the boy up in his arms, holding him up toward the stars.

"Blood of my blood, from my loins and your mother's womb, you have come forth. A child of the Kham-Ridhe, waiting to be taught. From your mother, you shall have all the promises of the heart; from me, a sword that will bend and not break, a shield to protect you as you grow into knowledge, and a voice that will teach you of the long tradition of the Kham-Ridhe. I name you Drados, a fire arrow, signaling the coming of a new path."

"It is a worthy name, Seth," Lianre said.

"I can only hope that he becomes a man worthy of it," Seth said. He handed her back the child, who had slept through all the fuss. "Or that we can become worthy of him."

Lianre cradled the sleeping infant to her breast. "What did you see, Seth?" she asked.

"I saw two victories for our people, but only one did not lead to ruin." He shook his head. "It will be hard to tell them of all this."

"They know the prophecy as well as we do. They will believe," she said firmly.

"In time, maybe," Seth said. "For now, we have a long journey ahead of us."

"Will you continue on to Kathas?" she asked. "Defeat the elves as you've intended?"

Seth stared into the fire, seeing the long shadows of war play amongst the flames. "No," he finally said. "We will go east. There to make a new home and new lives for ourselves." He looked out over the hills and thought of all those who had died tonight, and other nights, when the Kham-Ridhe, the Knights of Shadow and Light, had attacked.

"Is there a place for us there?" Lianre asked.

"There will be in time," Seth said. He turned to where Marikus was watching them, his eyes ablaze with interest. From where he was standing, he couldn't have heard much, but must have known something was going on. "Marikus?" he called.

The knight stepped forward. "Yes, General?"

"Recall the unit commanders and arrange for the withdrawal of our troops from Parthanor."

"Sir?" the knight asked.

"We are leaving this place," Seth said. "Never to return in our lifetime."

"But . . . but, General, why? We have them beaten," he said, spluttering. Obviously, the idea of the Kham-Ridhe leaving the field was a bit much for him. "They're beaten, sir."

Seth grinned. "No, Marikus, they're not. Not yet, anyway. And if we do beat them, we'll end up the losers. Our people will lose."

Marikus shook his head in disbelief. "What shall I tell them, sir?" he asked.

"Tell them . . ." Seth trailed off for a moment, looking at his wife, and his sleeping child. "Tell them that every shadow can exist only in the light. Tell them that we go to a new place, where the sun warms the ground all year, and the shadows play on the lee of every hill. Tell them that for the Kham-Ridhe, the time to conquer the world has not yet come."

"Sir?" Marikus said.

"You're a good knight, Marikus," Seth said. "Tell them that my son brings with him the prophecy of peace, and we shall find it in the east."

Marikus nodded, and walked away to gather his horse. He climbed aboard, and then said, "General, what did you name him?"

"Drados," Seth said.

Marikus was silent for a moment. "A good name, sir. What shall I tell them to do about the elves?"

Seth grinned again, and felt in himself the release of all the tensions he had been feeling. He knew now why the destruction of Parthanor was unsatisfying. "Tell them to let them go."

"Free, sir?" Marikus said.

"Free," Seth said. He turned his back on Marikus who rode away to find the commanders and crossed the clearing to sit by his wife and child. Along the way, he unbuckled his swordbelt and set it next to him on the ground.

"We're free," he repeated softly to himself, looking with wonder at the child sleeping, innocent and wise, on his wife's chest. "And we'll never be the same."

Lianre looked up at him. "What's that?" she said.

"Shh," Seth said. "Let Drados sleep. He has a long journey ahead of him."

"As do we all," Lianre whispered. "As do we all."

IN A LIFETIME

by Kristin Schwengel

Kristin Schwengel's work has appeared in the anthologies *Sword of Ice and Other Tales of Valde-
mar, Black Cats and Broken Mirrors, Legends:
Tales from the Eternal Archives,* and *Warrior Fantastic.* She lives in Racine, Wisconsin, where she
works in a bookstore. She says, "My life is surrounded by books; I'm either selling them, reading
them, or writing for them. Who could ask for anything more?"

A FLICKER of his opponent's eyes was all the warning
Gedyr had. Relying on instincts honed from decades of
fighting, he slid to the right and brought his blade up, slashing
to the bone one of the bare arms that swung a mace down into
the empty space where his head had been. The weapon dropped
from nerveless fingers and the big man fell to his knees, clutching at the wound with his uninjured hand. From the corner of
his eye, Gedyr saw one of his fellows finish him off. His foe's
eyes glazed, and Gedyr guessed that there were no others to
surprise him. He lifted his blade back to a guard position, ignoring the aches of strain in his muscles.

The attack during their midmorning dismount to rest the
horses had not taken them wholly by surprise, but it was closer

than he would have liked. Had he been the guard-leader, he would have—no, he would not have been given the command. Lord Devran only put his own bonded men in such positions, even when they lacked the intelligence to guard a piss-pot, much less a caravan of tribute for his lordship.

The bandit he matched blows with now was another such as the guard-leader, stocky and predictable, depending on the smashing force of his attacks to wear his opponent down. Gedyr feinted to the left, then stepped to the right, drawing the man a little away from the rest of the fighting, under the trees. As he had expected, the recent rains had made the leaves slick, and he kept his feet beneath him to retain a solid footing on the earth. His opponent wasn't so cautious, and a single misstep found him sliding forward onto Gedyr's waiting blade.

With the deaths of the mace-wielding giant and the man Gedyr had faced, the rest of the bandits lost heart and melted back into the woods, soon lost in the underbrush. The guard-leader at least had the sense to call the hotter-blooded men from futile pursuit, gathering them together to check for and tend to injuries.

Gedyr, as always, remained apart from the rest, walking the slight stiffness from his body and cleaning his sword. He had decided at the beginning of the journey that, when they returned to Devran's keep, he would not renew his contract, no matter how the old man pressed him. It was time and past for him to move on, before the men around him noticed that his face never wrinkled, his weight never settled, and his hair never turned gray. His body was always that of a warrior in his prime, around twenty-five years of age.

Ever since he had realized that he did not grow old, Gedyr had made a practice of moving often from place to place. The history of a sellsword was not often scrutinized beyond the most recent employer, at least not among those petty lordlings to whom he offered his services. They were happy enough to get a man in their ranks whose skills were equal to those of the king's personal guards. They didn't need to know that he had once ridden to battle under this aging king's grandfather's grandfather.

The fleeting thought of that long-ago war brought with it an unexplained pain that tightened his heart. Gedyr frowned, probing the pain with his thoughts. Once, the heat of a sword fight had sufficed for all his needs, driving him to greater feats of sword skill. Now, the end of the battle left him feeling some-how empty, with an indefinable ache of pain and loss deep in-side him.

The troop of guards remounted, and the caravan moved on, only a day's journey from Devran's lands. His weight settled on his horse with unconscious ease, Gedyr turned his mind inward once again.

Loss. He considered the idea for a moment, tasting the thought and turning it in his mind, exploring it. Loss of . . . what? He certainly lost nothing of his skills, for those grew only greater with the years. He kept to himself and made no close friends, so there was no companionship that he could miss as his posts changed. Yet he felt that something greater rested behind this feeling, something that years of fighting had dulled in him.

He thought back through his life, trying to remember any-thing that would still call to his soul, and was stunned to see gaps in his memory, holes that he had never noticed before. His youth was surprisingly clear in his mind: the keep that he had played in as a boy, the fortress where he had fostered and trained as a squire, the day that he had gained his spurs and given his service to his king. The early days of his knighthood, hovering on the outskirts of the court, all stood fresh in his mind when he sought them, as though only years rather than decades ago. The next memory he found was some years later, an image of leaving the battlefield with the king's guard. He could not even recall the battle itself, only riding, blood-spattered, from the field. He frowned at the road before him. Now that he knew the blank in his memory was there, it nagged at the corners of his mind. Somehow he was sure that it was connected to the ache in his soul, as he also knew that he must find out what had once filled those gaps.

The years slowly brought Gedyr back to the south, to the plains where he had been born. The estate of his parents had long since fallen into disrepair, untended after his brother had squandered what little wealth the family had had. He recalled that he had chosen to remain in the king's retinue when the war had ended rather than claim a worthless keep in the middle of a barren field. He stood in the empty Great Hall, the wind knifing through the gaps where stained and glazed window panels had once glittered in the sun. A flicker of motion caught his eye, and he turned to the raised dais at the head of the room, his eyes picking out the flapping of a tiny piece of tapestry, left behind in a crack where it had caught on a block of stone.

His eyes widened and some instinct drove him forward to that block. His father had never quite trusted his feckless oldest son—had he told him all the keep's secrets? Gedyr mounted the dais and reached for the stone, one of a pattern of blocks around the room set to jut forward from the wall. His fingers found their places in the shallow indentations on the right side, and he pulled forward while his other hand pressed the left side of the block up and in. With a rough grating sound, the block turned a slight hand's breadth, then stuck. Pulling his dirk, Gedyr slipped it through the gap, expecting no resistance and cursing in amazement when the blade struck something. He sheathed it and applied himself to the pivot mechanism one more time, pushing on the block with all his might, skin tearing off his fingertips. Just when he was about to go to the dead rose garden for a hooked branch to pull the unknown object forward, the block shifted again, sliding open and allowing light into the tiny hollow in the wall.

A leather drawstring pouch the size of his two clenched hands rested in the center of the space, holding something rounded in shape. Old habits and suspicions made him reach for his dirk again, sliding the blade through the string and lifting the pouch out and placing it on the dais.

Still using the dagger, he opened the drawstring and pushed and pulled at the bag until its contents rolled out and rested in the center of a lone sunbeam, winking at him in the winter air.

His jaw dropped. Surely his brother would never have left behind something so priceless—had he known of its existence. Gedyr chewed at his upper lip and thought for a moment. He had acted as his father's seneschal for a few years, after he had completed his fostering but before he had earned his spurs, and nothing to match this had been in the family treasury. Nor could his father have afforded its purchase at that time, for the estate's resources were already dwindling. It must have been a gift to his father, although Gedyr could not recall any who would have owed his father this kind of debt. Perhaps it was yet another memory that fell during his lost years. Leaving the sack, which in the light showed signs of rotting leather, he bundled his find into the pouch that hung at his waist. Despite its obvious value, he would not sell it, not yet. It raised questions he wanted to find the answers to, and his sword still provided him with wealth enough, even though it had been a score of years since he had taken his last long-term contract, with Lord Devran in his keep far to the west.

The thought of the western lands filled him with a strange sense of purpose, much as a memory of his father had driven him here, and he trusted that instinct. His travel was slow, interrupted as it was by periods in which he hired out his fighting services until he earned enough coin to move on, but he had yet to see any reasons for haste.

Decades had passed before he traveled again through the west, guided by what whims struck him. High summer was brutal in the western kingdoms, and only in the deepest of the forests could one find relief from the blazing sun. Gedyr rode slowly, allowing his horse to choose his own pace on the road threading through the trees. It would be suicide to ride the beast to foundering in this wild place. Even the birds were still during the heat of day, emerging to court and feed and sing in the early morning and evening hours. Not a hint of breeze lifted the heat, and only a few insects raised their buzzing songs.

In the oppressive silence, a welcome sound reached his ears—the gentle bubbling of fresh water. The stallion perked up, flicking his ears to the right. Gedyr tightened his leg, the pressure of his knee guiding the horse off the main road and onto a narrow grassy path that led deeper into the woods.

The path opened onto a grassy glade, at the center of which stood a stone basin framing a natural spring. Gedyr let the horse drink first, pulling him away from the water before he could injure himself with overdrinking, and looked around him. Another path led away from the spring, and he could just hear a chanting murmur. He tied the horse to graze and walked down the second trail.

A larger clearing stood beyond the first, this one occupied by a chapel and two other buildings, which could only be the dwellings of the hermits or monks who chose this distant solitude. The chanting came from one of those buildings, and Gedyr turned to enter the chapel, seeking a moment of that same solitude.

The chapel was a plain building, stone and wood with a thatched roof. The inside of the tiny place was filled by an altar of the same dark wood, simple but made with care, covered with a plain cloth. As he had on the vigil before his knighting, Gedyr knelt before the altar, although he offered no prayers. One who could not die has been abandoned by what gods might exist, and prayers from such a one are fruitless. Instead he turned his mind inward, as he did more and more, seeking answers from that shadowed place within his memory.

On impulse, he stood and unbuckled his sword belt, unsheathing the blade and laying it flat along the altar. The sheath and belt he left on the floor in front of the altar.

His heart lighter, he left the chapel in the same silence with which he had arrived, returning to his horse. He watered the beast again and refilled his flasks with the sweet spring water before riding back to the road. A breeze rustled the leaves, sifting through his hair in what felt like a familiar caress as he rode to the north.

Many years later, his wanderings brought him again to the west, where he heard a ballad of a chapel near a spring in the deep forest, and the night that a beacon of light had shone down upon the building, transfixing all who saw it. When the light had passed, so the song claimed, the monks had entered and found a shining sword driven point-first into the altar. He had smiled to himself and slipped out of the common room of the tavern, wondering who had told the fanciful tale first: the monks, or the bards.

The ache in his heart grew greater as he traveled, pulling him onward without guiding him. When needed, he still hired himself out as a guard, although some instinct made him choose only posts in which his dagger would suffice him for a weapon. Those who hired him thought him a knight doing penance in refusing to use even a loaned sword, and perhaps they were right.

He sought more often the company but not the friendship of others, spending his nights in the common rooms of inns. Once, he had heard a bard with a harp singing a ballad of a nameless man and the woman whose name he had defended, and something deep within him had rung with recognition. He had stumbled from the common room into the dark night, his eyes stinging with tears he could not explain. Thinking perhaps another song would tell his own story, he had begun to pay closer heed to the minstrels, listening to the tales and rumors of the lands he walked. Some of these stories called to him, drawing him to the places where legend said great heroes and fair maidens had lived and died. A feeling of desperation began to drive him, a sense of urgency moving him from place to place.

Gedyr rode, expecting nothing. He had lost count of the trails he had followed, the stories he had heard. How many mysterious valleys had he seen, how many dark legends had he tracked? A glance at the mountain that was his destination, another glance to the setting sun, and he urged the tired gelding to a faster pace. After all these years, he no longer bothered to name the horses he rode. He cared for their needs and they carried him on his search, and that was enough.

Now he rode into the forests fringing the eastern mountains, his mind wandering back to the latest inn, the latest minstrel.

"They call it the Glen of Tears, though legend has it that once it was called the Glen of Laughter." Gedyr's head had lifted at that, and his hollow stare had made the minstrel shiver. "I have seen the place myself. 'Tis but a vale like any other, nestled in the foothills of Mount Kedwyn, with a little stream flowing through it. But no matter how the sun shines, it seems always dark and foreboding there. It has a feeling of tragedy from long ago. They say 'tis even more so at night, that dark words echo and nothing good comes near."

Little enough, but it had drawn him on. He had begun far to the south, ranging across the kingdoms, racking his mind to just *remember.* But memory was too completely gone, and so he crossed the country, backtracking over it again as rumor and legend reached him and tugged at the edges of his recollection. His hand stole to the pouch knotted at his waist and he clenched it in his fist, willing himself to believe that he would know the purpose of what lay within when the time was right. He had carried it close to him ever since he had removed it from his father's secret hiding place, and he was sure neither his father nor anyone he once had known had placed it there. Every time he had thought of selling it, some impulse had stayed his hand, and thus it traveled with him on his search.

The horse pulled up, snorting and fighting his hand on the reins. Gedyr glanced at the sky again. Dusk approached, but he was near enough that tonight would bring his answers. He tightened his grip and squeezed with his knees, reminding the gelding that, though he seldom used them, he still wore the spurs he had earned so many years ago. The gray steed shook his head but obeyed the pressure, his weariness buried under mounting nerves. He danced and sidled into the deepening gloom of the forest, his ears twitching.

Gedyr shared his mount's edginess, glancing from side to side, searching for the landmarks the minstrel had spoken of as the night fog thickened around them.

The mists cleared briefly, and a pillar of silver-gray stone appeared on the roadside just ahead of them. He nodded, turning the gelding off the main road onto a narrow path. The horse fought, trying to go back to the well-worn track, but Gedyr touched his sides with his heels, and he moved on, ever more unwilling.

The grassy trail wound through the trees, sometimes not

even a discernible path, but he guided the horse unerringly deeper into the forest. Looking at the trees, he recognized oak and hawthorne, and pulled to an abrupt halt when he saw a holly tree growing on one side of the track, an ash on the opposite side, their branches reaching toward each other overhead. He reached out to the holly, brushing his fingertips against the leaves, and a breeze blew against him, pushing the boughs beyond his reach. His lips thinned, and he rode on into the wind.

The clearing, when it came, surprised him. Somehow he had not expected it to be so close to the main road, though he knew it must have been. Twice as long as it was wide, the vale was divided by a stream that traveled its length, curving around the ruins in the center. The forest had encroached upon the glen, closing in over the years until the smaller saplings brushed the crumbled stone.

Gedyr dismounted, grooming the horse with care before tying it just inside the vale, then walked to the ruins. The wind and rain of decades had worn them down, softening the shattered walls into moss-covered mounds. Passing through what once had been an arched entrance, he placed his hand on the stone that remained. Closing his eyes, he saw the ruins as the small keep they once had been, nestled within the forest, and he knew his search was over. He opened his eyes and the shadow of what once had been still hung before his eyes, an image laid over the true picture of the crumbling walls.

He cleared a circle of stones where two walls stood together in the corner of what had been a large room, building a small fire not for warmth but for the comfort he somehow knew would be needed. His pack he set against the wall, not bothering to remove his bedroll, and he leaned against it to wait.

Night fell quickly in the foothills, and the tiny blaze before him cast flickering shadows between the gaping holes in the walls. His ears strained, seeking anything beyond the silence of the ruins. He heard his horse snorting restlessly once or twice, before the gelding held his uneasy peace.

It was the wind that he noticed first. So accustomed had he become to the rush of it in the leaves that its absence startled him. After a long moment of dead calm, a gust of wind howled inside the ruins, nearly snuffing the fire, lifting the dried leaves from the still-smooth flagstones and dancing them around him. Then that blast died into stillness, and he heard the soft brush of a tread in the leaves beyond the ring of light his fire created. He lifted his head, staring at the arched entrance, his body an agony of anticipation and dread.

"Gedyr." The voice was soft as the merest whisper of a breeze brushing at one's ear, but still he heard and rose to his feet.

"Fianna." The name rushed out of him as soon as it had entered his mind, his brain flooded with the past, and long-lost memory built a picture of her in his mind's eye a moment before the fog that held her drifted into the fallen chamber.

She stopped just within the circle of firelight and the mist melted away, revealing her tall, slim form, achingly unchanged. He took a breath to speak, but she held up a pale hand.

"What right have you to return to this place?" Her face was hard, her voice cold.

He looked at her, one eyebrow quirked upward at her stiff manner. "The right of one who has sought this place for seven lifetimes." He took a step toward her, then another, until he stood not quite close enough to reach out and brush her white arm.

She eyed him, perplexed, then bit her lip in an incongruous gesture and turned her face away, staring down at the dancing flames. "Seven lifetimes?" he heard her whisper. "What manner of fey thing have I then become?" she asked the fire.

"What manner of fey thing have I become?" he asked in response, drawing her mind from its inward focus.

Her dark eyes shimmered when she glanced at him, and she blinked in rapid succession to clear the traitorous moisture.

"You are as you have always been," she said bitterly, "a knight with his steed, seeking honor in battle."

"Since the memories of you and this place were taken from me, that honor has meant little, and then nothing," he said, his voice more tired than defensive. "I have known to seek something, but have never known what until I arrived time and again to find that it was not what I sought. Until this night, I have chased shadows and fancies—and it seems that even here I do the same."

She tilted her head and looked at him. "You were not to remember anything," she whispered. "Those of my grandmother's blood swore to me you would not, and that you could not return."

"Nevertheless, I am here now, and to stay, so long as this unnatural life is in me."

She looked away, refusing to meet his seeking eyes.

"Fianna, what know you?"

"More than what lies between you and me is involved here. You never did believe the tales of my mother's mother, and loved me despite them, but for all that, they were true."

He stared at her face, the flickering firelight dancing over the narrow lines of her jaw and cheekbones, the slight tilt of her eyes, and the dark shadow of her hair falling over the long tips of her ears. She saw the widening of his eyes, and nodded.

"What is closest to us is that which we fail to see. The blood of the fey flows thin in my veins, but still it flows. When they came to me with their demands, I was still able to call upon the powers of my ancestors and be answered. I wept three tears upon the Stone of Ereman, one for myself, one for you, and one for the love we shared. The Stone disappeared, but the fey still took me unto them, hardly more than a year ago. Every night I walk here, though the fey destroyed the place when they came for me."

"Not every night," he answered, "for legend speaks of a woman who walks this place once a year, on the eve of the month of FirstFlowers."

Anger filled her eyes then, but it was not directed at him.

"Thus is time in the realms of the fey," he added softly.

Something within her seemed to collapse, and she sank to the ground, wrapping her arms around her legs and burying her face against her knees. He walked around the fire and knelt beside her, reaching toward her shaking shoulders. When his fingers were a mere hand's breadth from her, she flinched away, and his hand jerked to a stop against an invisible shield around her body.

He pulled away from her huddled form and stared into the flames. A cold rage seeped through him, a fury both at her and those who had carved the rift that had come between them. He stood, his hands clenched in fists at his sides, and his sudden movement caused his belt pouch to thump heavily against his hip. Realization dawned, and he opened the pouch and pulled out what he had carried for so long.

It nestled in his hand, larger than his fist, a raw, unshaped piece of amber. When the firelight caught it, it seemed to flash with light from within. Looking deep into the stone, as he had so many times, his eyes widened. The dark shadows within the amber melted away, and it glowed with its own light, a solid flame cupped in his hand. It shone brighter and brighter until he winced with pain. He glanced away, and when his eyes returned to the stone, the glow had lessened and the shadows had returned in its depths—except he could see that the shadows were himself and Fianna, he standing and she crouching, and both of them ringed by flickering shadows of *others*. Seeing those other shadows surrounding and separating the two of them, his anger peaked, and he cast the amber into the fire at his feet.

It should have made a sound like thunder, but if it did, he heard nothing. The shock of it rippled through the ruins, disturbing Fianna from her grieving trance. She raised her head and stared at the amber in the flames, her eyes wide.

"The Stone of Ereman was lost to the fey the night that I—" She stopped and bit her lip. "How came it here?"

Before he could answer, the flickering shapes that he had seen in the amber came to reality. Tall, slim forms appeared, one group lining the ruined walls, another group standing protectively around Fianna, and one figure alone standing in front of him.

"Grandmother," Fianna began, but the one in front of him gestured for her silence.

"This was of your making, but its solution shall not be." The speaker tipped her head to the side, holding her head at the same angle that Fianna always used when she was deep in thought. Her green eyes were a shade darker than her granddaughter's, but their shape and intensity were the same.

The circle of the fey around Fianna linked their arms together, and he moved toward them, his instinct driving him to protect her as he always had so many years before. His hand went to his waist, reaching to close around the hilt of the sword he no longer carried. The woman in front of him reached out and touched his sleeve.

"Fear not, she will be well. She is one of us, and we do not treat our own so ill as you humans do."

He glared at her, then looked back to Fianna. Her face was abstracted, as though she heard and saw nothing of what was before her.

"Now, human, what would you have of the fey, that you cast the Stone of Ereman into the flames?"

"I would have an end to this curse that keeps us separate,

to live together as once we did in this very place, the keep that was her mother's legacy." He looked at Fianna's grandmother, but she, too, was looking at Fianna, her eyes soft with affection and an emotion that, in anyone other than a fey, he would have called regret.

"That cannot be. Your hand is stained with the blood of a prince of the fey, and therefore to us you are accursed."

The last memory jolted into place, of the crusade for his king, and of that last battle. As though he were there again, he saw the pale figure in leather rather than chain mail riding toward him. He felt his body strain with the swing of his sword, biting deep into the man's unarmored side. He saw again the strange, wild look in the young man's eyes, those eyes that had seemed so familiar even in the heat of battle, and a chill rippled through him. He looked down at his hands, expecting to see traces of the blood that had covered them when he had left the battlefield.

The woman continued, her voice rolling over his recollection.

"Because of her fey blood and her love for you, Fianna was given the choice of your fate. You would live your days either with or without the memory of her, and she chose for you the latter. Although you may wish it otherwise, once a spell is cast on the Stone of Ereman, none can break it, not even the Queen of the Fey. The Stone is a wild magic, more ancient even than the fey, and cannot be controlled."

"Then why did you come to us, why do you bring her here each year for all this time, if nothing can be done?"

"We come tonight brought by the power of the Stone of Ereman, though I know not how it came into your hands. As for the other, that I have no answer to. Her insistence on returning to this place is beyond my understanding, for she only provides herself with pain by doing so."

He smiled inside, knowing that a fey, even one who had

taken a mortal to her bed and birthed a half-mortal daughter, could not fathom a love that stretched beyond the limits and bonds of time and magic.

"Have I not proved myself something more than a murderer of her kind? Is there naught redemptive in all these years of seeking, even for one whose hands bear the blood of her half brother?"

"Perhaps there is. Beyond all expectations, you have defeated the magic that was wrought and have found your way back to this place. Perhaps it is time that a peace was built between you." A speculative half-smile lifted the corners of her mouth.

His eyes narrowed in suspicion. "At what cost? I know that the fey demand a price for any boon."

"Her love for you combined with the half mortality of her mother and full mortality of her father has made her mortal. If she were to leave the company of the fey, our magics could no longer keep her alive. She will pass on with the dawn to what you humans call the next life. If you choose to release the hold your love has on her, she will return to the life of the fey, remembering nothing, as though her time with you had never been."

"And what of me?"

The fey woman looked away, unwilling to meet his eyes. "Your blood is fully mortal. Only the power of the Stone of Ereman has kept you unchanged over the centuries. It has a strange magic, one whose effects cannot be predicted."

"Perhaps that same magic that brings Fianna here to seek for me has helped me to seek her until the time was right to find her."

The woman shrugged. "It is possible. Whatever choice you make, you yourself will die. Perhaps you will live out a natural span from this night forward, perhaps not. Your choice is for Fianna alone."

Though she did not meet his eyes, he knew deep within him that even so, she spoke the truth.

"May I speak with her?"

"No."

He thought for a long moment, staring deep into the amber stone in the flames, then raised his head.

"If her love is great enough to make her mortal, that is her choice already. I cannot deny her that, though she sought to do the same for me. My life these many years has shown me that it is better to live only one more night with the knowledge of that love and mortality, than to live forever without knowing it had ever existed."

A flicker of emotion danced across the fey woman's face, too brief for him to know whether it was scorn or approbation, and she nodded once. She bent, reaching unscathed into the flames, and scooped up the Stone of Ereman. She closed her hand over its glowing light, and all the fey vanished into the misty darkness. An echo of her silvery voice danced in his mind, coalescing into words that vanished in the silence. *"Perhaps worthy of more . . ."*

Fianna, still sitting by the fading fire, looked up at him. A welcoming smile spread across her features as she reached her hands up to take his and draw him down beside her.

The minstrel walked down the trade road through the forest, humming echoes of the birdsong that rippled in the leaves above him. The first day of the month of FirstFlowers was always like this, he thought, so bright and full of life. He had come this way but two days past, and if he didn't recognize the pillar of stone where the path forked off the main road, he would think he was in a different place entirely. The birds were silent for a moment, and in that peace he heard the whinny of a horse and the jangle of harness from down that track. Remembering the swordless knight with the desperate, hungry eyes, he turned onto the path.

Just inside that gloomy vale, he found the horse, tethered and reaching for the fresh grass just outside of his reach. The minstrel moved the beast's tether, scratching the gelding under his mane as he looked into the valley.

His eyes widened in amazement. The ruins were still ruined, moss growing over the stones, but the atmosphere was one of peace instead of tragedy. Bright flowers bloomed throughout the vale where days ago even the grass seemed barely alive, and tiny blossoms carpeted the moss-covered walls. He walked into the ruins, finding the large room he had seen two days ago, and stood as if elf-shot, stunned by what he now saw before him.

Only two days previous, the floor between the crumbling walls had still been smooth flagstones, hidden under moss or fallen leaves. Now, the stones in the center of the room were ruptured, the moss that had coated them dying.

Two trees, an ash and a holly, each as tall as he, grew twined with each other, their roots melded beneath the stones.

AND THE WIND SANG

by Bradley H. Sinor

Not long ago Brad Sinor ran into someone who he hadn't seen for several years. The friend asked if Brad was still writing. Brad's wife, Sue, said "There's still a pulse. So he's still writing." His short fiction has appeared in the *Merovingen Nights* series *Time of the Vampires, On Crusade: More Tales Of The Knights Templar, Lord of the Fantastic, Horrors: 365 Scary Stories, Merlin,* and *Such a Pretty Face.*

THE man who now called himself Eric Karlson sat on a rock near the tree line. From that perch he could look down the hill, toward the castle and the town that had grown up around it. As the sun began to burn off the night fog, the view got better and clearer.

He could see the roads leading in and out of the gates and figures moving to and fro along them. If anyone happened to look in his direction, it was hardly likely that they would notice him, save as an unmoving shadow that was just another part of the forest.

This was a place that Eric had not seen for over five years. A place that he hadn't expected to see for many more years, if ever again. The place he had called home for more than two decades. The place where he had lost his heart, had fallen in love, and had died.

"Camelot," he said softly to the wind and memories that surrounded him. Tethered a few feet away from his perch, Eric's mount stirred, drawing his attention, but the horse settled back after a moment; whatever had bothered it was now gone. The pack animal next to it hardly stirred, lulled into sleep by the concert of the night insects and the song of the wind as it moved among the trees.

"Camelot," he sighed.

No, he corrected himself. It was Camelot no longer. With Arthur's passing, the entire area was now held by Earl Seamus MacLeod, who had renamed the castle and town Camlin. Not nearly as striking a name, Eric observed, but good in its own way.

The name Camelot was now the property of bards and story-tellers, some of whom said it was easier to make rhymes with than Camlin. Not that Eric could have told; he was tone deaf and on the rare occasions he had attempted to sing, it was not a sound that listeners had rejoiced in hearing.

Eric reached inside his tunic and pulled out the letter: a single, carefully folded sheet of parchment, unchanged since the first time he had laid eyes on it. Had that really been only eight weeks ago when he had found it, buried deep inside his saddlebag, in a place that no one else knew about? The firelight had been enough to see the wax seal—a crow and an owl holding a single chess piece in their claws.

The hand that had penned the words was all too familiar, the words still the same ones he had read that night.

> IT HAS COME BACK TO CAMELOT. PEOPLE
> ARE BEING KILLED. YOU ARE NEEDED.
> NIMUE.

The words sent a shiver through Eric, and brought back memories of things best buried and forgotten.

An hour after sunrise Eric knew that there was no putting off what he had to do. As much as he had dreaded it, the time had come for Lancelot du Lac to come home. Pulling himself into the saddle, he headed his horses out of the forest and onto the road toward Camlin.

Behind him, a single figure, clad in armor that seemed to glow green in the darkness of the trees, watched Eric's departure.

The Three Hearts Inn was not the most luxurious accommodation the town had to offer, but the place suited Eric's needs exactly: a private room, a well-tended barn for his horses, and an innkeeper who, for enough coins, asked no questions.

With the ease of a practiced campaigner, Eric opened each of his saddlebags and inspected the contents. Clothing, armor, a few mementos, all seemed to be in good shape. From under the carefully rolled bundle of chain mail he extracted three leather bags. Hefting one of them, he rolled it over in his hands. Even through the leather he could feel strength radiating from it. A thief would only find dirt inside and perhaps make some comment about a knight's peculiarities.

But, for Eric, the rich and fertile dirt inside each of the bags was as valuable as gold. It was his native earth. He wondered if any of the bards who told the tales and sang the songs of Lancelot could ever in their wildest dreams imagine that their hero now bore the curse of the vampire.

The irony was not lost on Eric; he was not that far gone in cynicism. But practicality was habit he had learned long ago. Native earth was necessary to his survival, so he kept it close to him. Let any who saw it just assume it a bit of eccentricity. Eric Karlson, Lancelot du Lac, and the several other names he

had worn in the last few years had all seen their share of ec-
centricities; some far stranger than carrying bags of earth.

"Some of them make me seem almost normal," he smiled.

"Some things never change," said Eric, turning his face into the
breeze and wrinkling his nose. The wind had shifted, out of the
south now, and bore with it the highly distinct smells coming
from the tannery and the small lake where the town's refuse
was emptied.

The streets were muddy, wagons flinging it up as they
passed, while passersby sometimes sank up to their ankles in it.
A pair of young boys came dashing out from behind one cart,
sticks in hands like swords, dueling away, laughing with each
stroke of their weapons. Moments later, their trousers stained
knee-high with mud, they headed off, their quest taking them in
search of some goal known only to them.

This was the norm, Eric reminded himself. Kings might
come and go, battles rage, people die, but always would children play, be it in the center of chaos or calm. He smiled and
wished them well.

As he walked, Eric cast a wary glance along the street,
studying everything. Five years did much to change memories
as well as people, but he still worried that someone might recognize him.

Despite the fact that he much preferred to be clean-shaven,
letting his beard grow had seemed a wise precaution. Not a
piece of his clothing, armor, or weapons was native to England,
and he hoped his years among the Germans and Northmen had
blurred his French accent. If the circumstances were right,
memories could be rearranged. Ideally that was a problem that
might not have to be dealt with.

Eric had come only a little way down the cobbler's street

when he heard a scream. Just ahead of him a group of people had gathered around a rider who had come from the east.

The man was mounted on a small dark warhorse, with a second horse tethered behind him. The rider wore chain mail and leather, a heavy cloak that had seen better days around his shoulders, lance and shield strapped to his mount's saddle.

It was what the second horse carried that seemed to hold everyone's attention. A body, wrapped in a roughspun blanket, had been strapped in place on the animal between several saddlebags. A single bloody hand dangled free, bouncing with every step the horse took.

"It's happened again!" someone yelled.

"Who is it?" demanded a man in a blacksmith's apron. In spite of the question no one moved forward. Everyone just stood staring, at each other and at the body. Finally two men stepped up to lift the blanket clear.

It was a woman. Flies had already found the body. There were sounds of revulsion as people saw what had happened. Her throat had been ripped apart, not enough to pull her head away from her body, but nearly so. Dried blood stained her features, marking the maze of cuts and bruises; one eye had been ripped from its socket and was nowhere to be found. Eric couldn't help but think that there were more injuries, concealed where people could not easily see.

"I think it's Marie O'Connor," said one of them.

"I've know her since my girls were small," said a woman. "What happened?"

"It's obvious, isn't it! That thing is back, back murdering people." Those words raised the hackles on the back of Eric's neck. He'd hoped against hope that Nimue's words had been wrong, but the scene in front of him said otherwise.

"Good people, please!" said the rider. His voice was clear and strong, with the tone of command in each word. "Someone summon a priest, so that he may see to this poor woman's soul.

Then send someone to your constable and the earl's seneschal. Tell them what has happened and that I will come to report in a few minutes. It is unseemly to stand here with this woman newly dead, gawking."

People scrambled in several directions at once. The rider slid from his saddle, patting his horse on the forehead, and produced something from his pocket that he offered the animal.

From his position Eric could get a better look at this stranger. He was perhaps an inch or two shorter than Eric, but he had broad heavy shoulders, and moved with the manner of an experienced soldier.

His mail and sword were worn, but looked of quality make, lacking either badge or device to identify the rider. In addition to the weapons on his saddle there were daggers protruding from his boots and one strapped to his arm.

"And who might you be?" Before the man could answer, a woman came toward him, her brown hair streaked with gray, shaking her head as if she could not be certain of her own memory.

"I . . . I . . . know you," she said.

"I am Lancelot du Lac of Joyous Guard, once of the table round and King's Champion to my best and truest friend, Arthur Pendragon," said the horseman.

It was true, Eric had to admit. This man who was calling himself Lancelot did bear a passing resemblance to him. At least the image of himself that Eric remembered; he hadn't actually seen his own reflection in some years. Though to be brutally honest, he suspected that this stranger more resembled the idealized paintings that Eric had encountered from time to time.

"Your pardon, good knight," Eric said, deciding to make himself known. "Everyone assumed you dead, slain in the final battle; or returned to France and taken holy orders."

Both tales were rumors that Eric had done his best, at various times, to spread. If someone thinks you're dead or cloistered, they won't be looking for you.

"I've heard those stories myself, along with half a hundred others," Lancelot nodded. "Some even had a kernel or two of fact in them. I was indeed sorely wounded in the final battle. It took nearly two years before I recovered, at my home in Joyous Guard. Since then I have traveled much."

An interesting tale, thought Eric, as the other man said, containing a kernel or two of truth in it. Eric had indeed returned to Joyous Guard after the last battle. But he had remained there only briefly, seeing his lands into the care of cousins. As accepting as his people were, they would not have been happy to find their ruler was one of the "undead."

There had certainly been no mention of another "Lancelot" recuperating there at the time.

"Lancelot du Lac! You heathen sinner! How dare you return to Camlin! You should be spending the rest of your miserable life on your knees pleading for god to forgive you the sins that you have committed!" The voice belonged to a man in the robes of a priest who came pushing his way through the crowd. A cross of rough-hewn pieces of wood hung around his neck.

"Who speaks?" asked Lancelot.

"Aye, Lancelot du Lac, I'm surprised you don't remember me, Father Xavien! I know you," said the priest. Eric remembered him, much to his chagrin. The man was a self-righteous prig convinced that even the most minor deviation from holy scripture would damn someone to hellfire.

The priest walked over to the woman's body. He rudely pulled the head up and stared at the damaged face and neck. "Another sinner gone to face God's wrath," muttered the cleric. He growled something to several members of the crowd. They came forward and made quickly to bring the body off the back of the horse.

"Take her to the church," said the priest. "Is this your doing, du Lac?"

"Hardly," said the man who called himself Lancelot.

"Mayhap you didn't wield the sword, but I know you were hip-deep in responsibility. I have prayed and beseeched God for a sign, a sign that would awaken these people to the danger their souls are in. I've asked Him to give me the way, the way to save them," the priest proclaimed. "This is the same curse that rang across this land in those last dark days before Arthur's death. Death walks among us as it did then, taking the guilty and the innocent. And with it you have come, du Lac, your hands as bloody as ever."

"Believe what you will, priest. Just know that I found this woman a few miles from town. I would say she was killed sometime last night. Now, Father, if you will excuse me, I must make a report, one I wish to God I didn't have to," said the man who called himself Lancelot.

With the advent of this other Lancelot, Eric decided it might be time to retire to the Bearded Cockerel. He had feared being recognized at his old haunt, but now he felt the need for familiar surroundings.

He had spent far more time at the inn than many at court thought proper. It had been the place he would seek out when he wanted not to be the King's Champion or "Sir Lancelot" but just another person. A place for thought and dream and forgetting himself for a time.

The only thing that seemed to have changed about the Cockerel was the freshly painted sign that hung over the door. When Eric walked through the door, he felt as if the last few years hadn't happened. The big heavy tables, the soot-covered beams, and the enormous fireplace were all there and virtually unchanged.

Taking a table back against the wall, he settled into a chair and motioned for one of the serving girls to bring him ale. The dozen or so other customers had looked up when he walked through the door, but then turned back to their own business.

Bits and pieces of conversation drifted to Eric. He could put faces to most of the voices, but that was of little import at the moment. For the most part their words dealt with everyday life: who was rebuilding a barn; the need for a new wall at someone's farmstead; how much the earl might increase taxes next year. The words of two men sitting near the door dealt with something entirely different.

". . . neck was ripped out just like Sean Farina last month. I don't care what the seneschal says. It were no wolf! They say that a couple of the dead'ns looked like big chunks had been ripped out of them and eaten. Martha Tattershall said that she saw something, a man she thought, standing over the body, and 'e was glowing green."

Eric considered the possibility of striking up a conversation with the two men; if he stood for the drinks, it might loosen their tongues even more.

"Your drink, m'lord." Instead of the young girl he had given the order to, an older woman, perhaps thirty, stood next to Eric, holding a wooden mug of ale.

"Thank you," he said, holding two coppers out to her. Her fingers brushed Eric's hand, and the Bearded Cockerel was gone.

Eric looked around in stunned silence. He still sat in the same chair, but now it was in a room filled with shelves and tables, covered over with apparati, books, scrolls, and sputtering candles.

He knew this place. Merlin's Lair. Not the tower, the one that everyone in Camelot had known. No, this was a private place, buried deep in the catacombs beneath the castle. Here,

Merlin did his real work, delving into dark secrets that few beyond Nimue understood.

"Good evening, Lance."

Sitting in a chair only a few feet from him was Nimue. Her ink-black hair and dark blue eyes glistened in the dim light. When he had first met her, a few weeks after arriving at Camelot, Nimue had seemed no more than one and twenty; not a spinster, but more than a bit past prime marrying age. Yet she had moved through the court, a force to be reckoned with as Merlin's public voice. The passing of the years not seeming to affect her, only added to her mystique.

"Still good at making an entrance, I see," said Eric.

"One does what one can. Of course, if you can do it with a bit of style, that does help things along." Her lips never moved, her eyes never left his. The only sounds, besides Eric's own voice, were the shifting of air and what might have been the slow dripping of water in a cave.

Nimue spoke in his mind, her voice his memory of what had been.

"Doing things with style. Yes, that suits you." Eric reached across and touched Nimue's hand. It was real, warm, and soft to the feel.

"Old friend, I am here and yet not here, locked away in a place of safety if not of my choosing," she said. "But we must speak quickly as I can only hold you here a short span of minutes."

"Is this Merlin's doing? Did you two have a lovers' quarrel?"

"Nothing of the sort. Know that Merlin is elsewhere and cannot take a hand in these matters, no matter how much he would desire to do so. I cannot either; my powers are, for the moment, limited. It has fallen to you to do again what you had to do before."

"You're being as obscure as the Old Crow." Nimue inclined her head toward him as he spoke.

A broken piece of metal appeared on Eric's lap. He let out a long sigh, but didn't touch it. There was no need. The carved rune representing a name was quite familiar. Loki.

The seal, the sight of it made his stomach revolt, was a thing of evil, used to lock away a thing of worse evil. When that had been done, he'd prayed it could never be undone. But it had been.

"Why? That armor was to be locked away forever. Even Arthur admitted that it did more damage, destroyed more dreams than a hundred armies," said Eric.

"On that there is no disagreement. Armor forged for the trickster should never have been brought into this world in the first place. It was a mistake, one of many that cost Arthur the throne. But that is the past. This is the present. The seal is broken; Loki's armor is loosed again in the world. People are dying, and without cause. It falls to you to stop it, Lancelot du Lac." Her pronouncement was solemn and final.

"I am not so sure any . . ." Before he could complete the sentence, the Bearded Cockerel was once again around him. The woman's fingers had lifted the coins from his hand.

Day gave way to night and Eric again walked the streets of Camlin. The darkness brought him more-than-human strength. Merlin's magic let him walk in the daylight, but only with the strength of a normal man. The night gave him more, and he would need it.

The armor of Loki. Eric spat at the very thought of it: helm, breastplate, gloves, and ax. At Arthur's behest, Kay, Galahad, and he had brought it back from a place that would have put fear into anything that drew breath. Laid before the king, who had proclaimed it the answer to dealing with Mordred and his invaders.

"Poor, poor Arthur, if you had only known." Death had followed in the footsteps of whoever wore it. Not just the death of warriors, but of the innocent, as well. Once someone wore the armor, he was beyond control.

Only by chance, and Eric's own uniqueness as a vampire, had they been able to seize it and lock it away. "So much for forever," he muttered.

Then, without thinking about why, Eric drew a deep breath, closed his eyes, and let his mind reach inward. The moment of transiting from solid form to mist hurt as much as anything ever had.

Drifting over houses and streets, he let the wind take him. The temperature had begun to drop before sunset, so there were bits of fog lingering on the street, mixing with plumes that came trickling out of smoke holes in various roofs. One more bit of mist was hardly noticed.

The sound of metal striking metal caught his attention. It was not that of honest work, a smith laboring long after dark, but the familiar sound of combat coming from an alley just ahead. There were two men attacking a third. The victim was on one knee, but still held a sword and was giving a good account of himself to fend off his foes.

Eric came to human form without thought to the pain, and in a single move his own sword slid free, almost before he was fully materialized. He'd never liked two on one, no matter who was involved. Besides, he admitted to himself, he was in the mood for a fight.

The advantage of surprise was enough for him to put an end to one of the attackers; a blow with the hilt of his sword across the man's face, and swift kick to the knee brought the man down. Perhaps it wasn't the most knightly kind of tactic, but it worked.

The other was more of a problem. Eric dodged the man's sword thrust, but a dagger in his other hand drove into Eric's chest. Had he been wearing his chain mail shirt, it might have deflected the blow. Instead, the blade cut through leather and cloth and into flesh itself. It was more surprise than pain that made Eric's fingers go loose from his sword.

Not that it didn't hurt; it hurt a lot, enough to reach behind the walls he had fought to hold in place since *that* night that he had died and been reborn as a vampire. The Beast, the animal who considered humans his rightful prey, roared in pain and took Eric in its grip. Fangs sliding into place, the vampire that had once been Lancelot du Lac stood in his place, savoring the pain and the fear that hung in the air like solid objects.

Iron-muscled fingers grabbed the attacker, grinding through cloth and into flesh as Eric lifted the man off his feet. A look of uncomprehending surprise was the bandit's only reaction.

Eric drove for the man's neck. Flesh parted beneath fangs, and fear roared through the man, radiating out like heat from a blazing fire. He could feel the liquid rolling down his throat, over his lips, staining his teeth. The bandit thrashed about, but Eric's grip was tight and unyielding.

In a single fluid movement Eric lifted the man above him. Blood from his victim's neck dripped down like a slow rain. Then he slammed him hard onto the ground, mud splattering over the body like a shroud.

Eric turned toward the victim of this attack. He arched his eyebrow in surprise, coming back to himself, the Beast sated, more easily pushed back into darkness. It was the "other" Lancelot.

Instead, Eric didn't move. He locked eyes with this stranger who wore his name, pushing his own thoughts into the man's mind. The memories of the last several minutes were exactly what Eric expected to find; exhilaration and fear, all pulsing like a single torch in the darkness.

It took only a moment for Eric to wrap those memories in a cocoon and push them so deep into the man's memories that he would never recall them. In their wake he whispered a slightly different version of what had happened.

"I thank you, sir, for the aid. I could have handled these ruffians, had I not tripped over a thrice damned dog whose rest we seemed to have disturbed," he said.

"I'm sure the dog felt as upset as you."

"Damn!" Lancelot moved several steps, shifting his weight from one leg to the other, testing them with a few steps each. The pain that shot through his features told the results. "I appear to have twisted my ankle."

"I wouldn't try running any foot races for a day or two, at least," said Eric.

"The problem is, I don't have time to wait for it to heal," he said. "My friend, I must ask for your aid again. Are you willing to fight at the side of Lancelot du Lac?"

"Lancelot du Lac? I would be honored," said Eric. The irony didn't escape him. "How came you here? Who were those two assassins?"

"I know not who they were. Earlier this evening one of the night watch reported seeing a figure in green glowing armor in this area of town. I have been searching for him most of the evening," he said.

Loki's Armor! There could be no other like that. "You think it perhaps the killer of that woman you found today?"

"Indeed." He nodded. "I hoped to find and face him. But with my ankle injured, I am at somewhat of a disadvantage."

"We will try to change that," nodded Eric. "I will stand

with you this night. But I do not think we will need to search far for the one you seek."

"Why?"

"Because we are not alone." Eric gestured toward the far end of the alley. A figure stood there, dressed in breastplate and helm, gauntlets with inches long, flesh-tearing claws built into them, a tattered cloak, and holding a large ax in one hand. The green glow only emphasized the danger.

"Lancelot!" The newcomer's voice echoed from several directions at once.

"Loki," muttered Eric.

"I am Lancelot. Who calls me?" said the man at Eric's side.

"Lancelot."

Eric considered their options. With Lancelot's injured ankle, escape, while not an impossibility, would not be that easy. He also had the distinct feeling that the man was not the sort to be willing to run from a fight, even when prudence might demand it.

"What do you want?" demanded Eric.

Lancelot did not wait for an answer. Moving awkwardly, he pushed in front of Eric and waited, sword drawn. The green warrior's first blow, though stopped by the flat of his sword, had enough force to knock Lancelot off-balance and almost off his feet. He had to struggle to keep from going down.

The man raised his ax and began to bring it down in a final swing. That move was interrupted when the ax went flying forward and so did its wielder, sailing headfirst into the wall just behind Lancelot. He lay there in a heap, mud half-covering him.

When Lancelot managed to turn, he found Eric with a long piece of broken marble in his hands.

"That was hardly fair," said Lancelot.

"Fair is surviving, my friend," said Eric. "Anything damaged?"

"Nothing. Did you really have to attack him from behind?"

"It struck me as the safest way." He knelt at the fallen man's side, extracting a knife and cutting the helmet's chin strap. "Now, let's see who you are."

Once neatly trimmed gray hair and beard, now scraggly and matted with blood and dirt, surrounded a face that Eric knew all too well.

"Hello, old friend," the man said in a raspy voice.

"I would hardly call you a friend, Merlin," said Eric.

"Merlin?" asked Lancelot.

"Aye," muttered Eric. "Merlin."

Eric began stripping every piece of metal off of the old man, throwing it all as far away as he could. "Why?" demanded Eric as he worked.

The magician shook his head. "Call it the fault of my own vanity," he said. "That we weren't able to destroy the armor has always nagged at me. I should have had the power! But it eluded me! Then a few months ago I found an ancient text that suggested a way it might be done. I felt I had no choice but to try."

"Then it was you who broke the seal and breached your own spells," said Eric. "Why couldn't you leave well enough alone?"

"I only wish now I had. Help me up," the magician had to grab Eric's arm to brace himself, but managed to get to his feet. "As you can imagine, the results were not what I anticipated. Part of the spell required my wearing the armor and invoking Loki himself."

"Loki!" said Eric. "Merlin, I'm beginning to think you more of a lunatic than I ever did before."

"I deserve that remark. However, I never got to that particular part of the incantation. The power of the trickster's armor was too much for me. I lost myself to it. I don't even want to think about the results."

"Think about them! With every breath you take, think about them. Let them remind you that you cost innocent people their lives, and by your own hand, not through some political manipulation or magic spell," Eric told him. "But your own hand!"

"And Nimue could do nothing?" Eric asked.

"She also, in her own way, was my victim. I tricked her into a place of safety and by my arts sealed her away. I imagine she is not particularly happy with me right now," admitted Merlin.

"I'll leave her to express her feelings on that matter to you herself. But you should know that it was by her doing that I am here at all."

"Resourceful as always, isn't she, Lancelot?"

The "other" Lancelot had not spoken since they had freed Merlin. "What did you call him?" he asked.

"I called him by his right and proper name, Sir Lancelot du Lac, Knight of the Round Table, onetime Champion to Arthur Pendragon, High King of Britain," said Merlin.

"This cannot be!"

Merlin walked slowly toward him. The magician's eyes had always been his most striking feature, capable of causing terror in the heart of an enemy or bringing happiness into the smile of a small child. The man looked to either side of Merlin, refusing to look him in the face.

"Who are you?" Merlin said. He spoke so softly that Eric doubted the man's voice could be heard more than a few feet away.

There was no answer.

"Who are you?" he said once more. "What is your name?"

The man who had called himself Lancelot seemed to have to struggle to find his voice. His eyes had grown glassy and unfocused. "My name is . . . Collum Naismith, from the village of Myra in Weston Shire."

Eric knew that place. It was fifty or so miles southwest of Camlin. An isolated place as he recalled, quite nice, quite peaceful. Far from the madness that seemed to have engulfed much of England these last few decades.

"So why have you laid claim to my name?" asked Eric.

"I was a soldier in Arthur's army. I fought in many battles. In the last battle I saw the High King fall. Try as I might, I and the others couldn't reach him before that happened. If I had been closer, and a better soldier, perhaps it would have made a difference," said Collum.

Eric reached over and patted Collum on the shoulder. There were no words, at least none that were worth the saying at that moment.

"It took time for me to recover from my own wounds, to regain my skill with a blade. By chance, some mistook me for you, and I did not disabuse them of that belief. Because of that, I was able to help them. Then I was able to help others, to keep the dream that all of us had fought for alive."

"You are not a knight?" asked Merlin.

"No. As the son of a blacksmith, I was not a noble and could never aspire to the spurs of a knight. I would have liked to have been one," he said. "But I did what I did, not because people thought me a knight, but because they needed me. I gave them hope." Eric remembered the people in the plaza when Collum had arrived. Their fear was gone, they had hope. It was something that Arthur would have approved of.

Eric stared into Collum's eyes. To him it was like looking at his own reflection. He knew what he had to do. "Know you, Collum Naismith, that I have found you as noble and worthy as any man who sat at the table. In your heart is everything that

Arthur lived and fought for at Camelot. I have no children; I will have none. Will you allow me to adopt you as my son?"

Collum looked from Eric to Merlin, puzzled, uncertain of how to react to the offer. "I would be honored."

"Then, as was the custom of our Roman forebears, I formally adopt you as my son and heir. You will always be Collum Naismith, to honor the parents who bore you, but from here on you will also bear the name Lancelot du Lac, the younger. Now kneel, my son," said Eric.

Collum complied, uncertain of just what would happen next. With Merlin nodding his approval, Eric took out his sword and touched it to Collum's shoulders. "As my son and heir, I pass to you all my titles, and the obligations they carry. Lancelot du Lac, I charge you now, as a knight, to carry on the traditions laid down by Arthur Pendragon and to bear my knighthood as your own. Do you so swear to do this?"

"I do so swear." Tears rolled down the new knight's face. It was not the ceremony that Eric had taken part in when he won his spurs, but for Collum it would be enough.

"Then arise, Sir Lancelot," said Merlin. "I agree with Lance, Collum. Arthur would be proud to call you a member of his band and have for you a seat at the table."

Father and son embraced.

"Oh, such a sweet scene." Standing near the end of the alley stood the priest, Father Xavien. In his hands he held the breastplate worn only minutes before by Merlin. The sickly green glow had flared to life at his touch.

"What do you want, priest?" demanded Merlin. "You are playing with forces that you know nothing about."

"Oh, I know about them, you pagan devil, Merlin. I had thought you dead and sent to the fiery fate that you so richly deserve. I know exactly what this is, what has happened and what is going to happen. You have laid the groundwork, which I shall carry on. This is the answer to my prayers." The priest buckled the armor on over his robes. "I shall bring terror to the hearts of the people, drive them from sin and back into the arms of our Lord. I shall be the hand of God among them!"

"You would use the weapons of a demon like Loki to do God's work?" demanded Eric.

"If necessary," growled the priest. His face began to shift into something not quite human. The flesh of his arms merged with the metal gauntlets.

"No! God himself would deny you!" yelled the newly christened Lancelot du Lac, the younger. He threw himself at the priest, sword drawn, but was met by the green glowing ax that moved seemingly with a will of its own.

"Who do you think you are?" roared the priest. "How dare you interfere with God's Work!"

"I! I am a knight!" Lancelot drove his attack harder, both of the combatants striking so quickly at times that Eric could not see the blows being thrown. One stroke of the priest's weapon drove hard against Collum's shoulder, cutting leather and mail and flesh with a dull thud. Blood spurted, following the weapon's edge as it pulled free.

Collum made a sound, deep in his chest. Perhaps it was a word, perhaps something else. He threw himself against the priest, pushing the man's weapon aside, grabbing him in a bear hug. Then with all his strength, Collum crashed Xavien down across his knee. The sound of bones breaking rang in the darkness of the alley as both men collapsed in a heap.

Eric was on them in a moment, pulling his son away. Then, as he had for Merlin, he stripped the armor away from the priest as swiftly as he could. Only then could he turn back to Collum.

"Alive?" asked Merlin.

"Xavien is dead, a broken back."

"What about Collum?"

Eric didn't have to answer. "I live," the voice was whispery and rough.

"Had I my full powers, perhaps I could heal you," said Merlin. "But my magic has not returned." The three of them knew it would only be a matter of minutes.

The wound on Collum's shoulder was worse than Eric had expected. Try as he might, Eric could not stop the bleeding. The ax had cut too deeply.

"I thank you, Merlin. But even if you had your powers, I'm not sure I would want you to use them. I've never trusted magic all that much," said Collum.

"You sound just like your father," said Merlin.

Both father and son smiled.

"Am I truly a knight?" asked Collum.

"You are, my son," said Eric.

Collum said nothing, only smiled as he closed his eyes for the last time. As the night insects and the wind sang around them, Lancelot wept for his son.

KILLER IN THE REIGN

by Rosemary Edghill and India Edghill

Rosemary Edghill is the author of *Speak Daggers to Her, The Book of Moons,* and *Fleeting Fancy.* Her short fiction has appeared in *Return to Avalon, Chicks in Chainmail,* and *Tarot Fantastic.* She is a full-time author who lives in Poughkeepsie, New York.

India Edghill's interest in fantasy can be blamed squarely on her father, who read her *The Wizard of Oz, The Five Children and It,* and *Alf's Button* before she was old enough to object. Later, she discovered Andrew Lang's multicolored fairy books, Edward Eager, and the fact that Persian cats make the best paperweights. She and her cats own too many books on far too many subjects.

USUALLY they come to me. It's not that I'm picky, but my profession isn't one in which you go looking for work. Work finds you, and it doesn't much care about the window dressing.

Not that it's a bad office, all things considered. On a clear day you can look out over the Bay and see the Siege Perilous, providing you stand on a chair, of course. The sign on the door says "Pendragon and Lake, Licensed Hermeticists." I'm Pendragon. Lake is dead, and has been for some time. The people who come to me don't care much about the door or the view.

Of course, my clients usually aren't Table Knights, either. Table Knights have as much need for my services as I do for a fancy office. Table Knights can go to the Grove or the Wheel when they need services like mine. They don't have to leave the Court and come slumming down in Appletown.

But here they were, two of the Table's finest, bandbox neat in their blue satin tabards and bright shiny armor. They were standing in my outer office—the one that hasn't had a receptionist in it for a very long time. I didn't recognize either of them. I searched my conscience while I was holding up the wall beside the door, and couldn't come up with any reason I'd come to the attention of the Table. It's better that way. If you lose your license, it's even money you'll lose your thaumaturgy permit as well. That means being taken to the Grove and forced to deliberately break the prohibition that comes with your power. It's something to avoid.

The door to my inner office was open, and I knew they'd been in there already, but if they'd been looking for me, they hadn't found me. Business was slow, and most of my clients aren't morning people. These boys were, and had probably been waiting for me since the start of business hours. They didn't look happy about it. I thought of telling them about the view.

"What can I do for you, gentle knights?" I asked.

"Are you Artos Pendragon?" the short one asked. He was pale and handsome—fairy blood somewhere in the background, I was willing to bet, but it wasn't the handicap it'd been when I was a kid.

"It says on the door." I jerked my thumb at it.

"Show some respect to an officer of the Court!" the tall one snapped, taking a step forward. He was a good head taller than I was—not Giant blood by any means, but sizable. It was pretty clear he'd been tagged to play Bad Cop today. I was betting he was pretty good at it.

The wall seemed to be able to get by on its own now, so I walked past them into the inner office and sat down at my desk. I pulled open the bottom drawer—the emergency bottle of Old Overcoat was right where I left it, which was comforting. I expected to need it once these bright lads were gone.

"All right," I said, leaning forward and resting my elbows on the desk. "We've established that I'm Pendragon, and unless fashions have changed at Court, you two gentlemen are Table Knights. It is now your turn to add something substantial to the conversation, such as your names."

They'd followed me into the office. Tall, dark, and surly was looking outraged. Handsome was looking thoughtful.

"I'm Glendower; this is my partner, Sir Percival," he volunteered.

"Percy. Glen." I'd have offered them a seat, but it doesn't work out too well when you're wearing parade plate. I knew that from experience.

"You used to be a Table Knight," Glendower went on, as if expecting me to contradict him. It's a matter of public record, along with the requirements of my magic, which are on file down at City Hall along with every other public wand's.

"Him?" Percy couldn't contain his rapture, or maybe this was part of the act. If so, I wished they'd can it and get to the point. I might be at liberty at the moment, but I wasn't getting any younger.

"Me," I agreed, though that had been a few years back. Some Table Knights are hermeticists—but they're the ones whose proscriptions are easier to work with—like virginity or teetotalism. Mine got in the way—or it might someday. And I'd never been cut out to be that morally upright in the first place. "We're getting somewhere now, gentlemen, but kind of slowly.

Would you care to speed things up, or shall I plan to order dinner in?"

Glendower grinned, but not like he was happy to be doing it. "It might come to that," he agreed. "Your old oaths still bind you, don't they?"

"Some of them," I agreed cautiously. Service to the King, sure: it goes with the license. But no longer being a member of the Court, I'd been released from my oath to uphold the King's Grace—a nit-picking distinction, except for the fact that where the Art Magical is involved, there are no nit-picking distinctions.

"So you'd be willing to do some work for us?"

"Order him," Percy growled, looking like his teeth hurt. They probably did, the way he was grinding them together.

Glendower sighed. He couldn't do that, and we both knew it. "The Table needs your help. We'll pay."

I sighed. This setup smelled like week-old kraken: Table Knights do not come asking favors of people like me. "I don't do unbindings. I don't scry. I don't talk about my clients. And there's a lot of other guys who've worked the Table and then gone private. Why me?"

"You've been to the Wood," Percy said.

"So I have. And so have a lot of other guys." I wasn't going to make this easy. My head hurt, trying to figure their angle, and walking catalogs of knightly virtue tend to get on my nerves. Even today, I could recite the Twelve in my sleep: Chastity, probity, honesty, kindness, cleanliness, willingness, honor, strength, wisdom, trust, courage, and faith. It's quite a list. Table Knights take them seriously. I'd been serious once.

"Please," Glendower said. He looked like it hurt, but not too much. "We'd like to purchase a little of your time—in the King's name—to discuss a certain problem. If you decide to take the case after what you hear, fine. If not, you're free to refuse."

"In the King's name," I echoed. Talk was cheap. Not free, in my business, but cheap. "Let's see your coin."

Glendower reached into his wallet and pulled out a handful of worn metal. He set it in the middle of my desk. I looked at it. Not Castle-minted electrum: silver demilunes and gold crowns. But it was silver and gold, and would do for the binding.

I sighed, and reached out to touch the coins, feeling the faint buzz in my fingertips as the magic settled. "Silver and gold to bind it," I agreed formally. "Talk."

He did.

"There's a place up north called Carterhaugh. Know it?"

"Only what everyone knows." It's an abeyance-manor on Huntley land, and technically within the earl's gift, but it's one of those places that can only be held by someone with a particular set of qualities, and those in a rare enough combination that several generations could pass before Carterhaugh was under someone's direct control. I cudgeled my memory for what else I knew about the place and came up slim.

"There's a rosewood there. Eight women have died there in the last four years." Glendower took a scroll out of his surcoat and opened the case. I spread it out on my desk, using the crowns to hold it open. The illuminations were clinical, and quite pretty if you didn't realize what you were seeing. The women were all blonde, all young, all pretty. Each of them had been stripped, strangled, and hung on a rose tree. The staging was elaborate. Someone up north had too much free time on his hands. That would be a pity instead of a problem, except for the fact that all of the dead girls looked enough alike to be the Queen's twin sister, and according to the forensic necromancer's report, all of them had died on one of the Cross-Quarter Days.

What they'd been doing at Carterhaugh was anybody's

guess: after the first death, the Earl had declared the place off-limits, but that's never stopped a woman yet.

"And?" I prompted.

"The Court is going on progress. North." He left me to fill in the details. It wasn't hard.

I've got nothing against the Queen, but everyone in Avallach High and Low and most of Logres knows that Artos made a political marriage. He holds the Northern Kingdoms through the Queen. He couldn't leave her behind if he went north, and any northern progress would include a stop at Huntley's estate. If the King went to Huntley, the Queen would go to Carterhaugh. God help the High Kingdom if anything happened to her there.

As I recalled, the White Rose of the North didn't take constraint well: there'd been a rift between her and the Table a few years back. After my time. The Table no longer guarded the Queen's person. She had an Amazon bodyguard now, by the King's command.

"I'm afraid I still don't see where I come into this," I said politely. "Weregangers, wood-wosen, trolls . . . any of them could have done this, and they were Table business the last I heard." If they couldn't keep the Queen out of there, the next best thing was to clean it out before she got there.

"No man can enter the rosewood," Percival said. He glared at me as if he suspected I'd be an exception.

"The Table still has lady-knights, doesn't it?"

Glendower pointed at the last illumination on the scroll.

"That's the Lady Bradamante. She'd been missing since spring. Some charcoal burners found her body last month."

As I recalled, Bradamante had been a good knight and a fair thaumaturge. I was sorry to see her dead, but Table Knights don't make old bones. It comes with the oath.

"There's more," Glendower said. There always is. He glanced at his partner.

"The Queen. The other Queen." Sir Percival seemed to be a man of few words, and at this point it looked like he'd used all of them.

"*She's* involved?" I said.

All this catfooting started to make sense. The Queen of the Wood was one frail you didn't want to run afoul of, especially if you were the High King ruling an assortment of petty kingdoms on both sides of the Veil. Conquering them was one thing. Holding them when they didn't want to be held—and might get downright shirty about border crossings and sanctuary laws—was a can of worms the High King didn't want to open, and I couldn't say that I blamed him. The Table oaths bound its knights directly to Crown Puissant, so that anything they did, they did in the King's name. The Great Bear might as well go and offend her in person as send one of his knights.

That left me. Or someone like me. I'd been to the Wood on my Maiden Quest, and the Table knew it.

"We think so," Glendower said. "We hope not. There's an outlaw in the area named Tam Lin. We think he's behind the murders. We also think he's using Carterhaugh as his hideout, but if he is, he has help. Magical help."

Which meant either a bent hermeticist, or something from across the Veil. And a rogue wand would leave more tracks behind him than a few dead girls. That left Elphame.

Glendower waited. We both knew there were things he still wasn't telling me. We both knew he wasn't going to tell me. But that was business as usual. I've had clients lie to me before. It always leads to trouble further in, but trouble is my business.

"So you want me to go and ask the Queen of the Wood what she knows about the murders. Unofficially."

"Yes."

"And if she is involved, you want me to find out why, and make her stop."

Percival smiled then, a strangely sunny smile. "Oh, no,

Pendragon. We want you to pray her, most humbly and prettily, to stop."

Sometimes the quiet ones surprise you.

I took the case. Maybe I wanted to see the Wood again. Maybe it was the bright shiny stack of Castle-minted angels that he offered up front, or the fact that it never does any harm in my line of work to have the Table owe you a favor. Maybe I was tired of looking at my office walls.

Or maybe I wanted to find out just what it was that Glendower didn't want to tell me.

The moon would be full in a few days. Any mortal who dares can cross the Veil then. I had a few arrangements to make before I left town. One of them was a visit to an old friend. I waited until it was dark, then put on my best coronet and my worst cloak and paid a visit to Dragontown.

The Fortunate Pearl Tavern is down at the edge of the docks, where the big bard-sung clippers that ply the Ocean Serpent dock. It's the kind of place even Table Knights enter in twos. They knew me there, but memories are short in Dragontown, and I carried my 357 openly as a warning against rash actions. It's a heavy professional model, Persian ebony inlaid with silver serpents, and it's got one hell of a big point: over 300 grams of optically-pure crystal.

First Mists of Autumn Along the Yellow River greeted me even before I got in the door.

Come in, Artos. We've been waiting for you.

I smiled at the barkeep, who didn't smile back. I was used to that. I went around the end of the bar and started down the stairs.

I hate coming here. The stairs go on forever—I always mean to count them and never do. But First Mists of Autumn doesn't go out. If you wanted to see him—and not many do—you went to him.

He was playing chess with Liu Hsi when I got there.

The whole room shimmered like summer lightning, in a constant flicker that hurt my eyes. It'd surprised me when the two of them had struck up a friendship—creatures of magic tend to be solitary beasts—but I suppose it was inevitable. If most people found out that Liu Hsi was the Palug Cat, they'd probably run screaming—even after four centuries, she's still got a certain reputation in some quarters, even if she's done her best to live it down lately. But even without Taliesin Silvertongue's magic collar she's impervious to all magic but her own, and I expect First Mists of Autumn liked having someone around who didn't have to worry about looking him in the eye.

Liu Hsi jumped up when she saw me and bounded over. Halfway there she turned from a large golden cat to a small golden woman. The transformation, as always, was interesting to watch.

"Artos!" she said happily, flinging her arms around my neck, then sniffed and made a face. "You're in trouble."

He's always in trouble. He likes it. First Mists of Autumn said. I didn't say anything. Dragons have a different perspective on things than mortals do.

"I'm going out of town for a while. I wanted to let you know."

"Take me with you," Liu Hsi said instantly.

"No," I said, just as fast. It wasn't that I hadn't thought about it. The Palug Cat would be an asset in any fight, and certainly had nothing to fear from the Queen of the Wood. But she'd also be a hostage to fortune, one I didn't dare lose. And I'd been asked to go precisely because the situation was so volatile. Dropping Liu Hsi into the middle of it would be like dropping a chunk of phlogiston into hot oil. The results might be both spectacular and entertaining, but they wouldn't be useful.

Disappointing a lady, Artos? First Mists of Autumn asked lazily. He sounded amused. Damned dragon.

"She's no lady," I said, although Liu Hsi was an enticing golden armful that made me glad the gate to my Powers didn't involve chastity. "And I'm no gentle knight."

You're running their errands, aren't you?

I'm not sure how he does it, but First Mists of Autumn knows everything going on in Avallach almost before it happens. It was one of the reasons I'd come here tonight.

"I'm being paid to ask some questions. It's a job like any other." It sounded a little defensive, but I let it rest. "I'm wondering what you know about a place called Carterhaugh. It's up north."

An abeyance-manor in the Debatable Lands, surrounded by a rose wood no man can enter. Only the rightful lady of the manor can harvest its roses. You don't pick the easy ones, do you?

"So sue me," I muttered, disengaging Liu Hsi and sitting down on a chest. The local Protective Associations stash their gelt here for safekeeping. First Mists of Autumn is the closest thing to a bank that Dragontown has. "I suppose it's a little far outside your usual neighborhood."

No. If dragons weren't remarkably vain and easy to manipulate I'd have gone mad years ago. *There've been more killings there than you know about. They go back fifteen years, not four.* On the other hand, I almost never hear anything I like. *They're right to suspect the outlaw. Tam Lin, as they call him. Of course, he has another name.*

I should have figured it out then, at least enough to ask questions. I didn't. I was tired, and had the start of a long ride tomorrow, and I wasn't really sure any more why I'd come here tonight. Certainly I could find out as much about Carterhaugh and the Queen of the Wood in the archives of the city broadsheet or the public pages of the Court circular as First Mists of Autumn seemed willing to tell me.

"Were all the victims similar?"

All maidens who entered the rose wood: young, blonde, willful. There are some remarkably fine specimens there—roses, not maidens. You should bring me back some cuttings when you go.

"I'm not likely to be seeing the rose wood."

Liu Hsi, having seen that she wasn't going to get her way, reverted to her cat form and had stretched herself out across my lap, purring maliciously. Fortunately, she'd chosen the smaller of her forms. The larger one is the size of a carthorse and has fangs as long as my hand.

You'll be surprised, First Mists of Autumn said. I let that one lie, too. There are some things not worth knowing.

"Tell me about the Queen of the Wood," I said instead. "How is she involved in this?" That was the part that didn't make sense, assuming I was buying Glendower's line about Elphame's involvement. The Fair Folk cannot kill. Cross one of them and you might spend the rest of your life as a tree, or an owl, or drowse away the centuries in an enchanted sleep, but you aren't dead. You can't lie to them either—not safely, anyway—and they don't like murder. But the Table was sure there was some kind of connection.

The usual way. She pays her teine to Hell and her taxes to the King, and keeps to her side of the Veil except for the rades and dances. By treaty, any mortal who crosses over is hers to do with as she will: she's been using mortals to pay the teine for some time now. Most people take the hint and stay home.

"But not all," I said. Liu Hsi purred louder.

Not all, First Mists of Autumn agreed grudgingly. *And since the teine only has to be paid every seven years, crossing*

*the Veil usually involves nothing more serious than a hangover
and an embarrassing* geas *or two. Providing, of course, you go
home again.**

"Is she killing those women?" I asked bluntly.

Why? First Mists asked simply. It wasn't an answer, either way. I knew better than to think it was. But it was the question I needed an answer to.

There'd been no point in trying to take a look at Carterhaugh—
assuming my information was correct—but I'd gone anyway.
Tavern rumor along the north road had given me a full, if un-
likely, history of the outlaw Tam Lin, along with the information that there used to be a house in the wood in the last lady's
time. If there was, I couldn't see it from the road. The rosewood
covered the road between Huntley and Erceldoun, the nearest
market town, which was one explanation for the number of victims—another being that they hadn't all gone there willingly.
There were roses everywhere, despite the fact that summer was
all but over: huge blooms the size of cabbages, in every shade
from moon-silver to a red as dark as old blood. I dismounted
and walked up, then reached out to pick one. The branches
lashed out like a medusa's coils, flinging themselves across the
path. I jerked back, looking down at the bracelet of thorn
wounds that circled my arm.

Fair enough. Proof is always nice to have. I rode on, made
arrangements for my horse, and proceeded on foot. Getting a
horse through the Veil doesn't mean you'll get him back, and I
didn't want to walk all the way home.

I'd been across the Veil a few times in the past, but I never
got used to it. There's no sun, just damp air and fog and trees
big enough to park a coach and four in with room to spare for
a gryphon or two. But I knew the way—through the forest, then
up through the orchard, along the Middle Road, and across the

Sangue Real, into the Eildon Hills. The fog that came up off the river smelled like fresh blood, and the interlaced swords of the bridge made singing sounds as I crossed over. It's the hardest part of the journey—most people prefer to ford the river, but I needed to look respectable when I got where I was going.

You always forget how lovely it is in Elphame; the green hills and the silver sky, and every inch of it manicured and false. Fog hung low on the Eildon Hills, covered the trees with bright spangles, and made my cloak drag at my throat, sodden and heavy with damp. When I'd gotten a mile or so into the hills, I could see the Glass Castle shining in the distance. It looks like it's hanging in the air, but it really isn't. I'd been there before. I'd been young and immortal in those days, and with every step I took, I was reminded that those days had been long ago. Of course, I'd had a horse then—a horse and bright armor and an invincible set of scruples I'd since turned in on a half-good bottle of Scotch and an office with a sometime view. Crossing the Veil brought all those memories back, sharper than they'd been in years.

I wasn't expecting to get all the way to the castle unchallenged, Middle Road or no, and I didn't. But I didn't expect the welcoming committee I got.

I heard him before I saw him, of course—the Queen of the Wood is mad for bells, and her Court uses enough of them to keep Dagonet and his descendants in full motley for several generations. The knight riding toward me was wearing more than his fair share. He rounded a turn in the road and I could see his horse, its white coat glowing in the eternal twilight. A little longer, and I could make out the rider, a courtly sort in full kit, his armor enameled green to match his horse's trappings. They don't use iron on the other side of the Veil, of course, but over the years they've developed the knack of blending silver with titanium to make an alloy that's almost as good as steel. It's a little more brittle, but I wasn't likely to have the chance to test that. I wasn't wearing a sword—most of the time, in my line of work, a sword only gets you into trouble. I'd left everything that had iron or steel in it back at the inn, and had my wand tucked away out of sight under my coat. There was no way I could bull my way into the Wood Queen's court by force, so I might as well be polite.

I stopped and waited. The knight rode up to me, and he stopped. He stared down at me for a long moment.

"Artos . . . ?" he said slowly. "Is it you? By Arianrhod, you've grown old!"

He put back his helm and let me see him. It took a long moment, but the demilune finally dropped.

"Thomas," I said.

Thomas Learmont and I had been partners at the Academy. We rode out on our Maiden Quest together. After that, we were partners for a while. Then we weren't partners. I heard later he'd died. Now I found out he hadn't. Nor had he aged. You don't, in Elphame. He looked the way he had the last time I'd seen him, almost twenty years ago. Whatever'd happened since then, it looked like he'd done well for himself. He was wearing a fancy coronet under his helm, gold, with a repeating pattern of stars in gold enamel.

"How are you?" He swung lightly down off his horse—fairy armor is more forgiving than mortal forging—and flung his arms around me as if we'd been better friends than we had. "You've left the Table," he said, holding me at arm's length and studying me.

"So have you," I pointed out. He waved that aside.

"You've come to see the Queen, haven't you?"

"Is that difficult?" I asked, not committing myself. I was sorry I'd asked. Thomas had to tell the truth. True Thomas, I'd nicknamed him, when the gate to his Power began to open. He could stand silent, even if asked a direct question, but he could never lie, not and keep his magic.

"She rides out tomorrow night. You can see her then if you go to the crossroads," he said easily. "But what brings you north?" He turned away, and began leading his horse up the hill. I followed.

There was a lot of chat—his—and not about anything important. The Court and his place in it, mostly. Local politics. He left plenty out, not that I knew what it was. But a man's secrets are his own business, Tom's more than most. He had a flask on his saddle. We had a few drinks of something that had been brewed far from the fairy court. He'd always favored a good Scotch. The fairies hate the stuff. They stick to milk and honey, sometimes wine. There's an ale they brew for mortals, but it isn't anything you'd want to try.

"Why don't you come back with me, Tom?" I said after a while. "You know the Queen will send you back if the King sends someone to take your place. I can ask her. You know the Table takes care of its own."

"I can't," he said. There was an awkward silence. Then he broke it. "Tell me how things are going back on Earth. The Queen—is she still firm in the King's affections?" he asked.

"It isn't like I still run in those circles," I demurred. I remembered Thomas had been hell-bent on joining the Queen's Guard, back when the Table still guarded her. "I know what I read in the broadsheet. They're still married. He'll be bringing her with him on progress."

"The Court is coming north." It wasn't a question. "I think they'd worry about lying at Huntley." There was something in his voice I didn't like, even more than I didn't like the notion of a Table Knight who'd come to Elphame and stayed put.

"Huntley might have cause to worry," I allowed. "I had a taste of the rosewood on the way here." I held out my arm. The scratches showed black in the dim light. "The locals think an outlaw is using it as his lair. Have to be a damned peculiar outlaw, considering the rosewood won't allow any man to enter."

"Oh, that's just from the Earthly side," he said cheerfully. "If you go from this side of the Veil, you can get in and out pretty easily. I do it all the time."

He stopped, realizing what he'd just said.

I ducked then, but I wasn't fast enough—not against a changeling knight who would never grow old. The green hills of Elphame came up and kissed me on the brow. There was a dark well with stars at the bottom. I fell in.

I came back from dreamland still kissing daisies. Thomas was standing over me, talking just like I'd been awake to join in the conversation.

"You don't know how it was," he said. "She was so fair, so beautiful—Arthur's unattainable bride, the White Rose of the North—leading men on, laughing at them. I can't forget that. The way she laughed. I never meant . . ."

I groaned, and tried to get my face out of the mud. My head echoed, and something inside was trying to tell me there was something wrong with this picture. They don't have mud in Elphame. After a few tries I managed to roll over and pry my eyes open.

Leaves. Sunlight. Roses. I was back on Earth.

Thomas stopped talking when I moved, and when he started again, it seemed to be on a different subject entirely. "I'm from around here, you know. My father was Huntley's man, and my mam was a Carter—her sister always said she could have tried for the manor, but she didn't want to take the risk. Got married instead."

After a few tries I made it to my knees and shook my head to clear it. Thomas was leaning against the biggest rose tree I'd ever seen. There were roses all around us; the air reeked of them. We were deep in the rosewood. It looked like once you got far enough into the wood, it left you alone. Or maybe it was the company I kept. Behind him was the manor. The roof had fallen in a while back, and the roses had taken care of the rest. First Mists of Autumn had been right. He'd known I'd end up here, even before I left town.

And Glendower had known Thomas was alive. Or suspected it, without proof enough to take to the Grove. That was why he'd sent me. I was his stalking-horse. Whether I vanished or came back, he'd know more than he had before.

Thomas was still talking.

"I always used to think how different things would have been if she'd taken her rights instead of marrying the first hedge-knight that came along. I could have been sponsored to the Grove or the Wheel instead of scraping my way up to a place at the Table."

"You've gotten by," I said neutrally.

He laughed. It had a jagged sound. "Oh, yes. Serving one queen is very much like serving another—I'm her favorite, don't you know? Her favorite. A mortal knight of great renown. She calls me that. She lets me have any thing I want."

"Congratulations," I said. Things were falling into place. I didn't much like where they were landing. Thomas could get in and out of the rose wood whenever he chose. Unlike the fairy kind, he could kill. He'd even gone by his own name—they'd make "Tam Lin" out of "Thomas Learmont" in the northern cant quick enough.

Means and opportunity. But motive? What could reduce a Table Knight to this?

"Why don't you tell me about it?" I suggested. I managed to make it to my feet. The roses stayed where they were.

He laughed again, high and wild and mad. "You would have gone to the Queen. You made me tell you where to find her. I knew you'd go. And you never knew when to leave things alone, did you, Artos? You never did."

"No," I said. "I never did." I started edging closer. I wasn't sure I could take him—not where Bradamante had failed—but I had to try. He didn't seem to notice.

"I'd been going to leave the Table—after the whole thing with Ancelet and the Queen's diamonds, how could I stay? I knew they were talking behind my back, but they wouldn't say anything, not to my face. So I took leave, came home to think it over."

He seemed to think I'd know what he was talking about. I didn't, but it didn't matter. He was quiet for a long time, as if there were things he wanted to leave out but still had to tell himself. I waited, telling myself that when he'd talked himself out he'd be willing to listen to me. Sometimes that's all it takes. I guess down deep inside I still thought of him as my partner— True Thomas, repository of the Twelve Virtues that every Table Knight is sworn to. But these days Thomas seemed to be a few virtues short.

"What happened then?" I asked, just to keep the conversation going.

"When we were kids, we all used to play down here in the rosewood," Thomas said. Whoever he was talking to, it didn't seem to be me. "Until you hit your teens, no problem, and I guess if I'd been thinking clearly I wouldn't have gone. Or if thought about it at all I figured the wood would make an exception on account of my Carter blood."

I was almost close enough.

"It didn't. When the rose vines came at me, my horse shied and I fell. I must have been stunned. I don't know how long I lay there, but when I finally noticed anything, I saw that *she* was looking at me. I had no choice but to go with her. And here I am."

The Queen of the Wood had taken him fair and square— there are rules against sleeping outdoors for just this reason— but he could certainly have petitioned to be returned to mortal lands, sent a message. It occurred to me then that young Tam

Lin *had* been sending messages, and I didn't much care for where the thought led me.

"And the girls?" I knew he'd killed them, but it was still the one piece that still didn't fit.

"The Queen was talking about the teine. I knew she'd use me to pay it when it fell due. I lured a girl into the rose wood. Jonnet. We'd used to play together, but she didn't recognize me now. She wasn't afraid of me—thought I couldn't be mortal if I was here. I tried to explain. I gave her roses. But she got spooked and began to struggle. Things got out of hand. You know how it is."

I did. He'd killed a woman, found out he liked it, and decided he'd keep on doing it. Maybe he told himself each time he only wanted to take her across the Veil with him. Maybe it was even true.

"You're still here," I noted.

"She got someone else." And Thomas kept on killing anyway, working his way up to killing the Queen he could in place of the Queen he couldn't.

But why did he hate her? And if he hated her, why did he stay?

"You lied to her," I said, guessing. "You broke your prohibition, and you didn't dare come back to mortal lands after that, not to stay." Broken prohibitions didn't count on the other side of the Veil, but he couldn't spend a full day on Earth without paying the price.

"She asked me if I wanted to stay with her. She *tricked* me! The bitch tricked me! *Whore!*" His face contorted; for a moment I couldn't tell whether he was going to scream or cry.

He did neither. He smiled.

"Clever, clever Artos. Too clever."

He turned and ran, and like a fool, I followed him. He was making for a gap in the rose hedge that grew over the old manor. I was pretty sure of cornering him there. The thorns tore at my cloak and tunic, but only in the ordinary way.

The Great Hall was weirdly empty. For some reason, the roses hadn't come inside, though they covered every door and window. I could feel him somewhere nearby, listening.

"It's over, Tom," I called. "Don't do this. We can work something out."

"I have," he called back. "I *have* worked something out."

I reached into my tunic. My wand was still there. But I had to draw him out, get a line of sight before I tried a compulsion.

He stepped into sight then, on the other side of a rose-choked doorway. I could see the green of his surcoat against the duller green of the vines, but I couldn't reach him easily, not without getting myself half-shredded. I raised my wand, but I knew the vines were bespelled and might stop the shot. There was no way he could reach me, and if he'd been carrying a wand, he'd have used it already. But we both knew he didn't dare let me go. Once I reported back, the Grove could drag him through the Veil, willing or no, or get the Queen of the Wood to send him out.

Standoff. I stared at him, wondering if he meant to hang himself in the brambles the way he'd hung Bradamante. Then he pulled something out of his coat.

A rabbit, I think it was. He held it up by the scruff of its neck while it kicked and struggled and fought for freedom. And then he took the knife in his other hand and started to skin it alive. I rushed him, but I couldn't get through the brambles. I tried. The rabbit screamed the whole time.

The requirements for wielding magic are different for every thaumaturge who comes into his power. Some can't kill. Some can't do other things. Me, I can never stand by and allow an animal to come to harm.

But I just had. Because I *could* have gotten to it, *could* have saved it, if I hadn't been watching for him to try anything but this.

There was a tearing in my guts as some heartless celestial judge kicked me in the teeth. Thomas threw the rabbit down when he'd finished with it. I'd already dropped my wand. On its way out the power ripped through all the places inside me where magic lay, burning them cold and hollow and dead.

It hurt.

For a while there wasn't anything but that, and by the time I could think again, True Thomas was gone, back across the Veil. I got to my knees and emptied my stomach in a series of meditative heaves. It didn't quite take the top of my head with it. After that was over, too, I got to my feet slowly, feeling old and fragile. My power was gone, but I was still alive.

If you want to break your gate, you do it young, and even then there's still a chance you won't survive.

I wasn't that young. I should be dead now.

Thomas was counting on me being dead. If the Queen asked, if anyone asked, he could say he hadn't killed me. But no one would ask. No one in mortal lands knew he was alive to ask. Except maybe a young knight named Glendower, who'd be riding north with the King.

I reached for my wand out of habit, and dropped it immediately. It didn't recognize me anymore, and its innate magic burned. I stood there for a moment looking down at it where it lay on the ground and sucking on my fingers. If I got out of here alive, I'd have to send someone back for it. Right now I still had a job to do, and Thomas had told me how to do it.

I reached Miles Cross just ahead of the rade. It's one of the cornerstones that marks the boundaries of Elphame—a place where three of the Nine Worlds meet—and the Fairy Court rides its boundaries through the mortal world every month when the moon is full. The night was dark and cold, but not as cold as I felt inside. I could hear the bridle bells chiming in the distance.

He was riding his white horse at the Queen's right hand, wearing his crown of stars. The fairy kindred change and dwindle, but mortals who live in the fairy lands endure forever. I jumped out and grabbed his bridle. The rade stopped.

The Queen looked down at me from the back of her blood-red roan. "Who halts our rade?" she asked. Her voice was as cool and disinterested as the silver bells she wore.

"I. Artos Pendragon of Avallach." I'd never seen her before, but just as I'd suspected without ever really knowing why, she looked like the Queen. The other Queen, the one back in Avallach, the Queen through which the Great Bear held the North, and more than the North. The one all those murdered girls had resembled, in the way a crude wooden doll resembles a china figurine; the one Thomas had loved to disaster. The White Rose of the North was related to the Fairy Court, and if that became public knowledge, the High King would have more than territorial squabbles on his hands. He'd have war.

"Do you claim this man?" the Queen of the Wood asked, and laughed, chill and heartless.

"I claim him by right of the oaths we both swore," I said. I reached up and pulled him off the horse.

He fought. Suddenly I had my arms around a thrashing snake, its torso as thick around as a young tree. You don't need either a wand or a spellskin to shapeshift in Elphame, and Thomas hadn't wasted his time here. But I held on. That's the Law, if you want to take a changeling out of the rade. Stand your ground and don't let go, no matter what.

Its scales began to heat up. I smelled burning hair, and then burning flesh, but I was long past feeling anything. He'd done that when he cut me off from my magic, back in the rose wood. I held on.

Chastity, probity, honesty, kindness, cleanliness, willing-ness, honor, strength, wisdom, trust, courage, faith. . . .

The rade sat and watched, not taking sides. Just waiting to see who would win. The serpent cooled and dwindled away, and now I was holding a dead man, his cold skin slick and black with rot, sunken eyes staring at me in terror.

I held on. It seemed as if we stood there long enough for the moon to rise and set. I could feel worms and beetles scut-tling over my skin, looking for a better place to hide than the corpse in my arms. The scent of roses welled up, sickening me, but the worst battle was yet to come.

Voices whispered in my brain, telling me things I already knew, some of them even true. I could keep my magic even now. True Thomas had. All I had to do was let go of him. Admit defeat. Stay here, with him, with the Queen and her court, for-ever young, undying. I could become the greatest thaumaturge the world had ever seen: greater than Silvertongue, greater than the Oak-King. . . .

But some oaths bind forever. And some oaths, broken, are sharper than glass.

At last he had to take mortal form once more. I let go of him then, and he reeled back. I whipped my cloak off and cov-ered his nakedness, then slung him over my shoulder. He didn't fight. He couldn't, now. I'd won. I'd held him and clothed him, and now he was mine. That, too, was the Law.

"He is yours," the Queen said, "and I wish you joy of him. What will you do now?" she asked, sounding faintly curious.

"Take him home," I said. Then I took the step back across the stones that would place me firmly on the mortal side of the Veil. The Court rode on. Dawn was coming. The sky was al-ready gray.

I set him down and folded back the cloak. The change had been immediate. All the years he'd set aside caught up with him—that, and more. He wasn't the Wood Queen's beautiful knight now. He was an old—a very old—man. By noon he'd be a dead one. He'd broken the gate to his power years ago, but he'd never paid the price.

Now he would.

Thomas began to cry weakly, an old man's tears. He didn't ask me why I'd done it. We both knew.

Chastity, probity, honesty, kindness, cleanliness, willingness, honor, strength, wisdom, trust, courage, faith.

Virtue dies. But some oaths bind forever.

IN DAYS OF OLD

by Esther Friesner

Esther M. Friesner is no stranger to the world of armed-and-dangerous warriors having (a) created, edited, and written for the *Chicks in Chainmail* series, (b) graduated from Vassar College and (c) raised a teenaged daughter. Her son, husband, two cats, and warrior-princess hamster treat her with accordingly appropriate awe which has nothing to do with the 30 novels she has had published, the two Nebulas she has won, or the over 100 short works she has written besides this one.

T HE guards who kept the western gate of fabled Camelot smelled the rider approaching well before they saw him. At first the poor fellows thought that some overzealous hireling, on spring cleaning bent, had dropped a bucket full of dead rats off the battlements again, but after a brief discussion they agreed that they had not heard the customary pit-a-pat-a-THUD that accompanied days that were cloudy with a chance of scattered rodents. They leaned upon their spears and scratched their heads as they tried to puzzle the matter out. It was no easy task, for the stink was quite distracting.

"Think it's the moat, then?" the taller and thinner of the two suggested to his companion. He was called Baird, his partner

Llew. Both wore tabards of ivory silk trimmed with gold braid and embroidered with the face of a purple dragon, the required uniform for all the guards of Camelot. The design was Guinevere's own confection and hell to keep clean. The beast was supposed to be snarling, but by an unlucky quirk of the needle it instead grinned like a prize-winning village idiot. Baird and Llew always spent part of their watch debating whether this was an accident or if Arthur's queen had done it on purpose. Perhaps she thought that when confronted by gatekeepers thus attired, invading enemies would pull up short and fall out of their saddles laughing, breaking their necks in the process.

"The moat?" Llew echoed. He appeared to think this over, at last concluding: "Naaaaah. Still a bit of wintry nip left in the air. Too early for the moat to be, well, properly *ripe* yet, if you get my drift."

"Could be coming from the stables," Baird offered.

His friend disagreed. "Any other gate and you might be right, but this one? Too far from the stables. *Or* the kitchen middens, *or* the rubbish dump, or even the pages' dormitory. Besides—" He stuck one pudgy finger in his mouth to wet it, held it high in the air, then studied the results. "Just like I suspected. Wind's coming in from the sea. We couldn't smell the stables even if they were right behind this gate, not with a brisk little breeze like this'n blowing landward."

Baird sniffed the air. The ocean breeze blew with might and main, but the refreshing tang of salt and seaweed was overwhelmed by a rank stench of eye-watering power. "Only means one thing, then," he concluded.

Llew nodded. "Only one."

Baird sighed. "Right. All signs concur. No getting around it, no other explanation possible."

Both men took a deep breath and said, independently yet as simultaneously as if they'd rehearsed it: "*He's* coming back."

Baird shaded his eyes with one hand and peered down the

road to where the stone paving that led up to Arthur's stronghold faded away into a winding path of beaten earth that ran along the seaward cliffs below Camelot. "Yes, I think I can see the dust rising already. He's taking the scenic route. If he'd come 'round to the front gate like any respectable knight, it'd be *those* fellows' hard luck. Instead, we're the ones stuck with the chore of telling the king."

"Do we have to?" Llew asked, almost pleading with his comrade-in-arms. "He always seems so . . . let down, like, when he hears that Sir Weylin's returned. You'd almost think he didn't want him to come back."

Baird spat. "Nonsense. Everyone knows how highly Arthur values his loyal knights of the Table Round."

"Same as everyone knows how badly Arthur handles disappointment. Tends to take it out on whoever's handiest, he does."

"And how would you propose we avoid the task?" Baird inquired, adopting a lofty, sarcastic attitude. Like his sovereign lord, he had a propensity for expressing his own dissatisfactions by making the nearest innocent bystander suffer along with him. "Run away?"

Llew lowered his eyes, toyed with his fingers, and said nothing, all sure signs that *Run away* had been right on the tip of his tongue and that he'd only just managed to gulp it back down in time.

"Shame on you!" Baird proclaimed from the dizzying heights of his own unearned moral superiority. "Shame for even considering such a thing as fleeing your assigned post! Just for that, *you* go tell the king that Sir Weylin's returned."

Llew's head jerked up as if some playful giant had yanked it by an invisible string. "You *dog!*" he cried. "Shift all the dirty work onto *me?* You'd like that, wouldn't you? I never *said* anything about running away, and you can't hang a man for his thoughts. Where do you think we are, Gaul? Find another cat's-paw; we'll tell the king about Sir Weylin's return together or not at all!"

"Why?" Baird countered. "Where's the sense in both of us bearing the king's wrath? I've got a wife and children to think of."

"And I don't?"

"Yes, but yours are uglier."

"If you think for one instant that I'm going to go tell the king about this by myself, then you've got another—"

A clatter of hoofbeats over stone and a relative augmentation in the ambient level of fetor might have served the two bickering guards as a warning that they would do well to reach a decision soon. Yet no matter how foul the air around them became or how loud the sound of galloping hooves, they were too enmeshed in their quarrel to notice. Though sound and smell increased and bore down upon them relentlessly, Baird and Llew might as well have been a hundred leagues away, for all the heed they paid. In fact, they had set aside their spears and were literally at one another's throats with bare hands when the rancid rider crossed the drawbridge of the western gate and plunged right past them, through the archway, and into the heart of Camelot.

The two guards paused in their tussle and exchanged a look of panicky realization and culpability.

"Oops," said Llew.

"Uh-oh," said Baird.

They leaped apart and pounced upon their discarded spears in a frantic effort to cover their dereliction of duty, snapping to attention at their posts and looking more military than they'd done in years.

"Maybe they'll think he came in by the north gate," Baird said through lips held in a grim and rigid line.

"Could be," Llew replied out of the corner of his mouth. "If we're lucky. They always set the new recruits to mind the north gate. We'll keep our story straight and swear that he got in that way, no matter what the young snotnoses claim. Can't see 'em taking the word of a couple of cadets over the sworn testimony of a pair of loyal veterans like us." He tried to sound hopeful, but there was a quaver in his voice that put his partner in mind of a dog caught killing chickens with his tail already tucked between his legs, guilty as sin even before being charged with any crime.

"Well, done's done." Baird didn't sound any more confident than Llew, but he was trying to put a good face on things.

"Right. No use crying over spilled dragon's blood."

"Is *that* what was making that stench?"

"Usually is, when Sir Weylin comes back," Llew said. "Arthur keeps sending him off on quests to slay this monster or that ogre and he always comes back drenched in sweat and blood, his and theirs, respective. A few hours' ride in that condition conjures up a smell fit to stun an ox."

"Why *does* the king keep giving Sir Weylin those quests to do, hey?" Baird asked. "It's not like it's some monster's been despoiling the local countryside and wants having his head cut off as a lesson. The way I've heard it, most of 'em were minding their own business when Sir Weylin lopped them in two."

"Yeah, and it's not even like they were a clear and present danger to the security of the realm," Llew put in. "What *I* heard was that every last one of 'em dwelled far, far away from Arthur's territory, at least three months' hard ride."

"Three months?" Baird repeated. "No wonder Sir Weylin reeks like an August slaughterhouse!"

"You know, it's not my place, but I think I'm going to tell Sir Weylin that it's all right to take a bath or a swim or just a quick wash up after he's achieved his quest but before he takes the Camelot road," Llew remarked.

"*You* tell Sir Weylin something like that?" Baird was incredulous. "You, a mere guardsman, telling a knight of the Table Round like Sir Weylin *anything?* Oh, I'd like to see that!"

"And so you shall," said a third voice from just within the shadow of the castle gate. It was an old voice and a cold voice, a voice that held much wisdom, much power, a bit of menace, and a more-than-average helping of vexation. Baird and Llew stiffened where they stood, too terrified to turn their heads and face the speaker. Soft footfalls came up from behind and passed between them as the king's wizard and counselor-in-chief, Merlin Ambrosius, emerged from the western gate of Camelot.

"So you have something you want to tell Sir Weylin, do you?" he said, leaning one hand against the castle wall at Llew's back and bringing his nose to within a hair's breadth of the guard's own.

"N— n— n— n—" was all Llew could reply.

The wizard, gaunt and gray and wrinkled as an oak root, chuckled. "Eloquent. Most eloquent." He turned his attention to Baird. "And what about you, my fine buck? Do you have anything to add to what your well-spoken friend here has said?"

Baird tried to say something, anything, but was unable to summon up so much as a peep. His eyes rolled back in his head, and he began to crumple to the earth, but Merlin shot out a remarkably powerful hand and yanked him back to his feet by the front of his cream-and-purple tabard.

"Oh, no, my poppet, you don't get out of doing your duty twice in one day. Not while I'm around. Which brings me to the point of this little impromptu inspection: Sir Weylin's return. His *unheralded* return."

"Please, sir," Llew whimpered. "Please don't be wroth with us. We were going to follow our standing orders and report his return to the king, truly we were, only we—we rather got to wondering why such an order's posted at all. You know, the one that says every guard must make haste to inform the king of Sir Weylin's return from questing as soon as he's within sight."

"True," Baird added. "There's no order like that for the other knights."

"So, you want an accounting of the king's will from *me,* do you?" Merlin purred. The two guards paled and shuddered, bleakly aware that they'd stuck their feet in it knee-deep for certain.

"No— No, sir," Baird said. "We just said we were wondering about it, and that's how Sir Weylin slipped past us. Because we were, um, wondering rather lively at the time."

"Right, just wondering, idle, innocent, no answer wanted," Llew reiterated. "Certainly not from *you.* In fact, the less we have to do with you, the bet— Uh, that is, what I *meant* to say was—"

Merlin held up his hand in a gesture bidding silence. "Enough. I quite agree with you. I am not the one who ought to explain these matters. It is only right and fitting that you hear the reason for our Sir Weylin early warning system from the fount thereof, namely—"

King Arthur sat behind a table of the common oblong breed, heaps of scrolls and loose parchments before him. He had been doing the castle accounts, and he was in a foul mood that Merlin's news had just made fouler. He looked over the top of the shortest heap and continued to hold the two squirming guardsmen with an eagle's gaze. A beauteous maiden with hair of golden hue, her slender form clad all in scarlet samite stood at his elbow. She scowled at Merlin's prisoners with a face like a squashed honeycake, sweet, yet anything but inviting.

"So these are the men who failed to warn us when Sir Weylin was within sight of Camelot," Arthur said. He didn't sound happy. "As a result of which, Sir Weylin is now dismounted, disarmed, stripped of his gear, and up to his neck in hot bathwater."

"That's a mercy," Llew muttered.

"Worse," the maiden said. "He has received the silver

chalice of welcome from my own hands and drained it to the dregs in a single gulp. Such an action seals and sanctifies his return to Camelot past all hope of remedy."

Baird and Llew exchanged a look.

"Ummmm, and that is a dire thing because . . . ?" Llew asked timidly.

"Because for the first time in slightly over three years, Sir Weylin has not come *in* through the gate of Camelot only to be sent straight back *out* again!" the maiden shouted, stamping her dainty foot. "Because our sovereign lord the king was not given sufficient warning of Sir Weylin's return, he was unable to come up with a fresh quest to give him even before the dust of the previous one had time to settle. Here he is and here he stays, and it's all your fault!"

"My lady, my companion Llew and I are not knights; we're just simple guardsmen," Baird said a little sheepishly. "I fear we still don't understand. If you want Sir Weylin out of Camelot, for whatever reason—"

"—and we're sure it's a very good reason, too, because obviously it's one of our beloved king's reasons and he has nothing but the best reasons for everything and we love him a lot on account of him being so reasonable and just and merciful," Llew put in, lavishing an ingratiating grin on Arthur, who merely scowled.

"—then why can't you go to him *now* and tell him there's a fresh ogre to slay?" Baird managed to finish. "That ought to get him back on the road in a jiffy. We've never heard tell of a knight who could resist hunting down an ogre, though they are getting harder to come by, these days. But a troll would do in a pinch, wouldn't it?"

It was Merlin's place to answer thus: "No, it would *not*. According to the rules of chivalry as set forth by Arthur himself, once a knight of the Table Round has returned from a successful quest and has sipped from the chalice of welcome, it behooves him to cede the next opportunity to win glory and fame to one of his boon companions."

"There's a waiting list for deeds of derring-do," the maiden said, seeing the bewildered expressions on the guardsmen's faces. "A roster. They go questing in rotation."

"This is Camelot," King Arthur added, mixing in nicely. "We share, we play fair, we take turns. It's our motto."

Baird and Llew glanced down at their tabards, then up at the king. "Sire, by any chance did our revered Queen Guinevere come up with that, too?"

Arthur made a face. "It sounds better in Latin."

"No, it doesn't," the maiden said. "Nothing that Guinevere comes up with sounds better in Latin or looks better in silk." She glowered at the guardsmen's embroidered purple dragons so intently that Llew imagined he saw some of the looser threads begin to smolder. "That woman is a ninny, a booby, a tweedle-brain, a complete and total waste of time and space. If there were any justice in the universe, Sir Weylin would have come back from one of his quests with a *live* dragon so it could gobble her up and spit out her crown like a peach pit! And then it could turn around and devour *him,* too!"

She ended her tirade at the top of her lungs. The silence that followed was like a plunge into ice water. Baird and Llew froze where they stood, awaiting what must come, for the maiden had spoken patent treason, defaming and demeaning the good name of their king's royal lady, Guinevere, and such temerity certainly could not be allowed to pass unchallenged or unpunished.

Indeed, King Arthur rose to his feet, his eyes burning with an unfamiliar light. He closed in upon the lissome girl while Merlin observed indifferently and the guardsmen swapped questioning looks and many helpless shrugs, wordlessly inquiring of each other whether they should play the gallants and step in to shield the unlucky lass from the king's wrath or stand back and preserve their own skins.

Braver (or more foolhardy) than he'd ever been in his life, Llew was on the point of taking a step forward to intervene when Arthur seized the maiden by her shoulders and said: "Now, now, sweetums, you mustn't carry on like that about silly old Gwennie. We all know she's a cow—pretty enough, but a cow nonetheless. Still, she's a *rich* cow and she *did* come with the Table Round and a dowry that would choke a sea serpent. You mustn't let her bother you; it'll put a nasty ittoo wrinkies all over that darling li'l facie-poo of yours, yes, it will." And he kissed her.

It was a kiss of heroic proportions and staying time, as befitted a king of Arthur's legendary prowess. It was also a very absorbing kiss, for it was still going on, hellbent for the all-Britain freestyle osculation record, when Merlin turned to the two appalled guardsmen, raised one hoary eyebrow, and said:

"*Now* do you get it?"

Baird swallowed hard. "Oh, yes," he said, unable to tear his goggling eyes away from the sight of his sovereign liplocked with the maiden (though he was more than a little sure that "maiden" was probably just an honorary title at this point, judging by the way she gave as good as she was getting, kiss-wise).

"Definitely," said Llew, his head bobbing like a cork in a whirlpool. "And, um, would we be right in assuming that the reason this young lady and our lord the king are so insistent on keeping Sir Weylin out of Camelot is that he is her betrothed?"

Merlin smirked. "You're pretty smart for a guard too stupid to raise the alarm. Sir Weylin is indeed the affianced husband-to-be of the Demoiselle Desiderata whom you see before you. Ironically enough, it was Arthur himself who awarded the lady's hand in marriage to Sir Weylin upon the successful completion of his first quest. Unfortunately it was while Sir Weylin was off on his second quest that Arthur and the damsel developed the mutual admiration and respect that you presently behold demonstrated with such, *hrrrmph,* enthusiasm."

"He got a *damsel?*" Llew was astonished. "All we ever get in the Guards for a job well done is a pat on the back and a bottle of mead."

"Yes, but at least there are no grave political repercussions if you share the bottle of mead," the wizard said. "Sir Weylin is the son of one of Arthur's most powerful barons, a man whose pride is as great as his domain. If Sir Weylin discovers that his bride-to-be comes to him minus her maidenhead, *he* might believe she lost it horseback riding, but his father never will."

"Sir Weylin would believe *that* old excuse?" It was Baird's turn to stand amazed. "How stupid *is* he?"

Merlin sighed. "Sir Weylin is not stupid, *per se.* Rather he is honest, forthright, trusting, and virtuous to a fault. In other words, he's a bit of a chump, but it does make him the perfect knight. If his father sets him wise, he'll have no honorable choice but to withdraw from the Table Round and to take his attendant men-at-arms with him. Moreover, his father will sever the alliance with Camelot and make sure that Guinevere's father, King Leodegrance, hears all about it and does the same. That's two immensely powerful allies lost, taking a huge complement of our military manpower with them, and the Saxons prowling our borders like a pack of randy tomcats." Merlin glanced where Arthur and Desiderata were still going strong. "An unfortunate simile under the circumstances," he muttered.

The king's lips pulled free of the maiden's mouth with a sound like an ox's hoof coming out of a mudhole. Panting for breath, he still managed to say, "Now do you two see the harm you've caused? It will be months before Sir Weylin's name comes to the top of the quest rota again! In the meanwhile he'll be more than justified to demand that his promised marriage take place, and once that happens, can his wedding night be far behind?"

"The consequences of which you already know," Merlin added.

Llew pursed his lips. "Maybe Sir Weylin won't notice that the maiden isn't— doesn't have— lost—" He stopped, aware of the venomous look Desiderata was shooting his way. Maiden-by-courtesy or not, she was still the king's light-o'-love and as such had the power to make a mere guardsman's life a juicy slice of hell if he provoked her. "I mean," he said hastily, "that there's no reason for word of it to get back to Sir Weylin's father, is there?"

It was Arthur's turn to sigh. "I have done a great thing in establishing the fellowship of the Table Round, bringing together in amity the great lords of Britain. Together we hold this isle against the Saxon hordes. But even though I have created this grand alliance, I don't for a second believe that my knights have abandoned their old enmities and rivalries. They break bread together, yet would as gladly break each other's necks."

"Camelot is an ideal," Merlin said. "It shines bright as a new-made suit of armor. But the knights of the Table Round are like dogs who circle it relentlessly, trying to sniff out a chink, a weakness that will permit them to return to the old ways of bashing each other's skulls and snatching each other's lands."

"All except Sir Weylin," the king reminded the wizard. "*He's* bought into the whole chivalry bit up to the eyeballs."

"As I said, he's a bit of a chump," Merlin replied. "And his father is well aware of this, which is why, like so many others among our allies, he has seeded Camelot with spies to watch out for his boy's best interests."

"Do you know how much damage a vigilant laundress can do to a girl's reputation?" the Demoiselle Desiderata whined.

"As long as we could keep on intercepting Sir Weylin before he'd drunk from the chalice of welcome, we were safe," King Arthur said. "The drink seals the ritual of return. No worthy knight can in good conscience turn down a fresh call to arms while he is still in the saddle."

"And there was always the chance he'd get himself killed on one of those new quests," Desiderata put in.

"Beggin' your pardon, m'lady, but you're wrong there," Baird said. "The more practice a knight gets at slaying dragons and ogres and such, the less likely he is to get himself killed while hunting down the next one."

"True," Llew said. "We guards overhear the knights when they talk amongst themselves. According to them, ogres and dragons and giants and trolls all tend to fight the same. Slay one, slay 'em all. I wouldn't be at all surprised if there's not a single one of 'em left living within a decade, if the knights keep on cutting 'em down like weeds. Poor bastards, too thick to know that it takes more than brawn to get along in this world. Nowadays you can't hope to survive unless you've got imagination."

"How perceptive," the king remarked in a voice that was first cousin to a mastiff's nice-little-throat-you've-got-there-pity-was-something-nasty-to-happen-to-it growl. "By which I may assume that you *do* have some imagination?" He looked from Llew to Baird and Baird to Llew, a look which made the pair of them squirm like transfixed angleworms.

"Er," said Baird.

"Uh," Llew elaborated.

"Good," said the king. "Because you're going to be using that precious imagination of yours in one of two ways. Either you can use it to come up with a way to get Sir Weylin out of Camelot again before he has the chance to wed my darling Desi—"

"—with the ensuing consequences that the wedding night must bring," Merlin interjected.

"—or you can use it to foretell all of the very creative and highly painful entertainments you will both be enjoying in my dungeons," the king concluded.

"We'll take the first one," Baird blurted.

"See that you take it soon, then," Arthur said. "For unless Sir

Weylin is on the road by tomorrow's sunrise, then the second option goes into immediate effect. Is that clear?"

"Oh, yes, sire, certainly, sire. Don't you worry about it any further." Baird was babbling like a brook at the springtime flood as he hustled Llew toward the chamber door. "By tomorrow's sunrise you won't see hide nor hair of Sir Weylin, we promise!"

"I had better not," Arthur said. "Or more than just your promise will be broken before tomorrow's sunset."

The two guardsmen conjured up sickly smiles, bowed low, and dashed from the room.

They didn't stop running until they reached the comparative safety of the kitchen garden. Once far enough from Arthur's presence to cast off the dread chill his threats had lodged in their bones, Baird and Llew sank down amid the mint and sage to take stock of their situation.

"We're doomed," said Llew. "How are *we* ever going to get Sir Weylin to leave Camelot before sunrise? You heard what those highborn bullies said: He's the perfect knight and as such he plays by the rules and the rules say that once he's sipped from the chalice of welcome, he can't leave Camelot again until his name comes back up to the top of the questing list."

"Stupid system," Baird grumbled. "If a man wants to go out and risk his neck chasing dragons and fighting black knights and getting fleas in his personal crevices, I say we should let him."

"Me, too," Llew agreed. "But it's not up to us, is it? It's the bleeding *rules*. And why do they *have* the bleeding rules to start with? Just so no one knight gets to hog all the glory!"

"Glory." Baird made a deprecating sound like a horse's whicker. "Where's the glory in another dead dragon? The knights are fed up with slaughtering 'em left and right. The only ones left aren't even full grown; it's not a challenge anymore, and they're bored with it."

"Is that so?" Llew rested his face in his hand, elbow on knee, and studied his knowledgeable friend. "I never heard any of 'em say that where either of *us* was in a position to overhear. How do *you* come off acting like you've got the inside story on how the knights feel about the whole dragon-slaying question? A little armored birdie tell you?"

"No," Baird replied with a shrug. "Just Lance."

"Lance?"

"Sir Lance, I should say. Sir Lancelot du Lac, if you're going to get formal about it."

"*Sir* Lancelot du Lac?" Llew was now regarding Baird as though his companion had sprouted horns. "A knight?"

"A new one. Just come over from Little Britain, he has, over on the Continent. Good lad, a trifle shy at first, but friendly enough once he warms up to you. We met in a wineshop down in the town proper, and it didn't seem to bother him at all when I told him I was just a guardsman."

"Oh, great." Llew shook his head. "A democrat."

"And what's wrong with a little democracy, I'd like to know?" Baird protested. "Especially when it's willing to buy the drinks?"

"Nothing," Llew answered. "Except that it never lasts. How long ago was it that you made this fellow's acquaintance?"

"A month," said Baird. "Maybe month-and-a-half."

"Time enough for him to make some *real* friends among his own kind," Llew said, a man who knew whereof he spoke. "I'll wager he wouldn't even give you the time of day if you hailed him now."

Baird's face fell. "The only time of day we've got to worry about is sunrise tomorrow. After that, it won't matter much, will it?"

Llew's whole body slumped. He had been enjoying himself, holding forth on the vagaries of knightly affection, but reality was once more knocking at the gate and was using the Reaper's own scythe to do it.

"I wish that you'd become this Sir Lance's bosom chum last

week instead of last month," he said glumly. "Maybe then we'd have half a prayer of asking him if there's any way around our problem. If we want to get Sir Weylin chivvied out of Camelot before sunrise, there's no better advisor we could find than one of his fellow knights. Set a thief to catch a thief, my old mam used to say."

Baird snapped his fingers and brightened up. "That's brilliant!" he exclaimed. "We *will* ask him!"

"As if he'll even acknowledge he knows you." Llew was bound and determined to remain sunk in gloom.

"It's worth a try," Baird said. "After all, what have we got to lose?"

"Call me Lance," said the affable young knight, filling three cups with some of the wine he'd brought with him to Arthur's court from his home across the sea. "I insist."

"Very well . . . Lance." Llew accepted the cup charily. He was not used to knights treating guardsmen as other than semi-intelligent articles of furniture and Sir Lancelot's friendly attitude made him nervous. He took a deep draught from his cup and let the potent vintage work its magic on his tightly-wound nerves. "So . . . you'll help us?"

A rueful smile curved Lancelot's lips. "I would if I could. I'd like nothing better. However, it's rather difficult to do that since you won't tell me *why* Sir Weylin needs to be out of Camelot again so soon after his return."

"We can't," Llew said. The extended version of this reply would have been *We can't if we value King Arthur's blessing and his continued permission to go on breathing,* but for obvious reasons this had to remain unsaid.

"Why not?"

"Whyyyyy . . ." Baird bit his lower lip in thought, then flashed a grin. "Why, because it's a matter of honor."

"Oh, *honor*." That was enough for Lancelot. "In that case, I won't press you for details. But you do understand that any advice I can give you will be sadly limited?"

"Better than nothing," Baird said, looking hopeful.

"Not by much," the young knight cautioned. "You see, apart from an act of God, the only way a knight can leave the gates of Camelot on quest before his turn comes 'round again is if his services are vital to the welfare of one of his brothers-in-arms. Say, for instance, that Sir Gawain does battle with the Dolorous Knight of the Forest Perilous and loses a passage-at-arms and winds up languishing as his foe's captive in the Dungeon Malodorous, it would be all right for Sir Weylin to sally forth in order to rescue him."

"Oh." Baird thought this over. "I don't suppose you'd be willing to go out and get yourself captured by the Dolorous Whozis of the Thingie Perilous and wind up in the Dungeon Smelly, would you?"

"Well, I would, but there's no way I could arrange all that *and* get word of my plight back to Camelot before sunrise. Dreadfully sorry, but there it is." To his credit, Sir Lancelot did look sincerely regretful. "Besides, it's not yet my turn to leave Camelot either. I've only just returned from my own quest. You might say that the chalice of welcome has barely left my lips."

"*Again* with that thrice-damned chalice!" Llew cried out, slamming his fist into his palm. "Does it all depend on *that?* If the so-called Demoiselle Desiderata had had the brains to *lose* the bloody thing before she could offer it to Sir Weylin, his return wouldn't really count, would it?"

"Well, not officially, but—"

"Right. No chalice, no return, and nothing to stop the king from drumming up yet another poor, innocent dragon for Sir Weylin to ride forth and slay. But no. *She* couldn't think it through. She had to *find* the stupid chalice and *fill* the stupid chalice and *offer* the stupid chalice and—!"

"*That's it!*" Baird grabbed Llew in a bear hug whose vigor crushed the breath from his comrade's body. "By all holy, that's *just* what we'll do!"

Llew broke free of Baird's grasp in time to pant: "Wha— wha—what?"

"*We'll* lose the chalice!"

"While we're at it, why don't we lock the stable door after someone steals all the king's horses?" Impending doom had soured Llew to the point of entrenched cynicism.

"No, no, it's perfect. Don't you see? The moment the alarm goes up that the chalice of welcome has vanished, it'll start off that whole help-your-brothers-in-arms bit. For until the chalice is found again, no knight of Camelot can ever truly be said to have returned from his quest!"

"By heaven." Llew rubbed his chin and stared at Baird with nothing but admiration. "That *is* perfect."

"Of course it is! If Sir Weylin's half the loyal knight they say he is, he'll be out the gate before we've finished raising the hue and cry."

"My friends," said Lancelot, "I hate to cast a cloud over your plans, but the chalice of welcome is kept beneath the high altar of the chapel royal. There's always some young knight-postulant or other standing vigil over his arms in there. How will you manage to spirit it out?"

"Oh." Baird's exhilaration went out like a blown candle.

On the other hand, Llew's own level of optimism appeared to take flame at precisely the same instant. "*Spirit* it out, did you say?" he asked. And thereat he began to laugh with such abandoned diabolical glee that it took Sir Lancelot and Baird and three more cups of Gaulish wine to calm him down sufficiently to tell them his plan.

*   *   *

Thus it was that while young Sir Perrin of Lower Scudleigh knelt at vigil over his arms that night, a ghostly shape did drift out of the shadows behind the high altar of the chapel royal. Resplendent in his wife's best white undershift, his face and hands liberally dredged with flour, Llew pitched his voice as high as he could without doing himself a permanent injury and informed the already highly strung youth that a great and glorious quest such as the world had never yet known now awaited all the goodly knights of Camelot.

When the young man asked what manner of quest the ghostly figure meant, Llew briefly ducked his head beneath the high altar and extracted the chalice of welcome in short order.

"See this?" he said, waving the silver cup so close under Sir Perrin's nose that, had the knight-postulant been less on edge from keeping sleepless vigil, he might have smelled the lingering tang of old wine clinging to the bottom. "Well, you only *think* you're seeing it, because this isn't under *there* anymore." He pointed dramatically at the altar. "This is just a what-d'you-call-it, a *vision* of what *used* to be under there until it went missing. Because it is missing. It's gone. Vanished. Wouldn't be there if you looked. Trust me."

"Gentle spirit, how came you to this knowledge?" Sir Perrin gasped. He hailed from a gravely afflicted region of King Arthur's realm where the land yielded more poets than peasants. It was an impoverished place, but the natives were able to describe their poverty in terms so flowery and rhapsodic that the sheer beauty of their words often allowed them to forget they were half starving to death. "Prithee, impart thou until me thy nature. Be thee ghost or goblin, imp or angel?"

"Errrr, the last one," Llew said, making what he hoped was the right choice. "And because I'm an angel, like you said, this falls under the whole act of God thingie that you knights have to obey even if it means leaving Camelot on quest before it's your proper turn."

"By all that is holy and blessed, so mote it be!" Sir Perrin exclaimed, staggering to his feet, his vigil-weakened knees giving him but tottery support. He brandished his sword dangerously close to the supposedly phantasmal chalice. "And holy be our noble quest for this, the missing grail!"

"Beautiful," said Llew, who didn't even blink at the lad's preference for the more archaic term. "Now why don't you just run along and rouse Sir Weylin and the two of you can be packed and out the gate before—"

"Sir Weylin?" the postulant echoed. "Why he?"

"Because—because you're new to the game and he's got experience and—and—and who do you think you are to question *me?* I'm an angel! I outrank you!"

"Sweet messenger of the Most High, take my words not amiss," Sir Perrin soothed. "Nay, by my troth, I but questioned why I might not summon full many more of our goodly company than Sir Weylin alone. Such quest as this commands it! Yea, though this were the very cup from which our Lord Himself did quaff, I would not stint from—"

"Yes, yes, no stinting, that's nice." Llew waggled the chalice at Sir Perrin in a shooing gesture. "Now run along, run along, time's a-wasting and they're expecting me back in heaven soon." Having completed his mission as he saw it, Llew whirled around and beat swift feet out of the chapel. Had he lingered only a little longer he might have been gratified to see with what alacrity Sir Perrin sprang to obey the heavenly charge.

He would also have seen how the young knight, his stance and gait still unsteady by reason of long vigil on his knees on a stone floor, only managed to take half a dozen steps before he tripped and went sprawling, striking his head a stunning blow against one of the thick stone pillars holding up the chapel roof. Sir Perrin lay there dazed a little while and when he came back into his full senses it was with a fragmented and jumbled recollection of what the angel had told him.

He would not have wagered his immortal soul upon it, but there were several points on which he was certain:

Imprimus, that a holy quest was called.

Secundus, that a chalice, likewise hight a grail, was missing and needed to be found.

Tertius, that heaven was taking a personal interest in the matter and that somebody had better go and tell the other knights (especially, for some reason he was still too addle-headed to understand, Sir Weylin).

He picked himself up and dashed off smartly to serve his God, his country, and his king.

"Well, there they go," said Baird. Back at their posts with the sunrise, he and Llew watched the fast-retreating cloud of dust that hid most of the knights of the Table Round as they galloped away from the gates of Camelot, Sir Weylin in the lead but Sir Lancelot not far behind. "How in hell do you think it got *this* far out of hand?"

"Don't ask me," Llew replied. "I never thought that the sight of me in my Malvina's shift could do all *that.* What did you say they're calling this foolishness?"

"Quest for the Holy Grail, I think. It's all over Camelot."

"Hunh. Stupid name. Stupid knights. Well, at least the king's not mad at us any more."

"Um, actually, he is, a bit."

"What?!"

"Something about draining Camelot of manpower, sending most of his best knights off on a wild goose chase so that if the Saxons should attack in the meantime—"

"Oh, for—! Damn royals, never satisfied! Didn't we get rid of Sir Weylin for him?" Llew ranted. "Isn't he free to play sword-in-the-stone all he wants with his little popsy? What more does he—?"

Baird had endured a trying twenty-four hours and was ill-disposed to enduring Llew's diatribe. Better than many a knight of the Table Round, Baird knew the strategic value of a good distraction.

"I hear there's venison for lunch," he said, in a bid for peace.

At once all thoughts of King Arthur, his knights, the Table Round, fair Camelot, and that ridiculous quest flew clean out of Llew's mind like a covey of startled quail in order to make room for the things in life that really mattered to an honest man:

"Mmmmmmm, venison . . ."

And the thin trail of drool that escaped from the corner of his mouth glittered as brightly as the edge of great Excalibur.

KNIGHT MARE

by Josepha Sherman

Josepha Sherman is a fantasy novelist and folk-
lorist, whose latest titles include *Son of Darkness,
The Captive Soul, Xena: All I Need to Know I
Learned from the Warrior Princess by Gabrielle* as
translated by Josepha Sherman, the folklore title
Merlin's Kin and, together with Susan Shwartz,
two *Star Trek* novels, *Vulcan's Forge* and *Vulcan's
Heart*. She is also a fan of the New York Mets,
horses, aviation, and space science. Visit her at
www.sff.net/people/Josepha.Sherman.

WHEN they came for him, Andris was in the royal stable,
currying his chestnut mare. At her warning grunt, the
young knight glanced sideways over his shoulder. Not a
friendly group of courtiers. And guards with them, hands not
quite resting on sword hilts.

"Meg, Meg, you were right," he muttered into the mare's
ear. "We never should have come here. The court's corrupt, and
our . . . king . . . Bah, but what choice did we—"

"Sir Knight," a precise voice said. Andris hadn't been here
long enough to recognize it, but guessed it to belong to Minis-
ter Varik—ah, yes, he did recognize that thin, long-nosed face.
"Your presence is requested in the royal presence."

"Now?" Andris' sweep of a hand took in his horsy cloth-ing: the leather apron over tunic and trousers. "I am hardly dressed for—"

"Now."

This time the guards did tighten their hands on their hilts. *It's true, then,* Andris thought. *Severik really has singled us out for . . . special treatment.*

The result, of course, not of any crime on his part, but of someone's jealousy of him, the young knight who'd come at the royal command to pay his requisite homage to the king. There was, Andris knew, always jealousy of newcomers at court, even though he had done his best to avoid trouble.

Let's be honest. It wasn't just the courtiers. Severik wanted *to stir up trouble.* A bored king was a dangerous creature, all that power and no decent outlet for it. *At least he doesn't yet know* all *the truth . . . I hope.*

If he fought now, one against many, it wouldn't get him anything but a painful defeat. Andris glanced back at Meg, who pricked her ears at him, then gave what looked very much like a shrug. Andris shrugged, too, and threw off the leather apron. Brushing himself as clean as he could with both hands, he said, "Lead on."

Andris glanced subtly about: A crush of courtiers in bright, multicolored tunics, guards in gleaming mail, red-and-gold banners hanging from rafters, torches on every column . . . He fought down the urge to hunt for one friendly face in all that colorful, smoky, hall, knowing all too well he wouldn't see it. Besides, the young knight told himself, he downright refused to give that throng of gawking, gossiping courtiers the satisfaction of seeing him panic.

If I must die, let me die with dignity. Which would proba-bly surprise the life out of Meg.

Never mind that. Severik, a tall, lean figure on his gilded throne, was leaning forward, chin on one fist, watching him. Severik was all golden handsomeness as befitted a king, the illusion almost successfully hiding the graying hair and the worn face.

Vanity? Or desperation? I'd pity a man so fiercely clinging to his youth, had I not heard the tales of— But I will not listen to tales! Andris bowed his most courtly bow. "You have summoned me, Sire?"

"Indeed. Sir Andris, you are new to our court, yet I have already been listening to some most impressive tales."

Oh. "Sire?"

"Of you, Sir Andris. Tell me, did you not capture the bandit who called himself the Wolf?"

"Well, yes, Sire. But my mare was the true hero. Her hoof caught him on the side of the head and stunned him." Which, Andris thought dryly, was true enough, even if the whole thing had been an accident.

"How . . . modest. And surely you are the only knight ever known to prefer a mare."

Yes, that was an insult. And no, Andris knew he could not retort. He merely waited.

Do you think you're the only one to have mocked me for my "unknightly" mount? But I wouldn't trade Meg for a hundred destriers.

Not that she'd let me.

"Yet I have heard other accounts," Severik continued after a moment, and if he was annoyed that his jibe had missed the mark, he showed no sign. "Did you not slay a dragon?"

"By sheer good fortune, Sire." Again, true enough.

"And not by the Lord's will, Sir Andris? Are you, then, so vain?"

"Sire, I . . ." *Will be trapped by my own words if I don't stop now.*

"Perhaps the other tales are true as well."

"Sire?" Andris repeated, swearing silently.

"Why, Sir Knight, the ones flooding in from all sides. The ones that say you are a wonder of a hero. The ones that say you hesitate not at letting all think you are a modest, humble man— yet one who may, indeed, think himself greater than the Almighty."

Oh, a thousand hells, he's snaring me nicely. No way out of it: This was why he'd been summoned—to be rid of him. *I wouldn't listen to the tales, I wouldn't believe that Severik would be so jealous of the young and active . . .* "Sire, what would you have me do to prove my worth?"

"Will you first give me your vow as a true knight to fulfill what I may ask of you?"

Do I have a choice? "Sire, you are the king. I am yours to command." Solemnly, angrily, he swore by his knightly honor to . . .

"There is a demon terrorizing the land," Severik said smoothly.

"A . . . demon."

"A monster, at any rate, come from the Pit to torment honest souls. Up to this date, it has slain several head of cattle, and five peasants." Severik's lips drew up ever so slightly in what could almost have been a smile. "I would have sent my armies against it, but my wise men assure me that there can be no hope of success for an army. Only one hero may conquer it. And you, sir knight, have no kin here, no ties to bind you to our court."

Which meant, of course, Andris translated silently, that he was expendable.

"They will tell you where the demon may be found," Severik continued, "and what is known about its weaknesses." *If any,* went the unspoken addition. "Bring me its head, sir knight. Succeed, as you are a knight."

Fail and be dishonored.

Andris bowed his most courtly bow. "So be it, Sire. I shall bring you the demon's head, on my honor as a knight."

And I can already hear what Meg is going to say about this.

Meg, of course, had quite a few choice things to say—once they were safely out of the keep and beyond any chance eavesdroppers. "You had to agree," she said over her shoulder as they rode out of plowed fields and on into forest. "Had to send us out on a—a—"

"Hero's quest?" Andris suggested, ducking under a low branch.

The mare snorted, shaking her chestnut mane. "Idiot's quest, more like."

"Meg, what else could I do? I swore an oath!"

"Humph."

"Knight's honor, Meg, I can't—"

"I'm a horse. What has knight's honor to do with me?"

"Meg! You know—"

"I know that one of these days *you* are going to get *us* killed—no, no, never mind that *us,* make that *me!*"

"Meg, love, if I want to kill us, all I have to do is let someone know I ride a talking horse."

"Humph."

"Besides, who's to say we can't take a demon? Didn't we kill that dragon?"

The mare glanced back at him. "Which one? The lame, broken-winged one? Put the poor thing out of its misery is what we did."

"Well, then, what about . . . uh . . ."

"Never mind." Meg snatched a mouthful of leaves, chewing them vindictively. "We're not about to let Severik win, we both know that, so let's stop wasting time and get at it."

"Humph." This time it was Andris who said it.

They rode on together into the deepening forest and twilight, two companions not needing to talk to know each other's habits.

He and Meg had been a team ever since the days when he'd been hunting a suitable knightly horse, hunting (of course) for a knight's proper steed, a stallion. This most unknightly horse, this mare, had fixed him with her usual cynical stare and said, "You going to get me out of this mess?"

How was it that she could speak? Meg wasn't sure, or else claimed she wasn't sure. Andris had already seen enough evidence to disprove his original theory that she was an enchanted maiden: Meg was definitely equine in everything she did, thought, and remembered, and possessed a vocabulary that never would have fit anything as delicate as a maiden. The odds were good, from the way she literally shied when he tried to mention it, that she had escaped from some sorcerer.

But what did it matter? They'd been together for . . . what was it now? For nigh five years. And you didn't question a friend too closely, after all.

Even a friend who shied so suddenly that she nearly sent Andris flying. "Scent," she whispered as he clutched frantically at her mane. "Bad."

"Demon?" he whispered back.

"How should I know? Never smelled a demon!"

"Good point." Andris slid from her back and edged his wary way through the undergrowth till he could see . . . whatever that thing was. Meg's muzzle brushed his cheek. "Ugly," he murmured.

Her nostrils flared. "Very."

The, well, demon was large, furry, horned, and walked upright. It also, Andris noted gloomily, was almost twice his height, moving, there in the dim light, like a true predator. He was hardly surprised to see that it also had claws and fangs.

"Want to bet it's a creature of the night?" he breathed, and heard Meg grunt softly.

A sapling blocked the creature's path. Hardly noticing, it tore the sapling up with a casual hand and threw it aside.

The sapling stabbed into a tree like a javelin.

Andris and Meg let out their breath in twin sighs. "Forget it," Meg muttered. "Get on my back, we get out of here and—"

"And I lose my knighthood. And become known everywhere as a liar and coward."

"A living one."

"I swore to kill it."

"Yes? How?"

"Haven't a clue," Andris muttered.

With that, he drew his sword and charged. The blade ricocheted off the hairy hide, the force nearly tearing the hilt from his hand. The demon whirled with alarming speed, and an arm that felt like an iron bar hurled Andris aside, slamming him against the ground so hard he couldn't catch his breath. The demon snarled, fangs glinting, looming over him like every painting of the devils in hell he'd seen on church walls. Andris hastily consigned his soul to God and hoped that Meg—

Meg charged, screaming like a stallion, then whirled to catch the demon a solid kick with both hind legs. Andris, struggling to move, heard the solid impact.

The demon staggered. But that was all.

"Hurry!" Meg all but snarled at Andris.

He caught a dangling stirrup, just in time, because Meg wasn't about to wait for him to gain the saddle. Half-dragged, Andris struggled until he could manage enough of a leap to sprawl across her back, then squirm upright. Good thing Meg didn't need reining, because he couldn't do anything useful but hang on as she tore through the forest like the wind.

"Meg! *Meg!*" Andris saw an ear twitch back and shouted. "It isn't following! Dammit, Meg, *stop!*"

She did, sliding back on her haunches so suddenly that Andris almost went over her head. He dismounted instead, catching her by the forelock. Meg stood splay-legged, panting and slick with sweat.

"Come on, Meg, walk with me. You know you have to cool down slowly."

She plodded along beside him, ears drooping. "Now what?"

He ran an affectionate hand along her sweaty mane. "Now we get out of here."

"To where?"

"Anywhere that doesn't involve seeing you risk your life for me."

She butted him with her head. "The same is true on this end. Not that I'm getting sentimental about it, understand. But what about your knightly honor?"

"It's not as important as your life."

Meg snorted. "I agree. But this is a human thing, and no matter what you say, I smell the regret in you. There must be a way . . ."

"How? Iron doesn't work on the cursed creature."

"Hoofs don't either."

"It would be just like Severik to put us up against a demon that couldn't be hurt by normal means, only by—"

Meg and he stopped short, staring at each other. "By magic," Andris finished. "And who at court has that magic? Severik's wise men."

"But what good is that? You swore an oath to slay the demon."

"Ah. True. Whoa, now."

"I'm already stopped."

"No, I meant, let me think for a moment." Andris frowned.

"I'm not so sure I did swear that. Not . . . exactly . . . no! Meg, Meg, Meg, we have a way out! Listen: Here's what I *did* vow."

He told her, and Meg gave a horsey lip-curl of a grin. "Sounds good to me. I already proved I can outrun the thing. But not now," she added. "Your poor human eyes can't see in the dark."

"And your poor horsey body can't act without rest."

They made camp. Convenient, having an intelligent horse as colleague: Meg could keep one ear alert even when asleep, so that no one could steal up on them.

The morning and day they spent resting and grazing in their separate ways: Meg easily finding greenery and cadging handfuls of grain from Andris, who in turn added edible greens to his store of dried meat. There was not the slightest whiff of demon.

The day crept on toward twilight.

"Time," Meg said shortly.

"You're fully rested? You're sure?"

The mare tossed her mane. "When am I not sure?"

"Modest, aren't we? So be it!" Andris leaped back into the saddle. "Let's go, my friend. Let us keep my word to Severik!"

Finding the demon again was no problem: Meg, shuddering despite her determination, scented it as it tore a deer to shreds. Andris took a deep breath and shouted, "Hey, ugly!"

No reaction.

"Demon! We challenge you!"

"'We'?" Meg muttered.

Ignoring her, Andris leaned sideways in the saddle, grabbed a rock, and threw it—

The demon whirled with a roar.

"Now you've gotten its attention," Meg said.

She turned and fled. Andris risked a glance over his shoulder. Sure enough, the demon was racing after them, crashing through the bushes, branches flying in all directions.

"Slow down," Andris hissed to Meg. "You're outracing him."

"Yeah. Right. Just what I want to do: slow down."

But she did, just enough to keep the demon following them without letting it quite catch up.

"That's it, Meg, brave Meg."

"Winded Meg," she snarled.

"Not much farther, see? We're out of the forest."

"Delightful."

Andris leaned forward over her neck, lashed by her mane, trying to spare her as much as possible as they raced across the night-darkened fields. Ahh, yes, the hulking shape of the demon was all but invisible in the darkness. This might work, this might truly work . . . if only Severik was as contemptuous of him as it seemed.

"Now, my brave one, now!"

Gasping, Meg put on a fresh burst of speed. They clattered up the gravel road to the royal keep—and sure enough, the guards saw only Andris, the knight turned craven coward, calling piteously on them to let him in.

Andris had a moment of utter terror. *What if they think it's more amusing to shut us out here?*

But there was Severik behind them, wrapped in a richly furred gold robe, dark amusement on his face. At his gesture, the guards swung open the gates. Andris and Meg raced past them into the courtyard—and the demon raced with them.

"I have kept my word!" Andris shouted at the king. "I have brought you the demon's head!"

As the wise men frantically scurried forth, as the demon roared and slashed out with its claws, as magic flashed and sizzled, Andris and Meg raced back out of the keep. No one thought to stop them; no one had the chance.

No one was going to see them in the now-total darkness.

Meg stopped, panting, and Andris slipped from the saddle to walk beside her.

"I think we'd better not linger," he said.

"Not wise, no. Where, then?"

"Oh, maybe to a cathedral, or maybe all the way to the emperor. Prove my case. And then . . ." Andris shrugged.

"And then we go cause trouble somewhere else," Meg said.

Andris opened his mouth, shut it, opened it again. "Meg, my friend, you are a wonder."

"I am," she agreed.

The two friends walked on together into the night, on into the coming dawn.

FAINT HEART, FOUL LADY

by Nina Kiriki Hoffman

Nina Kiriki Hoffman has been writing for almost
twenty years and has sold almost two hundred sto-
ries, two short story collections, novels (*The
Thread That Binds The Bones* and *The Silent
Strength of Stones, A Red Heart of Memories,* and
her most recent novel, *Past the Size of Dreaming*),
a young adult novel with Tad Williams (*Child of an
Ancient City*), a *Star Trek* novel with Kristine
Kathryn Rusch and Dean Wesley Smith, *Star Trek
Voyager 15: Echoes,* three R.L. Stine's *Ghosts of
Fear Street* books, and one *Sweet Valley Junior
High* book. She has cats.

O F a surety, I received my knighthood. After years of rigor-
ous training as a squire, at Pentecost I had a ritual bath in
rose water to cleanse me of sin. Then I was dressed in a white
robe to signify the cleanness of the body, a scarlet cloak to remind me to always be ready to shed my blood in defense of the
Church, my king, all women, and the poor and oppressed,
brown stockings to remind me of the grave where I would ultimately lie so that I would always be prepared for death, and a
white belt signifying chastity. I spent my vigil night in the

church, praying to God to purify me of earthly desires and to make me a fine and upstanding knight.

The next morning I heard mass. Afterward, I knelt before my king, who gave me a blow on the shoulder. "Arise, Sir Bran, Knight of the Realm," he said. Then the king with his own hands took a sword from the altar and girded it around me, and two knights fixed golden spurs to my boots to remind me to swiftly follow God's commandments as a pricked charger follows the commands of his knight. I arose in my third self since my birth, second since my baptism.

In the first days of my knighthood, I clove to God and honor.

But in the months that followed, with no war, no prospect of war, no one to fight save each other, we knights at court were at loose ends. We jousted and tourneyed for the amusement of the court and to demonstrate our prowess. We told stories and sang songs and dallied with the court ladies; we listened to minstrels and watched jongleurs and attended raconteurs who spoke of glorious adventures to be found just over the next hill; we lost our fire.

I discovered my own sins and weaknesses, of which sloth played a part, but looming larger (though not as mortal) was cowardice.

I did not begin a coward. I went to all my knightly studies with a good will and a clean heart. But somehow I could not get my limbs and my weapons to act in concert.

I knew I lacked jousting skill before I was knighted, but thought application would overcome shame. No matter how much I practiced against the quintain, I did not improve. A wooden dummy could unseat me, and left me with bruises to the head and dignity. Even the meanest of the other knights could unhorse me.

I became a laughingstock in the court. If not for some little skill at hand-to-hand combat and sword fighting, and enough skill with flute and fiddle to keep others entertained, I would have been wholly humiliated.

My father was slain when I was a child, and he did not leave me much more than a competence, a too-large suit of chain mail, and his horse; I could not afford to tourney, for I risked losing all my possessions to whoever beat me, and everyone could. It was due only to my skill with dice that I managed to pay for stabling and training while I was a squire, and after my dubbing, I was enjoined by my king in the interests of honor against playing games of chance.

Of my secret dream to be a bard, I never spoke. In the resting hours between arms practice, sleep, and meals, it was not thought unseemly for knights to take up the arts of music; one could pursue anything which would entertain the ladies, and so I learned from the castle bard some basic fiddle techniques and tunes, though I kept most of my practices secret.

Alas, for a lad whose noble father was killed by a wicked knight and whose noble mother's heart was full of vengeance, there was only one future; one must become a knight and avenge one's father's death. My mother told me that my father had been like me, gentle and not good at jousting. He was beloved of everyone, a raconteur around whom people gathered wherever he went. He could jest even the sourest knight out of ill humors, and his words lent brightness to many an ordinary day.

Would that I had such skills; I was only a shadow of my father, save for my luck, which often ran strong, stronger than his, I hoped.

Why did the Knight of the Pearl, a stranger to our court, arrive on a tourney day and insist that my father meet him in a joust? Why, after he had unhorsed my father, did the Knight leap to the ground and strike off my father's head after my father had laughed and yielded to him? My mother said my father had no enemies but his creditors. Who was the Knight of the

Pearl? No one recognized his devices, and he rode off directly following his base and cowardly act.

My mother told me the story of my father's death many times as I grew up. She planted the goal of vengeance in my heart. I, in my clumsiness, planted my own fears almost as deep.

No matter how many soothsayers I consulted, the fates always fell out the same way. Somewhere along my path, I would meet the man who had killed my father. I had the subsequent outcome told a dozen different ways, but that one point they all agreed on.

Any road, I had to make shift to prove myself better than I knew I was, lest I be cast out of court by the king and sent to guard some fortress at the far end of the wind-whipped world, where perchance I might never see another human face.

When I heard that Sir Wulfric, strong and brave and in all matters of arms and warfare knowledgeable, though known to be headstrong and fearless to the point of foolishness, was about to set off in search of adventure, I asked if I might accompany him. He granted me permission to join his quest, or to join mine with his. Sir Wulfric promised that if we heard rumors of the Knight of the Pearl we could pursue them.

Before we left court, I talked to all the ladies, begging one of them to inspire in my heart the knightly virtues of prowess, loyalty, generosity, courtesy, and an open and honest noble bearing. Most of the ladies laughed, but one of the queen's attendants, Amicia, kindly granted me permission to enshrine her in my heart, and gave me a red sleeve to bind around my sword arm to remind me of her regard.

She was not the most lovely of those who waited on the queen, but her brown eyes were merry, her brown hair curled softly about her face, and her figure was plump and generous. Her lips were plump too, and red as berries; in all, a lady about whom one could dream fine dreams.

It was only later that night when I was having a farewell ale with the other knights that I learned Amicia was beloved of a number of us, mostly the lowest among us. The others' favors were green, blue, white, and yellow; it warmed my heart that to me Amicia had given a red sleeve. Better an overgenerous love than none at all. I hid my favor and stayed out of the ensuing quarrels to see who ranked highest in her regard.

The next morning Sir Wulfric and I set out. Sir Wulfric had a squire named Eudo, and I, impoverished, had none, nor was my gear in good shape, since I had to polish everything myself, and I was not handy with mending leather or reweaving chain. When I myself was a squire, my knight booted me for my shortcomings until I learned to pay one of the pages with my winnings at dice to do my work.

My horse, however, was a good one, though elderly; he had been my father's destrier.

Sir Wulfric's squire Eudo was a kindly lad. He helped me with my armor after he had tended to his lord's, and managed fire and food and pack animals and weapons for the three of us without complaint. In this wise I traveled in more comfort than that to which I had been accustomed.

We had been three days on the road, beyond the edge of our best maps, and found ourselves in a deep, dark forest, with trees so dense they eclipsed the sky, when we met with our first adventure.

Sir Wulfric had chosen the least-traveled path, for he feared that other knights who had gone ahead of us would dispose of any adventures on the well-trod ways. As a consequence, we often had to pick out traces of the path through the underbrush. We were searching through brush for our path that afternoon and did not notice we had arrived in a clearing until we heard the noise.

A sliding, slithery, scales-scraping-on-rock sound it was, and then the moaning of a maiden. We looked up and beheld a horrid sight: a giant silver-green serpent as thick through as a man's chest had wrapped its noxious coils around a golden-haired damsel, encircling her in its cold embrace so completely that only her head could be seen. She appeared a high-born damsel, her skin pale as lilies, her forehead broad and high, her eyes a fine gray.

The serpent's hideous long-nosed head, which bore a red fanned frill and waving whiskers, lifted high above its prey. Golden eyes with narrow pupils regarded us.

The creature hissed. Flame shot from its mouth. The scent of scorched grasses surrounded us.

My heart quailed. I had never seen such a monster. Fear urged me to turn and ride back into the forest any which way, so long as it was away.

"Eudo! My lance!" cried Sir Wulfric. His squire handed him his lance, and Sir Wulfric charged the creature.

Eudo glanced enquiringly at me. He had all our extra arms on his pack mules.

"Let us see how Sir Wulfric fares," I muttered. Perhaps this caution could pass for wisdom rather than cowardice.

The worm's head lifted higher, then shot forth as Wulfric approached, and knocked him out of the saddle. His lance fell to the ground.

Sir Wulfric struggled to his feet and drew his sword. The serpent's head was so high Wulfric would never lay a blade on it. He should attack the body, I thought, but he waved his blade at the head.

Meanwhile, the serpent watched me, ignoring the threat closer to it.

"Now, sir?" Eudo asked me. The trapped damsel treated us to a wide array of screams.

I marshaled my fears and nodded. I had made myself a vow ere I started this journey that I would no longer run from danger; henceforth I would be foolhardy and hope that somehow I could win regard, if not from my peers, at least from God, who saw into all hearts. If the dragon ate me, still the court would respect me more than they did at present. "The light lance." I had no finesse with the heavy lance.

Eudo frowned. He was not allowed to question my choices, but I could nearly hear his thoughts. The light lance, not tipped with iron like the heavy lance, would not even pierce the monster's hide, should I be lucky enough to land a blow.

I held out my hand, and he put the light lance into it.

I thought fondly of my lady Amicia, in whose honor I had vowed to fight. I couched the lance and charged, my heart pounding faster than my horse's hooves. I pointed the tip of my lance at the damsel's head.

"What ails you? Are you a lunatic?" she screamed.

Sir Wulfric cried, "Thou hideous, stinking worm!" and thrust upward with his sword through the air, a blow so strong it nearly overturned him. "Engage!"

Nearer and nearer the serpent's coils I drew, my lance point unwaveringly aimed at the damsel. Truth to tell, I had no finesse with the light lance either, and I never hit what I aimed at, so I conjectured that if I aimed at the one thing I wanted not to hit, I would hit something else; if the fates smiled, something vital belonging to the serpent.

At the last moment, while the damsel screamed and Sir Wulfric raged (he had never even turned to see what she was crying about), the monster shifted, and I charged past without striking anything.

A familiar feeling of futility washed through me, seasoned with a hearty dash of terror.

"Curse you for a black-hearted knave!" the damsel cried. "May you never love until you love the one who overmasters you, and may you suffer from that love as long as you live!"

Her words did not inspire me with courage and the will to

save her, but nevertheless, I managed to wheel my destrier and gallop back in the general direction of the serpent.

Then a startling apparition charged from the forest, a be-smirched boy on a shaggy pony, yelling and brandishing a short sword. The beardless youth wore a soup pot on his head with the handle to the back, and a ragged dun surcoat under armor pieced together from mats of woven straw, the sort of figure of a knight one saw in comic plays.

He charged straight at the serpent and jabbed its hide. To my astonishment, he opened a wide slash in the serpent's out-ermost coil. Green ichor boiled forth, and the monster poured out an ear-splitting cry of rage and pain. The lad sliced it again with the short sword. His blade gleamed with green fire. Again he opened a wound in the serpent's side.

Wailing and spitting flames, the worm relaxed its hold on the damsel and fled into the forest.

"My savior!" the damsel cried to the lad.

The boy slid off his pony's back and wiped his blade on the grass, then took out a rag and cleaned the blade and sheathed it. His face suffused with crimson at the damsel's words, and he ducked his head.

I pulled up beside him just as Sir Wulfric, apoplectic with rage, charged forward, sword extended. Whether he intended to spit the boy, I did not wait to determine. I grasped the boy by the scruff of the neck and dragged him onto my horse. My mus-cles, hampered by chain mail, protested such a maneuver. For-tunately, the boy was agile and scrambled to safety behind me. My good horse bore us both a little ways off. "Well done, lad," I said.

Sir Wulfric ran after us until the weight of his mail and shield and sword slowed and stopped him. When at last he halted, puffing and huffing, I pulled my horse up.

"Sir," said the boy behind me, "thank you, sir. May I be your squire?"

"Are you of noble birth?"

His arms, which he had closed about my waist in our flight from the foot charge of Sir Wulfric, loosened their hold. "No," he murmured.

"One must have noble blood to be a squire," I said. "Only the king can else appoint a candidate to knighthood. It is not in my power."

"I humbly beseech you," he said.

"Listen, lad. I would love to have you as my squire, you and your sword and your skill and luck, but there are rules. I can take you as my servant, but I cannot elevate you to squire. I am sorry."

For a moment we sat. I watched the berserker rage drain from Sir Wulfric's face. He lowered his sword and reached under his helmet to scratch his head. "What happened?" he asked.

The damsel, behind us a ways and beyond sight, cried, "Where are you, sirs? Where are my protectors? The beast might return at any moment!"

"You drove off the serpent," I told Sir Wulfric. The boy's arms tightened around me again, perhaps in protest. "You were magnificent. I shall sing your praises: Sir Wulfric, mighty in battle."

Sir Wulfric chewed his ginger mustache. "There was a boy," he said. "I am certain there was a boy."

"Yes. He's up behind me."

Sir Wulfric toddled closer and peered up at the boy. "Had a notion he interfered with my fight."

"You saved us all," I said.

Sir Wulfric smiled.

"Help? Help? Help!" cried the damsel.

Sir Wulfric shook his head, then trotted off toward the clearing.

The boy poked me in the back. "Why did you tell such great lies?"

"Didn't you see he was ready to slice you lengthwise and spill your guts over the ground? He doesn't remember what happened. What use have you for glory? You'll never be a knight. This way praise will be heaped on Sir Wulfric, and he will be happy. Unless," I muttered, sotto voce, "Eudo tells him a different story. We'd best go back so that I can warn him." I wheeled my horse and we cantered back to the clearing.

We arrived a little in advance of Sir Wulfric. "Help!" cried the damsel. I glanced toward her, and saw that though her garments were somewhat crushed she seemed otherwise in good spirits. The monster was nowhere in evidence.

I rode directly to Eudo. "I've told Sir Wulfric he routed the beast," I murmured to him.

"He believed you?"

"The madness of battle overcame him. He remembers nothing."

"Does that stripling on the back of your horse have aught to say about this?"

"Yes. He complains about my choice in tales. Convince him I am correct."

The lad's arms loosed from about me, and he slid to the ground. "Never mind who tells what tales. I'll get myself gone from here now."

"Wait." For some reason I didn't want the boy to leave us, and it wasn't just a matter of treasuring his skill with the sword. There was something about him I liked.

I wanted to dismount, but it was a difficult maneuver when one was wearing mail and still clutching a lance. I was a champion at falling off horses fully armored. I didn't enjoy demonstrating that particular skill. I handed the lance to Eudo, then rode to a nearby fallen forest giant of a tree. I gave my good horse the command to stand. The boy watched sullenly as I maneuvered myself off my horse with the aid of the log and slid to the ground.

"Moon curse you, have you lost your wits, such as they are?" the damsel cried. "How dare you dismount when danger is still around us? Suppose the monster returns? How will you fight it from the ground?"

Sir Wulfric puffed up then and bowed to her. "Damsel," he said.

"And you, you fat, worthless fool!" she cried. "What ails you? Where are all your knightly skills?"

"Is it thus you address your deliverer?" asked Sir Wulfric.

"My deliverer! Devils pull out your hairs one by one, fool! What had you to do with anything besides irritating the captor worm?"

I had forgot to straighten out our story with the damsel, but then again, she didn't seem like the sort with whom one could reason.

"Wait," I said to the boy. "Who are you?"

"I am Nix of the Wilderland."

"I am Sir Bran of Elstan. Won't you bide with us?"

His frown was ferocious. "No. Somewhere I will find someone who will help me become a knight. I see no profit in staying here."

He had the right of that. I had no money or goods to offer him, even if he decided to accept a post as my servant. "I cannot offer you material things," I said, "but I can instruct you in matters of chivalry. Even if one cannot be a knight, one may assume the virtues of one."

The boy glared at me from under the rim of his soup pot.

"Yonder stands my savior," cried the damsel. Nix and I glanced at her. She pointed at Nix.

Sir Wulfric's face took on a dark and purple hue.

"All your knightly virtues didn't teach you to aim a lance," Nix said.

I sighed. "Sadly true. Perhaps you are right. You would do well to seek someone who could teach you truer than I could."

"All you've taught me so far is that you lie when there's not the least need."

"Oh, there was need," I muttered. Sir Wulfric was a powerful knight, and not to be thwarted lightly. He craved any excuse to fight, and regarded as insults remarks which others would see as innocence.

Sir Wulfric, sweat dotting his brow, came toward us, sword unsheathed.

"What transpires?" screamed the damsel, rushing toward us. "Sir Knight! What are your intentions?"

Sir Wulfric turned toward her, and at that moment Eudo rode past the knight, leading his pack mules so that he separated the boy and me from Sir Wulfric.

"I intend to see you safe from all base creatures, damsel," Sir Wulfric said.

"If you mean to retreat, now would be a good time," I murmured to the lad.

Nix nodded and let out a whistle. His pony galloped up and the boy jumped up on the log I had used to dismount, then leaped into the pony's saddle and galloped away.

The damsel, of course, had no mount, no palfrey, not even a hackney. She would not ride one of the pack mules. She would not ride Eudo's rouncey. Only a destrier would do.

The damsel managed to arrange herself on my saddle as though it were an accustomed mode of transport.

After aiding Sir Wulfric in remounting his destrier, Eudo helped me remove my mail and store it on one of the laden pack mules. He offered me his horse, but I decided to stretch my legs. The soft spring evening was pleasant for walking, and I felt light without my hauberk.

"What is your story, damsel?" I asked. "How did that serpent get you in its coils?"

"I do not converse with lunatics who mean me ill."

"Nay, but it's a solid question," said Sir Wulfric. "How came you to be in such straits, and whither are you bound now, that we may help you get there?"

"Neither do I converse with blind, fat fools," said the damsel.

"This should make an interesting journey," I said to Eudo, beside whose horse I walked. Even Sir Wulfric could not start a duel with a lady, no matter how rudely she behaved.

Eudo laughed, and the damsel turned to glare at us with fire in her eyes. "Do you make sport of me?" she cried.

"Pay us no heed; we are people with whom you do not deign to speak."

"I will speak with the squire, whom I hold blameless."

Eudo looked to his master. Sir Wulfric's face bore purple banners in its cheeks; he snarled beneath his mustaches, but gave Eudo a curt nod.

"How came you into trouble, maiden, and where do you desire to go now?" Eudo asked.

"I was stolen from my older sister's castle in the night by that creature. I thought it was a very nightmare of mine, but found I could not wake. It stole me the night before I was to secretly set out for the king's court in search of a knight to defend my sister from a marauding knight who has laid siege to her castle and who wants to marry her. For many days I have been in the monster's clutches, and it has defeated and devoured knight after knight who would save me." Her head drooped. "Finally, I found and lost a savior in the space of half an hour," she murmured.

"Where lies your sister's castle?" Eudo asked.

"In the north country, where the sea meets the feet of the mountains, and all the beach is cobbled stones. I wit not how far the serpent carried me, for it moved not like a horse; there was no measuring its stride. I have been in this forest a fortnight, I trow, while it went widewhere with me."

"Who is the knight who lays siege to your sister's castle?" asked Eudo.

She shuddered in the saddle. "The Knight of the Pearl," she whispered.

"Damsel, may we carry you home?" I asked. Bitter bile was in the back of my throat. I swallowed. "For I am fated to meet that knight. He slew my father."

Crimson touched her cheeks. "Why did you try to kill me, knave?"

"I didn't try to kill you. My luck is such that I never hit the thing at which I aim. I meant to keep you safe."

"This is a strange tale," she said. Slowly she smiled. "But perhaps true. Yes. You may accompany me home."

We traveled all the rest of the day, but no sign of human habitation where we might overnight did we see, nor sign of aught else but the puissance of trees. In the dustier stretches of our way I covered my face with a kerchief and let the others move ahead of me. After they had pulled too far ahead one time, Eudo rode back and urged me to take his horse and let him walk. Thrice I said him nay, but the fourth time I accepted his offer. Thereafter we traded the horse between us.

In the stretches of stillness when I was like to be alone in the forest, I was sure I heard the sound of something not on our trail but somewhere nearby. Something pursued us, but not fast enough to overtake us. I rested my hand on the hilt of my dagger, which was hammered from sky iron, a bequest from my mother's father and always lucky for me. Our pursuer never broke cover.

When Sir Wulfric decreed we must stop for the night, I

suggested we take watches. He grunted. "You watch first," he said. I was near to falling down with exhaustion, but I shrugged and agreed.

Eudo cooked a pot of porridge for us, dropping in dried apples and meat. The smell alone was heavenly, and the taste was ambrosial after all the dust I had eaten that day.

The spring night turned chilly. I offered the damsel my best cape for her bed, and she accepted it. My second best cape was threadbare, torn in places, but good enough for a man who shouldn't sleep through his watch.

"Wake me when your head nods too often," Eudo murmured to me. I told him I would.

But withal I did not. Despite the chill and my determination, my grinding fear that the serpent had followed us and wanted to eat us in the dark, I fell asleep beside the ashes of our fire, and only woke when iron scraped stone.

I startled up. All around me was darkness, for we were close in under the trees so that only a star or two glimmered between branches thick with young leaves. Then I saw a glow of green fire only a few feet from me. The monster's eyes? I leaped to my feet. "What goes there?"

Something clinked and clunked. I unsheathed my dagger. "Answer me," I said.

"Shh," said something near the green flame.

A hiss! Surely a serpent! My sky-iron knife outstretched, I started toward the noise, but tripped on one of the firestones where Eudo had cooked our dinner and fell headlong. My front smacked the ground. My breath flew out of me.

"Fare you well?" asked a low voice.

I waited till my breathing smoothed. What of the others? Had they heard my fall?

Nothing else in our camp stirred. Small wonder if they were all tired after such a day.

I groaned. "Not well, but not too ill."

Something knelt over me, tugged at my arm. I heard its breath, and knew from its size and sounds that it was no serpent. It helped me sit up.

"Fare you well?" I asked Nix, for it could only be he by the size and familiarity of him.

"My hunger overmastered me," he whispered. "I smelled your supper. I sat amongst the trees as long as I could. Is there any left?"

Eudo had sliced the cooled porridge into portions for tomorrow's breakfast and wrapped them in linen, then hid them in a saddlebag against marauding vermin. I unbuckled the straps around the saddlebag and gave my morning portion to the boy, whose hunger was no doubt greater than mine.

"Gramercy, noble knight," he whispered after he had finished.

"Here's a change in tune," I said.

"How and I should insult one who has succored me?" Since he spoke in a whisper, I could not tell whether he mocked me.

"How and you should lie? I thought it was a fault not in your character."

"For all I know, you may be noble, by birth if not by deed. In balance, you must be; you are a knight, are you not? And the very one who told me one must be noble-born to be a knight."

"I'm not the one who fashioned these laws. I imagine some time in the dim past it was not so; who was the first knight? I only tell you what I know to be true in the present day. There may be a way around this. Distinguish yourself with deeds so that the king hears of it, or sees it. If you display your prowess, he may elevate you, as was done in the romances of ages past."

The boy sighed. "Here's a tale I would hear more of."

"Why not speak of it tomorrow?" muttered a voice from the darkness.

"Eudo. Sorry we disturbed your rest," I murmured.

"Since I wake I may as well watch. What o'clock is it?"

"There are not enough stars to say." I yawned.

"Well, well," he grumbled, and sat up, a dim form in the darkness. "Rest you now. I'll wake you later."

So Nix joined our company, by stealth, in dark of night, under my aegis.

In the morning Eudo and I drew the damsel away from our camp and spoke to her before Sir Wulfric woke.

"The boy has rejoined us, and might stay, if we are careful," I told the damsel.

"The lad is as shy as a wild bird," Eudo said. "The merest word might make him take flight."

"Please, as you value the boy's life and his service to you, don't point to him and call him savior," I added. "Sir Wulfric is testy about such things and might take offense, and in so doing, harm the boy. He is a man of much wrath, quick to strike and powerful. Pretend the boy is only my squire; perhaps the knight won't notice him then."

She frowned a mighty frown. "You would ask me to betray what I know as truth?"

"No, no!" Eudo flapped his hands in the air.

"Keep the truth in your heart, not on your lips," I said. "Silence is all we ask."

She heaved a great sigh and nodded.

So we went back, and some of us had cold porridge for breakfast. Sir Wulfric took no notice of the boy; in like manner he had never taken notice of servants at court.

Another day we traveled, the boy and I to the rear. Sometimes he led his pony, and sometimes he rode it. I took out one of my willow whistles and tried to remember tunes from court, when I had breath to blow and there was not too much dust in my mouth. Nix listened closely, and sometimes whistled with his mouth when he caught a tune. I was more pleased than I had a right to be that he could carry a tune. Were we to stay together, music would add to our pleasure in each other's company.

Other times I told the boy about court life, and marvels I had heard, and ways that knights had earned glory. He had a great hunger for such stories.

Just after we lost the sun, we fought free of the dark forest, and saw before us a fine castle built of black rock, surrounded by a moat of dark water, with torchlight gleaming from some of the embrasures, and flickers of fire reflected on the water's surface. A soldier strolled the wall walk above against the soft blue spring evening, then stopped to watch us.

"God's mercy. Tonight we will feast, and sleep with a roof over our heads," said Sir Wulfric. He urged his horse to the drawbridge, which was down, and hailed the gatekeeper. "Who lives here? Will he give hospitality to two knights and a lady?"

"It would be his honor to aid you," said the gatekeeper, and stood aside so we could enter the inner courtyard.

Stable boys came to take our mounts. Eudo followed them to see that the stables were clean and well-stocked with hay, and that they took proper care of our horses, then joined us in the great hall.

The lord and lady of the castle made us welcome. They were both handsome, though the brown of their hair had silvered over with age. The lady took our damsel away with her to wash somewhere else. The lord summoned servants to disarm us and to fetch ewers of warm water for us to wash, and they arranged for pallets to be laid by the fireplace, where we could later sleep. The boy would not let the servants touch his armor, and washed only his hands, leaving his face dirty. I opened my mouth to speak, and he glared at me with his honey-colored eyes.

"Supper will be served directly," said the lord after we had finished our ablutions. He showed us to table.

Then they served us a marvelous meal, bread, wine, venison, salt to our tongues' content, and asked that we share our story.

At this Eudo and I exchanged glances, for who would tell a story that each of us knew variously? Would the lady speak her truth? Would the boy speak at all? Eudo and I had arranged that he sat farthest down the table from our hosts, for we knew he was untutored in manners, and hoped he would escape notice.

The damsel began the tale. "I am Tegwen of Morcant." She told how the serpent had ravished her away from her siege-embattled home in the north country, and how she had endured days as its hostage, and how knight after knight had come upon her and the serpent in the forest and tried to rescue her, but died in the attempt, and how finally we came and set her free.

The lord and lady praised us.

Sir Wulfric took up the tale. "I challenged the great beast! When it saw well what it would have to fight, it released the damsel and departed!" He smiled and stroked his mustache.

Eudo and I stared anxiously at the boy. He sliced off a morsel of venison and ate it from the point of his knife, then drank wine from a silver goblet, and said nothing.

"How fortunate that your fierceness inspired such fear in a creature more like to eat knights than run from them," murmured the lady. Her brows drew together in confusion.

"And now we are returning the damsel to her home," I said before questions could be asked. "We hope to overcome the knight who is besieging her sister."

"Who is that knight?" asked the lord.

"The Knight of the Pearl," whispered the damsel.

The lady blanched, and the lord straightened. "We have heard of this perilous knight. His prowess is unmatched and his reputation is cruel. They say he hangs the bodies of those he defeats from trees so the ravens may sup, and leaves them there unburied, showing them greatest dishonor."

"He slew my father, after my father yielded to him," I said. Fire kindled in my gut, fear and anger mixed. "All my life I have known I must face him."

"God protect you, then" said the lord, and the lady murmured assent.

I felt a heat against my face, and turned. The boy stared at me with his honey eyes, his face a fierce mask.

"God protect me," I repeated. For my mother's grief, for my father's dishonor, for my own purpose in life, I must go forward, though in my heart I knew there was no chance of victory for me. I would end up a hanging corpse, no doubt, which fate was better than to have all honorable knights laugh at me living.

I turned from the boy's gaze, and for a moment let my mind wander through my own dream of a future, one where I went armed only with my dagger and fiddle and whistles, and my treasury of stories and songs, and traveled not to battle but to entertain.

"I will face this pearly knight, too," Sir Wulfric said, his voice hearty. "I search out adventure. I fear no knight. Sir Bran may have first battle with this knight to satisfy his honor. I will face him after, and I will beat him."

"But how unkind to say such a thing," said the boy, "as though there were no chance Sir Bran might beat him."

"Hush," I said. "He knows me well."

The boy gave me a scorching look such that it made me wonder where his thoughts had traveled.

Eudo turned the subject to news from court, and we spoke no more about our future that night.

*   *   *

In the midst of the night, when the fire flickered low and the wine I had drunk whispered to me it was ready to quit me, I rose to find a latrine, of which I knew there were three in the walls off the great hall. I saw that two other pallets were as empty as mine, the boy's and Eudo's, so I took a taper, kindled a flame in the fire, and went to the farthest latrine, reckoning the closer two would be occupied. I came silent down the narrow crooked hall to the seat, and there beheld—

For the first time, I saw the boy without his helm and such armor as covered his lower half. When he saw me, he sprang to his feet.

I could not help seeing what I saw.

A curtain of red-blond braids hung from his head, each long enough to reach his waist.

Her waist.

I turned so swiftly my taper blew itself out. I stood with my back to her. The light of her taper threw my shadow on the wall before me. "I beg your pardon a thousand times," I said.

"You may not have it," she said crossly.

I bit my lip and left the latrine hallway, waited in the great hall until she emerged, wrapped in her straw and surcoat, her hair hidden up under the soup pot again. She waved her taper out and leaned against the wall beside me. For a while we watched the flicker of firelight across the rushes on the floor and listened to the thunderous snores from Sir Wulfric. Need overcame me, and I went into the latrine in the dark, which was not wise, but I remembered the turns in the hall, and only scuffed an elbow; I relieved myself into the chute, and came back out, wondering if she would still be standing there or would have retreated into sleep.

She waited, brave in this as in all things.

"I have never heard of a lady knight. I don't know how you will make a knight," I whispered.

"By deeds. As you said."

"By deeds and deception?"

"Sometimes deception is necessary, even to knights. You taught me that."

"Why do you want this?"

She looked away. "I will not be locked in a house. I was born in the wild, and I have the heart of a warrior. I must fight, or I will go mad."

I had seen knights who had a like problem, berserker blood that could not be denied. They were those who took affront easily and forced fights on others, taking offense at innocent words turned insult by misapprehension. They were never more alive than when battling anyone or anything. One walked wide around them, unless one were another such hot-blood.

Yet Nix did not seem wild in that way. She hunched like a falcon, though, who spots prey. It seemed to me that maybe she hosted a different wildness, the wild of the hunt.

She said, "When we reach the castle where the Knight of the Pearl holds sway, if you are as ill a knight as you profess to be, you must let me face him first, Bran."

"No."

"But it seems you have no hope of winning against him."

"You are a maid, and half a head shorter than I. This is my fight, has been my charge since I was a child. How could I be chivalrous and let you risk yourself?"

Her eyes seemed lit by yellow fires within. She leaped on me then. There had been no challenge, and I was unarmed and surprised. But still, by my greater size and my small skill in hand-to-hand, I would have thought I could overmaster her.

It did not thus transpire. Soon she sat atop me, her hands crushing my wrists to the floor despite my struggles. "Yield," she whispered between clenched teeth.

I fought to flip us over, and could not. Her muscles had set like iron; she sat unmoving on my stomach, heavier by far than her appearance had suggested, her face a foot above mine, fierce as a falcon's. "Yield. You cannot overcome me, for my mother was a water maiden, and gifted me with powers of which you wot not."

Sweat bloomed on my brow. I brought my knees up against her back and felt as though I had knocked them into a stone wall.

"Yield, Bran."

I thought of the fair Amicia, wondered what she would say if she could see one of her many champions now, helpless beneath a maiden. Once more I threw myself into every effort to escape Nix's hold. Nothing I tried dislodged her, or even shifted her. I sank back and whispered, "I yield."

She was off me and back on her feet in an instant. "I claim first battle rights with that knight," she said.

Filled with shame, I knelt before her. I felt faint and confused, but I remembered what chivalry demanded of me. "I swear my homage and fealty to you," I whispered, staring at the rushes on the floor. "All that I own is at your service."

"What nonsense is this? Get up, Bran." She prodded me with her toe. A moment longer I stared at the floor, as I released all hold I had on dreams and vows and vengeance, and, indeed, on my lady Amicia. I gave myself leave to feel how now I was born yet a fourth time, out of my old self and into this one who owed life and service to Nix.

Then I felt cheerful, and got to my feet. Whatever came next lay in a pattern I had not yet foreseen. We went back to our pallets and I thought of men hanging dead in trees, with ravens eating out their eyes, and for the first time since the lord's tale at supper I did not picture my corpse among theirs.

In the morning we heard mass and broke our fast with the lord and lady. The lady saw to it that the cook gave Eudo supplies.

"Have you all else that you need for your journey?" asked the lord.

The damsel Tegwen said, "If it chances that you have a palfrey I might ride, I could return this noble destrier to Sir Bran."

I said, "If it chances you have mail that would fit Nix—"

All turned to stare at me, lord, lady, Eudo, Sir Wulfric, Mistress Tegwen, and Nix. Nix's eyes were sharp and harsh, her yellow falcon eyes. Eudo and Tegwen looked confused, and Sir Wulfric dubious.

"The lad needs mail," I said. "He means to fight, and who can he fight in such garb? Suppose the dragon had set his armor afire. What would have happened then?"

Sir Wulfric frowned. Tegwen glanced askance at him, and Eudo made a motion to me of his hand cutting his throat. The lord and lady, of course, did not know of what I spoke.

"I have a hauberk my son outgrew before he went adventuring," the lady said. "The child is welcome to it; would that it protects him as it did my son, in God's good name." She went to fetch it.

"I cannot offer you a palfrey, but I have a hackney I can spare," the lord said. He sent a servant to fetch it.

Presently returned the lady with youth-sized mail, a keton, a shining helm, a milk-white coif, a round green shield, and a clean whole surcoat in white and green, which she offered to Nix.

For a moment Nix just stared. Then she said, "Oh, thank you. Thank you." She took the clothes inside the keep.

I searched my saddlebags for aught I could give in return for the horse and mail. I found no money, but an emerald brooch my mother had given me which I had never gamed away, the only token of hers that I carried with me always. "Please, for your kindness," I said, and offered it to the lady. She refused it three times, but the fourth time, she accepted.

Nix emerged, her face at last washed. She was clad in real mail, with the green-and-white surcoat overtop, and again all her hair tucked up out of sight under the new helm. She looked a faerie knight.

She was not like any lady I had ever seen or courted. Yet I felt such stirrings in my breast as signaled the start of a fortunate fall. Just so I had felt when first I beheld the queen's fairest attendant, Catrin, whom all the knights courted. Yet, as I studied Nix, I felt something more, something strange and new for which I did not yet have words.

Eudo's eyes widened. He watched Nix a moment, then glanced at me.

I stepped forward and held Nix's stirrup so she could mount. She climbed up onto her pony, then dug her toe into my stomach. "Stop it," she whispered.

I smiled and turned away.

The damsel gave me back my destrier and consented to ride on the lord's hackney. Thus we proceeded, with other adventures, into the north country whence she had been abducted, until presently we approached her home. We passed through a village she knew. When they heard the sound of our horses' hooves on the packed earth streets, the dwellers came out of their wattle-and-daub houses. "Where are you going?" some asked.

"Morcant," said the damsel.

"Turn back," the men told us. "All who travel there die shameful deaths. The air is full of the stench of bodies rotting. Turn back."

"Is that you, Mistress Tegwen?" asked an old woman.

"It is, and I have brought these champions to face the Knight of the Pearl."

"It is a wicked day when a damsel brings men to their doom," cried the old woman.

For the first time since I had met her, I saw Tegwen stop and think. She studied each of us in turn. "Truly," she said, "I may be doing you great ill."

"Had I not met you, still, fate would have brought me here," I said.

"I am ripe for any challenge," said Sir Wulfric. "An he had killed a hundred, still would I face him, for he has never yet met me."

"I will fight anything that brings shame and dishonor to women or children or knights," said Nix.

Everyone looked at Eudo. He shrugged. "I live and learn, and hand them their arms."

"Still, I release you all from any pledge you may have made to uphold me," Tegwen said. "From here on, accompany me by choice or turn back. I must go on. When last I was home, my sister and her family and vassals and servants and soldiers were close to the edge of starvation with this siege. I must do what I can to aid her."

"Let's go," said Nix.

We rode on through the village. The villagers did not seem to know whether to cheer for us or mourn. Some few trailed a ways with us, but then we went through a slender pass in the hills, and lost our followers.

On the crest of the last hill, we looked to the land below, a dark-treed wood, a few buildings beyond, huddled at the base of the curtain wall of a castle built of pale green stone on a spit of land. And beyond the castle—

For the first time in my life I beheld the sea.

It transfixed me. Something strange and light rose in my chest. How could such a great gray-and-green expanse stretch out into eternity before one and not rouse a spirit of wonder?

"Bran," Nix murmured. She touched my sleeve.

I blinked and looked at the company. I realized that I held one of my willow whistles. That I had been playing it, all unknowing. Tegwen and Eudo stared at me with wonder in their faces.

Sir Wulfric's face was purple with impatience. "Let us not tarry for such silly tootling," he said. "If fear has seized you, turn back."

"Fear," I murmured. Strange, but I had forgotten my fear. I put my whistle away, and we rode on down the track to the wood.

"That deaf fool," Nix muttered. "'Twas eternity and ocean you played. Who could hear and not understand?"

I took her hand and kissed the back. She jerked away from me, spurred her horse, and caught up with Eudo.

Now, I thought, I have dishonored my master. I will have to make it up to her somehow. Still, I smiled.

My smile vanished when the road took us into the trees. Just as the lord had said, as the villagers had said. The stench of death was so thick it made us choke and cough. Knights, dead knights, in various states of decay, hung by the neck from low branches all through that horrid wood, their shields and swords hung up beside them in a dreadful display of evil and dishonor. Clouds of flies attended them; crows pecked at them. At the Last Judgment, how should they rise up from such a place?

Even Sir Wulfric was quiet as we traversed that wood.

Beyond it we came to an open field that might once have been a fair jousting ground. In the meadow was pitched a magnificent pavilion, and beside it lay a black dog large as a pony. As soon as the dog spied us, it rose to its feet and howled, and out from the pavilion strode a knight, attended by a host of servants. At the same time, above, on the wall walk of the castle came many people.

"Sister!" cried a beautiful golden-haired lady from above.

"Sister!" cried Tegwen. "How fare you?"

"The better for sight of you!" she cried. But all on the wall walk looked gaunt and weary.

I stared at the knight, the man who had killed my father and whom I had never before seen. All I could discern was that he was a large man and wore black mail beneath a black surcoat, and in the center of the surcoat's chest there was a circle of pale pearls.

"Have you come to challenge me?" he called. His voice was smooth and sweet as hot cider.

"We have," said Sir Wulfric.

I kneed my horse to the fore. "I am Sir Bran of Elstan. You slew my father and dishonored my family, and I must face you."

"What a barking pup to put out of its misery," he said. "This should take but a moment of my time."

Nix rode in front of me. "Now, Bran. I accept your fealty and homage, and press you into my service," she said. "Give me your favor. I will be your champion."

I had forgotten everything at the sight of this man but the ancient goal carved into my soul. I blinked three times, for a moment mazed in mind by what Nix said. My stomach jumped as I fought to change course. Then I remembered my fourth self, which I had pledged to her. I took three breaths and glanced down at what I wore, then tore the hem off my blue surcoat and held it out.

She presented her right arm, and I tied my favor about it. I still felt as though sword-smote.

"What are you playing at?" asked Sir Wulfric.

"Nix will be a knight," I said, "and is already my master."

"I claim first battle right," Nix said. She rode to the pack mule and took the heaviest lance we had. "Knight! For all the evil you have done, repent you, and prepare to die!"

"I do not fight children."

"Call me a dwarf, then, and have at you!"

The Knight of the Pearl laughed.

Nix sat her pony, with her lance couched, and waited.

Sir Wulfric turned three shades of purple. Eudo spoke softly to him and they both rode to the side of the ground. Tegwen stared long at me, then bit her lip and looked away. I watched Nix.

When the Knight finished laughing, he said, "So be it," and told his servants to set his spurs on his heels and bring him his black horse and black spear, and then he mounted and withdrew to the far end of the jousting ground.

I could not let Nix do this.

I must abide by my word to do her bidding.

I must protect her, protect what was beautiful, fierce, wild, and precious. Suddenly it was more important than even my honor. I would willingly die for her if need be.

How could I protect her when I couldn't protect myself?

She had the strength of her mother's people. She could overmaster me in a trice. I couldn't protect her. I must trust she could protect herself.

Sickness roiled in my stomach.

The Knight shouted, and they set off toward each other, gaining speed as they grew closer. Each smote the other in the midst of their shields with such force that both fell from their mounts and lay stunned upon the ground, the reins still in their hands.

Did they live? Did Nix live?

The people on the castle's wall walk raised a cheer. "No one has ever unhorsed him before," Mistress Tegwen murmured.

Nix and the Knight sat up slowly.

I pressed my palm to my chest.

When each saw the other awake, both jumped to their feet.

Nix struck her pony's flank. He trotted straight to me. I took his reins.

The combatants retrieved their shields and drew their swords, and then they fought, raining strike after strike on each other's shields and helms, the Knight big and powerful, Nix small and agile, dancing away from blows, dancing inside his reach to strike at him with her green-bladed sword, harrying him like a hound a boar.

The sun moved across the sky and still they fought, evenly matched despite the disparity of their sizes. They bled from a dozen small wounds.

"Fall, dwarf," the Knight cried.

"Die, breaker of women's and sons' hearts," cried Nix, and then she drove a blow of her short sword straight through his mail and into his shoulder. When she drew the sword out, he dropped his sword, his arm dead from the shoulder, blood streaming down over his surcoat. Anon he buckled to his knees before her.

She set the tip of her blade beneath his chin. "Will you yield?" she asked.

"I do. I yield me to thy mercy."

"I shall have just as much mercy as you had when you slew Bran's father," she cried.

"Nix!" I dropped the reins of her pony and cantered toward her. "Stop!"

She glared up at me, her eyes full of golden fire, her body braced to give the killing blow.

"If you strike now, you will be a false knight or no knight at all. Stop."

The fire left her eyes. She jerked her blade back, and the Knight of the Pearl collapsed. She stepped away from him and cleaned her blade on the grass, then wiped it with the hem of her surcoat and sheathed it.

He struggled to sit up again, though weak from loss of blood.

"Through the mercy of my sworn man, you yet live," Nix said. "So now, do whatever he asks of you."

The Knight looked up at me.

"Swear homage and fealty to Nix. Make over all your lands and possessions to Nix for the purpose of making reparations to those you have harmed. Spend the rest of your life making amends to all those you have trespassed against," I said. "Swear by everything you hold dear that you will abandon all evil and work to right the wrongs you have wreaked."

He bowed his head. "I swear."

My heart was sore. "Why did you do all these evil deeds?" Why had my father died such a senseless death?

"She whom I loved above all others charged me with this mission. I had given my word to do her bidding," he said. "A knight who laughed dishonored her. She made me swear to avenge her, to kill all knights who laughed. First I sought out all knights who laughed and killed them. Then she said perhaps I had not killed the one who defiled her, and told me to kill all knights from the court of your king. So I set myself that task." He wiped a hand over his bloody face. "At last she died of her derangement, but she never released me from my vow. I thank you, Sir Dwarf, for honorably defeating me. I have longed for nothing more these past many years."

Later, our company and all those who had been besieged sat down to a feast prepared by the Knight of the Pearl's servants.

"Do you write lyrics?" Nix asked me.

"Once upon a time," I replied. They still sang some of my songs at court, though no one remembered where they had come from. I had given up tunesmithing when I put all my heart into practicing the arts of war.

"This is the service I want from you," she said. "You'll follow me everywhere, and watch my deeds, and make them into songs for the bards to sing. We will have many adventures. You'll write many songs. My reputation will precede me. When we have done enough great things, we'll return to court. How then can the king do other than make me a knight?" She smiled and gnawed on the wing of a fowl.

Of all the possible futures no soothsayer had ever told me, how came Nix to pick the one closest to my heart's desire? I felt warm clear through. Already words shaped themselves in my head around Nix's fight with the dragon.

Eudo tapped my shoulder. "How came you to be his squire?" he whispered.

"I'm not a squire. I'm a bard," I said.

"Or something more and less," said the damsel Tegwen, who stared at a couple of Nix's braids that had escaped her helm while I was tending her wounds, "but withal, still a lunatic."

THE CAPTAIN OF THE GUARD

by Fiona Patton

Fiona Patton was born in Calgary, Alberta in 1962 and grew up in the United States. In 1975 she returned to Canada, and after several jobs which had nothing to do with each other, including carnival·ride operator and electrician, moved to 75 acres of scrub land in rural Ontario with her partner, four cats of various sizes, and one tiny little dog. Her first book *The Stone Prince* was published by DAW Books in 1997. This was followed by *The Painter Knight* in 1998, *The Granite Shield* in 1999, and *The Golden Sword* in 2001.

CASTLE Jorgen-Tor stood on the edge of a precipice in the Talnek Mountain Range, hundreds of feet above the River Ivar. Its walls encircled fifty acres of field and orchard, its wells followed chasms deep within the rocks, and a single road, one cart-width wide, to the south was its only approach. It had been the central stronghold of the Malikan Demon Lords for nearly eight hundred years; unassailable, impregnable, and, until the armies of King Ludik had somehow fought their way to within half a mile of its gate six months before, virtually unknown.

Viktor Endrik, the Captain of Jorgen-Tor's Castle Guard,

stood on the gatehouse battlements, looking down on the besieging army. He had served Jorgen-Tor's most recent master for over a decade, rising from the ranks to become the one sane voice of counsel to the dangerously unstable Malik. But one sane voice had not been enough to prevent the ill-conceived war which had shrunk the Lord's southern holdings by half. This siege was the latest result of a series of disastrous decisions made by Lord Malik's generals, decisions which had seen three of them flung from the castle battlements in under a week. At the time, Endrik had not mourned their passing; too many of his own Guard had died by their order.

There was movement below. His foot on the battlements, Endrik leaned forward.

King Ludik's soldiers had been working day and night to widen the road so that his heavy siege engines might be brought within range of the castle. They'd made little headway, and their casualties were enormous—Lord Malik had an inexhaustible supply of projectiles, some of them human—but as King Ludik's victories had increased, so had his allies. Four southern kingdoms had joined with him as word of the siege had spread. King Ludik, it seemed had an inexhaustible supply of soldiers.

A blue glow rose over the road, then dissipated. The King's mages had been working day and night alongside his soldiers. Come nightfall there would be another foot of melted rock anchoring the new patch of road. They might not be making much headway, but they were making some, a little bit each day, like extremely persistent snails. Someday soon they would be in range, but not this year.

Sucking in a deep breath of air, Endrik tasted the hint of frost on the breeze. It was nearly autumn. That gave them all four, maybe six weeks to prepare for winter. No one was looking forward to being bottled up in Jorgen-Tor for five frozen months, but it would be worse below. After eight centuries, the sheer cliffs were barren of timber and, although there were caves enough to shelter King Ludik and his officers, there were not enough for his soldiers. Without the protection of rock, the bitter cold would sap their strength, making them easy prey for Lord Malik and his griffins, and as the Lord's restlessness grew, so would his attacks. If they didn't take the castle by the onset of winter, they'd have to withdraw, losing all the ground they'd shed so much blood to achieve. But they could not take the castle, not from without.

The harsh cry of an eagle seeking its own prey sounded in the distance. Endrik's gaze followed it as it soared above the cliffs, remembering the first time he'd watched Lord Malik take to the skies. In all his life he'd never seen anything so strong and so powerful. He'd stood, rapt, on the gatehouse wall, indifferent to his own danger, even after the Lord had returned to the battlements in a great beating of wings, one of his own sentries hanging limp and bleeding in his arms. The guardsman and the demon had stared at each other for a long time and then, as Lord Malik's human seeming had returned, Endrik had gently removed the body of his friend Kender from his master's claws.

Lord Malik no longer hunted his own people, for love of the man who'd shown no fear or revulsion at his approach, and for ten years Endrik had stood on this spot, a silent witness to his Lord's departure and a beacon for his return. In those few hours the walkways and corridors of Jorgen-Tor were safe for its human inhabitants as long as their Captain stood watch on the gatehouse battlements. Tonight would be no different.

Tonight.

"It will be tonight," he said, loud enough for the sentries on guard to hear him. "He will fly tonight."

"Captain?"

Sergeant Pendik. Endrik hadn't heard him come up, but

then the older man had always had a light footfall, despite his size.

"He will fly tonight," he repeated. "Pass the word." Regardless of Lord Malik's promise, force of habit made Endrik turn to give the same order he gave each time the Demon Lord took to the skies in search of sport and blood. "Stay alert. Don't look at the sky. He can see your eyes, and when the hunger's on him it will draw him to you. Stay at your posts. Concentrate on the road. King Ludik's engineers will likely be taking advantage of the shadows to creep about looking for places to hide his sappers."

The sentries stirred nervously, and Pendik cleared his throat. "I thought His Majesty didn't like Ludik called a king, Captain."

Endrik shook his head. "He is a king, Sergeant," he said with mild reproof. "If you don't accord your enemies the respect they deserve, you'll never defeat them."

"Bollocks. A good trebuchet will defeat anyone."

"And they have a good trebuchet, so let's hope they never get close enough to use it."

"General Colar said Ludik was a hill bandit," one of the sentries offered.

Sergeant Pendik shot the man a wrathful glare. Ever since the General's death, Captain Endrik had been uncharacteristically withdrawn. Word in the barracks was that he was still angry over the number of sentries General Colar had co-opted for the war, but Pendik suspected it was something deeper. So far, however, the Captain had not seen fit to confide in his Guard Sergeant, something that was also uncharacteristic of him.

"General Colar is the reason we have a besieging army at our gate," he growled at the offending sentry. "So I wouldn't be so quick to hold him up as an expert or you might end up just like him."

As one, they glanced down. The remains of General Colar's body had lain on the rocks below the gatehouse for less than an hour before the castle griffins had finished devouring him. But then, there hadn't been much left of him to begin with. Lord Malik had always been very fond of organ meat. His jaw tight, Endrik turned away.

That night, as the moon shone down on the battlements, Lord Malik stepped onto the southernmost battery. His human seeming was large and muscular, topping seven feet by a good three inches. His hair, worn long and loose, was as gray as a winter storm, as were his eyes, the pupils standing out like bright, red coals. Immune to both heat and cold, he stood naked, allowing the wind to tickle across his body, raising the fine hairs along his arms and thighs and stimulating his vast appetite as it stimulated his erection. Feet planted firmly in the rock wall, he raised his arms, spreading out his chest like a huge bird of prey.

The change came slowly, first tendons, then muscles, flowing and merging into new forms. The thin membranes between his fingers grew and stretched across his forearms and along his shoulders and back. His legs lengthened and his chest widened and flattened while his fingers became curved and sharp. His eyes opened impossibly large in a face becoming narrow and hawklike as the crown of his head pulled back into a crest. Fully changed, he stood frozen in the moonlight for half a heartbeat, then dropped.

The updraft caught him fifty feet down. He banked sharply, heading for the besieging army as, behind him, a dozen smaller shapes soared out from the castle rock. As one, they followed their Lord to the hunt. There would be human prisoners in Jorgen-Tor's dungeons come morning.

*   *   *

Standing on the gatehouse battlements, Captain Endrik watched the demon's great shadow flit across the moon, sadness overlying the familiar sense of awe. Then, his face twisting in distress, he looked away.

Tucked inside the darkness of a nearby sentry box, Sergeant Pendik lit his pipe.

"He'll take you down with him one of these day," he said mildly, "if you keep making yourself a target like this."

Endrik shrugged. "He hasn't yet. He knows me. Even when the hunger's on him."

"When the hunger's on him, a Malik Lord doesn't know anyone. He killed his last Guard Captain, as you well know."

"That was different. Tolek was a traitor," Endrik answered without enthusiasm. "He broke into the griffen aerie and killed the Lord's only breeding male."

A puff of smoke left the sentry box. "One might say he sacrificed himself for his people; the griffins were overbreeding and beginning to prey on the sentries. One might say he was a hero."

"One might, but one would be wise not to say it too loudly."

"True enough. But he cared about his sentries, as you do."

"As I do," Endrik echoed quietly.

"Captain?"

Nothing.

"Are you all right, sir?"

"I'm fine."

Far below, a streak of clear magic lit up the sky.

"They're looking for him," Pendik observed.

"Even if they find him, it won't matter."

"Likely not. The last archer that drew blood paid for that accuracy with his own."

"It was a foolish attempt. A single arrow, no matter how bravely shot, would never be enough to slay a Malik Lord.

He'd have needed an arbalest at the very least, or a ballista, and even then it would have taken a shot of unnatural precision."

The Sergeant's brows drew down in reproof. "You shouldn't talk about such things, Captain," he admonished.

"Why not? It's the truth."

"Which doesn't mean it should be spoken out loud. You have a dangerously romantic streak of nobility that's always worried me. Lord Malik may love you, but even you're not immune to his wrath. I don't want to lose another Captain. It's bad for morale."

"Then, for the good of morale, I'll keep your warning in mind."

The familiar blue glow lit up the distant roadway and Endrik shook his head.

"Even when they know he's on the hunt, they still struggle on. You have to admire their tenacity."

"And wonder at their stupidity."

"It's not stupidity, Sergeant, it's fortitude."

"Not if he catches up one of their mages, it isn't. King Ludik hasn't enough to spare. It's poor tactics."

"You could go down and tell him that."

"Don't think I wouldn't love to, on the point of a sword, preferably. A siege is a bad business for all concerned."

"Especially when the Lord of the besieged has wings."

Pendik snorted. "I wish we all did. Then we could go out and fling the lot of them over a cliff."

Endrik chuckled. "We might've if we'd have had more griffins, but then your hero killed our only breeding male."

Another puff of smoke made its way into the air.

"Do you suppose that was what Lord Malik had in mind, Captain?"

Endrik shrugged. "Likely not," he admitted. "He's only ever used his griffins for sport, never for war."

"I wonder why?"

"Probably because a single arrow is enough to slay one of them."

Below, another blue glow grew and died. Pendik frowned.

"Do you think they might get close enough to use their siege equipment before winter, Captain?"

A thin scream sounded over the wind.

"Not at this rate."

"They'll be planning something desperate, then."

Endrik nodded. "I would be."

"He'd have needed an arbalest at the very least, or a ballista."

Allowing the cool breeze to whisper across his face, he stared up at the moon.

Sergeant Pendik had returned inside, leaving his Captain to his own thoughts. Lord Malik had passed behind the cliffs, but after all these years of watching, the Captain could still sense the hint of musk and blood on the wind as surly as he could still smell the Sergeant's pipe smoke. Accounted the most powerful Malik Lord in the history of their empire, the master of Jorgen-Tor had a powerful hunger for violence. He would fly and feed until dawn and then, his appetite sated for a time, he would return, his great wings spread across the sky like a God's.

". . . even then it would have taken a shot of unnatural precision," his mind echoed.

"A precision no ordinary archer of King Ludik's could possess," his mind pointed out.

"No ordinary archer, no."

"Even if they knew where to aim."

"No one knows where to aim. No one's ever gotten close enough to find out."

"You have."

"Yes, I have."

Staring into the night sky, Endrik watched Lord Malik pass across the moon.

The Demon Lord and his creatures returned just before dawn, their flight hampered by the burdens in their claws: human captives to feed the Lord's appetite for meat and sport, cattle and pigs to feed his garrison. Even in the midst of his hunger, Lord Malik remembered his people. After accepting his Captain's salute, he swept into the gatehouse, a robe-clad body slung over his shoulder and, with one last glance at the moon, Endrik followed him inside.

That afternoon, the castle prepared to feast. Kegs of beer had been rolled out into the main courtyard where a steer had been roasting above a bonfire all day, and the great hall had been cleared of furniture and weapons with the exception of a single bare sword lying in the center of the floor. The Lord's sport would begin as soon as the sun touched the blade.

Standing beside the throne, Captain Endrik went over the afternoon's itinerary with the Chief Handler. He'd been down to the dungeons that afternoon to inspect the prisoners and make his recommendations. Of the six brought in, one was already dead and another would die by nightfall. They'd be given to the griffins. Of the remaining four, two were private soldiers, young and terrified, and one had the look of a mage. He would provide the most interesting sport and would be saved until the end. The last man had stood, arms crossed, in the center of his

THE CAPTAIN OF THE GUARD   259

cell, glaring at Endrik with a look of virulent and defiant hatred. The Captain had studied him carefully.

He was a large man in his late twenties, black hair tied back in the southern manner, hands and arms scarred by sword work. He wore a simple tunic, now tattered and bloodstained, with no sign of rank or position, but he had the look of a seasoned veteran. Endrik wondered how he'd been caught. He came forward.

"Sergeant?" he asked.

The man drew himself up stiffly. "Knight."

"Nobility or Royal Guard?"

"Screw you."

Endrik smiled faintly. "Royal Guard. Captain Viktor Endrik of Tol Mazkol."

The man's eyes narrowed but, after a moment, he shrugged. "Lieutenant Sir Jehan Albek of Cruska."

"You're unarmed."

"I was sleeping. Stepped outside for a quick piss."

"Poor timing."

"It happens. What now?"

"You'll be brought upstairs to the great hall where you'll be offered the opportunity to fight for your death."

"For my death?"

"Yes. A good fight, a good death. A poor fight . . ."

"I go off the battlements?"

"Possibly."

"So, who would I be fighting? You?"

"It depends on whom Lord Malik chooses. If it pleases him, you might even get the chance to fight the Lord himself."

"Really?"

"It's not unheard of."

"And if I refuse to fight?"

"You die, so you might as well die fighting."

"And that's it? No questioning, no torture?"

"What could you know that we don't also know?"

"King Ludik's plans?"

"King Ludik's plans are written in the movement of his troops."

"And the torture?"

"Is for others."

"I see. Very well, then; I'll go down fighting for the honor of the Guard and the amusement of the enemy. I just have one question for you that I'd like answered before I die."

"Which is?"

"How do you live with yourself, Viktor Endrik of Tol Mazkol?"

Endrik's expression darkened. "I serve the greatest Malik Lord ever to take the field," he answered harshly. "Your King Ludik is a weakling in comparison."

"And that's enough to justify swearing oaths to a monster who kills and eats your own kind?"

Endrik met his eyes. "Yes."

The setting sun touched the sword blade as the first of Lord Malik's prisoners was brought to the great hall. A farmer's son in King Ludik's pay for less than a month, he put up as good a fight as he was able but died in less than hour. He would have died sooner, but Jorgen-Tor's Guard knew their Lord liked his sport to last. Finally, Sergeant Pendik had thrust his dagger into the youth's eye. Lord Malik feasted on the body while the second prisoner was brought in. Too terrified to even pick up the sword, he could only stand and shake, staring at his dead comrade in horror. At last, the Chief Handler released the oldest of Lord Malik's griffins. She made short work of him, dragging the body off herself to eat it in private. This left the mage and the Lieutenant.

Sir Jehan Albek strode into the great hall one step ahead of his guards. Crossing to the center of the room, he picked up the unbloodied sword and studied the blade critically before glancing about him with studied indifference. His gaze took in the line of sentries, the off-duty spectators, the Demon Lord with his grisly meal, and Captain Endrik standing to the left of the throne. He smiled tightly.

"Your Guard Captain has blood on his uniform, Lord Malik," he said with deliberate scorn.

The sentries glanced nervously at their master, who peeled his lips back off his teeth in appreciation of the man's bravado.

"He stands too close to the fray, Sir Jehan," he answered, his bass voice reverberating throughout the hall. "I often fear for his safety."

"You should. Someday a desperate enough man might make a lunge for him."

"Someday? Why not this day?"

"Why not, indeed."

Albek leaped forward, the sword jerking toward Lord Malik's breast at the last minute. It stopped an inch away, caught on Captain Endrik's own blade.

"If that blow was meant for me," he said mildly, "You've missed."

The other man shrugged. "A predictable attempt, but one worth making all the same."

"Did you honestly think a blade like that could harm a Malik Lord?"

Showing his teeth, Albek raised his sword in a mock salute. "What could honesty possibly have to do with it?" He attacked.

They fought up and down the hall as the sun crossed the floor, climbed up the far wall, and touched the dark-beamed ceiling above. They were equally matched in size and ability and, although Cruska and Tol Mazkol were a thousand miles apart, they often mirrored each other's moves with ghostly precision. His eyes narrowed, Lord Malik sent for his mages.

The floor became treacherously slippery with blood as each man made contact, but neither showed any sign of weakening. Finally Albek brought up his blade a second too slowly and Endrik darted inside his guard. Catching him with his elbow, he knocked the Southerner to the floor. He raised his sword and a red glow sprang up all around them. He paused.

Mage-fire tickled along his legs and back, around his head, and out through his arms to dance across Albek's face and chest. His sword tip an inch from the other man's throat, he straightened and turned a hard stare on the three mages huddled to the right of the throne.

"What?"

They looked to Lord Malik, who cocked his head sideways.

"Nothing at all, My Captain," he rumbled. "Do, continue."

They fought for another half hour, the mage's red glow occasionally flickering up between them. By now the Southerner was visibly tiring, the attack by Lord Malik's griffins the night before having taken more out of him than he cared to admit. Finally, he stumbled, and Endrik ran him through with a quick, economical jab. He fell. Clutching Endrik to him like a lover, he tried to speak and coughed blood onto his shoulder. There was the tiniest flash of blue in his eyes and then, his lips pressed against the Captain's ear, he whispered one word.

"Zerek."

Endrik jerked away, letting the body fall. He was covered in sweat and blood, the single word buzzing faintly in his ear like a tiny midge. Shaking his head to clear it, he turned to Lord Malik. The Demon Lord showed his teeth.

"A good fight, My Captain," he purred.

"Majesty." Endrik raised his blade, then dropped it, overcome with weariness.

"A pity it ended so soon. You had so much in common." Malik glanced at his three mages. The oldest shook her head.

"Nothing, Your Majesty."

Endrik's jaw tightened. "Nothing of what, Vashka?"

She met his hostile glare with a cold stare of her own. "Nothing which links you magically to Sir Jehan, Viktor. That we could discover in such a cursory examination, that is," she added pointedly.

"Why would there be?"

"You tell us."

He took a step forward and Lord Malik flicked a spray of blood between them.

"Enough bickering." He pushed the body off his lap with a satisfied belch. "I feel warm and sated after so much lovely violence and I want something tastier than the age-old squabble between Magery and Barracks. Where's my Chief Handler?"

"Here, Your Majesty."

"Send for my final prisoner."

His name was Misko Inek, a mage of above average ability newly arrived to King Ludik's service on loan from his allies on the coast. Two of Lord Malik's Senior Mages escorted him into the great hall, the red glow of their warding magics all but obliterating the sight of him.

At first he made a pretense of defiance, but as the red glow tightened around his face and throat, he began to babble, giving up as much information as he possibly could in one breath. Finally he pleaded for his life, promising service and loyalty.

Pavel Gries, the Lord's Most Senior Mage folded his hands into the sleeves of his robe with a satisfied air.

"He would make a powerful addition to Your Majesty's Magery," he urged. "He knows the road working and King Ludik's magical plans. And, come spring, he would be useful in any counter assault Your Majesty might be considering."

Lord Malik glanced coyly at Endrik, noting the disapproving frown and narrowed eyes.

"And what say you, My Captain?"

"He's been primed, Sire," he answered sharply without bothering to look across at Gries.

"And wasn't Sir Jehan?"

"My Liege." Endrik bowed slightly, conceding the point.

"But primed or not, shall I keep him? What is your counsel?"

His expression hard, Endrik looked from Albek's body to the man groveling on the floor beside him.

"I wouldn't advise it, Sire."

Malik glanced sideways at Gries who bristled indignantly, then back to his Guard Captain.

"No?"

"No, Sire. A man who'll betray one Lord will betray another."

"Pavel?"

"He can be spell-bound, Your Majesty," the Mage sniffed, "If Captain Endrik is afraid of betrayal."

"Spells can be broken."

"Spoken like a man who knows nothing about spell-craft."

"Maybe not, but I do know something about loyalty."

"Enough." Malik's inner eyelids slowly raised themselves over his eyes, then snapped back down again. Gesturing at Sergeant Pendik, he stood. "Bring him to the wall. We'll play a little game."

As Inek had his feet forced up on the gatehouse battlements, he began to scream, calling on Gries to save him. The Senior Mage kept his face expressionless, and Lord Malik thrust his chin out in a toothy smile of anticipation.

"What chaos," he tisked. "My two most trusted counselors locked in opposition." Looking to the setting sun in mock distress, he raised his hands. "And how to resolve it?" He glanced down, past the shaking Inek, to the jagged rocks below. "Both loyal and long serving, both nearly indispensable." He cocked his head to one side. "Of course, I have other guards and other mages. I could toss them both off as a warning to their successors." He glanced slyly at Endrik who met his Lord's eyes with a neutral expression. "What do you think, My Captain?"

"Well, I'd rather not die just yet, Sire."

"Do you think Pavel does?"

"I doubt it, My Liege."

"Let's find out, shall we? Why don't the two of you climb up there with our guest while I make up my mind?"

The Mage looked appalled, but Endrik simply stepped up onto the battlements into his usual position. Back to Lord Malik, he stared out at the orange-tinted sky while, behind them, the watching Guardsmen stiffened. The Demon Lord grinned to himself, then turned a flat stare on Pavel Gries. Hesitantly, the Mage took his place to the other side of Inek.

"One little push," Lord Malik mused as he touched each of them in the small of the back, grinning to himself as both Inek and Gries flinched away. "And that's it. I wonder if my griffins would catch the bodies in midair. They never have before. It might be interesting to find out."

He shoved Inek over the edge.

The Southerner screamed, sending out a bolt of blue magefire as he fell. It caught Endrik in the side of the head, knocking him against the left merlon. He nearly went over after him, then twisting violently, he fell backward toward the gatehouse.

Lord Malik caught him one-handed before he hit the stone catwalk.

"Well, that was a relief, My Captain," he said, peering down at him, his red eyes warm. "It looks like you just might be indispensable after all."

Endrik met his gaze and, for an instant, a flash of pain came and went in his own blue eyes. Still cradling him in the crook of his elbow, Lord Malik glanced at Gries who stood frozen, his hands clenching the stone wall in a death grip. "Come down from there at once, Pavel," he admonished. "A man of your years shouldn't be playing such foolish games." Setting Endrik on his feet, the Demon Lord started to laugh, the sound booming off the surrounding cliffs. He turned toward the inner courtyard.

"Feast!" he shouted, "and be grateful that I didn't send your beloved Captain to the end he so richly deserves for denying me a new mage." With one last bellow, he made for the gatehouse stairs. With a hard look at Endrik, Gries followed.

Leaning against the battlements, the Captain touched the side of his head gingerly. Beside him, Sergeant Pendik lit his pipe before glancing over.

"What did I tell you about morale just last night?" he asked dryly.

"I forget, my head is still spinning."

"Are you all right?"

"I think so." Endrik looked up at a sentry hovering in the doorway. "Yes, Lenka?"

"His Majesty is demanding your attendance, Captain."

"I'm on my way." He glanced over at the Sergeant. "No rest for the wicked, eh, Natan?" he said, trying to make light of the matter.

"No rest for anyone, Viktor, wicked or righteous, as long as they live," the Sergeant answered in a sour tone, refusing to be mollified.

"Then we should make the best of it while we do."

"I imagine so, Captain."

"Sir?"

"I'm coming, Lenka."

Together, the two men followed the sentry back to the great hall.

A month after Misko Inek was pushed to his death, Captain Endrik stood in his usual place on the gatehouse battlements, staring up at the moon.

The night was cold, frost sparkling on the rocks below. Winter had come early to the Talnek Mountains, but King Ludik's troops still huddled half a mile below the castle, widening the road, one foot at a time.

Endrik took a deep breath. There was an air of anticipation on the breeze tonight. He could almost feel Lord Malik step onto the southernmost battery and lift his arms to the moon. When the change came, it raised the hairs on the back of his neck, and when the Demon Lord leaped from the wall into the waiting arms of the winter wind, he closed his eyes, his lips moving in what might have been a prayer. Lord Malik passed across the moon and Endrik raised a cocked and loaded arbalest to his shoulder, the quarrel gleaming with a dull, magical glow. He waited.

A second later, a shaft of clear magic shot into the sky. It caught Lord Malik in a brilliant halo of light and, just before it winked out, Captain Endrik pulled the trigger.

The quarrel shot into the air like a comet trailing a great tail of blue magic. It caught the Demon Lord in a tiny patch of translucent skin deep within his left armpit where the wing met the bone. Lord Malik jerked backward as, undermined, the wing tore free. A spray of blood arched into the air as he cried out in pain and surprise. The hail of arrow-fire that followed could not help but hit its mark. Unable to fly, he fell, his griffins spiraling down behind him, drawn by the trail of blood. Darkness obscured Endrik's sight, but the cheering that rose up from King Ludik's army told him clearly enough that Lord Malik had hit the rocks below. No one else in the castle had seen him fall, no one else had ever had the courage to watch him fly.

On the battlements Captain Endrik of Jorgen-Tor fell to his knees, the arbalest tumbling over the edge of the battlements. The pain in his chest was almost too much to bear, and clutching at the wall, he pressed his forehead against the cold stone. When he finally looked up, Sergeant Pendik stood in the gatehouse doorway, his eyes wide with shock. No one else had the courage to watch Lord Malik, but Sergeant Pendik had always had the courage to watch Endrik.

"Captain?"

Endrik closed his eyes. "Sergeant."

"What have you done?"

"What only I could have done," he answered, his voice thick with grief.

"But . . . why?"

"It was my duty,"

"Your duty? To whom?"

"King Ludik."

"King . . . ?" Unable to even speak the name, the Sergeant just shook his head. "How?"

Endrik opened his eyes. "He was the greatest Malik Lord ever to take the field," he explained almost to himself. "For a hundred years his empire loomed over the southern kingdoms like a pall. Diplomacy could not deflect him, armies could not defeat him. He was as strong as the mountains themselves." His voice broke, but after a moment he continued. "So King Ludik sent three of his most trusted and loyal Royal Guard to weaken him from within: Tolek, Colar, and Zerek."

"Wha . . ."

Endrik turned a hard stare on the other man. "Captain Sir Boris Tolek," he said loudly, "Lieutenant Sir Ivan Colar, and Second Lieutenant Sir Viktor Zerek, son of Eliska Endrik. Each one sent in with the mission to find and exploit Lord Malik's weaknesses." He laughed bitterly. "Only he didn't have any, did he? Except one." He bowed his head.

"The only thing they could do was undermine his military might," he continued. "Kill his griffins and lose his battles, spill his soldiers' blood onto the field, and give up the position of his strongest fortress. It was a dangerous game, one that got both Tolek and Colar killed. I thought they deserved it at the time, maybe I still do."

"I don't understand. If you were one of them . . . ?"

"We were placed under magical geas. Colar remembered nothing until Tolek died and I remembered nothing until Colar died."

"Six months ago."

"Yes. That way, if one of us was discovered, there would always be another to take up the sword."

"But why didn't His Majesty's mages find anything when they spell-cast you and Albek in the great hall?"

Endrik turned, his eyes burning with a bright, blue light. "Because His Majesty's mages couldn't find their arses with both hands and a glow spell," he answered harshly. "All Royal Guard are trained as battle-mages. We three were the most powerful King Ludik had. The only one talented enough to break through our defenses was Inek."

"So you counseled Lord Malik not to trust him and ultimately to kill him even after you knew you were one of Ludik's Knights?"

The light faded from Endrik's eyes. "Yes."

"And Albek?"

Endrik returned his gaze to the night sky. "Albek. I don't remember him," he said thoughtfully, "but it's been so long.

King Ludik sent him as a signal that I had to do something to break the siege before winter or they'd lose the war."

"They'll be planning something desperate."

"Exactly."

"And Albek allowed himself to be captured and killed for that?"

Endrik shrugged. "He was Royal Guard. The King commanded, he obeyed." His tone was bitter. "That's how Kings use their people, Pendik. They don't snatch them off the battlements and feast on them in the throne room, they send them out ignorant of their mission and expect them to die carrying out their orders anyway. Once Albek took on the geas, he wouldn't have remembered anything until death released the binding spells on his memories."

He closed his eyes, suddenly unbearably weary. "I'm so tired," he whispered. "Ten years ago I knelt before Lord Malik and swore an oath to serve him loyally until death, and I meant every word. He was the most powerful being I had ever encountered. Serving him made me whole somehow, I couldn't even say why. I was proud to serve him; I would have died for him. And six months ago I learned that I had served him only to weaken him and defeat him and, bound by an oath to another Liege, I was to conspire to kill him." He looked up, his eyes wet. "I found it that very first night, you know. His wings were stretched out above my head and I saw a tiny patch of skin that seemed different from the rest." He looked at Pendik. "All creatures of power have a weakness somewhere. Guarding it is a matter of life or death; discovering it is the obsession of kings. No one else in history has ever stood close enough to a Malik Lord to see it and live to exploit it. And . . ."

He fell silent.

"And . . . ?"

"And I wish I'd never seen it."

He took a step forward.

"For six months I denied my own memories. For four weeks, I struggled over which Lord to betray."

"How do you live with yourself, Viktor Zerek of Cruska? Until six months ago that was never a question I needed to answer. I served the greatest Malik Lord ever to take the field, and he loved only me, his Captain of the Guard. That was enough. But now . . ."

He moved to the edge of the battlements.

"Captain?"

Endrik turned, his eyes dark. "He sent three, Natan: Tolek, Colar, and Zerek. Tolek and Colar made their choice and died in the name of duty. It's time for Zerek to do the same."

"Don't . . ."

"A man who'll betray one Lord will betray another, Natan."

"Viktor."

"Take care of my Guard, Sergeant."

"Captain, don't . . ."

Endrik stepped off the edge. A moment later a blue glow flashed in Sergeant Pendik's eyes. His jaw dropped.

Sergeant Sir Natan Pendar of King Ludik's Royal Guard stood on the gatehouse battlements for a long time, staring down into the darkness.

"King Ludik sent four of his most trusted and loyal Royal Guard—Tolek, Colar, Zerek, and Pendar—to defeat the greatest Malik Lord ever to take the field," he whispered. "That couldn't be enough for you to break an oath and sleep at night. It will have to be enough for me."

"Take care of my Guard, Sergeant."

*   *   *

"I will, Captain. Good-bye, sir."

Turning away, Sir Natan made his way down the stairs to open the gates of Jorgen-Tor for the armies of King Ludik.

THE KNIGHT OF HYDAN ATHE

by Michelle West

Michelle West is the author of a number of novels, including *The Sacred Hunt* duology and *The Broken Crown, The Uncrowned King, The Shining Court,* and *Sea of Sorrows,* the first four novels of *The Sun Sword* series, all available from DAW Books. She reviews books for the on-line column *First Contacts,* and less frequently for *The Magazine of Fantasy & Science Fiction.* Other short fiction by her has appeareed in *Black Cats and Broken Mirrors, Elf Magic, Olympus,* and *Alien Abductions.*

S ANNA brought beer and bread to the finest table in her parents' inn. She was dressed for the kitchen work, but it happened that the inn had a visitor her parents approved of, and she'd been ordered out from the hot, stuffy room, with its geography of dirty dishes, gray well water, and burning fires.

She smiled, her lips lifting in the half quirk of remembered mischief. This man had worn the first bowl of soup she'd ever been asked to serve; she could see it dripping from his beard if she closed her eyes for half a minute. Horror had frozen her limbs; humiliation had etched this picture firmly in memory. He had come to the inn for lunch, which was rare.

The only real inn in the town of Hydan Athe was large and roomy, and although it wasn't the merchants' turn of season, it was seldom empty and never closed; Hydan Athe was a village known for the prosperity of its outlying lands. That and more.

The inn was called Wayfarer's Retreat, and it crested the highest hill in the Andian plains. When the trees were sparse with spring growth, or barren with the fall, one could see the lay of the lands for miles around from its single, round tower: the striped, square lands, brown where fields were fallow; the trees that protected the young growth from the winds that swept up from the valleys; the rivers that ran, like exposed veins, from one end of the Athelands to the other. Those rooms were almost always empty, for they were the finest the inn boasted and few indeed were the customers who could afford their rent.

In the tower rooms, bed and table, desk, chair and lamp slept under the heavy fabrics that protected them from sunlight and dust. Only the maids and the servants—Sanna, her younger brother, her two aunts and her Uncle Kent, no blood relation— were allowed in and out, and it was from the heights of this hidden unused finery that Sanna might watch the winding caravans of the merchants in their season, after harvest but before the skirts of winter brushed the lands.

Those merchants were the source of news, gossip, and the letters that traveling townspeople cared to pass on, and she had come to know their routes by heart, for that reason. She had long since given up on asking for letters, but the hope remained to cause her a bitter pain long after the merchants had left, their hands empty of anything for her.

It was in these rooms that she would rest her arms against the carefully polished sill of window and gaze out, tracking the bend and tuck of winding road that led down through the valleys and into the unfathomable distance. Nev had gone that way, two years past, and he had never come back. He had sent two letters, both with the first of the merchant caravans to come this way, but even those had stopped; there was silence and it seemed to stretch from Hydan Athe to Faerlan, the capital.

Nev was happy, she thought, numb now with time and distance. The Prince of Everarre had called him, and he had gone, and what could Hydan Athe offer a young man that Faerlan couldn't better?

Aie, and what did you expect, you foolish girl: He's a knight's son. A knight's son, and what are you? The daughter of an innkeeper.

The daughter, her father had said, stung, *of the finest innkeeper in all of the Athelands. The daughter of the Innkeeper of Hydan Athe.*

Her mother had slapped his shoulder because he'd been smart enough to get his face out of the way. *And there you go,* she said, with frustration and scorn and something deeper and harsher than either. *You feed her this nonsense. You tell her to open her heart. And to what? You know your place, girl. Don't you forget it. Nothing good comes of not knowing your place.* Darkness in her eyes, then. Sanna's ma'am had traveled from one end of the kingdom to the other, and she'd seen everything—or so she said—but she spoke of it seldom. It was only at times like this, shadows in the corner of her eyes, lips tight and narrowed, that the past crept into conversation—but she never loosed it enough to give it words.

But ma'am, she'd answered, in that meek voice that fooled no one, least of all the mother who was so like—and so unlike—Sanna. *Hydan Athe is special. Even in the Athelands, there's no land so special as this. And the Knights of Hydan Athe are special as well—everyone says it. All the merchants—*

Merchants will tell you anything they think you want to hear if you'll look more favorably on their wares. They only care about what they can get from you; they have no shame about how they get it. But her voice gentled, even if her expression remained as constant as the river's voice. *Hydan Athe* is *special, Sanna, but it's still just a part of the world, and in* this *world it's safest to stick to your own.*

Sanna had known when to retreat. Her mother, after all, had come to Hydan Athe as part of a caravan, and had caught her father's ear—not so much his eye, for that roved freely even now—with her acerbic common sense. She had made Hydan Athe her home, but she had not been born to it, not bred to its wildernesses and its tame commons, its abundance and its health; she could not *know,* as Sanna knew, as her father, and her father's father knew, that Hydan Athe was the exception to all rules.

But on days like this, she wondered what the word exception meant.

Her mother, so quick to accentuate the distance between the mere daughter of an innkeeper and the son of a knight, was chatting with the knight himself as if he were a favored older brother; her father was tilting his chair back on two legs as he joined Sir Hyrtan in a drink. From the rise and fall of her mother's voice, Sir Hyrtan was not to be spared opinion or advice, but he smiled or laughed when she lifted her hand over the table in her habitually clenched fist.

He liked Sanna's mother.

This man, Nev's father, was so unlike the son; grizzled and aged, jolly where Nev was so dark and serious, burned and worn by years in the sun, years bent over the furrows in the earth itself, years in the small courthouse at the side of his manor in which the affairs of Hydan Athe were peaceably—for the most part—resolved. Nev was straight and tall, taller than his father by a good four inches and taller than the other men in the Athe by at least that much. But he had always been gentle, courteous, reserved.

Too reserved for her liking. She thought of those letters.

"Sanna?"

She looked up, lost in thought; met unblinking, dark eyes,

and realized with a sudden unease that some things about Sir Hyrtan and the son she so missed were alike after all. She put a smile on her face, and placed the tray on the table, but before she could retreat, he spoke.

"I've had word from Neville."

"Nev?" She spoke the name too quickly, and knew it. "Is he—has he—"

"I've come to tell you that he's coming home."

"He's coming home? To Hydan Athe?"

"Aye."

"When?"

"He's on the road now," Sir Hyrtan said quietly. "But . . . I am not sure that he is coming to stay."

The words stilled what little conversation there had been between Sanna's parents. "Not staying?"

"Perhaps. He wrote to say he would be coming to . . . visit."

He wrote. To his father. "He hasn't come home these two years."

"No."

"But—but when he comes—" she knew she was smiling. She knew it was silly; too girlish by half. She couldn't help it.

The old knight offered her no answering smile, no joy, and in the face of its absence, hers withered. "What's wrong? Is he injured? Is he ill?"

"No."

"Then what is it? What's wrong?"

He looked up at her.

Harvest had not yet come, but she felt the edge of winter as if she'd bypassed the season of plenty entirely. She had seen this man twice a month for most of her life, but she had almost never seen the expression he offered her now. Pity.

She flushed, and then she paled, and then she lifted the

empty tray from the table and made her retreat, innkeeper's daughter.

"Sanna!" Her mother's voice followed her, familiar, angry, embarrassed—all the things that had, over the years, caused Sanna to develop a reflexive cringe. But it wasn't enough to take the terrible dryness from the roof of her mouth, the thickness from the weight of her tongue. She could not go back to the great room.

She fled, instead, to the inn's finest rooms. They were so seldom used, so seldom entered, that she could be certain of a moment's respite among the sheets that hung over bed and chair, over table, over grand chandelier. Her hand brushed past cobwebs, catching them, dust and all, in the fingers and palms of her hands; she could not see them as they lay against her skin.

She saw the window instead, found the window seat, sat upon it as she had sat upon it many, many times in the last two years. She saw the road beneath the tower; the trees—now green and heavy with leaves, with hidden nests, the invisible lives of birds. She could not see the road.

But she looked for it, looked for some sign that it was bringing Neville home.

And then, because she could not sit by this window without looking, Sanna lifted shaking hand, trailing spider's home, dust, and the tremors of a bitter disappointment, and drew the curtains shut. She did not cry.

In the late afternoon, when the inn was busy enough that she could avoid both her mother and her mother's wrath, she slid out of the side door and down the road that led to the heart of Hydan Athe. She made her groveling apologies to the cook, and Tess, her cousin by marriage, but they must have heard something because they shushed her and held the door against her mother while she made her escape.

She knew, as any child did who grew up in the Athelands, that Hydan Athe was special. The land knew little drought, little famine, little pestilence; even in the seven year drought that cracked the parched earth beyond the Athes, the rivers had whispered in their near-empty beds.

It had been hard then.

The drought had brought the night of fires.

She had been a child, but she remembered the old knight in the great room of her father's inn, his face creased, his expression grim; she remembered that the light from the fire, burning as it was in the largest of the fireplaces—for dry wood had been easy to come by in the forests—had been reflected across his chest, his arms, his gloves. And she remembered, as she paused a moment to catch her breath from the long run, that she had been afraid.

Of him.

Of the Knight of Hydan Athe.

But the deaths—and she knew, at the remove of years, there must have already been deaths if he stood so grim and silent—had been hidden from the children who huddled in the depths of the inn. She remembered that, too: The children, carried in ones and twos, wailing and screaming as their mothers quietly left them in the care of the innkeeper and his wife. The town's children.

"I charge you, Marton," Sir Hyrtan had said, "with the safety of the Athe."

Her father—her father!—had fallen to one knee. "I'll defend it with my life."

And her mother had said, "If we have to defend it with our lives, we've already lost." But her voice was a tense and bitter whisper. She was thin, then. Too thin, and the screaming and wailing of too many children didn't sweeten her temper.

But Sanna, nine years old, had gathered those children as she could; she had taken them through the rooms of the inn, on a grand and mysterious tour that had ended with the splendor of the tower. Her father had been charged with their safety; she had taken it upon herself to see to their happiness. And those children that had slipped through her grasp, those children who had cried or wept, or clung to the mothers and fathers who were commanded away into the falling crimson of the evening, were gathered by another. A boy a few years older than she.

Twelve, she had thought him; almost old enough to be counted among the men.

It was not the first time she had seen Neville, Sir Hyrtan's only son. But it was the first time she had spoken more than two words to him, and although those words were more often than not shouted above the heads of moving children, with many syllables lost to the chaos of the same, she remembered him best that way.

Because that night he hadn't been a knight's son, denied his chance to prove his worth to father and town by a scant few months. Not to her. He had been a knight, shepherding these lost and terrified children to a place of safety and peace. And she had been his squire. His aide.

Even that wouldn't have made a difference in the long run; she'd been—in her boundless imagination—more than simple squire. She'd been knight, queen, sorceress, hero; the realms of day's dream and girl's desire were fertile, fraught with peril and sacrifice.

No, it was what happened afterward.

After he had heard the cries of the children and had come to the windows to see the fires—fires when water was so scarce and the grounds and grasses dry in the still air—that mesmerized them; when he had realized at twelve, as she had failed to realize at nine, that they meant death, that some of these children, in this tower, this inn, were now orphans, that she realized that she would always love him.

He had drawn the curtains. He had denied them the undeniable, savage beauty of the thing that was even then killing their families. He had, wise knight, young man, offered them instead stories of heroism and, yes, death and sacrifice. He had treated them not as children, but as people who would, this very evening, give the things they loved best for a good that they could, by dint of the soft gravity of his words, glimpse clearly.

They had been afraid. Even Sanna had been afraid. But that fear had mingled with pride, and the pride was almost enough when the evening and the burning ended.

And why was she thinking of this now? It was come and gone. It was history. The famine, the drought, all gone. The lands were whole; the harvest abundant.

She had reached her destination. She hesitated a moment outside of the tidy stone house that rested amidst the fronds of grass-cluttered plants. Bethda, a seamstress in the town, had, as payment for the old-wife's services, spent three weeks clearing out wild-grass and wildflowers in order to lay down a tidy, colorful garden. That garden had lasted one full season. Elements of it could be seen, in drift, between the slender green stalks that she had attempted to banish.

If the old-wife appreciated the effort, she had never let it show. She had told Bethda which plants were not, under any circumstances, to be removed, and had let her do the work with a bewildered shake of the head. But the cottage itself, for weeks, was so neat and tidy, so wonderfully well-ordered, that everyone had stopped to stare at it, as if half-expecting that its very existence would work a miracle of transformation upon its occupant.

That failed to happen, of course. The old-wife was set in her ways; as easy to change the course of moving rivers as it was to change her; as easy to change the ways of the Athelands.

Sanna straightened her shoulders and self-consciously adjusted the apron she'd forgotten to remove. Then she pushed the fence-gate open and stepped onto the path that the grass had not yet overgrown. Flowers lined it like foot soldiers in gaudy uniform, and at any other time she would have appreciated them, for they were not commonly seen in Hydan Athe; that was Bethda's gift.

Any other day.

She walked toward the old-wife's door and waited there until it opened. And although she lifted no hand, made no sound, raised no cry, the door *did* open. The old-wife was as special in her way as Hydan Athe, but more mysterious.

"No, the old-wife said, as she pulled the heavy, plain door into the house, "Less mysterious by far. Are you finally ready to come in, Sanna?"

Sanna replied by placing a foot squarely over the threshold. One foot. The second did not seem to want to leave the familiarity of the path that had brought her here; it was heavy, weighted to earth. She looked down to see the plain leather straps of old sandals, the browning of skin, her left toenail cracked because she'd not taken the time to cut it properly.

When had her feet grown so large, so cumbersome? When had they become so heavy, so graceless?

"What price?" she whispered, as she dragged her gaze up to the old-wife's face.

"I'm afraid that the price is not mine to set," the old woman said, wearing an odd expression.

It took Sanna a moment to realize why it was familiar; it was, line for line, the expression Sir Hyrtan had offered her. She hesitated between this world and that, and then she drew breath and entered the old-wife's home.

*   *   *

She had expected darkness, shadow, the absence of illumination, and these things were there, but they were there in the same way they resided in the inn itself. There were no magical orbs, no sigils, no wards; there was no small cauldron, no staff, no wands; the rings upon the old-wife's fingers were simple in type and few in number. She wore no loops in her ears, and when she traveled from the now-closed door, she led Sanna not to the hearth, but to the kitchen.

In the kitchen, though, Sanna found more earth, more life, more greenery, than existed—she was certain—in the whole of the midwife's garden. In boxes piled around the two windows, on counters, on small tables that must have been made for that purpose and no other, plants trailed toward ground at the weight of leaves, or rose toward ceiling or light. The smell was almost overpowering; here, a brief scent of cloves, and here, garlic; there something spicy and thick that she could not name, and ginger and clover, bay leaves, sweet mint. She might have spent the entire day drifting, eyes half closed, from one group of plants to another, but one caught her eye, and when she realized what it was, her feet once again grew heavy and cumbersome; she forgot how to walk.

White flower. Black soil.

The blossom itself was small; the petals so delicate she could see, in the failing light, the pale veins beneath the surface. But its stem was pale, pale green and it had no leaves. Nothing grew around it. Nor would it.

She could see at its base the fallen bodies of small insects, their legs curled, their wings splayed as if, in death, they had attempted flight.

Athe's Death.

"You know what it is," the old-wife said quietly.

Sanna nodded. She was afraid to speak. Afraid to give voice to the knowledge.

"Do you understand what it means?"

She shook her head. "It is *Athe's*—"

"It is called *White Athe,* Sanna. Of the other, we do not speak."

"Everyone calls it—"

"No one else has seen it. Aye, I know there are stories," the old-wife added. "There are songs. But they are hidden in the Athelands, and they are sung only to the children. You are not so far from childhood that you have forgotten. *White Athe,*" she added quietly. "That is what you must call it.

"I have grown many things in my kitchen, young Sanna. Many things. And I have killed a good many in the attempt," she added, with just a hint of wry humor. "It is hard, this growing of living things. That one needs water and light; that one withers and yellows if a hint of rain touches its quills. And that one needs sun and shadow in equal measure. It takes time to learn the needs of the mute.

"This past year is the first time I have had success in growing the *White Athe.*"

"W–why?"

"Why have I failed? Why have I succeeded?"

"Why would you try? It is—it is said to be—"

"The death of the Athelands? An exaggeration, surely." But the old-wife's gaze was remote, and her expression as tangled as the vines that grew from the plant boxes. "The Athelands are vast; they form the heart of the entire kingdom."

"The death of Hydan Athe."

"Well that is something else entirely. And a single flower? The death of Hydan Athe?"

"That's the story."

"That's a part of the story, Sanna. But only a small part, if you've a mind to learn it."

"But if it's even a risk—why would you try to grow it?"

"It is one of my duties," the old-wife said quietly. "Year after year, since I became old-wife, I have planted the seed of the *White Athe* in my kitchen, and I have watered it, and I have fed it. And every year, the powers that guide the Athelands have answered my prayer and the seed has lain dormant."

"You've tried to grow it, but you've prayed to fail? I don't understand."

"No. You don't. It's of no matter; when I first came to the old-wife's house, I didn't understand it either. This house, Sanna." She paused; turned her attention to the odd sprigs of mint in the sunlight. "Do you understand the nature of the *White Athe*?"

"It's—it's a poison."

"Aye, it is that. But it is more than that, Sanna. It's a judgment." The mint was forgotten; the old-wife drew close enough that Sanna could see the carved lines of her face, the thinning of her lips, the dark, dark centers of her eyes. "Why did you come tonight? What drew you from the Wayfarer's Retreat to mine?"

"You know."

"Aye. Do you?"

She looked at the tall, slender stalk, the stem of the blossom. "Nev is coming back," she finally answered.

"Yes." Just that.

"Did you know?"

"Not until I saw you at the foot of my garden path. It is starting to grow wild again, but you can see the roots of Bethda's work all through it."

"Yes," Sanna said weakly. "But—but what does Nev have to do with your flower?"

"My flower? You misunderstand me, child. I grow it. I am merely custodian. If it belongs to anyone here, now, it is you. I'll tell you why you came today."

"Why?"

"To take the *White Athe*, child."

"To take the—no."

"Oh, yes. It is almost past growing in the planter; it needs space, air, moonlight. You told me, when you first stood in front of my door years ago, that you wanted to understand all the secrets of Hydan Athe."

"I don't remember."

"It doesn't matter. The Athelands remember. What the wind hears, the Athe hears."

"I don't want it."

"I know. But it doesn't matter. I can see your name in every vein, in every petal, as the blossom unfurls. It is almost ready; it is almost ready, Sanna. You must water it. You must feed it. And when the times come, you must decide how to use it."

"Use it? But I—I don't make poisons. I don't—"

"Poisons? No. You don't. This is Hydan Athe, child. You were born and bred to the Athes, even if you don't understand what that means; you will know what to do when the time comes. My word, child. You will know."

"But I—"

The old-wife had already lifted the small pot that housed the deadly blossom. Her hands, as she carried it, shook; she was pale. The crimson of sunset had all but vanished; the moon was bright. Light seemed to vanish against the surface of white petal, and although it was pale and white, everything about the flower suggested shadow.

"Old-wife, a question."

"Ask it; you've the right."

"Did the *Whie Athe* bloom because Nev is coming?"

"Not because he's coming, child," the old woman said sadly. "Never that alone."

Still she hesitated; a question hovered just out of reach, and she felt it important to ask before she accepted what the old-wife offered—if a command could be said to be an offer. "Did the *White Athe* grow for Sir Hyrtan?"

The old-wife became completely still. "You have a touch of the Athes about you, Sanna. No. No, the *White Athe* never grew for Sir Hyrtan."

"And his father?"

"I was not old-wife in his father's time."

Sanna reached out for the planter; was surprised at the warmth the old-wife's hands had left upon it. As their fingers touched, the woman who had grown the blossom and the one who now accepted its weight, Sanna said, "Sir Hyrtan wasn't the eldest son."

And the old-wife closed her eyes. The memory was bad; it left a tremor about her thin lips, the line of her chin. "No," she said curtly. "No. He wasn't. Don't ask me, child. I will answer no more of your questions. I am old-wife, but the life I lived before I came to live in this cottage was *my* life, and I will not share it further."

Sanna thought she saw tears in the old woman's lashes, but it was a trick of the light; when the old-wife gazed upon Sanna again, her eyes were dry, and no wider or narrower than they had been when she'd first opened the door.

She had meant to sneak into the inn, but the light in the side-room was on; she knew that one of her parents was waiting for her.

She prayed prayed prayed it was her father, and when she wedged herself through the smallest—and therefore quietest—opening she could make between door and frame, she thought her prayers had been answered; her father came out of his paper room.

But as the lamp he held drew near—and it had gotten dark enough that he held one—the lines of his face, washed in orange and gold, dispelled relief. For he saw, clearly, what she held in the cupped palms of her hands, and although he recoiled, it was somehow clear to her that he had expected no less.

Bitterly, he said, "the Athe demands its test."

"Papa—"

"Don't let your mother see it," he told her. "I sent her to bed; I told her I'd wait. Sanna—" He fell silent. She started toward her room and faltered; to reach it, she would have to walk around her father, the lamp in his hands brighter and less forgiving than the flowerpot in hers.

But she would have to pass him sooner or later; by silent consent they had both agreed that whatever passed between them, this night, was to remain between them—and if it got much later, Sanna's mother would be up, haunting the halls, worry depriving her of sleep.

So she walked.

"Sanna, do you understand what a knight does?"

It was not the question she had expected to hear, but she held *White Athe* in her hands. "He collects taxes. He settles disputes, at least the ones he doesn't start. He—he runs the town. With the help of the old-wife," she added, although it was privately agreed that the truth ran the other way 'round. The thought would have made her smile, but her father's expression was so grim, the light beneath his chin so orange—

That she remembered clearly the night of fires seen through the illusory safety of tower window, the light gleaming off sword and armor. She repented instantly. She knew that knights were more than daily duties, more than just the work.

As if he knew the direction her thoughts had taken—and there were so many, scattered at the farthest reach of words, that there was no reason at all he should have, her father said, "Train all your men in the arts of war, and you have an army, Sanna, not a village, not a town. We are *Hydan Athe*. We do what we must, and we pay the price."

"And what does that make Sir Hyrtan?"

"No less than that."

"More?"

"Aye, Sanna, you sharp-tongued child. He's more. He's the Knight of the Athe."

But sitting in the dark, the flower hidden in shadow from the glaring face of moonlight through open shutters, Sanna realized that she did not understand what those words meant anymore. Sir Hyrtan had been as much a part of field as he was of manor; his shoulders bowed a little less than her father's by something as trivial as age, but his hands no less weathered by labor. He had owned—still owned—horses, and two just for riding, but the wealthy merchants that had chosen to leave off traveling owned at least as many. And his house, the manor house, was not exceptionally fine. She knew, of course; she had been in his manor, running from hall to hall, desperate for a glimpse of the hidden beauty and the sanctity that surely must accompany a man who was called knight.

It had been such a disappointment. She had come away with an understanding that this man and her father were alike; fallible. Human.

Well, Sir Hyrtan, what is *a Knight of Hydan Athe?*

She woke in the morning, although she would have bet—until the moment she squinted to keep sunlight at bay—that sleep would have eluded her. But it rested in her knees and her elbows, and she was reluctant to cast it off until she heard the sharp bark of her mother's voice. She fell out of bed; it was the quickest way of signaling compliance without having to speak.

But in the morning light, the *White Athe* stood, slender and tall, its shadow thin against the floor planks. She wanted to touch its petals. It had seemed dire, a thing of doom or death, in the old-wife's green kitchen; here, in the starkness of a room without so much as a planter, it seemed to be some part of life itself. She dressed quickly, glancing at it from time to time.

Had she been afraid of it?

Maybe. And maybe she still was. For she had the sense, watching it, that it did not like the light. *I'll move you,* she promised. *Tonight. When it's dark. I'll move you then.*

As if it could hear her. As if it could understand.

It was market day, which explained much of her mother's impatience. The farmers had already been offering their wares for sale in the common for the better part of an hour, and although the Wayfarer's Retreat was counted as the most important of any farmer's customers, with the exception of the house on the hill—the other, shorter hill—it was not by any means the majority of a farmer's business. And Marjorie Lesham drove a hard bargain, merchant's daughter that she was, so the farmers weren't unhappy to sell what they could to the villagers whose responsibility was a single household, not an entire dining hall. If they had less than Marjorie desired, they apologized and pointed to the height of the sun with a shrug; it was therefore her custom to arrive *early,* and Marjorie did nothing by halves.

To make Marjorie late was to therefore court the most severe disapproval, and Sanna was aware of nothing—not sun, not sky, not obdurate merchant—as much as that disapproval. But on this day, as she murmured something quiet and drifted slowly away from her mother's side, empty basket hanging from her hand like afterthought, she failed to notice the odd rise of her mother's brows, the momentary slump of her shoulders; failed to hear the pause between the sentences she was firing at the farmer that breath alone could not explain. It was easy

enough to miss; Marjorie Lesham shared vulnerability with almost not one, and all of these things were gone in an instant.

But so, too, was her daughter.

She found Sir Hyrtan in the fields behind the manor house; it
was where, this close to harvest, he could often be found. From
a distance, there was little to distinguish him from the other
men and women who toiled beneath the open sky; he was perhaps a shade taller, that was all. But watch him for long enough,
and one could see the way that the others would defer to him,
on those occasions when they stopped working for long enough
to make deference an issue; it was subtle.

She watched, and this watching was a luxury that she did
not normally have. It came to an end when Sir Hyrtan excused
himself from the fields and, trailing morning shadow, came to
greet her.

"Sanna," he said, when his voice could carry the distance
that separated them in near-silence.

"Sir Hyrtan." She dropped a curtsy that would have made
her mother proud.

"You went to see Magdalen."

She frowned. "Magdalen?"

"The old-wife."

Sanna hadn't even known that the old-wife had another
name; she could not remember hearing it before today. Somehow she didn't take comfort from the unfamiliar syllables.

"She gave you what you needed."

"She gave me something."

He nodded stiffly; his hands crept behind his back and he
stood before her, blocking sunlight. "Why have you come to
see me?"

"I don't know."

"Ah." He was, as older people often were, good at waiting. She made him wait a long time before she spoke.

"I wanted to ask you a question."

"Did you?"

She shrugged; a dark lock of hair fell across her lashes like a veil. "Well, maybe not a question. Not exactly. I just— I wanted—"

"Yes?"

"What makes a Knight of the Athelands different from other knights?"

He raised a brow, its arch ascending in place. "An unusual question. Have you met other knights?"

"No. But you know that."

"Aye, perhaps I do. I have . . . met other knights. Not all of the knights of the realm are landed; many serve as knights errant at the whim of the king. Or his sons."

"Nev does."

"Aye, he has."

"And you?"

"Oh, yes," he replied. He looked at her, eyes dark as night, remote as stars. Whatever memory her words conjured, it wasn't one she wanted to share. "In my time, I served. If you see Neville, you must ask him about Faerlan.

"Faerlan is a grand place, a beautiful place. Its towers are lofty, its sages wise beyond the ken of a simple old-wife. Women are seldom considered wise in the capital."

"But you came home."

"Aye. I came home. I came home in time for drought, and famine, and war. You are young enough—"

"I remember," she said softly.

"Do you?"

"Yes. The night of fires. I remember. I saw Nev for the first time."

"Your memory plays you false, Sanna. You saw Neville many, many times in your childhood."

"No, it was the first time I *truly* saw him."

"What do you mean?"

"Did he never tell you?"

"He told me little. There was much to do after the night at the inn. Much."

"Oh." It was a memory of such import to Sanna it seemed impossible that anyone could live in Hydan Athe and *not* know of it. But maybe it had never been as important to Nev. He was the Knight's son, and destined, by simple fact of birth, to become the Knight of Hydan Athe.

"Tell me, Sanna."

"It was—it was nothing."

Still he waited, but this time, she kept her words to herself, and after a moment, he sighed. "It is not a romantic duty, to be a Knight. It is not a bold adventure. There is no dragon to best, no obvious enemy to vanquish."

"But the night of fires—"

"It is because of that night that I say this," he replied, gaze intent. "Do you know who we fought?"

"Bandits," she replied.

"Aye, bandits. But when your children are starving, when they are dying from lack of clean water, it is easy to become a bandit. It is easy to come to the foot of the manor house with torches and staves and axes; easier to ride anger than face fear and death.

"We fought villagers," he added. "We fought the people who came from the edge of the Athelands, seeking what we had, ourselves, barely managed to preserve. Had we food, had we water, to spare, there would have been no swordplay, no fire." He turned his back upon her. "Need is my enemy," he said simply. "Fear. The desire to possess what others have. When I can—whenever I can—I fight them.

"And when I do not see them, I live a modest life. These fields are like fields across the Athes."

"They're *better*," she said reflexively. "They grow everything. Anything."

"Aye, if there are men and women to tend them." He was silent again. "But without those men and women, they would be fallow. The Athes do not need their knights, child; they need their *people*."

"You're wrong," she whispered.

"Am I? Look at Selina; look at her husband, Pieter. They toil, day in and day out. When the old king passes away, and the new king takes the golden throne, wears the golden crown across his pale brow, what will they know of it? The merchants will carry tales; the bards will sing songs paid for by the new, young monarch. Perhaps they will say that the new queen is beautiful, and perhaps that might even be truth. But will it be of value? Selina and Pieter will still tend these fields. They will feed their children. They will try as they can to curb their harsh words, to still their deep fears. Oftimes they will fail, but there's much to praise in the attempt."

"But people do that *all over.* There's more to the Athes than just that."

He said nothing.

"The Knights of the Athelands are special."

"So you've said, Sanna."

"They're special," she repeated, as if repetition itself were a kind of truth. "Everyone knows it. Everyone knows what happened when the king tried to replace the Knights of the Athelands with men of his choosing."

"Do they?"

"Yes."

His smile was cool. Hard. It was an expression that she seldom saw on his face, and she didn't much care for it.

"What happens, Sanna?"

"The Athelands die."

"Do they?"

"That's what the old-wife says. Without the Knight, the lands wither. And the Knight *must* be of the Athes." She smiled when his expression lost the sharpness of its edge.

"Those are true words."

"Some while ago one of the kings tried to take the Athelands for his own."

"The king owns all of the lands in the kingdom, Sanna."

"He tried to take it from the Knights. To give it to men he wanted to reward."

"A privilege kings enjoy."

"So he told the Knights of the Athelands that they were knights no more, and he left them the choice of overseeing the lands—for the knights of his choosing were not men who desired to live away from the lights of Faerlan—or of leaving them. What could the Knights do? They stayed. They were of the Athes. But even though they stayed, even though they worked, and resolved disputes and attempted to protect their people, the lands withered. It rained, but the ground absorbed no water; the land shed its seeds; the rivers stilled, the lakes shrank. Across the Athes, even the wild creatures vanished."

He nodded. "So I was told."

"And the old-wives across the Athelands traveled to Faerlan, and they told the king the herbs that the physicians prized so highly would not grow; that the lands would yield nothing for his use, or for theirs. The king was furious, and had them flogged, and sent them home. But he learned the truth of their words in time, when his sons sickened, and one by one, began to die. In the end, the king chose to return most of the Athes to their Knights, and the following year, the lands—those that had been reclaimed—were healed.

"But the herbs that he sought and desired still refused to grow. This time he sought the old-wives, and he was terrible in his fury, and they said, again, that the Athelands required their Knights. He removed all of his appointed knights, and when they were all gone, he had what he desired. And no king has acted against the Knights of the Athes again."

"But that is a story of land, of fecundity," he whispered, "and not of Knights."

"I tell you again, child, that these fields, those people, are the heart of Hydan Athe; the heart of the Athelands. And they have worked without me for long enough this day. Thank you for coming to visit, Sanna." He bowed. "Water and shelter the plant in the soil you find it best suited to.

"And child, when the time comes, *judge*. And judge wisely."

Before she could ask him what he meant—if she had the courage to do so at all—he was gone.

That afternoon, Sanna arrived at the kitchen in time for the evening meal. She wore a fresh apron, a crisp white linen shirt, and a cap to restrain her hair—but it was her expression that worried the cook and her cousin; she could see it in the sidelong glances they gave her when they thought she wasn't looking.

She mumbled her apologies to them both, well aware that in her absence, they'd each had to work twice as hard. Tess would have none of it. "Your mother's been looking for you."

"I'll find her after dinner."

But the cook shook his head. "No, Sanna, you'll find her now. Your father's coming in to help with the meal, and Uncle Kent as well."

"But why? Is it very busy?"

"Busy enough," the cook said darkly.

Tess looked at the floor, at her hands, and at the hem of her apron.

And Sanna knew. She *knew*. Neville was here.

But even knowing, she was unprepared for the grim, grim set of her father's lips when he entered the kitchen. "You go and help ready the rooms," he told her, before she could ask him what was wrong.

"Which rooms?"

"The tower rooms."

"But—"

"But?"

"Neville will stay at the manor house."

"Aye, that he will. But it's not Nev as wants them," her father replied grimly. "It's the Prince of Everarre."

"The—"

"Aye. The prince and his knights have come calling. Go, Sanna. Go now. Everything has to be right in those rooms; everything has to be perfect. But hurry, girl; I'm thinking the youngsters might come to the inn to get a glimpse of the prince and his men, the silly fools; we'll want you in the hall then."

If a prince had ever chosen to stay at Wayfarer's Retreat before, Sanna had never heard tell of him. Her hands shook as she tried to unlock the doors to the tower rooms; she dropped the keys once, and once again, before she managed to open them. They creaked, and she stopped at once to oil the hinges.

Then she entered the room, her bucket by her side, her thick cloths, waxes, and oils in a bag slung over her shoulder. Marina came moments later; she was breathless from running. "Your Da' called me in," she whispered. "He says the Prince of Everarre is staying in these very rooms for the night."

"If he finds they meet his approval."

"Well, then, they will." She was a chatterer, and usually Sanna liked that; two people to share the tedium of cleaning made it seem like less of a chore.

But she wanted the silence.

She started with the great sheets that covered the furniture, pulling them from embroidered chair and gleaming desk, from crystal devoid of the fire that would light the room; she pulled them from the great posts of the large bed, and from the canopy of the smaller ones; she pulled them from the dining table at which a guest might eat in privacy, and from the paintings of which her father was so proud. And each time she did, she paused as if she could hear the whisper of a story, an old story.

And the crackling roar of distant fire.

But the voices of the children had fallen into hush in this room; there was fire and story.

She did not want to share these with the prince who had taken Nev away from Hydan Athe.

When the rooms were finished, linens brought, sheets changed, and curtains hung, she came down to the kitchen. Tess was nowhere in sight, but the cook was toiling; whoever had come to the hall had to be fed, and fed well.

Her father came in through the swinging doors, carrying empty trays, and he paused just long enough to hear her tell him that the rooms had been readied before he handed her an empty tray and told her what to put on it.

She obeyed him because it gave her something to do with her hands; they were shaking. Exhaustion, she thought, but without conviction.

She followed him when he left the kitchen; he left her no time to master her nerves. She carried her fear with her into the hall.

It was almost drowned out by the noise.

There were eight men at the center table, and more dishes that eight men from the Athes would have used had they sat through breakfast, lunch, and dinner without pause. Had she not known these men were important by the cut of their very fine clothing, she would have known it by the dishes they used; her mother had chosen the finest of silver, the most delicate of plates, the most expensive of bowls for these customers. Those utensils lay littered across the linen cloth like fallen servants; the cloth itself was stained with the dark, deep red of her father's wines. Between them were elbows, boots, fists; the men were loud.

She had seen merchant guards behave like this a time or two, but her mother had offered them no honor. Which of these men was the prince?

Curiosity was stronger than dread for just a moment; she looked with care at the men at the table while she tried to make room for the food that she carried.

But her gaze never made it to the end of the table; it fell upon one young man.

She froze, and the lack of movement was obvious where bustle would have been lost. He looked up and met her eyes.

"Sanna?"

Her heart was stupid. Stupid, childish, reckless. Before she could stop herself, her lips lifted in a wide smile, and she spoke his name. "Nev!"

"What have we here?" The man to Nev's left turned toward her. "What *have* we here, Neville?"

Neville frowned. "One of the townspeople," he said at last. He shrugged. "Sir Hyrtan and I used to frequent the inn when the merchants came. I recognize her."

"And it would seem she recognizes you." The stranger smiled. There was nothing warm in the expression at all. "Come here, girl. You can smile like that for a knight, smile for me."

She tried. But the smile was fixed and wooden.

"Oh, come, come, don't be shy. I've a mind—"

"Sanna!" Her father shouted.

She put the tray down. "Your pardon," she whispered.

She worked for the rest of the evening, and it was one of the most terrible of her life.

She was a serving girl. Just a serving girl. If she was lucky and ambitious, she might one day be a merchant with her mother's family.

And Neville would be a Faerlan knight.

She did not approach the high table again; she did not loiter in its view. She did not wish to see Nev's face. He was mercifully silent; his voice did not drift, did not catch her attention. The others were less so, and their words were loud and ugly, but they were not as hurtful as Nev's, examined compulsively over and over again in the silence of humiliation.

She worked.

The miller's daughter was there with her brother; the tanner's cousin's daughters had also made their way to the inn. Conspicuous by his absence was Sir Hyrtan.

Sanna did not enter her room again until the moon had crested the clouds and the edge of her window was silvered. She stood a moment in the frame of the door, and then brushed it gently with her forehead; the kitchens were hot, and she wanted the coolness of untouched wood against her skin.

But she found no comfort in it, and entered her room, fussing with the knots of her apron; her hands were shaking. She raised them slowly toward her face and stopped; they were shadows; the slanted light of moon did not reach her.

She could not go to the tower rooms; they would be occupied by Neville's companions. She could not go back to the hall. Her teeth were shut tight against any sound, any hint of pain, but it was a bad silence, and she knew it. Innkeeper's daughter.

She walked to the window, knelt slowly before it as her knees gave way. Her elbows, like the corners of a door, spread against the sill, and she lowered her face into the crook of her right arm. But tears were a tight knot at the base of her throat; they would not come. Instead, she saw the ghost of a fire; there was no light to cast her reflection back at her, and that was just as well. She saw the dark shades of trees, the clear night, the stars; she saw all of these things as they had once been, and as they now were.

Nothing separated the moon of the past from the moon of the present; why had things changed so much in every other way?

But as the moon shifted, a wind raised the curtain of leaves, and she saw—although she could not see it—the white cenotaphs of the graveyard of Hydan Athe. She closed her eyes; felt shame at the smallness of her desires and her loss. The men and women of Hydan Athe slept there, where they had been laid to rest after the night of fires.

They had given everything to the Athes. And their children, weeping or silent, terrified, confused, or resolute, had paid a much higher price than she had, that night.

Nev's voice, higher and sweeter by far than the low, adult tones they'd been replaced by, was a muted whisper. She had treasured that memory for so long, she needed a reminder of the true gift of that evening: Her father. Her mother. They had been left behind, with Tad and Ramble, the last defense for children too young to lift weapons and fight.

Lifting her chin, she felt shadow in the full light, and she remembered the white blossom she had taken from the old-wife's house.

And she knew, then, where she must plant it.

*   *   *

Her hands were steady. The thin clay that held the roots of the *White Athe* felt cool and delicate, but that was only right; the blossom itself rested atop a stem that was so slender it should have bowed at the weight it carried. If it didn't, she wouldn't. She left her room; walked quietly down the back stairs and into the narrow hall that guests didn't see, and didn't use. She paused once, just once, before she left the inn because she could see the play of window lights against the tended grass.

But none of that light was hers.

She left it behind; the moon was bright and sky was now as clear as fine glass. She found the gardener's shed and, fingering the rough latch that kept its doors closed, she opened the shed and took a trowel from the neatly kept shelves. She would have to bring it back before she slept; he would fuss so in the morning otherwise.

She dropped the trowel into the large pockets of the apron she'd had no luck removing and made her way down the path to the graveyard.

There were no gates in the graveyard; it was not a place that was hidden or protected by fences. The land was adorned by chiseled stone, but the words on the weather-worn faces were lost to the night. She did not know what they said, but it didn't matter; she knew what they meant. They were symbols of loss, small temples at which the bereaved might find peace.

There were no ghosts here, or perhaps no angry ones, and for this reason Sanna was not troubled to find herself above the dead. She knew some of the stones by heart. Some carried words like son, and some simple names, simple numbers; her mother had taught her to use those numbers as a very crude map of beginning and end, and she had learned to glean the simplest of truths from them.

She paused to run her hand across the top of one stone.

Athe's Death she carried, and she felt those words not as a doom but as a benediction. For in dying, so many of these people have given the gift of life to those that remained.

They had let the children come to the funeral. Sir Hyrtan had insisted that they be allowed to bear witness to their losses in the comfort and company of the adults, and she had thought him brave and kind for his decree.

It was only in the last two years that she had come to understand that their presence had served a purpose: It reminded those who had lost much of what they had not lost. She continued to walk until she came to the heart of the graves; to the place where she—and Neville, of course—had stood, surrounded by children, arms aching, back compressed as they carried first one and then another, holding them tightly as if by embrace alone they could shield them from pain.

She knelt in the grass; it was short, but it was not so soft and not so green as it had been in the spring. It was here that she began to dig.

"Sanna."

It should have surprised her, that voice in this place, but it didn't. She looked once over her shoulder to see the young man between the gravestones, and then she turned back to her task. It was not so hard to turn the earth here, and she did not need to turn much of it.

"Sanna, don't be like that."

She measured the depth of the small hole with the flat of her hand; the width with her palm. The *White Athe* was small.

"Sanna, don't ignore me."

His voice—unwelcome, changed voice—drifted closer; she heard his heavy feet against the ground.

"It happens that I'm busy," she ground out, between

clenched teeth. "I've a task set by the old-wife, and I'm bound to complete it tonight."

When she spoke the words, she realized they were true.

"What task?"

She did not answer.

He came closer, and closer still; she could see his feet from the corner of her eyes. "What are you doing?"

"What does it look like I'm doing? I'm not so fancy and highborn that I've forgotten how to dig and plant."

He was silent for long enough that she dared her first look at his face. It was not what she had expected. The cool distance was gone.

"That's *Athe's Death*," he said, as softly as she had when she had walked in the old-wife's house.

"It's *White Athe*."

"Why are you planting it?"

"Well, why do you think?"

"I don't know. That's why I'm asking."

After a moment, grudging the words, she said, "Neither do I. It's a task set me, that's all." He reached out to touch the blossom.

She almost let him. But at the last minute she cried out, wordless, and slapped his hand away. "Don't. Don't touch it. It's . . . It's not to be touched. By you."

The silence descended again. He broke it. She wouldn't. "I'm sorry."

"For what? You're what you are, Nev. And I'm the innkeeper's daughter."

"I know."

She was surprised that she could still want words, but she knew she did because those were the wrong ones. She pulled the dirt from the planter a little too roughly as she freed the blossom from its confinement.

"You don't know what it was like," he said at last. "To go.

To Faerlan. To meet the knights of legend. To see the city. They have cathedrals in the city's heart that the whole of the Athelands could not afford to build. And books, Sanna, that would stretch for miles if you placed them end to end. They have competitions there, where men of the sword can test themselves against each other."

She said nothing.

"I wrote to you."

"You wrote twice."

"I wrote a hundred times."

Her eyes hurt. She rubbed them fiercely with the back of her hand. "You wrote *twice*."

"No. I wrote a hundred times. Exactly a hundred. But I—I sent only two letters."

"Why?" She turned, then, knees in the dirt, hands on her lap because it was the only way to keep them still. "Why did you send only two? Why didn't you send the rest? Why didn't you come home?"

He looked away from her. "I couldn't," he said numbly. "I could not come home."

"You could have come if you wanted to. Your father came home."

"Aye, my father did."

"Well maybe he didn't love Faerlan so much as he did these fields and his people."

He flinched. "Aye." His voice was bitter and low. "Perhaps he didn't. But he's a true knight. I understand that now. Faerlan taught me that. If you knew—"

"If I knew what?"

"The truth, Sanna." His voice was low; there was nothing of the storyteller in it at all. But it was the first time this evening that she could hear something close to that boy's truth in the man's, and, again, she betrayed herself.

"Was there a—a girl?"

His laugh was wild, bitter.

"How can I know the truth if you tell me nothing? How can I know—"

"Do you think I loved Faerlan? Do you think that of me? The things I've seen, Sanna. The things I've watched—"

"Hey, Neville!"

In the distance she heard an unwelcome voice. Neville was on his feet before the silence returned. He cursed. "They're looking for me. I have to leave now. It's best—it's best if we don't speak again."

He rose quickly.

"Nev!"

"I can't be found here, Sanna. Trust me."

"Nev—I want the rest of the letters."

"What makes you think I could bear to keep them?"

He was gone. He left her to the tears that she could no longer stop from falling; she wept bitterly as she placed the *White Athe* into the spot she had made for it. But although her hands shook, the flower was straight as steel; it did not shake or tremble even when she almost dropped it in her haste to be done.

If she had not been crying, she would have heard them. But if they weren't silent, they walked without speaking until they surrounded her like a ring of stones. She noticed them first not by anything they said or did, but by the light they carried, orange and gold in the silver of the graveyard.

"What have we here?"

She was done with tears. She looked up to see first legs, and then chest, and at last visage. The Prince of Everarre.

She had never felt unsafe in the graveyard, even at night. She realized that, in truth, she had never felt unsafe before. She started to rise and felt two hands upon her shoulder, forcing her back to her knees in the dirt before the blossom.

The light came close to her; it swayed between her face and the face of the prince. He smiled.

She tried to smile, but her lips wouldn't move.

"The little serving girl."

She tried to rise again.

"Not so fast," the prince said. "We've found that the girls in the Athes are not very friendly, and we've been traveling for many days." He put the lamp down and stepped over it.

She lifted her hands and tried to pry the fingers from her collarbone; they tightened.

"Come, come; do you not know who I am?"

"The Prince of Everarre," she whispered.

"Ah, so you do know. And what would you do in service to your prince and the men who risk their lives in defense of his kingdom?"

He reached out and caught her chin in his hands, holding it less gently than his knights now held her shoulders and her arms.

"Please—"

"There's no need to beg, girl. No need at all. We're here to give you what you want."

The apron strings that had not come undone for her hands offered the prince no such trouble. Neither did the buttons of her shift, or the fabric she wore beneath it.

She screamed; a hand covered her nose and her mouth and its weight bore her down, down until her back was pressed into the grass.

He laughed. Short sound, ugly sound. "Not so loud," he whispered, his mouth at her ear. "We don't want to be interrupted."

And his hands bruised her thighs, exposed her legs; his

fingers fumbled with her underwear and with something else that she could not see.

Other hands touched her skin roughly, poked and pinched; she heard laughter and the promise it carried.

"She fights as if she has something to protect, doesn't she?" Laughter again. "We've some experience, girl. And you won't fight as hard once there's nothing left to lose." He knelt between her legs.

She couldn't breathe. She wanted air as badly as she wanted freedom; she went limp beneath him and his hand inched free of her nose. "Good girl," he said quietly.

And then she heard a strange sound, something from her past. She did not understand its significance, but clearly the prince and his knights did; her left arm was freed as one of the knights rose.

The Prince of Everarre turned to the left; she could not see what he saw because the weight of his hand across her mouth prevented her head from turning.

But she recognized the voice whose owner she could not see.

"Let her go."

It was Neville.

The prince did not laugh. "Think carefully, Neville. Think very, very carefully."

Neville said nothing.

"You've drawn your sword. I know you well enough. You are no oathbreaker. You wouldn't draw sword against the man you're sworn to defend."

And she knew where she'd heard the sound before. The night of fires. Sir Hyrtan's sword.

"Let her go."

"I believe he's serious," the prince said, looking above Sanna to the men who had accompanied him. "Have you lost all wit?"

"Let her *go*."

"Why?"

"She is not yours."

"I have no intention of keeping her. If you want her, join us."

"Neville doesn't like girls," one of the knights said. "Remember? He's always absent when we play."

"Oh, not always. Not always, eh, Neville?"

"Not always," Neville agreed. "But I've seen enough. I've been idle too long. It stops here.

"Let her go."

"And if I don't?"

Neville *moved*. Sanna saw his foot lash out; her mouth was free in an instant as the Prince of Evararre leaped clear of the strike.

The knights in the graveyard unsheathed their swords.

Sanna rolled to the side; she started to scrabble to her feet when a foot struck her in the back. "Stay, girl." As if she were a dog.

"Your Highness."

Sanna could see Neville clearly now. But had she not known his voice, she wouldn't have recognized him. He looked like a dead man.

The prince turned to the four knights and nodded; they spread out, forming a loose wall between Neville and the prince.

Neville's smile was ghastly. "I am forsworn," he said softly, and he stepped forward, drawing his sword up to the line of his shoulder and turning the edge of his blade on its side.

The knights readied themselves. The graveyard was mercifully absent of laughter, their laughter.

"Kill him," the prince commanded.

As one, they moved.

But Sanna could not see what they were doing; the prince

was upon her again. It was much easier to fight him, and she struggled until he struck her once, cleanly, in the throat.

She gasped, raised a hand to her throat, abandoning the fight; he lowered himself down as she flailed. She turned her face away from his as it descended, as he descended—and she saw, in the moonlight, untroubled by the battle, the slender stalk of the *White Athe*.

Saw, as if she were now no longer a part of her own body, the flash of steel, the stillness that accompanied it; the slow fall of a heavy, wounded man as he toppled in time with her heartbeat, across the flower she'd planted.

She knew he was dead.

She almost wished she were.

". . . that's what you'll tell them," he whispered in her ear. "that the son of Sir Hyrtan raped you, and died when we came—too late, of course—to your defense. You can scream now, if you like, girl."

But it was not Sanna who cried out.

The prince did as something struck him in the side without enough force to dislodge him.

She rolled away; there was no foot to stop her, no hands to hold her down. She got to her feet, her knees shaking, her skirt slowly falling toward the grass over her ruined underclothing.

And saw Neville, his sword through the chest of a second knight, his face bloodied.

She did not understand what had happened, until she saw the tanner come out from behind the bent curves of an ancient oak. In his hands was a crossbow. There was no quarrel.

A woman joined him. His wife. Her crossbow was armed and taut, but not for long. She said, simply, "bad shot," and lifted her own bow.

The Prince of Everarre did not speak another word.

Her father came next; his crossbow was, like the tanner's and the tanner's wife's, spent. He looked at Sanna, and then dropped the bow and strode quickly to her side, removing the cloak from his shoulder and wrapping it tightly around hers.

It had been years since she'd been light enough to carry; he did not lift her. But he lifted a hand to her mouth when she tried to speak; to find words, any words, that might make sense of this evening.

"Sir Hyrtan." His chin rested upon the crown of her head; she felt his words as they resonated through that contact. "It's done. They're dead."

The old knight came out from treeside then, his sword drawn. "Neville," he said quietly. "Your sword."

Neville turned toward his father as the knight fell backward. He saw his father, and closed his eyes. His hands were shaking as he let go of the sword's hilt; it, and the man it was buried in, fell backward.

Sir Hyrtan approached his son; his son shrank away from him with a terror that Sanna had never seen him display. "You are forsworn," Sir Hyrtan said coldly.

Neville fell to his knees. "Yes, sir."

"What price will you pay for the breaking of your oath?"

Neville said nothing. He tensed as Sir Hyrtan lifted his sword.

And Sanna broke free of her father's arms, her clothing a shambles, all dignity forgotten. "Sir Hyrtan!"

The old knight turned. His expression was the twin of Neville's; they both looked like men who had seen so much death, so much horror, that they no longer knew how to fear it for themselves. Yet Sir Hyrtan's words were gentle. "Yes, Sanna?"

"I planted the *White Athe*."

"Did you?"

"Yes. In the graveyard."

"And will you cull its blossom now?"

She shook her head and pointed to the first of the fallen. "It's there. Beneath him. He crushed it."

"Did Neville touch the blossom?"

"No."

The knight nodded. "Marjorie is bringing the old-wife," he said quietly.

"But it's not her decision—it's mine!"

At that, the old knight smiled. "Would you save him, Sanna?"

"He risked his life to—to—"

But Neville cried out in denial and turned his face from her.

Sir Hyrtan did not flinch. "Tell her, Neville."

"No."

"Tell her."

"No. I would face *Athe's Death* first. I would accept it."

"Then convince her that you deserve it," the old knight replied coldly.

Neville shook his head, back and forth, back and forth. Like a child. Like a child on the night the fires had burned in the Athes.

"You have a choice, Neville. Tell her, or I will."

Neville's eyes widened. "You—you know, sir?"

"I know."

The silence lasted a little while longer, but Sanna knew that Neville would speak; she waited, for the first time in her life, with patience.

"This is not—this is not—the first time," Neville said, but he did not look at her; did not look up at his father. "This is what—what—they do."

"And is it what you do?"

His eyes widened; Sanna could have slapped him with less effect than his father's words had had. "Does it make a difference? I did not stop them. I have never lifted sword against them. Against my liege. And many of the girls were younger than you are," he added. She knew what it cost him to say the words. They were terrible. "Younger, and they wanted him no more. But after he'd finished, he didn't kill them. He didn't hurt them further. And they—they were afraid of ruin. Afraid of the accusations they would face if they—if they demanded justice. Their parents said nothing, nothing at all. It was as if—as if it had never happened.

"I told myself it was just—just the way of things. In Faerlan. Away from here. He was the *prince*. He—" Neville was wild-eyed. "I thought we would fight bandits. Or raiders. Or dragons. I thought we would travel from one end of the kingdom to the other, protecting the helpless. Until I got there. Until I *lived* in Faerlan, where everyone is blind, everyone is mute.

"Do you understand, Sanna? Do you understand why I couldn't come home? Why I couldn't write to you, why I couldn't—"

"But you did write to me," she said softly. "You told me. You wrote."

"I wrote lies," he answered. "What do the words of a coward mean? I did *nothing,* Sanna."

"Aye, and it was wrong, and it was evil, in its way. But—"

Silence; everyone in the graveyard listened.

"But I remember the night of fires. I remember you then. Can acts of evil destroy acts of good? Do they mean that no good can *ever* be done again?"

"A good question, Sanna." The old-wife's voice. "Where is the *White Athe?*"

"There."

"Then help me, girl. Lift the body—we'll have to move it anyway. No, not *you,* Marton. Not anyone else but Sanna and I will do it."

"But old-wife," her father said, "she's done enough for one evening, surely."

"If she'd finished, I wouldn't be asking. You mind your inn, let *me* mind my business."

"She's my daughter."

"Father, enough. It's my duty." Sanna walked away from Neville, aware that he had not yet answered the question.

They pulled the body aside.

Where it had lain, with careful searching, Sanna found the crushed flower.

She hesitated. "Old-wife, what should I do?"

"As you wish, Sanna. Not more, not less."

Sanna reached out with shaking hands, and after a moment, although she remembered the insects that had rested upon the surface of damp, black soil, she touched the bruised petals. In an instant, a fragrance sweet and bitter filled the clearing.

"Ah," the old-wife said. No more.

Sanna inhaled deeply and found a renewed strength. Very, very carefully, she lifted the blossom; it broke free from its stem.

"Neville," she said quietly, "look."

He waited as she approached him, the flower in her cupped palm.

"You're—you're touching it."

"Yes," she whispered. "Yes. I can touch it now."

Sir Hyrtan did not breathe. No one did, or no one seemed to; Sanna could hear her voice, and Neville's breath, and nothing else.

"You had to go to Faerlan," she told him. "You had to learn what *Hydan Athe* is not, and must never be. Come home."

"To what?" He asked bitterly. "We've committed murder. We cannot kill a prince and be forgiven."

"Bandits," Sanna's father said unexpectedly. "The Athelands have a history of difficulty with brave and foolish bandits. Not even the king's own men have ever been able to end their threat.

"Or do you not remember your history? The Athelands are special, yes, because the Knights of the Athelands have grown to understand what the Athes are, what they mean, and what they must always mean. The kings come and go, and once in a while, they attempt to take from the Athes what the Athes require. From this experience, they have learned that to challenge the Athes is to starve, and not for such a one as this would the current king take that risk.

"Come, Neville, take what Sanna offers."

"It's not mine," Sanna whispered. "It's not mine to offer. Do you not understand what it is, Nev?"

"No. *Athe's Death.*"

"It . . . is that," she told him, gazing at the crushed petals. "But only because of its nature."

"Its nature? Sanna—"

"It is *your* heart, Nev." She gazed up at him, her eyes as clear as the night sky. "And when the heart of a Knight . . . festers . . . in the Athes, when the Knight loses the path, and the truth, of the Athes, *that* loss is death."

"My heart," he said bitterly.

"Yes. Only that. Can you take it, Nev? Can you take it back? Can you see what you have been, and what you must be, and live with its truth? It is yours. Take it. Become either a corpse or the hidden heart of the Athe."

Neville hesitated for another minute, and then he closed his eyes and placed his hand upon Sanna's; they were cupped on either side of the flower.

He cried out in pain, in anger, in horror; he screamed in a voice much louder than Sanna's would have been had the prince allowed her her voice.

But she caught his wrist with her free hand, and she held it so tightly his skin around the edges of her fingertips was as white as the flower had been.

Sir Hyrtan stiffened, but he did not speak. He waited. Sanna cried out in fear and in fury, and she clutched Neville more tightly, as if her grasp alone could hold him here; could prevent him from leaving a second time.

He fell to his knees, his hand in hers; she fell with him. He whimpered.

And Sanna knew what to do. She began to tell him a story. A story of the Knights of the Athes. A story of the sacrifices that Knights make, the pain they must live with, the people they must succor.

Her words reached him through his pain; he stilled to listen, as the children had listened so many years ago. Her hand was numb from the effort of holding his wrist, but she felt, in the silence, the erratic beat of a pulse.

When he lifted his hand, the blossom was gone.

Neville frowned. He looked at his hand, at his palm; bent to search the grass at his feet.

"Don't be an ass," the old-wife snapped. Her own hand was closed in a fist. "Or don't be *more* of one. Hyrtan, take the boy home, tan his hide, and put him to work." But her expression had softened.

"Neville."

"Old-wife." He bowed, tears a silver mask across both of his cheeks. And his voice—it was his voice, the voice that Sanna had known, at nine, that she would love forever. Oh, there were hollows in, and depths to it, but that changed nothing. She was surprised at the tears across her own cheeks.

Almost as an afterthought, she released his wrist.

"Sir Hyrtan's brother faced the test you faced; he was the elder son. He failed. Sir Hyrtan was never tested by the *White Athe*."

"My father is a good man."

"Your father," the old-wife said severely, "saw what happened to his brother. Now go home. We'll tend to the cleanup here."

He turned to walk away, because no one—not even the Knight of Hydan Athe—disobeyed the old-wife's direct orders. He took three steps, his father by his side, old arm around young, curved shoulders.

Then he turned back, risking the old-wife's wrath. There was a fear in his face that made Sanna wince.

But he said, "I kept them," before his father caught him by the shoulders and led him away.

KRISTEN BRITAIN
GREEN RIDER

"The gifted Ms. Britain writes with ease and grace as she
creates a mesmerizing fantasy ambiance and an
appealing heroine quite free of normal clichés."
—*Romantic Times*

Karigan G'ladheon has fled from school following a fight that
would surely lead to her expulsion. As she makes her way
through the deep forest, a galloping horse plunges out of the
brush, its rider impaled by two black arrows. With his dying
breath, he tells her he is a Green Rider, one of the legendary
magical messangers of the King. Giving her his green coat
with its symbolic brooch of office, he makes Karigan swear to
deliver the message he was carrying. Pursued by unknown
assassins, following a path only the messenger's horse seems
to know, she unwittingly finds herself in a world of deadly danger and complex magic, compelled by forces she does not
yet understand. . . .

0-88677-858-1 $6.99

Prices slightly higher in Canada   **DAW: 109**

Michelle West

The Sun Sword:

☐ **THE BROKEN CROWN**   UE2740—$6.99

☐ **THE UNCROWNED KING**   UE2801—$6.99

☐ **THE SHINING COURT**   UE2837—$6.99

In the Dominion, those allied with the demons of the Shining Court fear the bargain they've made, for to the *kialli* betrayal was a way of life. And as the Festival of the Moon approaches, demon kin begin to prey upon those in the Tor Leonne. But even more frightening than their presence was their "gift" for the Festival, masks created not by human craftsmen but by the *kialli*. . . .

The Sacred Hunt:

☐ **HUNTER'S OATH**   UE2681—$5.50

☐ **HUNTER'S DEATH**   UE2706—$5.99